A WOMAN OF OPINION

Also by Sean Lusk

The Second Sight of Zachary Cloudesley

A Woman of Opinion

SEAN LUSK

doubleday

TRANSWORLD PUBLISHERS
Penguin Random House, One Embassy Gardens,
8 Viaduct Gardens, London SW11 7BW
www.penguin.co.uk

Transworld is part of the Penguin Random House group of companies
whose addresses can be found at global.penguinrandomhouse.com

First published in Great Britain in 2024 by Doubleday
an imprint of Transworld Publishers

A CIP catalogue record for this book
is available from the British Library.

ISBNs
9780857528032 (hb)
9780857528049 (tpb)

Typeset in 10.5/14.5pt Berling LT Std by Jouve (UK), Milton Keynes
Printed and bound in Great Britain by Clays Ltd, Elcograf S.p.A.

The authorized representative in the EEA is Penguin Random House Ireland,
Morrison Chambers, 32 Nassau Street, Dublin D02 YH68.

For Mia, Josh and Zachary

And men, I think, will never quite forget
My songs or me; so long as stars shall set
Or sun shall rise, or hearts feel love's desire,
My voice shall cross their dreams, a sigh of fire.

Final stanza of *Pieria's Rose* from
The Poems of Sappho, as interpreted
by John Myers O'Hara (1910)

This is a novel inspired by the life, letters and lost diaries of Mary Wortley Montagu. Much of what follows is based on the historical record, but on occasion I have taken liberties, invented incidents and changed dates. These liberties are confessed in the timeline of events and afterword to be found at the end of the book.

PROLOGUE

Autumn 1699

Thoresby, Nottinghamshire, England

Papa sends Johnson out for me again. He would never think to come find me himself, and anyway I should not like him to. It is always the under-gardener who is sent, even though he is an oaf. Everyone says so.

'M'lady?'

Johnson-the-oaf is yet further away. He does not know where I am, even though he should, since I am always at this place stretching out my hands to hold the fiery ball as if it could be mine, the sun and our world and everything that sits between. I do not want to own the sun, not truly, but how I should like to have more than just this body, this tongue, these words.

A crow flies across the disc, startling and close, and a moment later sets down almost at my feet, its oily feathers a rustle in the still of the evening. It is, I suppose, surprised to see me there, hands extended, worshipping that day's tired old sun, but crows are creatures of fierce curiosity. I have such an urge to stroke its feathers, to feel the beat of its small heart that I lurch forwards and to my surprise it allows itself to be caught. I am struggling to hold it when Johnson is there at my side. Before I can stop the halfwit, he has taken the crow from me and pulled back its wings, breaking them. The sound of those small, sharp bones cracking is a thing I already know I will never forget.

'No, Johnson! No!' I shout at him. He holds the bird out by its snapped wings, as if it were an offering. Its shining eyes, like jet buttons on hose, are upon me, injured and perplexed. 'Why, why did you do such a thing?' I demand.

'I sorry, m'lady. I afeard it attack you.'

I do not know if a crow can live with broken wings. I reach out to feel for the beat of its heart, as I'd wanted to all along, and it is strong and fast, but like something racing towards its end. Though I barely rest my fingers there, the crow seizes its chance and drives its beak sudden and sharp into the back of my hand, drawing a bead of dark red blood. The pain is startling, but I do not flinch, fearing that Johnson will drop the creature to the ground, but he does so all the same and we both watch the poor thing try to hop away, trailing its broken wings behind it.

'Bring him in, Johnson,' I command. 'I shall nurse him back to health.' I turn, and as I do I hear the under-gardener wring its neck. I am ignored too readily on this estate. It may be because I am only ten years of age, but more likely it is because I am female. They do not know, not Father nor my governess nor any of them, that I am a creature who knows how to hold the sun in my hands, and the earth and all that lies between. But they shall. Soon enough, they shall.

1

A MATCH MADE IN HELL

Spring 1712, London

(Frances)

My sister and I are brought to London to be married as a pair of horses might be taken to a country fair, with quiet expectation of purchase but little care as to future ownership. Yesterday I overheard Papa telling his steward that it was *high time his hands were free of us*, as if we were something he had held on to overlong, like fallow fields. An odd phrase, *hands full* or *free*. I cannot think when last I was embraced by him or indeed by anyone excepting Mary. She says that Papa is all bone, brittle and bleached, a faint echo of the living, but she is given to saying such things. Our father is in perfectly robust health and growing quite plump, and I take her comment as poetical. I do not generally admit to Mary when she has confused me, for then she explains and I do not much care for explanation.

Mary has a taxonomy for the male sex: men are heaven (very rare), hell (far too common), or limbo (barely sufficient, as might be expected). As for my views on marriage, I suppose I should feel either intense excitement at the prospect or, more likely, dread – but find that I suffer neither sentiment. Mary tells me I am numb, too insensible to my emotions, yet I cannot be who I am not, and I do not feel so passionately as my sister does about things. Indeed, I don't believe there is a woman in all England who feels quite so much about everything as Mary.

I asked as we were sitting in the coach on our way to London, 'Why is it that all the men who come to dances, whether we're in Nottinghamshire or Wiltshire, are so wholly uninteresting, Mary?' Since our only companion was Mrs Catt, our old governess, a woman held together by nothing more than the taut weave of her many prejudices, we spoke as freely as if we were alone.

Mary looked a long time out of the window before she replied, as if her answer might lie in the greening fields. 'It is because,' she said at last, 'they have no idea that a woman – any woman – cares to hear of anything but how pretty we are, or how fine our dresses, how bright our eyes, as if we were nothing more than lapdogs needing to be coaxed to sit upon their parts.'

'Mary!' admonished Mrs Catt, who was sent with us at Father's insistence and stirred by the word *parts* from whatever dark thoughts had been pinching her bony features; for a part may be innocent or lewd, and for Mrs Catt almost anything – a leg or spindle, a chest or a strand of hair – is as likely lewd as not.

Mary ignored her, as always. 'They learn these lines of inexpert seduction from their friends, and I fear there are young ladies we know –' she thought for a moment, needing to call up an example '– the Misses Simkins, for instance, who pretend to be flattered by them and so encourage them.'

The Misses Simkins are extremely foolish, it's true. Yet

their brother is not. Indeed, he is one of the few men we know who might qualify if not quite for heavenly status, then at least for limbo. He recently returned from the Grand Tour and came to visit us with wonderful sketches of the antiquities and enthusiastic accounts of the glories of Rome. He even brought us a beautifully illustrated copy of Andreas Vesalius's *Anatomy*, which must have cost him a great deal. It was a book he knew would please us greatly, as we both like to dissect and draw dead things about the estate, pheasants and rabbits and deer and such like. Mary has said she would like to dissect a man, though we are agreed it would be indecorous to make her wish too widely known.

'Why do you think George Simkins is not at all stupid when his sisters are?' I asked.

'It's infuriating, isn't it? He's had an education, of course.' Mary glanced quickly at Mrs Catt, for we both knew her strong prejudice against education, but she was engrossed in her needlework, which given the jolting of the carriage was a task both hopeless and infuriating and therefore greatly suited to her inclinations. 'Had Molly and Lizzie Simkins learnt Latin and Greek then perhaps they'd behave less like chattering chaffinches.'

I should have been perfectly content to take George Simkins for a husband, but Papa wouldn't countenance it, for though Simkins had an income, he had no title nor any prospect of one. My own prospects are anyway not equal to Mary's, and I'm glad of that. Mary possesses our father's air of authority and his handsome looks, though more finely drawn, as a piece of porcelain is when set against a clay pot of the same design. Her eyes are large and seem always larger still when she's listening to anything that is said to her, as if the person talking were the most fascinating creature imaginable. Her lashes are long, her teeth straight and even, her hair with a lustre like a chestnut fresh from its shell, her form slender yet shapely and though she is but short she conjures an impression of height (she's always telling me not to slouch). Above all it is that a light shines from Mary that seems to illuminate every place she goes, whether itself bright or gloomy. When I'm with her I feel the warmth of it, and I miss her terribly when we're apart. We have sworn that whatever man each of us marries, if marry we must, he shall be of sufficient temperament as not to seek to divide us.

All of this makes Father's determination to marry Mary to a perfect hell wholly inexplicable. Clotworthy Skeffington is arrogant, thin-skinned and a good deal less intelligent than he believes himself to be. He met Mary at last summer's season and seemed interested in her, and when a woman has attracted the interest of a man she does not like, as his interest grows so in equal proportion does her loathing, as a fox once pursued by a hound will run ever faster in its flight. His problem is not ugliness, but dullness coupled with shallow ambition. Even if Father is set on this marriage primarily to punish Mary for her defiance and outspokenness on every topic, Skeffington seems too cruel a sentence.

When we arrived at Arlington Street after two days on the road, our gowns dusty, our hair matted, a film upon our teeth, we were no sooner in the house than we were informed that the awful Skeffington was present and in negotiation with Papa, presumably on some aspect of the marriage contract. Mary showed the footman only the briefest flash of annoyance before calling for Betsy, her London maid, and announcing that she would retire to her chamber.

'I do believe, Lady Mary,' said the footman, nervously, 'that Mr Skeffington wishes to have the pleasure of your company and –' he glanced at me, the poor man altogether as uneasy as if he were addressing the Turkish sultan and had a scimitar hovering above his head '– and that of Lady Frances, and . . . and . . .'

'Then you may inform Mr Skeffington that he will have to wait,' said Mary, although not unkindly, for I never did see her be rude to a servant.

'Madam,' he said, bowing and withdrawing, his relief absolute.

More than an hour passed before we entered the drawing room, to find Skeffington pacing it like a boar caught in a cage. A plate which must an hour before have contained sweetmeats was set beside the teapot, though upon it were only crumbs. He turned at our entrance, and the scene played out thus:

SKEFFINGTON: *Bows to me, bows to my sister.* My Lady Frances, my Lady Mary. It is my honour.

I: Sir. *Curtsies.*

MARY: *Silent.*

SKEFFINGTON: *Bows again, this time with less irony and with more concern for his pride, which is already bruising visibly beneath the pressure of his long wait and my sister's plain contempt.* Your good father has no doubt made you aware of my suit, my lady?

MARY: He has. And let me not question it, for it is generous, and no doubt in the last hour he has squeezed from you further sums so that your generosity, sir, stands now in such heaps that it must demand the admiration of us all.

SKEFFINGTON: *Looks at me uneasily. Surely he does not imagine I will withdraw?* Coughs. *Turns to face my sister once more.* You shall have five hundred a year in pin money, madam.

MARY: Indeed. And must I come to Massereene to spend it?

SKEFFINGTON: We shall be obliged to spend some time there, certainly once I am viscount. My father . . .

MARY: . . . ails, sir. I am aware. And once he is eat by worms you shall be viscount until you, too, are eat by worms, when I shall have twelve hundred a year. I am familiar with the terms. So much to look forward to.

SKEFFINGTON: *Affronted. He loosens the kerchief at his neck.* I do not know why it is I displease you so, madam. Have I offended you? I will treat you with the utmost honour and respect, I assure you.

MARY: Do you gamble, sir?

SKEFFINGTON: Barely.

MARY: And whore even less, no doubt.

SKEFFINGTON: *Reddens.* Really, madam. That is most certainly out of the question.

MARY: But I did not ask the question.

I: My sister—

MARY: *Interrupts.* Will you love me?

SKEFFINGTON: Certainly. *Realizes he has sounded too casual.* Most, most certainly. I should like you to be mine and devote myself to you completely.

MARY: And that I have no wish for your devotion, is that of no importance? That I do not love you, is that a consideration in the arrangements?

SKEFFINGTON: *Turning to me, presumably thinking no one can be so unreasonable as my sister.* Is it not the case, my lady, that people come to love each other over time? That children bring a husband and wife together?

I: I should certainly like to believe so, Mr Skeffington.

MARY: My sister likes to believe in many things, Mr Skeffington. Why, she even believes there is a ghost at West Dean.

I: *Quietly.* There *is* a ghost at West Dean.

SKEFFINGTON: *Comprehending that he will get no further on this encounter.* I bid you ladies good day. *Bows, withdraws in a fluster.*

'What will you do now?' I asked Mary after he had left, leaving the odour of bergamot behind him, not unpleasant, though Mary disapproves of men who wear scent.

'I shall allow matters to proceed, since I have no choice. If Clotworthy Skeffington has half a brain he will realize that marriage to me will be an imprisonment for us both.'

'But has he half a brain?'

'Yes, he has half. He possesses at least the intelligence of a pineapple.' Her self-possession, normally so absolute, fractured for a moment. 'Oh, Fanny,' she declared in exasperation, taking my hands in hers, 'why is it that the terms of imprisonment are so different for a woman than for a man? It is monstrous. Skeffington can marry and have mistresses and travel, he can have a career and go off to parliament – he's in the Irish Commons, and so will be drinking and gambling and whoring in Dublin no doubt, while I'll be stuck in Antrim bearing his children and counting the candles. It's . . .'

For a moment I thought I might see my sister weep. Despite her immense passions I have only seen Mary cry once or twice, and then only in frustration at some great injustice, as when a groom was dismissed for making a horse lame, when Mary had argued that the horse was ill trained and always likely to injure itself without the slightest assistance from anyone else. But Mary would never cry out of self-pity.

'It is simply the way things must be,' she said, gathering herself.

'And what of Mr Wortley?'

'What of Mr Wortley?' she said, dismissively, and marched off.

My sister's affair with Edward Wortley Montagu is a thing no less persistent than it is improbable. It has been going on for at least three years and is ever more perplexing. He is not the only man who has ever interested Mary. There was Joseph Snape, the Thoresby parson's son, who was handsome and clever and wrote poetry that Mary helped him have published. She said that she had no interest in money and would rather live on three hundred a year than three thousand. But a man like Snape would not make two hundred, and for all that Mary says she does not care about money or rank, she could not marry a country poet. There was Nathaniel Shaw, our brother's Latin tutor, whom we liked a good deal, but he disappeared very suddenly and none of us knew why, though I have a notion that Mary, having squeezed from him all his Latin and Greek, had begun to find him tedious. She is drawn to excitement, as surely as a colt is drawn to speed. Sometimes I think Mary is always seeking to outrun something, and I cannot think what that something is, unless it is herself.

As for Wortley, he is brother to Anne, a great friend of Mary from Nottingham who was the handmaiden of their affair until she died no less suddenly than inconveniently, and I have since had to take on the role of intermediary as best I can. If I say I cannot understand what it is that my sister sees in Mr Wortley I believe I am only expressing Mary's own emotions, for I do not think she understands what she sees in him herself.

Sometimes Mary shows me her letters to Wortley and his replies. She writes now and then of her love, even of her great desire that they should always be together, and if she does so, he replies much as he would to a tenant who has applied to build on to a dwelling, with caveats and requirements and warnings of the cost of the thing. Mary will then write back a cool letter to him, saying that she has known all along the impossibility of even so much as a friendship between them. This then brings about a letter of passionate indignation from Wortley and exclamations of a life of misery if he cannot spend it with Mary. She in response writes to him of the many difficulties a marriage entails and the likelihood that she will have no dowry and declares some such as she would in any case prefer to live in a nunnery. And so it goes on, endlessly, this courtship that blows four seasons through the house of their liaison in as many days. We are all weary of it.

Father negotiated with Wortley on the possibility of betrothal. Wortley is a Whig, if a somewhat priggish one, who sits in parliament for Huntingdon. More usefully, he has the possibility of a peerage if sufficient uncles should die without issue and – most usefully of all – stands to inherit many coal mines. All these considerations stand in his favour as far as our father is concerned. What stands against is Wortley's refusal to accept Father's terms for a marriage, which demand that all inheritance be entailed on the eldest male child of any union. What, argues Wortley, if any son he and Mary should have turns out to be a sot, a drunkard, a rake? This alone singles out Wortley amongst men and goes some way to explaining Mary's passion for him (inconstant though it is), since men in general imagine any son of theirs to be a simulacrum of themselves and therefore entirely perfect. Come to that, most men would simply accept terms, since they are invariably interested in the easiest course, particularly when it is lucrative.

What Mary's strategy is in respect of Wortley we are all unsure, but I cannot think she will actually marry Skeffington, despite the date now being fixed, and gowns being made, and announcements placed in the *Gazette*. Papa has expressly forbidden Mary to write even once more to Wortley.

2

ACTON, SOON

Summer 1712, London

(Frances)

Hearing voices raised last week – or one voice, rather – I went to the morning room where Father was blasting Mary with cannon shot, none of which (it was clear to me, at least) was landing anywhere near her defences. 'You tell me that you will not marry Skeffington, yet only two days ago you consented to it.'

'I have reflected, sir,' said Mary.

'You are not a damnable looking glass, lady, who may reflect as long as you care to. The time for reflection is long past.'

'I understand, Papa, that if I am to wed, then the Honourable Mr Skeffington is the one I must take as husband. And I understand, sir, that I may exercise no further opinion on the matter.'

'You have at least understood that perfectly.'

'But if it is to be Skeffington or nobody, then I choose to take Mr Nobody as my husband.'

Our father is in general a man of even temperament,

inclined to sombre moods and only rarely towards a light comment or even a particularly kind one, but he is seldom raised into a rage, yet at this his fist landed so heavily on the breakfast table that the chocolate leapt from the pot across the white linen and looked for all as if it were trying to flee the scene.

Mary, who naturally knew what she was doing in her provocation, added, 'And I shall always then be here at your side, to honour and serve you, dear Father.'

'Dear God above!' he roared, standing and obliging Mary to take a step away from him. 'You think I would will such a thing? What a torture it would be. It has been torment enough being father to you and your sisters, though Frances is only difficult when under your influence –' (he seemed either not to have noticed me standing there in the doorway or considered me barely worth considering in his tirade) '– and Evelyn has done her duty in marrying Gower. But the notion that I should want *you* at my side a day longer than I must. It is . . .' He sat, exhausted, only then noticing the disarray of the breakfast table, and gently began to put the spoons and knives back into their rightful positions. More quietly, and with a hint of regret, he said, 'You will have not a penny from me, madam. Not any allowance, nor settlement, nothing for any children you may bear when, as you no doubt will, you take some other man as your husband. And you must, if this is your certain choice, abandon all hopes of inheritance.'

Mary allowed herself a small smile, as if of victory, though for any other person this terrible declaration would have been a calamity. 'Sir,' she said, bowing very low and withdrawing, almost bustling into me in the doorway.

As soon as we were away from the morning room, I embraced her. 'Oh, my poor Mary.'

She placed a finger upon my lips. 'Papa still believes I will marry Skeffington,' she whispered. 'He cannot conceive that any plan of his will not be executed precisely as he wishes it to be. But I have my own. It needs you to be capable, Fanny.'

I was surprised my sister should have chosen Colman's toy-shop as the location to meet Mr Wortley. It is used by lovers who may not meet respectably or correspond safely, suitable because it is a place of chaotic display, with puppets, tops, hoops, tin soldiers, animals stuffed in such manner as to bear very little resemblance to their recently living form, and birds which flutter about and are chased back into their cages by Mrs Colman, who is almost blind. She is oblivious to the many men and women who frequent her establishment without showing the slightest interest in her miscellany. But I was amazed my sister settled upon the place, because while Mrs Colman may not comment upon my sister's presence there, others surely would. Mary was already well known, the subject of tittle-tattle and rumour, as I hoped never to be. I was therefore to remain with her, arm in arm, at every step, so whatever intimacies might pass between Mr Wortley and herself would also pass by, through or around me.

We stood before a goose, a wooden toy the size at least of the real bird and with wheels and a seat upon which a child might ride. Though what child would ride upon a goose, I wondered, since they are such ill-tempered birds? Wortley approached, upon his handsome face an expression of absolute composure. He bowed his head, first to me and then to Mary. 'Ladies,' he said quietly, though we were hardly likely to be overheard above the great clamour of the shop.

'Mr Wortley,' said I, with a hint of genuflection.

'I am unable to write, as you know,' said Mary, briskly. 'I

meet you only to tell you that Father is to send me to *Acton* to be with my brother and his wife. Acton, you understand?'

'I understand it is a place.'

'And papers are shuttling forth between here and Ireland that will settle my fate for ever if action is not taken, and soon. *Soon*, you understand?'

'Soon, I understand. Acton. Yes.'

My sister's plan slowly revealing itself, I was about to urge Wortley out of his obtuseness (with which I was familiar, having had sight of his letters) and in the direction of some response more meaningful than *Acton* and *Soon*, but Mary hushed me. 'He thinks before he speaks, Fanny. It is a quality both rare and admirable.'

Since I was there, and since Wortley had nothing on his face but a smirk, and nothing on his tongue but silence, I decided to ask him a question: 'How goes it in the Commons, Mr Wortley?'

He smiled at me kindly. 'It goes in the Commons, Lady Frances, much as it has ever gone, with bombast concealing deceit and the shrewd fellows working quietly and without scruple.'

'Note, Fanny,' said Mary, 'that Edward is neither bombastic nor deceitful. It's a shame he is not shrewd, but that is the price he pays for having scruple.'

I wondered if Mr Wortley would react with some annoyance at this statement, some hint of peevishness, but he shook his head in slow and tolerant amusement. 'That, dear lady,' he said to me, 'is as much of a compliment as I am ever likely to receive from your sister, and like a beggar who sits beneath the rich man's table hoping for crumbs, I take what I am given.'

How oddly likeable he was, this serious, sombrely handsome man. A figure brushed past us and, recognizing

Wortley, greeted him warmly. 'If it isn't Wortley, be damned!' Seeing us, the gentleman – if gentleman he was – bowed and apologized for his oath.

Wortley somehow seemed to introduce us without offering our names and said, 'The ladies are here to purchase a mechanical duck. It is the latest thing, it seems, and we are all ever so committed to the latest thing, are we not, Sutherland?'

'We are,' said this Sutherland, who looked at us moonily. He had the foolish expression of the kind of man who is used to ladies, and possibly gentlemen, falling for him without hesitation.

'And what is your latest thing, Mr Sutherland?' asked Mary, tartly.

'Why, madam, it is very probably you!'

'Indeed?' said Mary, her expression that of a woman who has accidentally put lemon in her tea instead of sugar. 'And yet given a choice between a mechanical duck and you, I would choose the duck. Good day.' And with that we moved on.

'Is that it?' I asked Mary once we were out in the sooty street air.

'It is sufficient.'

'*Acton? Soon?*'

'We are to be sent to Acton tomorrow, which is soon, Fanny. Very soon. Horribly soon. And if Edward waits another three days, I shall be married to Skeffington and then . . .' She looked about her, as if seeking some object that would explain her predicament. Seeing a horse, blinkered and in the process of being harnessed to the traces of a wagon, she said: 'I shall be no better off than that poor creature, and no doubt regarded as less useful to the world.'

My next task was to send word to Wortley that *a service is to be given at daybreak this Monday.* Some papers had arrived from Ireland that morning, and even a pineapple could deduce what they must contain. Since there was no servant who could be trusted with Mary's message, I went out to deliver it to Wortley's residence myself, pulling up my skirts as best I could and hiding my watch in my stays, since thieves were common along Portugal Street and round about. But I was not daunted. I love my sister, and would do anything to help her, though what any of it meant I did not truly know.

Monday came, and I was bid by Mary to be up at daybreak, and we stood together on the balcony at our brother's house awaiting – what, I wondered? Eventually it became clear to me that we awaited nothing, for nothing happened. 'You await Wortley?' I asked at last, the sun well up and the silence now broken only by the cries of William's infant son. Why I had not wanted to utter Wortley's name before I was unsure, but I think it would have been like breaking a spell.

Mary gave me a look, and turned wearily back into the chamber, starting to take off her travelling coat and boots, for she had been ready to do whatever it was she had planned, which may well have been to jump down from the balcony and on to a waiting horse. She seemed resigned to what must come. 'Father has wind of the matter. He will have me sent to West Dean today.'

'Then I shall come with you.'

She placed a hand on my cheek. 'Thank you, dearest Fanny, but I believe Papa may not permit it. He fancies you are confederate in my schemes.'

'I know less of them than I should like.'

'You know enough. It is important in intelligence to share only what must be revealed to achieve the final objective. Bear that in mind when it comes to your own marriage.'

'After seeing all you have gone through, I think I should rather simply consent to whomsoever our father chooses.'

'Then others must ensure your interests are protected, Fanny, for Father will sacrifice your happiness most willingly for two thousand a year.' She said so without rancour, still less any humour.

I had no wish to reflect on my own fortunes, be they good or ill, and so, thinking to cheer her into contradiction, said, 'You will see the ghost at West Dean. Do you think it is Grandmama?'

'It may be, if there were such things as ghosts in the world, Fanny. But there are not. There are only memories, and we who live turn those who are dead into ghosts. So I do not say you do not see Grandmama walking the corridors of West Dean, only that what you see is from here –' she placed a finger at my temple '– and here –' and moved that finger to my heart. 'You have made a ghost out of love, and so when you are next there you must not be scared.'

How wrong it was that my sister was comforting me when it was I who should have been comforting her. 'Perhaps Mr Wortley merely misunderstood. *Acton, Soon?*' I said, forlornly.

Mary frowned. 'He is not a simpleton, Fanny.'

I was kept behind at Acton, as Mary suspected I would be. It near broke my heart to see her leaving for West Dean that morning, looking out from her carriage, knowing she was sent away almost to imprisonment while she awaited her unwilling betrothal to that most unworthy man. I spoke to my brother of it after Mary had left, being careful not to give away too much of the failed plan, saying only that I did not think Mary loved Clotworthy Skeffington in the slightest, and that she still held her affections for Mr Wortley Montagu, who seemed to me a respectable and kind gentleman.

William laughed, which I took to be unsympathetic. 'Our

sister has a way of getting her way, Fanny. You just wait and see.' And he tapped the side of his nose, as if he were in possession of some knowledge that I was not, which made me furious since was I not the one who had performed all the subterfuge on Mary's behalf, and what had William done lately but become a father?

On the Monday it was clear that Mary was condemned to that terrible marriage, yet on the Wednesday Papa entered the drawing room at Acton, dust about his coat so that he seemed to be Jehovah speaking to us from the clouds. We were gathered together on his orders: my brother, William, his wife, Lady Kingston, who looked most feeble and unwell, and myself. 'Your sister Mary has married Mr Wortley Montagu,' Father announced. 'The elopement was long planned. I know you had some hand in it, Frances.' He pointed an accusing finger at me. I saw that it shook slightly, though his tone was even.

I did not regard myself as having had much of a hand in Mary's elopement at all, since I knew so little of it. I was minded to say something of Mary's love for Mr Wortley, but thought better than to infuriate Father all the more.

'You knew of it too, William, I am sorry to say.'

My brother lowered his eyes, as if in consent, leaving me in little doubt that he had known more of Mary's plans than I had.

'She left here at Monday noon for Wiltshire,' announced Father formally, as if he were obliged to give us a full report, 'stopped the night in Berkshire and the next day was galloped back to London and married. And that is all we know of Lady Mary Wortley Montagu, as she will now be known, and all I trust we shall ever know. No one is to have anything to do with her or her husband. Do you understand?'

None of us made to reply.

'Do you understand?' he repeated, quietly but firmly.

'We are not simpletons,' said I.

He cast me a look of surprise, knowing it was just what Mary might have said, as indeed she had. 'Well, then.' And with that our father went back to London, for the world's business awaited him always, and there seemed to be a hint of relief rather than fury in his tone, for Mary was indeed off his hands at last.

It was only later in the day that I realized, with a feeling of distinct misgiving, that I must be next.

3

A WOMAN OF OPINION

Autumn 1714, Duke Street, Westminster

(Mary)

Edward surely knew me to be a woman of opinion. Did he imagine my brain would fall away as I uttered my marriage vows, as leaves from a tree in a November gale? We are married two years, yet I feel he is more a stranger to me now than when we first met. My husband is unyielding, stubborn, burdened by an undue sense of propriety and thus as wearisome as my father. How odd that they did not see how alike they were when Edward first proposed his suit – and how odd that I did not see it myself.

I knew him first through the eyes of his sister, Anne, and sometimes I think it is she that I hoped I'd marry. There was nothing we did not talk about when together, Anne and I, and when apart we wrote letters that would be thought scandalous if any other were to read them. She was bright and clever and tender, the very essence of female perfection, and if we were foolish together, as one is obliged to be at fifteen years of age, then we were at least not guilty of shooting any creatures and leaving them injured, or drinking until we vomited over our shoes, or indulging in bareknuckle fights as young men are wont to do when in love with their friends. I saw a shadow fall across Anne from time to time when she asked me to hold her close, to place my lips upon hers, and I see now that she had some premonition of what was to befall her. I remember thinking when she slept in my arms that she might indeed be too precious a thing to live at all.

It was the measles she caught, and from a maid who had but a few spots and a mild fever with it. Yet for my soft, gentle Anne, with whom I had lain and laughed, whose skin was silk and whose fingers upon mine gave me a thousand ecstasies, for Anne the measles brought a swift death. Measles!

I understood Death then, and how he waits for love much as a hound waits for a scent, and once he has it, then he will chase and chase until he has his kill. First my mother, then my grandmother, who died right before my eyes. We were out riding one day at West Dean, just the two of us, I talking away about birds and spiders and the likelihood of encountering a March hare – I was nine years old, and such things interested me then – when I saw that her face had turned quite blue. With difficulty I dismounted, took her horse by the reins and brought it to a halt, at which she slid from the saddle and landed on the ground like a sack of grain, her mouth frozen in some word she had been about to speak and that I would never hear. Dead from an apoplexy. Oh yes, I understand the wily ways of Death.

After I lost Anne, I sought out love where I could find it, but secretly. There was the curate's son, a very pretty fellow who wrote me poems in the style of Virgil, and I to him. He was one of those young men who is naturally learned, and when Papa was out of the house I would take him into the library, and we would spend hours at Ovid and Horace. His company, any man's company, is different from a woman's – like a dance in which the steps are never quite learnt, I'd say. There is hair in more places, of course, and the smells are of earth and the wild. But still, it was pleasurable. Yet when Joseph Snape told me solemnly, a bunch of limp bluebells in his hand, that he loved me, I could not confess how I truly felt, and so I laughed, and told him that love was impossible. I did not mean because of our respective classes, though that would have certainly been an impediment. I wanted to say to him, *I am saving your life, Joseph Snape, for anyone I love is sure to die*, but he would not have understood, and he fled from me, thinking my mercy a humiliation.

Next came Nathaniel Shaw, my brother's Latin tutor, a poor fellow William brought home to Thoresby from Westminster the summer I was seventeen, and with whom I spent many happy hours discussing *The Satires.* He asked me to walk the grounds with him, and one hot day asked if he might swim in the lake, and I watched him undress, since it seemed that he dared me to do so. First he removed his jacket, next his shirt and hose, to reveal a form much as I had seen in books of Greek statues; indeed, the band of muscle on his belly seemed as if made from marble. He swam up and down in the clear water, his pale, taut form almost other-worldly beneath the rippling surface. Next day he asked if I would swim with him and, thinking my body no matter of shame, I did as he had, though stays and petticoats are not easy to remove when one is eager to be rid of them, and I could hardly ask my maid to come undress me. Finding each other pleasing, this became our practice that summer when the weather allowed for it. We did not shiver long. But Death was watching us, I knew, waiting for some sniff of love, and so the time came when I was obliged to tell Mr Shaw that I could not love him either.

With Edward I have always known there is no danger of love. Amiable respect is our preservation. He and I had corresponded through the safe offices of Anne, my friend thinking it a fine thing that I pretend to a flirtation with her older brother, already successful in business and a Member of Parliament. Edward has Anne's features, drawn just as they are obliged to be in a man, the chin squarer, the nose longer, the brow heavier. He has her eyes, too, a very faint blue, always seeming to search for something in the far-off distance, no less alluring in his sober face than in her lively one. After Anne died, Edward and I continued to meet in secret, and in truth I consented to his attentions in the hope of seeing some glimpse of his sister. Sometimes when he observed me, I thought it was the very spirit of Anne looking out from him and begging me to hold her once more.

My sister read the letters which went back and forth between Edward and me, which I thought of as the feint and flèche of fencing more than as a romantic correspondence, but Fanny has always been more literal, and so she asked me one day early in our courtship whether I loved Edward.

'Love? No, I do not *love* him, Fanny. He interests me, I should say, and I think I interest him, and that a man and woman should interest each other is better than many marriages, where a couple may be chained together for a lifetime, and love is nothing more than the moment's inattention that slips on the shackles.'

'Goodness!' said Fanny. 'You say such things. I think you have so great an animus against marriage that I shouldn't wonder if you stay all your life a spinster.'

'Most probably I should, but Father insists that I marry

that oaf Skeffington. And so it may be that Mr Edward Wortley is my only means of avoiding that fate. To marry for love is bad enough, but to marry for hate is another thing altogether.'

'Is Edward very handsome?' she asked, not then having had sight of him.

'He may be. I haven't really noticed,' I lied.

Fanny, who has a way of getting lost in her thoughts and lapsing into long silences, said at last, 'He loves you. That is obvious from his letters.'

'I really do hope not.'

'How can you say so?'

I started to tell Fanny all I thought about love and death, and yet how could I deny my love for my sister and not hurt her? Yet to confess it too openly would have Death sniffing at her skirts. As I tried to explain I saw an expression first of puzzlement and soon of dismay bloom on her sweet face, and so I stopped myself from saying more, concluding with: 'It is simply that love leads a woman into danger. A man may love and flee, after all. But if a woman loves she cannot quit the scene once she sees her error. A man may go to sea, or join the army or, or . . . go into a trade. What may we do but lock ourselves in our chambers?'

'Oh, Mary. I do not think you would ever lock yourself in your chamber.'

Ten months after Edward and I married I gave birth to our son. I was very sick in those first months of pregnancy, as is common enough. Edward was away in London at the Commons, I spending my mornings vomiting into my chamber pot and my afternoons in correspondence with my writing friends Joseph Addison and John Gay, or in keeping my diary, which I began to do every day. I was trying to find a suitable home in which to raise our son. Edward had left me the task, thinking that a roof and beds and servants were domestic matters beneath his mighty intellect. I found a house eventually at Middlethorpe, near York, and engaged a housekeeper, Mrs Hills, a capable woman who was determined to give me a variety of country cures for my morning sickness, these including concoctions of yarrow, mugwort and purslane, which may or may not have made me sicker. The scientific method would have required their application also to a woman who was not with child to see if she, too, was made sick with all the hedgerow herbs I was being made to swallow. Still, the sickness passed and I busied myself, including in giving advice to Edward, since soon after our son, Eddie, was born the old queen had the good grace to die, making way for a reluctant Hanoverian prince to come and be our king, and a new parliament to be elected. After years of Tory misrule, venality and corruption, it was clear enough that we were to have sensible Whigs in charge at last. I prepared to make a return to London, but before I could do so, little Eddie fell dreadfully ill.

It is miraculous that any infant should live beyond three, since they are loved well, and Death likes to pursue all well-loved things. I hold as proof the irrefutable fact that those whom everyone detests seem to live for ever. I took care not to show Eddie too great an affection or allow my heart to break each time he fell ill, first with croup, then Boulogne sour throat and after that the quinsy. I dreaded most greatly the smallpox, but we lived well out in good country air, and I thought that a preservation. It was scarlatina that seemed ready to take him from me, for he lay in a high fever for a week, growing ever more enfeebled. Edward had the best physicians sent from York, but they all wanted to bleed poor Eddie, and I felt certain that taking what little blood the child had in his veins was the last thing he could endure, and so forbade them their practice. This prompted my husband to write to me with a firm rebuke for *not permitting qualified men to do their professional duty*. I replied, saying that if he was so concerned for his son he should ride up from London and join me in sitting by his bedside.

Night after night, I sat with Eddie's little hand in mine, from time to time feeling his feverish brow for any improvement. His innocent face, blotchy and red, looked so afraid that I prayed, and in praying confessed my love for him and vowed that I would exchange his precious life for any other, save Fanny's.

On the fifth day of our son's grave illness his father at last consented to take the stagecoach from London, and it was on that day that Eddie's fever broke. Next morning my sweet boy knew me, said, 'Mama,' and ate a little soup.

When his father arrived the day after, the first thing he said was: 'The child seems well.'

'You sound displeased, Edward, as if it were hardly worth making the journey from London but for his funeral.'

'Don't be ridiculous, Mary. It is natural for a mother to worry more for an infant than is strictly necessary.'

'*Strictly necessary*? How much worry *is* necessary for a child that seems about to die?' said I, trying to conceal my fury, since I knew all too well that men think women susceptible to emotional overreaction. 'An ounce of worry, five ounces, perhaps? A pound of worry, shall we say?'

'I was concerned about Eddie, I assure you.'

'Your physician told me to expect the worst. I imagine he meant that our son would not survive. Though if I had given Dr Bland his way he would have bled our son to death.'

'Really, Mary!'

After our row subsided into studied silence we ate dinner,

and following discussion of the household accounts, the inadequacies of the cook I had engaged, and the brightest figures in the new parliament, we discussed Edward's prospects of being given some position. Our friend Joseph Addison, an ardent Whig as well as a fine playwright, was certain to gain high office, and Edward hoped for a similarly exalted place.

'Have you made your ambition known? You must make your case, Edward,' I urged him.

He gave me that cool look of his. 'That is not my way. It is yours, to flatter and charm and write to all, but not mine.'

'You cannot expect to be favoured if you do not favour yourself.'

'Then perhaps it is best I return to Westminster as soon as may be,' he said, peevishly.

'And as soon as Eddie is well, we shall join you there.'

He gave me a look of great agony but did not demur. I knew that some husbands wanted their families far off so that they could keep mistresses and gamble and drink late into the night with their fellow rakes, but all that Edward desired was peace, which he was right to surmise I had no intention of giving him.

My prayer for Edward's life cost me dear, as I should have known it would. My love for my child, silently confessed, put the scent of my vow into Death's nostrils and he sought out some other soul he knew I loved. I received a letter informing me that my brother, William, was ill with smallpox on the Tuesday, Dr Garth pronouncing the contagion a bad case, for the pustules were large and full and the fever high. But I hoped all that day and the day after that this was merely the doctor adhering to his profession's invariable practice of spelling out the most terrible prognosis so he might then claim full credit for his patient's recovery. But on the Thursday my brother was dead. William was not yet twenty-one, his nervous young wife now left alone to care for two infants. I went straightway to Acton, and there the scene of desperate mourning was everything one might imagine, his wife pale and broken, the two infants oblivious to the calamity that had befallen them but wailing constantly, aware as children so often are of a distress they could not fully comprehend. Fanny was trying to console and organize, but she was so distracted with grief that she was unable to issue simple instructions to the household as to the proper placing of the black crêpe, and unsure as to whom the death notices should be sent.

'Where is Papa?' I asked.

'Oh, Mary,' she said, 'he is in his chamber.' She bit her lip and looked at me with eyes made red by endless tides of tears. 'He will not see anyone. Not any of us.'

I felt an urge to go immediately to him and offer what consolation I could. But my father and I were not yet truly reconciled, though only the month before he had paid Edward and me a visit so that we might belatedly present him with his grandson. I was fearful of causing him yet more pain. And I had other fears, too, afraid as I was of seeing my adamantine father broken by the loss of his only son, and a deeper, lingering, sinister, terrible worry that I might confess my great sin to him: for had I not prayed some other soul might lose their life so that my own boy would live? It felt to me that Death had taken William at my very bidding. Showing none of what I truly felt to Fanny, I said: 'He will have to face William's funeral.'

'Yes,' said Fanny, uncertainly.

'I had better manage matters, then,' I declared, and

Fanny's relief made my performance of cool reason seem almost believable, even to myself.

'He has forgiven you, you know,' said Fanny, her voice strained, as if fearing some rebuke.

'Forgiven me?'

'For marrying Edward. I know you and he have hardly spoken, and Papa has been so busy with the new court and all the demands upon him. But he was so pleased to meet little Eddie . . .' She gulped down a sob.

'I wonder whether Papa will be permitted three months' mourning, as he ought to be.'

Fanny looked at me blankly. She had a habit of pretending to perfect ignorance of any political matter, which I found irritating, playing as it did into the notion that a woman could not understand affairs of state as a man might, unless she happened to be queen.

The days that followed I took my grief and put it to work: arranging William's funeral, informing relatives, placing the necessary notices in newspapers, having the household placed into mourning, and giving instructions for my own to be made likewise. And still none of us saw Papa. The new king sent his condolences, a thing quite unheard of, though coming from such a small town as Hanover he had perhaps not understood the detached dignity required of an English monarch.

Fanny and I talked much in that week, of Edward and Papa, and of William, naturally. But since we had hours together, something we had not enjoyed since before I was married, we spoke too of other things. I told her that I had written a prologue for Joseph Addison's new play, having helped him with his *Cato*, which was such a great success, and this interested her, since we had always enjoyed play-writing. We talked of the new court, and when we might be presented there.

'And what of gentlemen?' I asked.

'Gentlemen?' said Fanny, as if I had spoken of a subject entirely alien to her.

'Yes, Fanny. Gentlemen. I did not say *what of camelopards*? Our father has surely been dangling matches before you. At least until . . .'

'There will be no more talk of that for now.'

'Not for now, no. But you never put this subject in your letters, yet it is one of great importance.'

'Don't I?' she said weakly, looking about her as if something might catch her eye and help her to change the subject.

'Has Papa not attempted any introductions since I last saw you?'

Her tone shifted from distraction to irritation. 'Not serious ones, Mary, no. You know how it is. Some widowed duke or other comes to town and I am introduced to him and invited to play the fortepiano and inspected like . . . like a . . . like a what? You always have the apt comparison.'

'I dare not say. I think *you* might be inspected like a pretty bird in a cage.'

'More like a heifer at a country show,' she said, not lightly.

'And did you not inspect them back?'

'No . . . no,' she said, stopping herself from saying anything more.

I wondered whether our father's intention was to keep my sister at his side, and hated to think of dear Fanny for ever in his shade, like an alpine flower struggling to grow beneath a rocky outcrop. 'Do not allow yourself to become Papa's companion, still less his slave, Fanny,' I urged. 'He grieves now, naturally he does, but you are too good a creature to live for ever in our father's long shadow.'

Fanny tapped the palms of her hands upon her knees twice, as if in resolution. 'He has his eyes on a new wife,' she declared.

This was a surprise. 'Who?'

'Lady Isabella Bentinck.'

'*She?* Isabella Bentinck!' I repeated, incredulous. 'She's the same age as me. What is it about old men? Why must they always take for a wife a woman young enough to be a daughter?'

Fanny smiled in weak agreement but said nothing.

'When I am old, I shall take for a lover a youth young enough to be my son!'

'Mary!' she said, almost ready to laugh, though she quickly placed a hand across her mouth, for laughter is unseemly in a house of mourning. 'There *is* someone that Father seems to have fixed upon for me,' she said hesitantly.

I had lowered her guard, as I had intended. 'Who?'

'I cannot tell you.'

'Why not?'

'Because it is a secret.'

'But we have no secrets, Fanny. We never have.'

'You are full of secrets, Mary. I know you are. I see into your heart, though you think I do not. Ever since you arrived here, I've sensed something more than grief.'

'Oh?'

'Tell me.'

'Tell you what?'

'Tell me that which you absolutely have no intention of telling me.'

This was a game we had played as children, to reveal to each other what we would never dream of revealing to any other. 'In proof that we do not have secrets, or at least that *I* have none, I shall tell you. It is that when Eddie was very sick and seemed on the edge of death, I prayed to God not to take him but to take some other in his place, save yours. And then . . .' I struggled to continue my confession. 'And then not two weeks pass before William is taken from us.' I struggled to hold back the tears I felt ready to spill.

Fanny reached out and placed a reassuring hand upon my arm. 'It was smallpox, Mary. Not a curse,' she said, almost too quietly to be heard.

'What is smallpox if not a curse – a speckled, monstrous curse?' I said, but I did not wish to say anything more about my constant bargaining with Death. Noticing that a lock of hair had come loose from her pinner I stood and tucked it back. 'I have told you my secret, and so you must tell me yours,' I said, standing over her. I couldn't see her expression but sensed her unease. In that moment a loud groan sounded above us, as if the house was shifting on its foundations, and not a minute after the footman was before us. 'His Grace the Duke of Kingston bids you attend him, Lady Mary.'

4

OF KINGS AND POXES

Spring 1715, Westminster

(Mary)

The rapprochement with my father was brief, but long enough to allow me to be presented at court, where I found myself seized upon as a flickering lantern is prized in a storm when every other has blown out, for the court I arrived at was extraordinarily dreary. All were agreed that since we had invited a cheerless German family to come rule over us, we were obliged to make the best of it. King George was fifty-five years old, endowed with a large belly, small chin, long nose, bulging eyes and in possession of a perfect lack of interest in his new realm. He spoke French tolerably well, and proved to be most susceptible to flattery from me, which was just as well, since it resulted in invitations to his evening parties, at which I paid particular attention to his mistress, who was considerably more intelligent than the king and yet all the while sensitive to his wishes, since she had no desire to find herself imprisoned in Hanover along with his wife.

Wortley and I dutifully attended concerts and cards and

took our places at long tables piled high with game both feathered and furred and drank the royal wine and ate the royal sugared plums and tried to amuse, since that was what we were there for, though amusement not being Edward's strongest suit the burden fell unduly upon me, and I walked that narrow path between attempting to charm all and infuriate none. It was a relief, always, when the evening came to an end and the king retired with his mistress.

'Why is George so stupid, do you suppose?' I asked Edward after we had been all evening at St James's and observed His Majesty asking if England had any towns that did not smell so strongly of their rivers. King George made this observation in German, which I was learning so that I could understand the smaller talk of the court, though I already knew enough to realize that much of what was said involved how best to cheat at *triomphe*.

'Why should a king be intelligent?' asked Edward.

'A king certainly need not be intelligent, and it may be better that kings are fools, happy to sit on the throne and have their portrait painted while those more capable run the country, but I did not mean that a king should be intelligent simply because he is king. I meant that this king has come from a family not known for its stupidity. His mother was a clever woman,' I said, 'a woman of letters, a conversationalist, a diplomat, an intellectual. Didn't Addison say so after he went to her court? And yet she produced an oaf, and we are obliged to exalt him.'

'Perhaps the king wasn't always so. As we age so we find the world grows away from us, and we from the world, and by the time one is old one is ready to depart this life, since one hardly recognizes it at all.'

Sometimes Edward sounded as if he was Methuselah himself. 'George is fifty-five, which is not so old,' I said, 'and besides, you are talking nonsense. I pity anyone who at the age of fifty-five has grown weary of the world! I shall die when I am good and ready, and until then I shall live as fully as I may.'

Edward gave me that look of his, which meant he could not stir himself to disagree.

When I finally wrenched from Fanny the truth of Father's proposed match for her, I was shocked into silence. At last recovering my voice, I asked her to repeat the name. 'He would have you marry *John Erskine*?' I said in disbelief.

Erskine, the Earl of Mar, was notorious for his weak and unreliable character, and it was universally known that he had been hunting unsuccessfully for a new wife for years, the mother of his son having died of childbed fever.

Fanny retreated bodily from my outrage, and though I pitied her, I felt certain that I could shake her out of her timidity and into repudiation of such an odious match. 'The Earl of Mar, yes,' she said with surprising indignation.

'He is but a Scottish earl. And he is shallow, Fanny. Shallow and vain. And moreover, he is a Tory.'

'He has been most solicitous.'

'I cannot believe you have been consorting with him behind my back!'

Fanny laughed at this, which was to her credit. 'You are not my keeper, Mary. I did not tell you because I knew you would behave exactly as you do now. And I thought . . .' Though as so often she seemed to forget whatever it was she thought and lapsed into silence.

'*What* did you think?' I snapped.

'I thought . . . well, hoped at first, and then feared, or I think I did . . . do . . . that his terms might anyway not be acceptable to Papa. You know how he is, and so it seemed best to see how matters progressed, if at all. Though I should have been sorry to see them snared on Papa's stipulations for what inheritance any son we might have should be given, and then how much to a second son, and what to a daughter and so on. John already has a son, of course. Thomas. He is twelve years old. Or is he eleven?'

'You will always play second fiddle to his first-born son, Fanny. You do see that?'

'Perhaps second fiddle suits me, Mary,' she prickled. 'I know you always need to be playing first violin, or perhaps a big bass drum.'

'Erskine is, what . . . fifteen years your senior?'

'And Wortley?' she parried. 'He is what? More than ten years yours?'

'But he is reliable. He is reliably what he is, which is not as much as I should like, but certainly no more than I can handle. I fear that Erskine is—'

'More than I can handle?' interrupted Fanny, still defiant.

'Very probably. He is intemperate. Known to be. Charming yet of ill mood and impatient. If you truly care for Erskine that is one thing, but—'

'I believe that I do. He is clever, and kind.'

Did my sister's naivety really extend to not knowing that John Erskine, the Earl of Mar, was regarded at court with contempt? Though I had no wish to hurt her feelings, indeed only wanted to protect her, I feared that her fond sentiments were growing around this loathsome man, much as mother of pearl grows around a rotten oyster that will still only stink. 'You do know what is said of him, since he veers one day in favour of Hanover and the next is with the Jacobites?'

My gentle sister looked up at me as if expecting a slap, which I proceeded to deliver with my next words. 'It is said that he worked first for the Act of Union, then decided he was against it when it seemed the Scottish parliament would never vote in its favour, and then at last, when the political winds changed, decided he favoured it after all, and that he was *as the dog to the vomit*. A man like Erskine is not to be trusted, Fanny, and but for his offices, which are now taken from him, he is poor.'

Fanny laughed at me, almost in derision. 'Really, Mary, you sound like Papa. Except that Papa likes him, and you do not.'

This was the mystery: Father – arch Whig, loather of Tories, suspicious of Scots, disliking of inconsistency – was seeking to match his one remaining unmarried daughter with the Earl of Mar, a man who exemplified every quality he detested. I resolved to get to the bottom of matters, for I knew that Fanny would do whatever she could to please Papa, and were our father to change his mind, Fanny would do so, too, and would be much the better for it. But before I could try to make my father see reason, I had to allay my husband's fears that he was not nearly so great a man as he supposed himself to be.

Edward had grown increasingly downcast because he had been offered only a very junior position in the Treasury, and that after almost every other post in the new government had been filled. 'I am obliged to turn it down,' he said.

'Whyever so? You will be working with Walpole, and he is by far the ablest man in the government.'

'I have *some* remaining shreds of self-respect, Mary.'

Edward was proud, which was his greatest failing, as I was often obliged to remind him. I knew that I had to work subtly to ease his sense of injury if I was to persuade him to take the post, as he needed to if he was not to be cast out from the circles of power for ever. 'The position you are offered is not one of great title or ceremony, it's true. But it is one of quiet influence. You will be able to write the laws, Edward, not simply make speeches for or against. You will improve the way we are regulated and bring fairness and propriety to the Treasury. I did not think you were much interested in grand titles like *Chamberlain of This* or *Chancellor of That*.'

He drew back his head, thrust his chest forwards, like a bird assessing its need to take flight, but said nothing.

'Besides, it is a good thing to start in government in the post you are offered,' I continued in a tone of mollifying reassurance, 'and you will, I have no doubt, show that you are worthy of higher office through your diligence and wisdom.'

He looked at me suspiciously. 'You counsel me to accept this office – which is an insult – for one reason above all others.'

'Which is?'

'It is so I do nothing to upset your father.'

'That is not true, Edward. I counsel you to take it because it is what you are offered.' That was perhaps harsh of me, but the truth was that my husband never made any effort to make himself amenable to those who decided these matters, and that, as anyone knows, is what truly counts above all else.

'Were we on better terms with your father then I might have been offered more,' he protested.

'I might be about to put us on worse terms yet.'

A look of despair crossed his face. 'Oh?'

'He wishes to marry Fanny to the Earl of Mar.'

Edward raised an eyebrow. 'That *is* a surprising match. Mar is—'

'I know what he is. Who doesn't? Well, Fanny apparently. But Papa most certainly does. I cannot think what he means by it.'

'Please don't enrage him, Mary, as you . . .' He stopped himself from saying whatever it was he was going to say.

'*As I what?*' I demanded.

'As you have such an inclination to do,' he said in irritation before taking up his hat and fleeing to the Commons, thus denying me the opportunity to interrogate him further on his true opinion of my character.

My father consented to see me at his offices at Somerset House. I was uneasy, indeed sick, at the prospect of the confrontation that I knew was inevitable but necessary in defence of my dear sister's happiness. I felt like the general of an army ill equipped, too long at battle and with supply lines exhausted, and yet certain that honour required me to make this last stand.

The building was from Tudor times, its upper floors low-ceilinged and dark, and the way to my father's offices was along narrow corridors and up narrower flights of stairs. At my entrance I prostrated myself before him, only to see when I looked up that he was continuing to read the many papers that were upon his desk, the feather quill in his hand hovering over them as if about to stab any word which met with his disapproval. He still did not look up as I stood, saying merely, 'Mary. You wish to see me on a matter of some urgency?'

'Yes, Papa.'

'If you are to make suit on your husband's behalf, you should know that I exerted myself greatly to have him offered any position at all.'

'And he is humbly grateful for it, as am I.'

At this he glanced up, no doubt thinking gratitude improbable and humility more so, before quickly resuming his reading, scratching out a word here and there. 'Then what?'

'It is Frances, sir. You have a match in mind for her?'

'I do not believe –' scratch, scratch at the paper '– that you are in any position to offer matrimonial advice, and I trust you do not intend to offer me any.' He looked up and smiled, chillingly.

'I should never in this life or the next be so impertinent as to imagine that I might offer you, sir, advice on any matter,' I said, my nerves so great that I spoke too fast, sounding impatient, which was precisely the opposite tone to that which I had intended. 'But I hardly think it necessary to remind you,' I continued, more slowly, 'that John Erskine, Earl of Mar, is in debt, a Tory and, if not today then most likely tomorrow, a Jacobite. If he seems unsuitable to be a son to you and a brother to me, then I am obliged to observe that he is most certainly unsuitable to be a husband to Fanny, for she has a tender soul.'

Scratch, scratch upon the paper. 'I am known, madam, for evenness of temper.'

'You are—'

He raised a finger. 'Do not speak!' His voice was high, unusually so.

I did not speak.

'Why is it only *you* that are so capable of stirring me into a fury, like some ill wind blown from a far-off place?'

Still I did not utter a word.

'Your sister is to be Countess of Mar and that is the end of it.'

'But why?'

'Why? *Why?*' His voice grew into a shout. 'Why, she asks!' he declared to no one in particular, though doubtless a battalion of clerks was also scratching away in the antechamber, listening to every word my father boomed at me. 'Because he has sworn his loyalty to the king and, moreover, to me. Because Fanny need be married. Because I am weary and want done of having to marry off daughters.'

Now I smelt the sulphur of the enemy's rifles, and heard the boom of their cannon, the thunder of their hooves, and I had no choice but to charge. I would not be intimidated. I feared death and I feared love, but I would not fear my unyielding father. 'I shall never again attempt to offer you advice or warning or even an opinion on any matter—'

'Good,' he declared, standing and ready to usher me from the room.

'But I love Fanny more dearly than anyone in the world, bar my son, and I think she of all people deserves a gentle, kind man as husband. I could not bear to see her married to Erskine.'

'Then you shall not, madam, for you shall not be invited to the wedding!'

'But—'

He raised a hand in finality, opened the door to make clear that I must leave. A footman appeared, ready to escort me from the building.

'You would not forbid me from attending my own dear sister's wedding?' I pleaded.

'Since you do not wish to see her married to the man, it is clear that I must satisfy your wishes. You shall not receive an invitation.'

I knew he would not be persuaded out of this stance, and though I should have retreated, I instead used the last of my ammunition against him. 'You want her married quickly so that you may take Isabella Bentinck for your wife. That's it, isn't it?'

'OUT!'

The day after my bloody encounter with my father I felt weak, exhausted, suffering with a sharp headache and a slight fever. I believed it must be in reaction to my confrontation, for in truth I always had high hopes of my father and whenever they were dashed – as they always were – it was as if I had been cast into a dark and tangled forest and had no hope of finding a path out. Thinking the best cure for my malaise was busyness, I went about my appointments, calling on my dear friend Lady Oxford and spending the afternoon revising some poems that I had been writing in the pastoral style in collaboration with John Gay. But by the evening I felt too exhausted to go to cards with Lady Bristol and retired early. The nurse bid me come and spend some time with little Eddie, and I was on my way to the nursery when I felt preternaturally certain that I should not sit with him but must instead go directly to my bed.

Next day I felt worse and was then certain I must have caught a chill. Going to the looking glass I noticed my skin was raised, and saw three spots on my right arm, and four more on my left. And I knew. I knew but spent an hour trying to convince myself that I did not. When Betsy, my chambermaid, came to dress me, I hastened her away before she could come close.

I knew.

I was violently sick at eleven and called through my door for Dr Garth to be sent for. He may or may not have come, for I remember nothing after but fractured dreams of crows flying across the face of the sun, of one bird landing upon my chest and driving its sharp beak again and again into my heart. Yet I did not wish the crow to flee. I embraced it, pressed its oily feathers into me, felt its heart beating, fast and strong and yet like something racing towards its end. I know now that Death must have come for me in the form of that crow. Yet I embraced Death when he expected me to recoil from him, and perhaps it was in that unexpected embrace that I cheated him.

I was told after that I spoke thus – of crows and suns and wings.

When I first became aware that I was alive, I could not see, and wondered then what a life of blindness would bring me, a life without books or art, without writing. Edward came close, his voice soft and solicitous. 'My dear Mary.'

'Do not come near, Edward, for you have never had the disease,' I croaked.

'Dr Garth says you will not infect now, because your blisters are scabbing.'

'Perhaps it is a blessing if I am blind, for I will not ever see the monster that the smallpox has made of me.'

He took my hand, squeezed it. 'You are no more a monster now than you were before.'

I gave a feeble laugh, and Edward laughed too, and what a cure for sickness laughter is, and how unexpected. Through dry lips and with scratched voice I said: 'Your compliments are always made, Edward dear, as if you expect some legal suit to be given in pursuit of their accuracy.'

He brought some water to my lips. 'True,' he said gently.

'You do not say I am no monster, merely no *more* of one.'

He left his cool hand on my brow. 'Hmmm.'

'But one of a different form?'

'You are changed, but since you have kept your wits, you

are not so changed as all that.' And to my amazement I felt the softness of his lips upon mine.

'Thank you,' I said, and was embarrassed to find myself on the brink of tears as I said so.

'*Thank me?* For what?'

'For the truth. Never lie to me, and I shall never lie to you.'

'I swear it.'

'It is our oath. And if I am blind it will be so easy for all to deceive me. I shall need a pair of eyes, some good servant who may tell me all that they observe, truthfully.'

'Dr Garth says it is not unusual for it to take some weeks for the sight to return, though sometimes it may not.'

'I pity the poor servant who would have to be my eyes, for I must see *all*, read *all*, know *all*.'

'I am sure every servant and every secretary in the land will be praying for your complete recovery, Mary. As do I, not least so no poor soul will be obliged to take on the task of seeing the world as you do.' He squeezed my hand again, but I could tell he was eager to leave.

'Where are you going now in such haste?'

'I am required to introduce a bill into the Commons.'

'There. You see! I told you that you would be given great duties at the Treasury.'

He gave a squeak, something like the noise a mouse gives out when close to being caught. Had I been able to see his expression I should have known whether he was amused or embarrassed. 'What is it, this bill?' I asked, afraid that he had already left the room.

'The bill raises duty on coffin nails.'

'Ingenious,' I said, but he had gone, and I was once more left to my thoughts and fears, though not for long.

Visitors came and went, as if I were an exhibit at the fair. Lady Rich declared that I looked very well and almost entirely like my old self, and Miss Calthorpe said she thought me miraculous. But dear Lady Oxford told me true, in part because she was my oldest friend and in part because she had not the sense to dissemble. I looked a fright, she told me, for my face was pocked and my eyelashes gone, and no one would ever think me a great beauty again, but for all that she would stay my friend because she loved me.

I wondered then whether blindness might save me from ever having to encounter the tattered remains of myself, but I knew I was not my face but my thoughts, and besides there were enough men and women at every corner, in every doorway, at cards and at court, who were pocked. A scarred face would hardly single me out.

My sight came back at first in bursts of bright light, and then in the blurred shapes of my room and of my maid and of Edward, who came to see me often, of my friends and of little Eddie, who seemed not to want to know me, such is the artless honesty of infants. I was determined to read so took up a recent work by Mr Defoe and found, with careful concentration, that I could make out the words and felt great joy at that.

I hesitated to approach the looking glass, but my fears of what I would encounter were so great that the image that confronted me was considerably less terrible than my worst imaginings. Still, I wept over that woman I had known for so long as myself, and who was now lost. I had been so casual with her and realized that she might have used her beauty more to her advantage. But there – she had quit the scene. Youth is anyway ridiculous: exquisite and fleeting and yet all life is somehow within it, and what comes after is only sorrowing, and so I wept – not from self-pity but for the very notion of youth and beauty, which is enough to make any person of sensibility weep. Why are we not permitted to live always in our pomp, but must instead lose teeth, hair, sight;

why must we ache and shrivel? The gods are cruel, to make us into ghosts long before we die.

I resolved to never do more than glance in a looking glass from that moment on, and then only to adjust a hat or pin up my hair. Vanity is for fools, pocked or pretty or otherwise. Betsy, though, would fuss about my hair, and offer me this gown or that, but could hardly bring herself to look at me. I could bear it no longer.

I: Betsy, I am pockmarked. I have not grown horns, or a second head. You must not be so upset about it.

BETSY: *Sniffling with unspilt tears*. Oh, madam. It's not my place . . .

I: Speak as you must, Betsy. I would rather you spoke instead of performing your duties about me as if I were a corpse dug up and being made ready for the dissection table.

BETSY: *Shocked*. It is such a shame is all, that you were once the prettiest . . .

I: Go on.

BETSY: Forgive me, but you were the prettiest lady in all London, in all the land I shouldn't wonder.

I: And now?

BETSY: Well, now . . . now you are not.

I: Just so. And now I am equal to all those who have suffered the smallpox, am I not?

BETSY: *Becoming suspicious, for she discerns some approaching cleverness, and she dislikes cleverness above all things.* I suppose.

I: I may look upon all those who are pockmarked with an equal eye, and they may look upon me in the same way. Beauty is a burden.

BETSY: *Purses her lips.* If you say so, madam.

Fanny came to visit me as soon as she heard I was ill, but I had her sent away from the house since she had not had the contagion. And though on my recovery I had begun to receive visitors, and though she implored me to allow her a visit, I found I could not face her: I could maintain my non-chalance about my disfigurement before friends, before Edward, indeed before all but my sister. I feared I would dissolve into a puddle of self-pitying misery in her arms, and I had no intention of doing that. I had to rehearse my part more thoroughly, pretend to a carelessness I hardly felt. Besides, when I did at last see Fanny, I knew I had to do everything in my power to make her see reason in respect of John Erskine. If I were well I would spirit her away to France or Holland or Timbuktu. As it was I barely had the strength to hold a pen.

Arlington St
London
5 June 1715

Dear Sister,

You might wonder at my reclusive state, and all the more so when you hear, as you no doubt have already, that Lady Oxford comes to me every day and some other ladies besides, and yet I have not yet admitted you into my chamber. You are ever the one I desire to see above all others. I cannot explain myself, can offer no defence, but to say that I am changed and for you I have always wished to be constant – constant in my affection, constant in my concern for your welfare and constant even in my visage. That is altered utterly, though my affection and concern are unremitting.

Come to me tomorrow but, I beg you, do not show me pity, for I neither wish for it nor deserve it. My maid pities me, and that is shame enough for any woman.

I am ever affectionately yours,
M

5

SISTERS AT WAR

Summer 1715, Westminster

(Frances)

That Mary is hungry for everything – for love, for sorrow, for adventure – is something I have always understood. Yet she also has a taste for conflict. Were she a man she would make a brave (though very probably reckless) general, always ready to lead her troops into battle and never doubting the righteousness of her cause. It was, then, unfortunate that the day I went to see her after her illness, my arms heavy with a bouquet of lilacs, my nose swimming with the flowers' heady scent, was also the day that my sister and I went to war.

As I entered the house from which I had been barred for the three weeks of Mary's illness, a maid tried to take the flowers from me, but I resisted, feeling a great compulsion to hand them to my sister myself, indeed to place them in a vase and arrange them, so that I might be with her day and night in the shape of those blooms.

On my entrance Mary was sitting at her desk, her back turned to me, absorbed in writing a letter as was her habit, and because I'd arrived unannounced she was unaware of my presence. I watched her, her body hunched over paper, her face a little closer to the page than was usual, and felt such a charge of love it was all I could do to stop myself from rushing to her and embracing her, but I delayed, wishing to observe a little longer until I said, softly, 'Mary?'

She turned, and stood, and I saw then how altered she was, her face covered in pits, her eyelashes gone, her eyes red and sore-looking. She seemed a creature startled out of its burrow. She searched my face for a sign of repugnance, but I gave none.

'Oh, Mary,' I said, throwing the lilacs to the floor and giving her the embrace that I'd held back. She felt so small in my arms, as if a part of her had been stolen away.

'Fanny,' she said, stepping back to regard me. 'My maid weeps each time she sees me, and Lady Oxford tells me I am hideous. You, Sister, will be no less honest, I trust.' She smiled without conviction.

'You are changed, Mary, but not so much. And besides, don't we both think prettiness overrated and spirit under-priced?'

'Edward says I am no more of a monster now than I was before!'

I thought that an awful thing to say, but then I understood from Mary's expression that he'd said it in jest and realized that she wanted me to make light of matters as he had.

'Perhaps Papa will let me come to your wedding now, since I might be in plain sight and yet unrecognizable?' she proposed, again in jest, or so I supposed.

'There is no mistaking you,' I said. 'Father has visited?'

'He has not, but he wrote, and kindly, and that is something,' she said, though it was plain to us both that it was not enough.

'If you were to come, I fear you would shout from the church door about just impediments and such like,' I said, meaning it fondly enough.

'I would, Fanny. Because you deserve a man who loves you; a man to make you happy.'

I looked about the room, at my dear sister's ribbons and slippers and at her hairbrush and the pile of books that teetered by her bed and tried to find a way of saying what I needed to say without anger and without pity. How could I tell her that I *did* love John Erskine? How could I explain to Mary, who knew so much about love, or seemed to, that I too deserved it? What I needed from a man was not the same as she needed or desired. It *could* not be the same, for we were not the same woman. 'I do love John,' I said quietly.

'How can you?' she fired back. 'He is so shallow, Fanny. So vain, and so preening and so . . . so . . .'

'Mary,' I said, striving to keep my tone sweet, 'you are talking of the man I will marry a week from now. Have some kindness.'

'A week? A week . . . oh!' she said, as if I had told her of the death of a dear friend. She reached for my hand. 'Believe me, Fanny, it is your happiness that makes me so . . . so determined to persuade you out of this match. A week is nothing, after all. I was to marry Skeffington the next day but escaped.'

'But you had someone else!' I declared, now failing to keep my tone as even as I wished.

'You will have other suitors. I cannot believe a hundred pretty men are not pursuing you night and day, for you are so gentle and delightful.'

I felt tears pricking at my eyes, and Mary reached a hand to my cheek. 'Is it that you fear being alone, Fanny?' she asked.

I pulled away from her. Who is not afraid of being alone?

But I *wanted* John Erskine, and not only so I could be Countess of Mar, not only to please our father and not only to displease Mary, though perhaps defying her was a part of it. When had I ever stood up to her? I wanted John Erskine because he made me feel like a woman, complete and desired and alive. 'You haven't even met him,' I said.

She smiled her smile of quiet victory. 'I have as a matter of fact, at court. He has been at court constantly since the king's arrival, wishing to ingratiate himself and plainly failing to do so. The first time he encountered me he flirted like a fretful peacock and was insulted when I did not respond in kind. The second time I was with one of the ladies of the court, I cannot remember which one – not a young or pretty one, anyway – and he was charming to me and rude to her, and that told me all I needed to know of his character, for we both know what we think of men who are hurtful to women they have no wish to bed.'

'You have him wrong, Mary. You have misjudged him.'

She threw back her head in disagreement, a gesture entirely familiar to me, yet it was a surprise, somehow, to see this new Mary, marked by the smallpox, behaving just as the old Mary had. 'I do not think so, but then again I am not permitted to come to your wedding, and so shall have no opportunity to shout out to the priest about just impediments.'

The room all of a sudden felt as if it had no air. I went to the casement, pushed open the glass and took a breath. Turning back to the room I saw the lilacs still on the floor, already drooping for lack of water. Mary was back at her desk, writing.

'Do I mean so little to you?'

'You mean everything to me, Fanny. Everything,' she said,

not even turning from her writing to face me. 'It is why I cannot bear to see you throw your happiness away.'

'You are not right about everything, Mary. Are *you* happy?'

She paused, then stood, approached me and brought her face close to mine. 'I am not happy about *this*,' she said, running her hand across her pocks, 'but I shall recover my happiness, because I am free. Edward and I have an equal understanding. If you can find such an arrangement with John Erskine then all may be well.' She glanced at the lilacs, as if seeing them for the first time, and rang for the maid.

'You do not know everything, Sister. You think you do, but you don't,' I said.

'Not everything, no. But I know enough.' She looked weary.

'I should let you rest.'

Mary looked at me with disappointment. She had wanted more of a fight than I was prepared to give. 'You will come again, before . . .'

I could not subject myself to more assaults on my choice of husband, more implications that I had woefully misjudged his character, or that I was marrying only out of fear of loneliness. But I *was* lonely. It was not that I had lost my sister, or that sister I'd always thought I'd known, but that we had always been allies – allies in family affairs, in friendship, in society. I could not think of a time when I had been the subject of her condemnation, even scorn. Yet now she seemed not only disapproving but unforgiving.

'Before I am married?' I said, for that is what she had been about to say, though she could not even bear to utter the words. 'And what will you do? Have me bound and gagged, Sister? Or make some speech, using every one of Cicero's tricks, to persuade me out of my decision?'

She smiled, but in her smile was her confession.

'Why cannot you see that I must . . .' I felt the anger in my voice, and knew that Mary did too. 'I *must* for once make my own way, make my own choice? Why can you not see that? You of all people, Mary, you who believe that a woman should be free to make her own life. Well, this is *my* life, and I choose the man I love!'

Mary looked at me coolly. She was unused to defiance, particularly from me. 'Where is that maid?' she declared, bending to pick up the lilacs and going to the door where the maid was standing just beyond, no doubt afraid to enter in the midst of our argument. 'You may take these, Betsy, and show my sister out.'

I went to give her a kiss, but she drew back. 'My skin is still tender, Fanny, and cannot bear lips upon it.' Was that true? I doubted it.

Once out in the street I could not contain my misery, my tears evoking a pity in passers-by that I felt sure they would not have done in Mary, so certain was she that I was in the wrong and she in the right.

6

TRAITORS AND POETS

Winter 1715–16, Westminster

(Mary)

What followed my illness were months of shame, but the shame did not – or not all – belong to me. That which was my own concerned not my wrecked looks but my literary adventures with Mr John Gay. He and I had been busy before my illness in writing witty poems which, while I'd lain close to dying, had caused a great furore. Had I not fallen ill I would have denied my part in the work, for it was not intended for publication, but (as so often) it was published, and with hints at its authorship. Edward had spared me details of the scandal, but as I recovered it became clear that it was thought I had been making jest of Caroline the Princess of Wales. This was unfortunate not only because she was Princess of Wales but more importantly because she and I had begun to form a friendship. I thought at first to deny my hand in the work, but then decided that boldness might be the better course, and wished to make clear to all that I was making jest not of Caroline but some of her ladies-in-waiting, who were like chickens clucking about her, their feathers ruffling alternately with pride or upset whenever one was favoured over another.

I decided, then, that my first sortie out of the house would be to the court of the Prince and Princess of Wales at Leicester House. My request for an audience might have been refused given the offence that I had apparently caused there, nor did I assume acceptance equated to forgiveness, for I imagined it was more than likely granted from curiosity about my changed looks.

At my entrance, announced by a gilded footman, I threw myself to the floor before her.

'Lady Mary. You are recovered?'

'As you see, Your Highness, mostly recovered, and with only slight injury.'

Her ladies-in-waiting observed me with satisfaction, though they had perhaps hoped for even more disfigurement than I was able to provide. Caroline dismissed them with a slight movement of her fingers.

'Come, sit, Mary,' she bid me, and since she was arrayed upon a blue velvet sofa that was not wide, and Her Royal Highness's girth was considerable, we were as intimate as sisters. 'You upset almost all my ladies with your poem, and their fury against you was only a little tempered by the rumours that you were sure to die.'

'They will have seen that as divine intervention, and my recovery as a great disappointment,' I ventured.

'Without doubt,' she said, looking not at me but at some object on the opposite wall. She was being careful to give no hint of her own true feelings, beyond having invited me to sit next to her. For a moment and in something of a panic I thought she had brought me so close to issue me with a banishment from her presence. She leant in and whispered: 'I thought your poem not only amusing but a portrait in words of perfect accuracy.'

'Oh?'

She turned to face me with a broad smile. 'Never be afraid of upsetting those who deserve to be ridiculed, Mary, though never do it cruelly.'

'I shall always be commanded by you.'

'You shall not! I do not think you can be commanded by any king or princess.'

'Not by *any* king or princess. Only by you, madam.'

'Then I shall have to issue my orders wisely. We shall bring my ladies back in and have polite conversation on the subject of literature and since you shall be sitting here by my side they will be obliged to join in politely. It will be an exquisite torture for them. But we must not giggle.'

In filed the Princess of Wales's ladies-in-waiting, all of whom I had mocked in my poem (though some of it was Gay's work), looking like ducks at swim, their tails flapping, their beaks dipping, in expectation of seeing me royally rebuked. Their disappointment as Caroline began a conversation about the appointment of Nicholas Rowes as poet laureate was indeed that of ducks who, having seen from a distance bread being thrown upon the water, find to their dismay as they draw close that it has all been eaten already. My shame was in such manner purged by royal amity.

My sister's shame, a matter of weeks after her ill-conceived marriage, was very much greater, though there was nothing she could do to rid herself of it. Mar was banished. After swearing his loyalty to the king, he promptly rode north and led the Old Pretender's rebellion. As in all else that man did, his generalship proved calamitous, and Hanoverian forces quickly routed the Jacobites. Mar skulked off to the Pretender's court in Avignon, where he was made secretary of state, which must have pleased his vanity, though being secretary of a state that was no more than a huddle of rebels in a far-off city was a thin sort of thing. Fanny was left in London, a wife without a husband and soon to be a mother. We had not fully repaired our relations in the weeks after her unwise marriage, but as soon as Mar revealed his hand, I spent what time I could with her, never once taking the slightest satisfaction that I had been right all along. In this way, little by little, we once more became sisters as close as kits in the same litter, though Fanny's spirits were low, and for good reason. It was a lamentable situation, and it was apparent that my sister was injured in some way deep within, something beyond the ministrations of physicians or friends. She loved Mar, and yet knew he did not deserve her love and never had.

My sister, being an unimpeachable Whig, did not get spat at in the street, or not often, although sometimes there was a rabble gathered before her door.

The scene: Forty-two St James's Square. Half a dozen members of the London poor are gathered at the railings. At my approach they stir.

BLACK-TOOTHED MAN: You go within to see that treacherous slut?

I: And what is that to you?

MAN: She is married to the traitor Mar.

I: Since she is my sister, I am aware to whom she is married.

WOMAN, BABY AT HER HIP: You should know better!

I: I should know better than to visit my sister, whom I love? What kind of sister would that make me, now?

WOMAN: I see yer point, missus, but still, she is a poor sort, marrying one such as Mar.

MAN: The fucker.

I: Should a woman be burdened with her husband's poor judgement, any more than with his bad debts and worse habits? Why, if every woman were to suffer such a fate, there would be few indeed who could hold their head up high.

ALL: *Laughter.*

I push the small crowd aside and rap upon the door with my cane. Once within I am led to where Fanny sits, in shadow, staring into space. Her belly is big with child.

FANNY: They're out there, aren't they?

I: Your admirers?

FANNY: *On the verge of tears.* Oh, Mary. Do not tease. They shout terrible things at me if I leave the house.

I: Why must I always remind you, Fanny dear, that it is not you they hate, but your husband?

FANNY: *Clearly not wishing to discuss her husband, changes the subject.* You saw the king last night?

I: I did. But it was a loud affair, and I did not have the chance to speak to him of Mar.

FANNY: *Failing to hide her despair.* No. I thought you would not.

I: If you must insist on joining your husband, wait at least until your child is of an age to travel.

FANNY: My child? *She looks down at her belly, as if she had forgotten she was carrying Mar's infant.* He will want a son, I suppose.

I: Men think they want boys, but they are generally gladder to have daughters.

FANNY: *Doubtfully.* You think so?

I: Not Papa, but then again he is displeased too easily. From me he wants obedience, which I do not have to give, and from you he wanted resistance, which you were unwilling to provide.

FANNY: *Her hand upon her belly. Vaguely.* I suppose it will be a boy . . . or a girl.

I: It will not be a rhinoceros, Fanny!

FANNY: *Smiles, weakly.* I trust not.

I: A daughter is to be preferred, for many reasons. I should like a daughter.

FANNY: But you love Eddie?

I: I . . . *Knowing the danger of confessing to love.* I like him well enough.

Silence. I summon Betsy, who having accompanied me to the house has gone below to gossip with the other maids. She enters bearing a bag of oranges.

FANNY: Not more oranges, Mary.

I: They will lift your spirits. *I proceed to peel orange after orange, the room filling with the smell of their zest.*

FANNY: Why can you not sympathize, Mary?

I: Sympathy? *I look at the pile of orange peel at my feet, and the peeled oranges upon the table, their thin skins already growing papery.* Is this not sympathy?

In such manner I did all I could to carry Fanny through her confinement and into the world of motherhood. She would not be the only woman to raise a child alone. What woman raises her children with the assistance of the man who fathered them? Edward had been of little help, and our father had generally taken the barest interest in his children except when it came to matters of marriage. For the poor there are sisters and mothers and aunts and daughters to help, and for those with means there are servants. And for those with neither there is gin.

My relations with the Princess of Wales repaired, and my poetic stumble pardoned, the time had come to extend my literary alliances, as a diplomat must after every setback speak only of victories to come. John Gay had urged me many times to pay a visit to Mr Alexander Pope. We had collaborated on a variety of works, and yet had never met, since Mr Pope being a papist was kept away from court, residing at Chiswick with his elderly parents. After an exchange of overly polite correspondence, it was agreed that I should call one Tuesday afternoon at three o'clock.

I was received with great civility by Mr Pope's father, who clearly regarded his son much as a magician might regard his rabbits on discovering they truly possess that ability to appear and disappear from hats that he had hitherto assumed dependent on his sleight of hand.

At my entrance Pope stood from where he sat in his study on a low chair of unusual pattern, putting aside a board held over his lap upon which he had been writing some such.

Raising himself to his full height, a foot less than mine, his back being curved most grievously with a consumption of the bones, he offered me a smile that was welcoming and sincere, yet with something questioning in it, as if he wished to see in that first glance whether I was truly friend or foe. He was not a handsome man, his nose too long, his mouth a little mean, but his eyes blazed with intense intelligence. He invited me to sit and proceeded without further politeness to interrogate me.

'What think you of rules, Lady Mary?'

Whether he expected me to be surprised by the boldness of his first utterance I was uncertain. 'I think we must know the rules so that we may break them with good intention,' I said.

He smiled, without revealing whether he agreed with my sentiment. 'And do you think old rules are to be preferred over new ones?'

I laughed, the question being of such deceptive simplicity. 'That is not one question, Mr Pope, but a thousand, each wrapped up in the other.'

He leant towards me, encouraging me to continue.

'The oldest rules, let us say of philosophy or design,' I continued, 'and of lyric and metre, are sound and worthy of upholding. And some new rules of taste are poor, indeed the very obsession with *taste* is absurd, as if there can be only one flavour or fashion, and all must follow it like sheep in a field being chased by a dog. Variety and unconvention are at the heart of all new art and science, and I fear that we live in an age where people are too inclined to follow fashion.'

He was so close that his knees were almost touching my gown. I felt that if anyone were to enter they would think that we had been startled in a moment of the greatest intimacy. Yet still Pope did not speak, and to fill the increasingly awkward atmosphere in that room, I pressed on. 'Yet there are times when the rules of society and of government work to the benefit of all, and others when the rules become twisted and cruel, so that men and women are burnt for being of one faith or another' – I gave him a look since in another age he might have been tortured for his faith himself – 'or never permitted to say anything against their rulers, as in France. And for a woman, Mr Pope, the rules are always harsher than for any man, for we may not be lawyers or priests or surgeons, we may not sit in parliament, and I may not write and publish a piece with my name attached to it, or not without attracting great odium.'

He leant back and regarded me as if I were a portrait he could not quite decide whether he admired or thought poorly done. This I might reasonably have considered the most grotesque breach of common courtesy since his only utterance since my arrival had been his two questions. I had not even been offered tea. But since we were discussing rules and the breaking of them, his behaviour was fitting and, moreover, he and I did in one sense already know each other well, since I had read and admired his *Pastorals* and, like everyone else, been agog at his *Rape of the Lock*, and he knew my contributions to the work we had undertaken with John Gay and Joseph Addison. He took my hand, another startling intimacy, and said, quietly, 'Lady Mary, it is apparent that you and I are destined to be the greatest of friends. Your sentiments are mine precisely. I shall have us brought tea, and I believe we should then set to work.'

'To work, Mr Pope?'

'Yes, to work, for there is a putrefying heap of hypocrisy out there waiting for us to poke at it, and I believe we may do so together.'

We spent our afternoon talking of all matters, from the rights of women to his friend and patron Lord Bolingbroke who had gone over to the Pretender, though Pope was at pains to make clear he was not himself of the Jacobite persuasion. We talked of the stupidity of princes and the grace of princesses, of the pompous and the humble, of the manners of the court, and of gambling at the basset table. We each wrote a verse about that, and read it aloud to each other, making ourselves howl with laughter.

'Yours is more amusing than mine,' he declared, not without a hint of surprise.

'But yours is cleverer than mine,' I parried, knowing that I must, though in truth I did think my verse sharper than Pope's.

'Perhaps a little,' he said, which I should have understood right then at our first encounter as a warning.

As the afternoon went along pleasantly he spoke of a subject that even he appeared hesitant to broach. 'The smallpox, Mary. Would you ever think to writing of it?'

I had not, or not until that moment. It was a matter both intensely personal and also universal and so perfectly fitting for poetry. 'I shall consider it.'

'Do. Write it in the manner of an eclogue. And let us henceforth be collaborators and equals.'

Equals! He had made himself irresistible.

'Let us toast our alliance before you go,' he declared, and stood in his awkward way to summon the maid and have her bring in two glasses of champagne.

'To equality!' he toasted.

'To humanity!' I replied.

'To wit!'

'To champagne!'

'To friendship,' he concluded, more quietly, his eyes once more intensely upon me, questing for something I felt certain I could not give.

7

A THOUSAND DIFFERENT MARYS

Summer 1716, London

(Mary)

I had cheated Death once and resolved that having survived I was destined to live an extraordinary life, and that life was not to be found on Arlington Street or floating along the Thames with a hundred thousand fish heads. My poems provided me with amusement and seemed to delight those I permitted to see them, but I had already experienced the outrage and indignity that ensued when I wrote what I truly felt. Besides, what adventure was there to be found in the dreamy pathways of my imagination compared to the bustling world beyond England?

Fanny, along with her new baby daughter, a frail little thing, but treasured, was soon to go to France to be with her errant husband, and while she had not the slightest appetite for the journey, I envied her the sights and smells of that foreign land, and the opportunities she would have to improve her French. I imagined myself in conversation with charming comtes and comtesses and dressing the French way. And yet France was not the world. Why not Italy, why not Egypt, why not India and China? I became more and more determined to devise some plan that would spring us from the trap I felt London was quickly becoming for me.

Edward was something of an obstacle to these plans, being comfortable enough in his position at the Treasury, and diligent yet wholly unmemorable in the Commons. I could not travel without him and leave little Eddie behind, not without causing a scandal too considerable to withstand. Motherhood was a duty I performed better than some and worse than others. Certain of my friends saw their children but once a day, if at all, and then only to be sure they were clean and suitably dressed, as if their little ones were a means of monitoring the performance of their servants. I had more love for Eddie than that, but I did not dote on him as some mothers did their sons. Eddie was small for his age, pale and overly eager to please by showing me his skill at reading a few words and writing his name and such like. I encouraged him but felt none of that natural pride I knew I ought. If I took him for a walk in the park, he would run ahead of me but would always turn before he had gone very far to make sure I was not far behind. I confess that in those moments I wished he would run further and be bolder. Not to be rid of him, not in the least, but so I could be free to think my own thoughts, to be Mary the woman, not Mary the mother.

As for Edward, his lack of interest was the product not of a hard heart but of the commonly held expectation that fatherhood requires an affection that must never be shown and a discipline that must ever be obvious. Besides, how could Edward perform fatherly duties when he was never present? When he was not at the Commons or the Treasury, he was off to Yorkshire to inspect his mines. We saw little of him. This was unfortunate, for my desire to see the world needed Edward's collaboration, whether given willingly or reluctantly or, best of all, unwittingly.

It was not easy to conjure favours for my husband, for although his diligence was noticed, so, regrettably, was his uncongenial nature, and the times were such that congeniality was considered of much greater importance than competence. Perhaps it was ever thus.

I collected rumours and gossip at court about which posts might soon become vacant due to illness or death or because the incumbent had fallen out of favour for one reason or another, and hoarded them like a bird in springtime bringing twigs to its nest. I then offered these twigs casually to Edward, since if I had said to him, 'Governor of Jamaica is to become free next month, you should make it known you are interested,' he would have rejected the proposal out of hand, believing in the paramount principle of resisting any suggestion from his wife as to how he should act.

When I heard at Easter that the ambassadorship to Vienna was certain to fall vacant, I felt compelled to mention it to him over dinner.

'It is a long journey to Vienna,' he said.

'Well, naturally, Edward. Any ambassadorial post will entail a journey since that is simply in the nature of *abroad*.'

He looked at me, uncertain as to whether I was laughing at him. 'The current war is very complicated,' he said. 'The Austrian interest is no longer one of defence, but is becoming one of attack, and England cannot support a long war against the Turks.'

'There, you see. You understand the situation, and your

calm manner and absolute honesty would make you ideally suited to be our ambassador.'

He put down his fork, lifted it and put it down again without taking a bite. 'What is it you are about, Mary?' he asked, his tone almost regretful. 'Would you have me abroad so you can pursue your literary and political career here without the constraint of a husband? Is that it?'

I laughed. 'Surely you do not imagine I would stay here if you were to travel, Edward? No, no. I will accompany you. Loyally.'

'*Loyally?* You may be loyal in spirit, Mary, but your tongue would be a constant source of controversy, as it is here. No, no. It is unthinkable.'

I knew that I would have to find a way of making my presence at his side unavoidable.

'Besides, there is little Eddie to think of,' he said, as if no child of three years of age had ever been on a journey.

'Eddie is much stronger now, and I think ready for seeing something more than the inside of his nursery and Kensington Gardens.'

He hesitated, and then asked, without malice but with an expression that suggested he knew he was playing his ace, 'And you would leave your sister?'

Fanny. How could I leave Fanny? Yet she would soon be on her way to France, and what use would I be to her in London? I tried almost daily to encourage her to come riding with me in Hyde Park, or join me at the theatre, but the most she would consent to was a game of *triomphe* at my home when I had ladies there she knew well enough to be certain they would not mention Mar. The spirit had gone out of her, and I was afraid that, far from Mar fading from her thoughts or, more properly, becoming a figure worthy of her contempt for his abandonment of her, her husband had become an almost heroic, mythical object of her passion. 'Fanny and her daughter will soon be permitted to go to France, and then there will be nothing to keep me here at all,' I said.

'Nothing? All your friends? Alexander Pope, John Gay? All your ladies? The Princess of Wales?'

'I shall write. I will write to them all. I am better with a pen than in person.'

Edward harrumphed. 'I have no wish to go to Austria. None,' he declared. He stood and left the room to avoid any further futile attempts on my part at persuasion.

The man chosen to go to Vienna was to be taken from Constantinople and moved to Austria in the manner that a knight is lifted on a chessboard and moved forwards and diagonally, thus leaving a vacancy in that tantalizing city. Our ambassadorship to the Ottoman Empire was a curious affair, the Levant Company being obliged to fund the position from its profits, and thus the ambassador expected to attend above all to the provision of a healthy Turkish trade. Since Edward had a great interest in profit, I formed a notion that the position might well be made to appeal to him. For my part I was seized by a great enthusiasm for Turkey and decided that I would do all within my power to gain him the position. As soon as I became possessed by this idea, London life paled further – I had no wish to play *triomphe*, or go to the theatre, or be a dutiful courtier, still less a loyal wife to a Member of Parliament.

I knew that Edward would have to be given no choice in the matter. I therefore went to see Robert Walpole, the leading man in the new government and with whom I'd lately become friendly.

*

Edward arrived home that evening in a thunderous mood. 'I am dismissed!'

'My dear?' I said, expressing absolute surprise.

'I am replaced at the Treasury by James Brudenell, a man of absolutely no distinction! And the explanation is that I am to be considered for greater things. Pah!'

'Edward,' I said, trying to calm him. 'Who has told you of these greater things?'

'Oh, Walpole. But one cannot believe a thing that man says. I know he is your friend, but I suppose his dissembling does not trouble you greatly.'

Edward was rarely so peevish, but he had been given cause, and I felt a little guilty for being the foundation of his dismissal. If he asked me outright whether I'd had some hand in it, I would have had to confess, since we had sworn always to tell each other the truth. But silence is not a lie, and I trusted that he did not suspect me. 'I am certain that it is in foreign affairs that the government will wish to use your services, since you are so very knowledgeable in these matters. Have you been to see Joseph?'

'I am to have supper with Addison tomorrow evening. I have already told him of my dismissal, and so he will know I am free to serve him in some capacity.'

How inexpert he was, my husband, how guileless, to tell a man, even a good friend such as Joseph Addison, now secretary of state, that he had been diminished and then to seek his help, instead of making it seem as if he was prepared to make some sacrifice. It was just as well that I had already arranged to see Mr Addison the next morning to urge him to oblige Edward to take on the role in Turkey. I planned to suggest he employ unbridled flattery and emphasize the complexity of the diplomatic task. Addison would understand the need for discretion. He knew how pig-headed Edward could be. I had in any case already been to see the governor of the Levant Company to smooth the way. And so within a week the *Gazette* made the announcement – Edward Wortley Montagu was to be His Majesty's new ambassador to Constantinople.

Mrs Hills would not countenance the notion of making a journey beyond Margate, and Betsy, my maid, chose the month of our departure to fall in love with a costermonger from Hoxton. Others of our household expressed either distaste at leaving English shores or unwillingness, and so I spent the weeks of the summer in recruiting, while Edward read histories of the Turks and engaged in correspondence with every ambassador in Europe, gradually becoming animated by a conviction that he and only he could bring peace to the Balkans. My plan had worked perfectly.

My only error was in delaying telling Fanny for as long as I did, since I couldn't conceive of a way of explaining why I was abandoning her before she had made her own arrangements. How ironic, that her husband was exiled and yet it was she who was in the more terrible state of exile at home. No doubt John Erskine, Earl of Mar, was having a high time of it pretending to be a figure of importance, while my sister sat in a house in St James's Square longing (however misguidedly) for reunion with him.

Though Fanny never read the *Gazette*, she had inevitably heard of my imminent departure from others. 'You are to leave England, I hear,' she said when I visited her one Thursday afternoon, as was my practice. There was a hint of injury in her voice, no more than that.

'Oh, Fanny,' I said, embracing her, almost stepping on little Frannie, who was in a crib on the floor. 'I kept wanting to find a way to tell you, and of course Edward's posting was not certain until very recently, and . . . and . . .'

'Hush, Mary. I'm pleased for you. You've always wanted adventure, and yet married a man so little disposed to it. How you persuaded Edward to take the position I cannot imagine.' She smiled at me and saw all, I knew, and we laughed together and that felt like a forgiveness. 'And I, who have wanted only quietness in my life, have somehow found myself in the midst of a great furore, and if Frannie is ever to see her papa I must set out on my own adventure very soon. I cannot think why John has not sent for me now that I have been given permission to leave England.'

I thought it all too probable that Erskine was a happy exile without the encumbrance of family but would not hurt my dear sister by saying so. 'I am certain he is simply making everything as it should be for your arrival in France, Fanny. He wouldn't want you and Frannie to be troubled with finding lodgings and servants and such like, and with his other responsibilities, well . . .'

'Yes, I'm sure you must be right,' she said, without believing it.

When I left her that day we held on to each other so long that when we pulled apart it seemed that our gowns had grown together. It was only a matter of buttons and hooks having become entangled in the strength of our embrace, but it felt that our silks were telling us what our hearts knew too well but our mouths could not utter. 'We are as two trees that have grown together, branch entangled with branch, and cannot be parted,' I said, with a smile.

'But we are parted, Sister. We are. And when shall we ever see each other again?'

'I promise I will write and write, Fanny. And whenever it

may be that we shall be together again, I shall make it sooner than seems possible to either of us just now.'

The baby stirred. 'I should see to Frannie,' she said, quietly.

Leaving her there, so defenceless, so at the mercy of her future and so condemned by her past, I felt a great guilt. I was afraid that Fanny had not the strength she would need to see her through the journey that faced her – a journey less of miles than of unfamiliarity. Yet leave her I must and leave her I did.

I asked amongst my friends for a maid who was intelligent and reliable and discreet, and who might have an appetite for travel. Weeks went by, and the date we were due to sail grew ever closer. Though we had taken on other staff, including a valet with a sharp eye and a good hand who would be an able assistant to Edward, and a nurse originally from Leiden and thus eager to travel, who was stupid but affectionate towards Eddie, I simply could not find myself a maid who met my stipulations. It was as if I had asked for a hound that could fly and sing and also dance a little.

Lady Wentworth at last mentioned an orphan girl who had some education and might be suitable, and next day this young woman, Nell, presented herself to me. She was of average height and slim, a little older than I had been given to understand, surely more than twenty, her dark hair almost black, her complexion sallow, and with bright eyes and a good bearing. She stood before me looking proud, almost defiant, taking in the disarray of packing cases and the furniture shrouded in cloth but making no comment upon it.

'You have a good education, I hear?'

'I would not say so, ma'am.'

'Oh? But you read and write?'

'I do.'

'Do you have languages?'

'A little French.'

'And your mistress tells me you play the fortepiano well.'

'Simple pieces.'

In other circumstances her terse modesty would have irritated, but with just a week before our departure I was in a degree of desperation. I had an urge to ask her to play the fortepiano for me, since I had the strong conviction that her modesty hid talents she did not care to boast of. 'Your duties in respect of me will be the usual.'

'Certainly, ma'am.'

'You might also need to care for my son from time to time, particularly as he grows beyond the capabilities of the nurse we have engaged, who is Dutch and very sweet but also insufferably stupid.'

A glimmer of a smile flickered across Nell's grave features, but it was quickly swept away. 'I am used to children. Indeed, when first I worked for Lady Wentworth it was as nursery maid.'

This was promising.

'The journey to Constantinople may be arduous, and life there might be comfortable or cruel, and no doubt at times it will be both. We shall need courage.'

'Courage is something I can say I know, madam.'

'Then good. You will start on Monday.'

And in such manner I engaged Nell, who became more than a servant to me, and became more to herself than she might ever have imagined.

The day we were due to sail was blustery, the sort of morning when it seemed as if the bright sunlight drove the wind into a frenzy, so that laundry was ripped from lines, flags flew from London's buildings straining at their halyards and clouds skittered across the sky in a chase. I was filled with an excitement such as I could not recall since one memorable evening when, as a small child, I was taken to my father's Kit-Cat Club to be toasted by all his famous Whig friends. I learnt only some years after from Mr Addison, who had been one of those friends present, that I was only brought there because my father wished to poke fun at their tradition of toasting the most beautiful woman of their acquaintance. I was eight years old, and even then knew that to be admired for one's looks was not only far less important than to be admired for one's character but also a steady insult to every woman: a low, grey cloud that darkened every female ambition, talent or skill. A man might be thought pleasing in his looks or no, but he would never be judged the better lawyer or more skilful butcher for the shape of his chest or the colour of his eyes; but for a woman it was her appearance that was always the first consideration. Yet for all that, I'd been exhilarated that day at eight years old, imbued with the conviction that I was stepping out of a familiar childish world and into a place of power and mystery and excitement, an adult realm and, most importantly of all, one I had been invited to join.

Just before Edward and I were to step out into the street to enter our carriage we saw that a large group of our friends had gathered to bid us farewell, amongst them Lady Oxford, Lady Rich and Miss Calthorpe, come to see me as if I were some sort of miracle, not only risen from my deathbed but now so thoroughly recovered that I was embarking on a considerable journey. But Edward held me back. 'What on earth do you have upon your head, madam?' he demanded.

I had decided to wear a full-bottomed brown wig, one of Edward's, thinking it looked comfortable and its weight would keep it upon my head in the blustery wind. I wore a sack dress, also for comfort and, besides, hoops were hardly practical on a coach journey. 'It is a wig, as you know full well. It is too windy for a hat, and besides, Nell could find no pins this morning. They must all be packed inside one of the trunks.'

'You look ridiculous. What woman wears a gentleman's wig?'

'This woman. And I might wear breeches tomorrow. Or a simple smock. I shall dress as it pleases me to dress.'

Edward, who never angered, regarded me with perplexity. 'I sometimes wonder whether I am married to one Mary or to many.'

In my spirited state, I announced, 'I intend to be many Marys! I shall be a thousand different Marys and, in such manner, shall find the one I wish to be.' I'd meant it as a light quip, though as I spoke I heard the fervent truth in my words, as did Edward. He took my hand and gave me a darting kiss on my cheek, which made the waiting crowd think him a husband who was a great deal more affectionate than his wife had ever found him to be.

As we mounted the carriage I saw a most surprising sight, for some distance away a short man was beetling along, his back bent, his stick flailing, his pace so rapid that the tails of his coat stirred a small cyclone of dust in his wake. Pope had accepted my imminent departure with a good deal less grace than my dear sister. He first asked me how he would be able to continue to write at all without me at his side and declared that I was leaving him but half of himself. Over the preceding months I had grown used to his self-regarding hyperbole and taken little notice, though I did increase the frequency of my visits to his home at Chiswick in the weeks before we were to set sail. We worked together on our poetry and went over his *Iliad*, which he'd begun publishing in instalments, and about which he was possessed by an almost unshakeable anxiety, which it seemed only I was able to soothe.

As Pope approached, he looked about at the small crowd with a sly, almost furtive squint. Naturally enough they recognized him, he being one of the most famous men in England, and a low murmur of awe greeted his arrival at our carriage door. 'Mary.' He kissed my hand, and greeted Edward with a bow. 'I feared I was too late.' He then held out a gift, wrapped in white silk cloth, and stood at the door of our carriage, clearly expecting me to unwrap it before him. Noting Edward's understandable eagerness to set off, I quickly removed the covering to see beneath it a collection of poems, bound in red leather, that he and I had written together, though I noticed that only Pope's name was there upon it, embossed in gold.

'I shall treasure these, and will write almost every day, I promise.'

'Every day, Mary. *Every* day!' he declared, but before he could utter another word the carriage jerked forward, and our journey began.

We were silent in our carriage, Edward and I. Mrs Van der Kamp – the nurse – and Nell were in the carriage behind with young Eddie and Joseph Knox, Edward's new valet. It was only once we reached the open country that lay between London and Gravesend that Edward spoke. 'Perhaps it is lack of moderation that draws you together,' he said, referring to Pope's display at our departure, 'and like Newton's law of universal gravitation, he fears that distance will diminish the force of that immoderation you both share.'

I thought of correcting his misreading of Newton's *Principia Mathematica* but, understanding that he was likely hurt not only by Pope's display of devotion but also that of so many other of my friends, felt the better course was to offer him a chilly smile.

I do not know what happened to that collection of poems Pope and I wrote together, for somewhere between London and Rotterdam it was lost.

8

HOLY RELICS AND HIGH HAIR

Autumn 1716, Vienna and Hanover

(Mary)

Rotterdam was neat, orderly and prosperous. Indeed, all Holland met with my approval, being something like a large garden. Germany less so, for its towns, particularly those ruled over by minor princes, seemed to me tawdry and poor. Yet in each German town we were required to pay our respects to the quality, to eat fatty, over-salted suppers and drink Rhenish wine. Conversation was mainly in French, and I kept my German in a pocket like a pistol, using it only when I heard some disparaging comment about England or the court at Hanover.

In Nuremburg, while visiting a Roman church, I found myself given the flattering attention of a young Jesuit priest who, on discovering my reading of some Latin inscription upon the wall, spoke to me in that language. He seeming to find me charming, and I finding him no less so, there followed conversation as lively as any possible in that tongue in that place. Nell observed us from a distance with quiet disapproval.

The church was filled with dubious relics and false jewels, as God demands of the credulous. The priest pointed out his church's treasures to me one after another with growing desperation for my approval. Seeing a casket covered in glass and making the bold claim that the tiny, blackened, gnarled object lying upon a blue velvet cushion within was not, as it so patently was, a piglet's trotter but the toe of Saint Peter, I asked the handsome young priest, 'How do you suppose Saint Peter's toe ever found its way here? Do you think it walked here all alone, or with the rest of the man's body attached?'

He blushed, not for the fraud of it, but because his faith in the relic's authenticity was absolute, and I realized his shame was not for himself but for me. Such are the mysteries and delusions of faith.

Outside the church I asked Nell what she had thought of the place.

'It was somewhat ornate for my tastes, madam.'

'Ornate, yes. But the priest was an uncommonly pretty fellow, don't you think?' I said, hoping to provoke her into laughter or even disapproval.

'He was the only holy thing there, because innocent,' she said.

I looked at her in surprise but did not comment. What a remarkably astute thing for Nell to have said, for that was precisely the priest's quality; and it was all the more observant for we had been speaking the whole while in Latin, which Nell had surely not understood.

We had been travelling only six weeks, but by the time we arrived in Vienna the nature of Edward's diplomatic mission had changed immeasurably, and in a direction that would make his task even less likely to be successful. The Austrians, upon whom he was to prevail for peace, had not only fought new battles with Turkey but had beaten them roundly, retaking the towns of Peterwardein and Temeswar. Edward, who was too easily disheartened, began to despair at the difficulties mounting up against him. I knew that I would have to work to create opportunities that would save his mission, and so set about gaining invitations to the houses of the great ladies of the place.

Society is sometimes likened to a ladder, and the comparison is fitting. One must place one's slipper first upon the bottom rung, that being a person familiar to one or at least the result of a personal introduction, and from that first rung the others come easily enough. And, as with a ladder, the trick of it is to never look down, but only ever upwards, and since we may not see the angels in heaven, at the very top sits a king and queen, or an emperor and empress.

I quickly ascended. I had persuaded Edward of the urgency of my acquiring a new wardrobe, for the ladies of Vienna dressed in gowns made of approximately an acre of silk and wore wigs high enough for birds to nest in. Indeed, seeming to recognize the vanity in those towers of hair, they decorated them with stuffed orioles and wrens and such like, which were pinned a foot or two above their painted eyebrows. Thus attired, I found myself in conversation with every powerful woman in Vienna, and like women everywhere, they saw the cost of war not in silver or in the edging forward of a frontier, but in the blood spilt by sons and husbands, and the prospect of an empty place at their tables, never to be filled. I listened with care to all that was said, and gave Edward advice which, since he had otherwise only the dissembling words of men to rely upon, he accepted with as much gratitude as reluctance.

We were weeks in Vienna, I delayed by my burgeoning friendship with the delightful Empress Elisabeth Christine, who quickly regarded me as a confidante, presumably since she knew I would soon be gone, whereas the ladies of the court were there to pity her for the constant pressure upon her to bear a male heir. When the empress and I were not talking of music and literature we went riding together or shooting, and I slowly came to realize that even if we never reached Constantinople, I was having the adventure of my life, the one I had sought so that I could throw it into Death's face, and declare: *See, see me – I live!*

Almost six weeks after our arrival in Vienna, Prince Eugene, the Austrian general, returned at last from the front line, and Edward, having quickly arranged a meeting, was filled with renewed confidence. 'What a very reasonable man the prince is,' he declared with approval.

'Reasonable?' I asked. 'I have heard princes called many things – monstrous, foppish, vain, brave, foolish, even learned. But reasonable? Never!'

'Eugene understands politics better than any politician. He knows England well – better than many an English prince if it comes to it.'

'That is not so surprising. And you made progress?'

'I did, for Eugene made clear what terms he would find acceptable for peace with the Turkish sultan, and they are not in my view unachievable.'

'Then you will achieve them.'

'Quite,' he said. 'After all, the Austrians could demand possession of a dozen cities and ports given their victory. But Eugene knows better than to gain territory that he cannot then govern well and would rather leave the misery of administering the Balkan provinces to the Turk. I shall not present it to the sultan in such a manner, naturally.'

'Naturally.'

And thus we prepared to set off at last for Constantinople, Edward filled with the confidence of a man of reason. But the course of war rarely runs as smooth as the course of love and love never runs smooth at all.

Disaster struck on the very day we were to leave. A letter arrived by messenger from Lord Stanhope. It came as our trunks were being loaded on to our carriages, the autumn air filled with flecks of sleet. Edward broke the seal, read what was within and for some reason looked at me as if I had been accused of a terrible crime.

'What is it?' I asked.

He paced the room, reading the note to himself silently, his lips moving slowly as if their recitation might make the words change their meaning. At last he thrust the note in my direction without even looking at me.

Dear Wortley,

His Majesty the King commands your immediate presence and that of the Lady Mary at his court in Hanover. There you will receive further instruction for your embassy to the sultan.

I am yours etc.,
Stanhope

It was a surprise, certainly.

'Hanover? Whatever for?' he said to me in despair, as if I might know.

'I have no idea.'

'And you are mentioned most specifically. Have you had some hand in this, madam?' he said, flaring in accusation.

'Certainly not! Why do you imagine such a thing?'

'You think I never know your schemes, but I do,' he said, though I felt certain he did not, or at least not all of them.

'Perhaps there is some development in the political situation at home that we are unaware of?' I offered, though I could not think what that might be.

For a moment Edward looked so despairing I thought he might weep. 'It is just,' he said, despondently, 'I have terms that I believe all may accept, and if we go quickly to Turkey before the snows set in, a breakthrough might be reached. But delay is impossible.'

'You could say so to Stanhope, or directly make your case to the king?'

'Even that will take a week or more.' He paced about the room once again, and though I knew full well what we would have to do, I forbore from saying so, allowing Edward to reach the inevitable conclusion.

'Well, at least our possessions are packed,' he conceded, 'and we may go today to Hanover.'

'Indeed.'

The journey from Vienna to Hanover was a terrible one. Our party and belongings packed into eight carriages which crept along roads little better than farm tracks through Bohemia and Saxony, and when in low country the wheels were deep in mud, and when in mountainous terrain, bumping and creaking across rocks. I took Nell and Eddie and Mrs Van der Kamp into my carriage and banished gloomy Edward into another with his valet. We slept, all our party, from time to time as we rode in hours of darkness as well as light since the days were growing short, and we changed horses at uninviting inns. On the third day, glancing out of the window as evening fell, I saw that we were on a narrow track on the side of a mountain, a drop of a thousand feet just inches from our wheels. Craning my head out of the window I saw that both the coachman and postillion were slumped, fast asleep. Only the good sense of the horses was keeping us alive. 'Hoy there!' I shouted. 'Hoy!'

Jerking awake, the coachman took the reins, and looked about him in great surprise.

I opened the little communicating slide and shouted through it, 'Best you keep us all alive, man!'

He turned and gave me a toothless grin.

A little further along we saw a terrible accident had occurred, only moments before we had come upon it. A coach had tumbled off the track and hit a rocky ledge perhaps ten feet beneath. A woman and child were standing upon the road, looking down in great distress at where a man, the husband and father, presumably, was trying to pull another from beneath the upturned carriage. Astonishingly, our own carriage, which was the lead, made no attempt to stop. I banged hard upon the roof and brought it to a halt, jumping down and seeing what we might do to assist. Scrambling down the bank as best I could in my gown, I saw that the man who was trying to perform the rescue was himself injured, with blood flowing copiously from a head wound.

'Sit,' I commanded, first in French and then in German, but still he did not comprehend me. I gestured to the ground and took my scarf from my neck and wound it about his head. Next, I looked to see what rescue he was trying to perform.

'Mary!' shouted Edward behind me.

I ignored him and went to investigate. The coachman's body was limp, and his flesh drained of all life. A leg was caught beneath the tumbled carriage. Death had been at his work, that much was clear, and as I stood looking about at the terrible scene I experienced the distinct sensation that the mortal apparition was lingering, as if he was not yet finished with the place. The thought of death, and the sight of it plain before me, made me hesitate.

'Mary!' called Edward again from where he stood up on the road, his coat flapping in the wind. 'Mary, this is not your business. Come away!'

It was the sight of the woman's eyes upon me, together with that of her child, seemingly imagining that I was capable of making all well, that shook me from my moment of fear and impelled me to set about issuing orders in affectation that I was bold and unafraid. 'We shall have to have a party of men sent from the next village to recover this man's body and dispose of the coach,' I declared. Where, I wondered, were the horses? The traces were snapped, and looking over the ledge I could see the twisted bodies of the poor creatures, faces contorted in their last agony.

As I went to help the injured man to his feet, attempting to make him understand that there was no more he could do for the dead coachman, he shook his head violently and pointed to the carriage. I could not see into it, the door being pinned against the ledge, and the upturned window too high for me to reach. Nell came behind me. 'I am slight, madam, and strong,' she said in her soft, calm voice, and next she had succeeded in scrambling upon the carriage and sliding down into it through the window. A moment later she emerged with the body of a small boy in her arms, perhaps three or four years of age. As I had suspected, Death had not finished his business in that cruel place. Nell placed him tenderly in his father's arms, who fell to his knees, sobbing. I clambered back up to the road, and went directly into my carriage, took Eddie from Mrs Van der Kamp, who had, to her credit, been shielding him from the scene of carnage, and did not let go of my child until we reached Hanover two days later.

I hear that father's sobs of grief still. I shall always hear them.

We arrived at Hanover after dark on the eighteenth of October to be greeted by a demand that we attend His Majesty immediately. Edward and I therefore appeared before the king with dust on our clothes and in our hair. He was playing cards with his mistress, Baroness Schulenburg, and both looked up with surprise at our entry.

'You're fearsome dirty,' said the king.

'Regrettably so, Your Majesty,' said Edward, 'but we made great haste to be here.'

'Come, join us at cards and tell us what you have been about.'

Edward raised an eyebrow.

'Mary,' commanded the baroness, 'tell us which great ladies you have been with, and what scandals you have heard.' She patted the cushion of the chair next to her, and I joined her. Edward was left standing.

'May I give you some report of progress in my negotiations with the Austrians, sir?'

The king regarded him with stupefied indifference. 'Oh? Yes, perhaps. Tomorrow. Will you join us for a hand or two of *triomphe*?'

'I, er . . .'

'Edward has some letters to write, majesty,' I offered, trying to save both Edward and the king from the embarrassment of neither of them wishing to engage in polite yet meaningless conversation. That was a duty I would have to perform.

*

And so it went. Weeks went by in Hanover – precious weeks – while the king took counsel on what Britain's stance should be on the war between the Austrians and the Turks, not only dismissing Edward's advice with a wave of the hand but finding my husband's poorly disguised desperation to be on his way to Constantinople a source of amusement. In our chambers – a grand but cold set of rooms in the ostentatious and impersonal Herrenhausen Palace – Edward accused me, as he so frequently did, of being an obstacle to his ambitions.

'Can you not try to be less amenable to the king?' he demanded, angrily.

'I should be unpleasant to our sovereign?'

'Not obviously so, no. But at least don't be so damned amusing.'

I looked at him, awaiting a smile, for he was capable of saying such things in jest, but I could see that he was in deadly earnest. 'Do you think I wish to be here?' I said. 'This is not the adventure I sought. I desire nothing more than to be in Constantinople. But George is king, and we are here at his command.'

'We may as well be imprisoned by him. He's like a fat lazy cat who prefers to torture his mice than kill them clean.'

I went to him, touched him lightly on the shoulder to see if he might be agreeable to an embrace (I could never be sure), and finding that he yielded, assured him that I would find some way to make our release both desirable and necessary to His Majesty.

One compensation of being in one place for longer than a few days was that I finally received a letter from my sister in response to the dozen or more that I had sent to her.

St James's Square
London
2 November 1716

Dearest Sister,

I am a poor correspondent, but then again I have never had your gifts, and should not know what to do with them if I had, for I have to confess the very thought of entertaining conversation, of travel, even of laughter fills me with such a great anticipation of exhaustion that I should most likely take to my bed.

Vienna sounds very rich in every respect, and therefore very expensive. How fortunate you are to have a husband with prospects. Mine has none, as you know all too well. I have at last heard from John, who tells me he will send for me when he is certain that he can offer me a home in keeping with my status. But what is my status, Sister? Is it not 'wife'? I may be Countess of Mar, but what an empty title that is now. Papa gives me my allowance and comes to see me sometimes, usually very late at night after he has finished some business in the House of Lords. We never speak of my husband. Never. It is as if he were dead – no, it is worse. It is as if John Erskine had taken his own life, which in a sense I suppose he did by siding with the Pretender.

Oh dear. I have read what I have written and see that it is all complaint and misery. I would screw up the paper and begin again, but this is the twentieth or twenty-first time I have tried to write to you, and each time it is the same, and my floor is littered with discarded letters, and so I shall let these words stand. Do not think I am miserable, Mary, for I love Frannie and still have hopes of a happy reunion with John, and believe we shall then make a life together, and if any man alive can gain my husband pardon it is our father, since he is now so very powerful. I have disgraced him, I suppose, in marrying John. You were right all along. But then you are right about everything, and your only fault is in knowing it!

Forgive me for writing but one letter to your dozen. I read all you write, and reread a hundredfold, so think of me as a spectator in a darkened theatre, appreciating the play you are acting out, but applauding only at the end of each act, for were I to applaud every scene then you should feel mortally interrupted.

I am ever your loving sister,
F

9

THE ROAD TO TURKEY

Winter–Spring 1717, The Balkans

(Mary)

It was as well we crossed the borderlands when the ground was frozen, the trees without leaves, the people invisible in their poor hovels where they huddled before what little wood they could find. Even though fresh snow had fallen I saw here and there bodies, or pieces of men I should say, frozen in the desolation. Close to our track, which followed no road but whichever course upon which the horses could find sufficient purchase to pull our sledded carriages most easily, the petrified fingers of some soldier, be he Austrian or Turkish or from another place, poked up through the ice, grey and bloodless yet seeming to plead for rescue. In any other season the limb would have rotted away. Even the rats must have frozen, or more likely feasted so well on that battlefield that their appetites had been sated.

On we went through the killing grounds, the sound of the steel runners on the snow like the swoosh of a sword slicing through air. There was a great, dense silence, and the white dazzle and smooth rush of the sleigh brought a stillness to our party. Eddie was wrapped up beneath a prodigious pile of blankets, lying sometimes on my lap and else with Mrs Van der Kamp, who had been her usual cheerful self all through Germany and Austria but since Buda had been mute with shock at the misery we had witnessed there, the women all senseless with grief and those few men who staggered the sorry streets mutilated or drunk or both.

Silence brings reflection, and I pondered the narrow divide between life and death: the beating of a heart; the warmth of a breath; the hope that fills and so often deceives the living spirit, be it in expectation of love or desire or the simplicity of a child's happiness – and sometimes nothing more glorious than the prospect of a piece of bread and dripping. Yet how complete is that divide between the living and the dead. We are told to have faith in an afterlife, but as we skated over the bones it was hard to believe in heaven's promise. Being in these lands reminded me once again that I was never far from Death, and that he could be defied only by living as fully as I could.

Thinking to break the long silence that had gripped the small space of our carriage, I said to Edward: 'You have seen the bodies on these killing fields?'

Startled out of his reverie he nodded solemnly. 'It is a vision of hell itself.'

'Might diplomacy have put a stop to this?'

'Perhaps.'

'Your diplomacy?'

He gave me a pained smile of defeat. 'That is its purpose, Mary.'

'What would you say, then, is the purpose of war?'

'One might just as well ask the purpose of the devil himself.'

Thinking that if we had made this journey in a more temperate season the stink of decaying flesh would have been in our nostrils every hour, every minute, day and night, I remarked, 'There should be an international treaty for the provision of burial parties, for there is no such thing as a Christian corpse or a Mohammedan corpse. Faith and titles, laws and ceremony are but the vanity of the living. The domain of the dead is one of absolute uniformity. No animal dies out in the open for all to see its corpse, short of a badger that might be crushed beneath the wheels of a coach. Wild creatures crawl away to die, but a man shot by a rifle or sliced by a sabre is left to rot. It is savagery that nature would not tolerate.'

He agreed, but then he agrees too readily, my husband, having no stomach for argument.

At the frontier we were met by a legion of Ottoman soldiers, and much ceremony accompanied the handing over of our party of carriages and wagons, almost as if we had been ten tons of tobacco and lace. The formalities were no less tedious than they were elaborate. Papers were examined by those who seemed incapable of comprehending them, and at least one hundred furious-looking young men gathered around our party dressed in flowing white robes, each carrying a rifle of improbable length across his shoulder. These, I was told, were the infamous janissaries, the elite soldiers of the Ottoman Empire. When, at last, we were given into the care of these Turkish guards, it seemed we were trophies to be carried across the ravaged lands as far as Belgrade, where we were to await our various permissions to proceed further into Turkish territory.

We could not make such progress as to arrive in Belgrade before dark, and despite our guards, it was pronounced too dangerous to travel through the night. We stopped in a poor village, I glad that I had my own divan to lie upon, for I should have been bitten to death on the straw beds we were offered. Our small army determined that we must be fed a banquet, though we had no need of one, and proceeded to commandeer from every cabin and hut a chicken, a goose, even three sheep, two goats and a pig; and our party, and most certainly every janissary, was fed handsomely, it seeming close to miraculous that such plenty had been conjured from so little.

In daylight next morning I saw how these poor people, already close to destitute, were now the poorer still for our visit, since the soldiers had stripped them of what they had need of and we had not. Some of these folk were protesting and I was obliged to witness them being beaten mercilessly, apparently for my entertainment since their protests were regarded as a great discourtesy to our party.

I flew from the scene to find Edward, who was writing letters, as always. 'Will you not put a stop to this?' I demanded.

'To what?' he asked, as unconcerned as if I'd asked him to swat a lazy fly.

'The inhabitants of this place are being treated brutally, and it is all a show, as if our guards think we will be impressed by their sway and swagger.'

'I'm sure you are wrong, madam,' he said in that manner that once more confirmed that Edward was not wholly immune from the prejudice commonly held by men that women are unduly subject to their emotions. 'We may not interfere in what must be matters of local jurisdiction, Mary. You know that.'

'Come!' I insisted, but Edward refused. 'Very well!' I went marching out into the village square and strode up to the chief janissary, not caring that the hem of my gown was trailing through mud and a heady blend of ordure – equine, porcine, bovine, ovine and no doubt human, too. I demanded that he cease. Even if he did not understand my words, which I declared in both English and Greek, he could not have doubted my intention. He raised the club he held high and struck the protesting grandfather before him with such force that the poor man fell to the ground clutching his shoulder. Before the janissary could move on to the next, a thin youth who cowered before him, I interposed myself between the lad and the soldier's raised arm. Observed by his men, the janissary brought the club down to an inch above my head. I saw from the corner of my eye, now fixed upon the oppressor's own, that Edward had appeared and was watching us, not without concern, but also with sufficient detachment that it was apparent he was content to see how matters would develop. Were I to be clubbed to death it would make a most unexpected start to my husband's embassy in Turkey, but perhaps one that would prove not wholly unhelpful to his cause.

It felt as if we were figures frozen in a scene painted by Mr Rembrandt: the chief janissary, the peasant boy, myself, the onlooking villagers and, lined up opposite, the soldiers. The only movement a thin curl of smoke from the chimney of a wooden cabin. It smelt of the reassurance that smoke gives on a cold, bright morning: the hope of a fire to warm oneself beside; of porridge or warm milk; of an end to loneliness. I thought that if it was to be the last sensation I should ever have it was a comforting one.

What was he to do, the janissary? Bring his club down upon my head? And yet for him to acquiesce to my demand would diminish him in the eyes of his men and ruin his authority before the villagers. I had to think quickly and act in such manner as the beatings would cease and yet still preserve this terrible man's authority. Mercifully I had my purse and pulled it from where it hung around my neck and took from it a sovereign, displaying it to all the villagers before I handed it to the janissary with a bow. I had given him little choice but to accept, and its meaning could not have been misunderstood. I gestured to the crowd of men and women who had gathered behind me, making clear that the coin was not only to spare the boy a beating, but all of them. The janissary flipped it high into the air, the low morning sunlight catching its gold again and again as it spun upwards, then seemed to hang for a moment until it fell, glinting, back into his outstretched palm. He closed his hand into a fist with a laugh, encouraging his men to laugh along with him. The moment of danger had passed.

As the troop of soldiers began to return to the business of preparing for the journey on to Belgrade, their interest in persecuting the villagers forgotten as quickly as a wasted bullet forgets its target, I was surrounded by the peasants who insisted on kissing the hem of my gown despite whatever filth had attached to it. I made noises as gracious as I could muster while endeavouring to pull away from them. I hardly deserved their gratitude. Our presence had robbed them of half their livestock and all their bread, and instead of compensating them, all I had done was save them a beating for their trouble.

Back at Edward's side at last, he said: 'That was not negotiation but bribery, madam.'

'And would you have done better?'

He drew out his bottom lip in careful consideration. 'I would not have had the courage you showed even to begin, Mary.'

We do not tend to pay each other compliments, and if

either of us inadvertently does so, we find it best to pretend it hasn't happened at all.

Once in Belgrade, our party was billeted with the pasha of the city, Achmat Bey. If my first experience of Turkish manners filled me with dismay, since they were those of the cruel janissaries, those impressions were handsomely gainsaid by our host. His home was arranged in the Turkish style, with simple low wooden seats around each chamber, a stove in each so that the cold was banished from the whole building, and carpets of rich reds and blues and yellows. The air smelt of sandalwood and pine and was a great deal more pleasing than the vaporous fumes of London.

Our host supped with us each night, and after our first meal together, where I asked many questions about the religion, culture and political organization of his country, Achmat Bey took me as his pupil. I began to learn the Arabic script, the expression in its poetry so different from English or French or Italian, because I found it to be a playful and musical language, with meanings shifting subtly with a syllable. It had perfect logic, even more than Latin, for a book became a library with a curl of a letter or two, and a library an author and an author a bookshop, and so it was also with a sword and a swordsman and a sheath and an armoury and so on. If English is a wild meadow, filled with flowers in gay disorder, and French laid out in geometric rows, its hedges low and clipped, and German a tall forest with paths crossing this way and that, Arabic is a riverbank, the water gurgling and tumbling over rocks, bubbling and full of cheer. Achmat Bey took pleasure in my every discovery; and in his kindness, patience and wisdom he was the embodiment of the tutor I had wished for as a child and never been granted. As with the best teachers, no question was deemed foolish, no challenge an insult, and no troubling doubt was heretical. I in turn taught him about our own faith.

'Why are your European churches at war with each other so much of the time?' he asked with perfect incomprehension.

'It is because in the Church of Rome they worship not God, or not God alone, but the Virgin Mary, and venerate saints and so forth and set their priests above the people, whereas in the Protestant Churches it is the word of God in the Bible that is all-important, and everything else is set beneath. The Roman Catholics take it as an insult that we Protestants should disdain their faith, it being venerable, and we Protestants, or some at least, think the Catholics aren't really Christians at all.'

'We also have our divisions,' confessed Achmat Bey. 'It is the result of putting superstition and revelation into our religion to win the credence of the ignorant. Such inventions bring advantage to the unscrupulous but plant the seeds for generations of misery.'

I agreed with him wholeheartedly but confessed that I was ill qualified to teach any person about religion, since my own faith leant in the direction of deism, and I found the trappings of almost all faith if not ridiculous, then certainly tedious.

'Then there is not so much that separates my own belief in Islam from your religion, madam, since my faith is one of pure . . .' He struggled to find a word that might match up to whatever purity it was he was about to avow. '. . . Morality!' he said with a flourish.

'I am pleased to hear it, effendi. But does Alcoran not forbid the drinking of wine?' I observed, perhaps a little unreasonably as Achmat Bey refilled my glass and then his own.

'Truly it is forbidden, but we must each make our own accommodation with God and with His word. The prohibition of the drinking of wine is of great importance for the poor since they are more likely to ruin their lives with it. I, madam, am fortunate enough to know how I may enjoy this blessing that nature has bestowed on us.'

I could not disapprove of an attitude not only so patently reasonable but also so manifestly convenient.

We left Achmat Bey's home with Edward in possession of certain assurances received from the sultan who awaited us in Adrianople, I in possession of some grasp of Arabic poetry and a degree of ability also in the Turkish language, and Nell in possession of a chill.

We stopped some days at Sofia, and I took the opportunity of going to the baths there. Nell, who accompanied me with some reluctance, would not consent to remove her garments, but eyed the form of so many naked women with ill-disguised awe. There may have been as many as two hundred ladies, some bathing in the very hot and sulphurous steam baths, others in the cold pool, but most of them resting on sofas and drinking sherbets, while their servant women braided their hair; though which woman was servant and which her lady it was only possible to tell by the service the one gave to the other, since none wore any garment, and their forms, whether graceful or no, were to my eye all beautiful for their lack of self-regard. It was very hard for me to imagine that, if ever such a scene were to come to pass in London, the ladies would not all be eyeing each other with disdainful smiles and cruel gossip about the shape of a breast or a sagging belly.

For my part I determined to enjoy the baths in the Turkish manner. As Nell began to undress me, I found myself surrounded by these women who, perfectly appalled by my stays, were clearly concerned that I had been imprisoned in them by my husband, who they surmised must be some kind of brute. Even without joining in fully with these women's discussions I gained a firm understanding of their intelligence and interest, and passed a convivial hour in their company, for much can be conveyed with gestures and nods, and my few Turkish words and their few Greek served to bring us somewhere near to mutual comprehension. I was left in no doubt that these women enjoyed a good deal of liberty, and their dress beyond the security of the baths afforded them a freedom that our Western costume most certainly did not.

Our entry into Adrianople was a literal leaving of winter and entering of spring as we descended from the hills into the rich fertile lands warmed by the now not-so-distant Aegean. Fields of young wheat were interspersed with the pale grey-green of olive groves, orchards of every kind of fruit were set out in orderly fashion, their branches jovial with blossom and, at the city's entrance, line after line of tulips in bloom, their colours as if the Almighty Himself had set down his palette there. Our quarters were on the river Hebrus, along which delightful gardens were set, lined with tall cypress trees. Each evening Turkish families came and sat by the banks, setting out a cloth and drinking their coffee and sherbets while servants sang or played instruments, so that when I had the window of my chamber open, I imagined myself – however improbably – raised to heaven, and thought that if heaven should be such as I witnessed there I should be well pleased to believe in its existence. It was captivating, but then we *were* captives of a sort, the sultan having chosen to place his court for the springtime in Adrianople; Constantinople, some one hundred and fifty miles to the east, being less suited for the hunting and country pursuits which it was said he exalted above all else.

I made a friend, the wife of the French ambassador, the Marquise de Bonnac, who was young, charming if rather naive, pretty, of excellent birth and with an admirable curiosity in all things Turkish. I encouraged her to wear Turkish dress as I did, which would have freed us to explore the town as we pleased, if only the marquise had not insisted on bringing a large retinue of servants, thus greatly undermining our attempts at discretion. On one occasion I convinced her to bring only her maid, and Nell came as my only companion, and we were able to visit the grand vizier's lady, and a dignified if rather dull evening was spent talking on most matters concerning the social life of the empire. Being the vizier's lady she did not speak of what I had heard: that Turkish ladies may have lovers more freely than the ladies of England, since they can go about without being recognized and even conduct an affair with a gentleman and that gentleman not know precisely who she be, since he may taste her lips and other pleasures yet never see her on any other occasion but veiled. It is a different sort of freedom from ours, and yet we are so constrained as women in what we may do and with whom we may converse that we might just as well be imprisoned. I have further been able to confirm another Turkish liberty that I shall strive to have introduced in England: that a woman's wealth is her own and does not pass to her husband when she is wed, or when they divorce, which may also happen without great difficulty. And as for the harem, far from being a place of lewdness and captivity, it is, as I have observed, rather a place of liberty and power.

Yesterday the Marquise de Bonnac and I were able to observe the procession of the sultan to morning prayers. It is an occasion of high formality and spectacle: he was preceded by several hundred janissaries who wore tall white-feathered headdresses, and paraded on foot or on horseback, the horses also all white; then came battalions of royal gardeners, for these men are a sort of army in Adrianople, keeping the legions of tulips and roses in order, and they were dressed in colours to match their flowerbeds; then came the kizlar agha, the chief eunuch, dressed in bright yellow silk which made him look like a splendid bumble bee; and after him, on a tall horse, the Shadow of Allah upon the Earth His Sublimity the Sultan, who, perhaps being told that the marquise and I were watching, brought his horse to a halt beneath the window from which we observed the parade. He cast me a look as chilling as it was regal. His eyes are dark, and though a handsome man, there is some haunted quality about his person, as I have seen sometimes in men of power, though not in our own king, who is not very interested in power nor greatly fearful of losing it, which is a happy position for a sovereign to find himself in.

Hearing a thump, I turned to find my friend the marquise had swooned at the sight of the sultan and fallen to the floor in a faint. I had been given rosewater to sip while we watched the parade and threw the contents of my cup on her face, which roused her, obliging me to pretend to a concern I hardly felt. Fainting seems to me something a woman should not do in public unless entirely unavoidable. I absolutely refuse to faint, even when it might bring me some advantage, for it is fainting that gives men the impression women are weak and foolish, though it has to be said that the Marquise de Bonnac is both weak and foolish if also admirably sweet and kind-hearted. She reminds me of my own beloved Anne, just a little.

Everything I have so far witnessed in Turkey has fortified the impression of where true power lies in this Ottoman Empire. It is form without substance since a frown from a janissary causes the edifice to shake. Turkey is not an empire but a wasps' nest, and for all its elaborate design not much more than dust and glue.

Edward and the Marquis de Bonnac both being new ambassadors to the sultan's spring court found themselves rivals and competed fiercely with each other as to which one of them would first be given an audience. In true Turkish style, the sultan consented to see them both on the same day and at the same hour, though in separate audience chambers. Given that he had so assiduously courted the good opinion of the grand vizier, Edward was sure that he had made great strides in the direction of peace. The French ambassador's purpose was the opposite, for he wished war against the Austrians to continue, so that a more general European war might proceed as soon as it decently could. I learnt little from my friend the marquise because she had no interest in matters of diplomacy, and found myself excluded from discussions with the grand vizier and his ministers. Though conversation with the ladies of rank was delightful, it was inconsequential on matters of war and peace. I was bound, perhaps for the first time in our marriage, to rely on Edward's own estimation of his skills. I trusted he was as able as he thought, though I never met the man who was.

We were soon to move with the court to Constantinople, and I was close to giddy with anticipation of the city, and of planting my feet on the spot where Constantine stood. How I longed to breathe the heady air of Byzantium.

10

DISCOVERING NELL

Summer 1717, Constantinople

(Mary)

'Do you truly believe we are not seen, my lady?' asked Nell, having removed three pins from between her lips. She was usually so respectful, and so quiet, yet she seemed barely able to contain her incredulity.

'I know that we are *seen*, Nell, but we are seen as Turkish ladies and so may pass more freely, and observe all that we please, which if dressed in our Frankish attire would be forbidden us.'

She stood before me, a puzzled expression on her face. She had replaced the three pins to her lips, for she was adjusting my *dimiye* pantaloons, baggy at the hips, tight at the ankle and tremendously comfortable. Removing the pins for the second time, she said: 'Excusing me, madam, but I see how heads turn when we pass. I say this only for . . . for –' she grasped for a word '– for the avoidance of some embarrassment, as I do not believe we are as invisible as you intend.'

'Nonsense, Nell. And how is it that you see heads turning when I have never observed such a thing?'

She squatted down to make the necessary adjustment to the hems, inserting the pins into the silk. 'I do believe it is because you always walk at such pace, ma'am, always being eager to arrive at our next destination. I walk a little way behind and observe.'

'Hmmm, well.' Much as I wanted to dismiss what Nell had said, I knew she would never speak out of turn or without good reason. 'I shall hereby appoint you as my rearguard, Nell.'

I found her observing me sometimes with the cold eye of a natural philosopher at a microscope, as if I were something curious needing to be recorded. I feared that she might be reporting my movements to Edward, though to have accused her of such would have been unproductive, and so I decided to set a test of her loyalty, the best I could devise and one which satisfied my own whims.

'I have a notion to see the Hagia Sophia mosque,' I said to Nell one morning as she was dressing me.

'Indeed, ma'am?' she said in her neutral manner, but by then I had grown as familiar with Nell's *indeeds* and *most certainlys* as a gamekeeper learns to interpret when a bird's cry is one of alarm or allure, and I knew that she thought I was being foolish.

'Yes. I would ask the Marquise de Bonnac,' I continued, 'but she has a tendency to flutter like a bird, and that would only draw attention.'

'Yes.'

'I think it would be better if you and I go together, just the two of us.'

For a moment Nell's hands stopped their busy work at buttons and hooks and laces. 'A woman is forbidden to enter that mosque. There are others that we may see, ma'am, mosques that have places set aside for women to worship, but . . .'

'. . . But I do not wish to see another. I wish to see the Hagia Sophia. I wish to run my hands upon the stones that the Empress Theodora herself touched. I wish to see the place, to breathe its air, to inhale time itself. But no matter – I shall go alone. Yes, perhaps that would be better . . .' It was mischievous of me to say so, for Nell had already set herself up as my guardian. She considered me reckless, and that her principal duty entailed ensuring that my rash behaviour would not bring me or anyone else peril.

'You might write to the grand vizier, madam, or to the sheikh, and be given some special dispensation? We might be permitted to visit at a time when worshippers are not present. Perhaps Mr Wortley might . . .'

'I have no wish to involve my husband in this,' I said sharply. 'Indeed, he is not to hear of it, do you understand?'

'Certainly.'

'We shall dress in men's attire and attend the *Fajr* prayers so that we may slip across into Sultanahmet before dawn.'

Nell did not speak, but I could see that she did not approve.

It was not that I did not respect Islam. Indeed, I had formed the highest regard for the faith. I simply wished to see that mighty building – and to test Nell. 'You are afraid?'

'There is danger in it, my lady, as you know full well, but no, I am not afraid. If we were to be discovered, it would cause difficulties for your husband's embassy. I believe you know this and have considered the harm that may do?' Her tone as always was calm and even. She was not threatening me, merely pointing out the truth and likely consequences of my plan. She had not only natural grace, but intelligence and good judgement, and I was in need of a companion who bore those qualities, particularly when I was free to ignore her warnings.

'There is danger in it, Nell,' I agreed, 'but we must live, we must breathe! What is it to be here if we do not see all, touch all?'

We set off for morning prayers the following Friday in heavy green robes over our baggy pantaloons, and above a shirt and waistcoat. Upon our heads we wore tall hats, large enough to hide our hair, and I had acquired from the ostler hair from the mane of a black mare which Nell had fashioned into excellent moustaches, which we affixed to our upper lips with gum Arabic, together with a sprinkling of dirt upon our chins. On our feet we wore splendid red leather slippers, which I had made so that they would suggest our feet were a good deal larger than they were, for nothing gives a woman away so easily as her diminutive shoes. Since we would be required to remove our slippers on entering the mosque, there was little I could do to enlarge the length of my toes, but I told Nell that we must both make our feet filthy with coal dust and put some soil beneath our toenails, so that they might pass better as a man's, since men's feet are ever dirty, even when washed.

It was an easy enough thing to slip away and so avoid the attentions of our janissary. Had I been with the Marquise de Bonnac she would have been giggling and I would most probably have caught the contagion. But Nell was imperturbable, her attention focused on getting me safely into the Hagia Sophia and out again.

I had chosen the holiest day of the week in the hope that the mosque would be particularly crowded and therefore give us the best opportunity of blending in with the other worshippers. I'd observed the Mohammedan members of our household at their prayers and knew what Nell and I must do in terms of cleansing ourselves before we prayed, and what kneeling and prostrating, and had practised these manoeuvres with her, and also some approximation of the lines of the Alcoran we must recite.

As dawn broke and the muezzin gave his mournful call from the minaret, I saw to my relief that we would easily be able to join the throng streaming into the mosque, and was even more gratified when I realized that, despite its vast interior, some worshippers went up the great staircase and prayed upon the high balcony. We followed, and from there I saw all and heard all and smelt all, for the odour was of bare, hot feet and unwashed clothes and morning breath, of worn carpet and sandalwood, and yet there was a sanctity in it, there in Justinian's holy house, built twelve hundred years before for the worship of a different prophet, but the same God. Had I not been with Nell, I would have been found out for who I was, for I gazed in such a trance at the vaulting ceiling, covered in mosaic of gold and blues, and at the Arabic script hanging on great shields, and at the Christian saints that had stood there for seven hundred years before the Ottomans had arrived in the city and had only half scrubbed them away, that I almost missed the call to pray. Nell abruptly pulled me down.

At the end of the service, I let the bodies of the hundred men who crowded about us stream away, their voices low and murmuring, and we followed, my sense that I had transgressed local custom growing so strong that I feared my folly had led us into great peril.

Just as we were leaving the building, a man, an official of the mosque, stopped us and addressed us in Turkish, some words I hardly understood, though they seemed to be about our dress. To my astonishment Nell spoke to the man gruffly in Turkish. 'My uncle and I are from Skanderoon, and unfamiliar with the ways of the city,' she said, in a voice that might have passed for that of an adolescent youth.

He nodded and let us pass with a blessing of welcome.

Once well away from the Hagia Sophia, I declared, 'You speak Turkish, Nell. That is extraordinary!'

'No, my lady. Not a word. And I had no idea what that gentleman said to us. You, I'm sure, did and may tell me.'

'Ah yes, well . . . there was something about our clothes, I think. Though I thought we fitted in with the crowd. But your response was so confident, so polished?'

'I had prepared a little speech, which I asked the under-Ayah to teach me. I did not tell her what we were about, naturally, but said that I should like to be able to tell any man that accosted me that I was from out of the city and pretend that an uncle was near by.'

'Nell, you are clever. Very clever.'

'It is not my place to be clever, madam. Only loyal.'

On our arrival back at the embassy Edward was in his office. I had hoped that we might slip up to my chamber and undress, but he'd been made aware that we were not at home and came out into the hallway to confront us. 'What on earth have you been about, Mary? And how are you dressed? And you too, Nell? What is going on?'

Nell curtsied, and gave a small smile, removing her moustache as if she were doffing her cap.

I was about to confess our adventure to Edward when, once again, it was Nell who spoke.

'My mistress thought to dress us as men today and venture down to the market to see if we were treated any differently when in male costume than in female. As you know, sir, Lady Mary is most interested in experiments.'

He looked at Nell quizzically, and then at me. 'Well,

madam? I have not seen the cat today that is so large that it might have got *your* tongue.'

I coughed, falsely. 'I swallowed a very dry almond at the market, Edward, and so Nell has been talking for me,' I croaked.

'Hmmm,' he said, turning back to his study and papers.

From that day on I knew I could count always on Nell's absolute loyalty. Until the day came, as it inevitably did, when I could not.

What Nell thought of the Marquise de Bonnac was all too easy to guess. She considered her too stupid for my company, though she never said so. Nell and I were often together last thing at night as she was obliged to undress me, and one evening she asked, in her usual tone of disinterest, what I truly thought of the marquise. Earlier in the day we had encountered two eunuchs in an animated argument, and the marquise had spent the next hour talking of how she would like a eunuch of her own, for she thought these poor men both hideous and amusing and compared them to the pug dog which she liked to carry about with her.

NELL: Were you surprised, madam, that the Marquise de Bonnac thought eunuchs so charming?

I: Your French is improving, Nell.

NELL: *With a flash of annoyance, for she does not care to reveal her many linguistic talents.* Perhaps a little.

I: Do you think the eunuchs repugnant? I know that many do.

NELL: No, madam. No, it is not that. It is that they are enslaved, not only robbed of their liberty, but of their very form. I think the Turks cruel.

I: Yet are not all nations cruel? In England we hang a man for stealing a sheep.

NELL: And worse.

I: Worse than hanging?

NELL: No, ma'am. I mean that a man – or woman – may be hanged for all manner of things.

I: *Thinking I might learn something more of Nell.* What things?

NELL: *Flushes red.* I know of a woman hanged for hiding the body of her stillborn infant. And she was only grieving over her lost child. That is not justice.

I: It is not. There is much that must be changed in the world, Nell. *I hesitate.* Was that woman a person you knew?

NELL: *Dismissively.* I was but a child myself. I was told of it.

I: *Gently.* Was it your mother, Nell?

NELL: *Places my gown upon its hanger and takes some time brushing it down. She turns to face me, her features perfectly composed.* We were speaking of eunuchs.

I: *Knowing that I cannot press her further.* It is a cruel thing, done to those boys. Yet the slaves of this empire are treated with more kindness than those of our own.

NELL: There is not an empire that is just but the empire of the mind.

I: *Thinking what a marvellous thing for her to have said! I could have embraced her then, indeed felt a great urge to do so – to take her in my arms and place kisses upon her clever mouth, her all-seeing eyes. I take a step towards her.* Nell?

NELL: *Curtsies abruptly.* Goodnight, my lady.

Eddie, just four years old, spoke to us only in Flemish. Edward thought it inconvenient, but not unduly so since he had little interest in anything our son had to say to him. I asked Mrs Van der Kamp why she did not speak to our son in English, which she knew well enough though her accent was unpleasant.

'It is the boy. He likes to pretend he is a little Flemish boy. I do not encourage him, madam. Sometimes I tell him a folk tale in Flemish, but that is all. Otherwise I speak only in English.'

'Folk tales fill a child's head with dragons and witches and are not to be encouraged, Mrs Van der Kamp.'

She looked as if I had driven a knife into her but nodded briskly. 'No folk tales? Very well.'

'Is it time for him to have a tutor?' I asked her.

'He is four years old. He likes to play, and perhaps . . .' She hesitated.

'Perhaps?'

'Perhaps to see a little more of his father and mother.' She looked down at her hands, which were knotted tightly together.

Thinking that, until a suitable tutor could be found in the city, Nell would be a good influence on the boy, I asked that she spend an hour or two a day with him. Since I had visits to make, and other engagements, I invited Mrs Van der Kamp to accompany me on those, as she would have no other duties at those times. The difficulty was that, whereas

Nell was both intelligent and quiet, Mrs Van der Kamp was stupid and loud.

I liked to sketch and paint in watercolours in the late-afternoon light on most days and, as part of her new duties, one afternoon Mrs Van der Kamp accompanied me to a park at the top of Pera Hill from where I had a splendid view of the domes and minarets and gardens of Sultan-ahmet, laid out across the narrow waters of the Golden Horn as if begging to be painted. I set up my easel and began first to sketch the scene in pencil. Nell would have sat some distance away, perfectly composed and silent, reading a book but glancing up from time to time in vigilance, but Mrs Van der Kamp peered over my shoulder and made strange grunting noises of disapproval. At last I could bear no more. 'Mrs Van der Kamp, is there something troubling you?'

'It is that you have missed out the boats in the water. And also the clouds in the sky.' She aimed a stubby finger at my sketch, pointing out where these objects should sit.

'The boats and clouds I may add later. Or I may not. It is not a perfect representation, but an impression of the city.'

'An impression?'

'Yes, it is what I see, or what I *feel* of the place, Mrs Van der Kamp. Art need not show nature exactly but must show it through the eye of whoever beholds it, and that is different.'

She tutted and moved away, muttering to herself that she had never heard of such a thing. I resolved that I would have to restore Nell to her former duties, for her presence was not only calming and graceful but, I found, increasingly necessary. When she was not in my company I found myself wondering what she might be doing and with whom she might be talking, as if I were suffering a fit of jealousy, which naturally I was not.

11

A VERY GREAT PROTECTION

Autumn 1717, Constantinople

(Mary)

Each time I went to a salon with Turkish ladies, and then in the evening to a party with ladies and gentlemen from European nations, all at war but at peace around a dinner table, I was struck by a great contrast: my Turkish friends never suffered a pockmarked face. Whereas in any gathering of Europeans, a third or more of us would bear the scars of that terrible disease. I began to make certain enquiries, and soon discovered that Turkish children were subjected to a remarkable procedure, which guarded them against a contagion that caused untold misery to every family in England and beyond, whether high or low. There was no protection from it in Europe, not wealth nor sweet water nor fresh air. Smallpox was merciless in its equality, unrelenting in its pursuit of young as well as old, rich as well as poor, thin as well as fat. Kings and queens suffered no less than their subjects, and royal houses were ended for want of heirs, so remorseless was Death's appetite in this regard. Yet here in Constantinople all were untouched. I determined to discover more, and next day sought out Dr Maitland, the embassy physician, for if there was some means of guarding my son from Death, I would never forgive myself for failing to seize the opportunity of protecting him.

Maitland was a neat, terse gentleman of about forty-five, who also served the factors of the Levant Company. He had the air about him less of a man of medicine than of a country parson with a better knowledge of his parishioners than of God. In short he was an amiable individual, often in attendance at embassy dinners where he made himself agreeable to all without ever saying a memorable thing.

'Dr Maitland?'

'Lady Mary,' he replied, with an awkward bow. It occurred to me that we had never been alone together, and he seemed embarrassed by his predicament.

'I have observed that the Turks and others in this city are unafflicted by smallpox and wish to know how this has come about, for every other contagion seems to bear down upon the place most terribly.'

'Ah yes, well . . .' He looked at the chair, and I bid him take it. 'It is a strange business, for the people of the city use a barbaric method, believing that it guards them from the disease. I believe they acquired the practice from the Circassians, who in turn acquired it from the Tartars or some such. They take the pus from one who is suffering from smallpox and next cut the arm of a child and pour a little of the pus into it and are convinced this offers them protection.'

'And does it?'

He looked dumbfounded. 'Does it what, madam?'

'Does it offer them protection?'

'How could it?'

'The evidence of my own eyes suggests that it does.'

Maitland laughed pitifully. 'I do not see how such a practice could possibly . . .'

'To learn one must have eyes to see, ears to listen and a heart that is open, Dr Maitland.'

'Yes, but really—'

'Dr Maitland!' I interrupted, before he could dismiss the idea again. 'I have a proposal.'

'Oh?'

'You believe in the principles of science?'

'Of course.'

'Then let us observe and record. We shall go and witness this process and note down the results.'

'I do not think . . .' he began.

'You may join me in this experiment or not. It is your choice.'

'I shall have to speak with Mr Wortley Montagu.'

'Speak to him all you like.'

I knew that Edward's efforts to impress upon the sultan and his ministers the importance of political relations with His Britannic Majesty were failing in the face of the lavish gifts which the French, the Dutch and the Poles were able to provide. Edward was constrained by whatever he could persuade the shareholders of the Levant Company to part with, which amounted to a few paltry clocks and bales of wool cloth. He took little or no interest in my activities, which was a mercy for us both.

Over the succeeding weeks Dr Maitland and I observed some twenty engraftings of children, attending each household, whether Greek or Turkish or Armenian, over the fortnight following to monitor the child's progress. In each case a very mild infection of the smallpox ensued, followed by the child's complete recovery. A handful of elderly Greek women were the surgeons, expert in knowing when there was a case of smallpox in the city, going to the sufferer, drawing off a little pus in a walnut shell and carrying it to their new patient. Convinced beyond any doubt of the efficacy of the treatment, as by this time was Maitland, despite his sincerely held but now defunct conviction to the contrary, I resolved to have Eddie inoculated.

'We shall have to await your husband's return from Adrianople, of course,' said Maitland, ever cautious.

Edward was away with the sultan's court, trying once more to broker an agreement for peace with the Austrians which seemed further away than ever. But what seemed an inconvenience was, I realized, an opportunity, for Edward was certain to object. 'I have already spoken to him on the matter. We shall proceed without delay,' I lied.

Eddie was running around in the grounds being chased by a janissary who was bearing down on him with his scimitar, for all the world as if he was about to slice off my son's head, yet the gleeful laughter of both child and man made it clear enough that, despite the terrifying scene, they were the best of friends. How I wished that Eddie might run so freely and gleefully with his father or for that matter with me.

Eddie was immediately suspicious that I wished to call him in, though the avuncular presence of Dr Maitland reassured him somewhat. We brought him to Edward's study, where the smallpox woman awaited, an old Greek widow who held in her hand the precious infection in a walnut shell. Once Eddie was seated the woman went at him with a blade, insufficiently sharp, causing my son, not unreasonably, to scream. She endeavoured to introduce the pus, but was nervous, never having performed the procedure upon an English child before. Indeed he was wriggling so much that Dr Maitland went to calm him, then took the shell from the woman, made a neat incision in Eddie's other arm, and the procedure was done. I wrote immediately to Edward to inform him, promising to report on Eddie's progress day by day. Edward was, naturally, furious that I had proceeded to perform the inoculation without consulting him, but I was serene in my conviction that I had performed an action that was justified by reason and love and, no less importantly, by my constant mission to deceive Death, who stood hungry over us all.

Eddie suffered a slight fever the next day, had some few spots over the following week and soon after was perfectly restored to health. Maitland said that he would write a paper for the Royal Society, and I assured him he would have my assistance.

Next, I decided that all my household who had not suffered the disease must be inoculated. Nell first, for I was growing to love her dearly.

'It is a great protection, Nell.'

'I am not eager to be experimented upon, madam.'

'Our experiments are over, and we are certain of the procedure, Dr Maitland and I. Besides, Nell, you have great beauty and in addition intelligence and refined manners. You might make a good marriage one day, that is supposing you are set upon such a foolish course, and yet should you catch the smallpox and survive, your looks will be ruined, as are mine.' I placed a hand upon my face to remind myself of the craters that disfigured it.

She looked at me doubtfully. 'Will Dr Maitland himself perform the procedure?'

'At my bidding, most certainly.'

'Then I will consider it.'

'Good.'

*

That night as she was undressing me, she let her hand rest a moment upon my belly. The gesture was so intimate, so wanted, that I placed my own hand upon hers, and there we stood, in a strange form of embrace.

'It is a girl,' she said.

I had not spoken to her or any other of my condition, but naturally she would be the first to notice. 'I should tell Edward that I am with child, I suppose.'

'And that he is to have a daughter?'

'You cannot know, Nell. That is superstition.'

'It is a girl, and she will live a long life . . .' She hesitated. 'Am I being impertinent?'

'Not impertinent. But I do not believe in magic, Nell. And I'm surprised that you do.'

She began to say something about sensing things that seemed to have no easy explanation but stopped herself.

'What else do you see?'

'Nothing.' She gathered clothes together, preparing to leave.

'There is something else, I know,' I pressed her.

'You must not expect too much of her, that is all. Your expectations are very great and may be disappointed.'

'You need not place your hand upon my belly to know that.'

She smiled remotely, and asked in her soft, musical way, 'Will that be all, ma'am . . . Mary?'

'That will be all, Nell.' But something impelled me to do what I should not have done, and I embraced her and kissed her upon the cheek, which caused her to give me a hint of a smile before she bowed, a little embarrassed, and withdrew.

12

RECALLED

Summer 1718, Constantinople

(Mary)

I loved Constantinople as assuredly as I ever loved any man or woman, save perhaps Anne, and my sister and now my children. My daughter, Mary, was born in January, a placid infant, healthy and untroubling. But it was the city that had taken my heart, with its hills and seas, its mosques and churches, its colours which made rainbows seem grey by comparison; its smells of spice and smoke and jasmine and sullied humanity; the sound of the muezzins' calls which rose like an overture five times each day; its swish of silks and wools and muslins; its shine of rain on two-thousand-year-old marble. The city seeped into my soul and changed me utterly, and because my love for it was so great it was, naturally, taken from me. Edward was recalled to London, his service over. To be torn from this place so abruptly was how a young tree must feel, having put down roots and produced leaves and settled into its place along an avenue with a fine prospect, thinking that it would grow tall and broad and make a home for generations of singing birds, only to be wrenched from the ground and told it was the wrong sort of tree all along.

Edward was informed by our friend Mr Addison, who was still secretary of state, that he was to return to London because his mission had been successful.

'It is a humiliation,' said Edward, holding the letter in his hand, tears on his cheeks testifying to his broken pride.

'Peace has come, Edward. You should be proud.'

'How can I be, Mary? You know full well it is not *my* peace, but Robert Sutton's. He has done all he could to undermine me from his embassy in Vienna. He has won an Austrian peace, and I have lost a Turkish one.' He looked once more at the letter and threw it across the room, which was not at all the imperturbable Edward I knew.

'I am sorry for it, my dear. As sorry for it as you.'

He came to me, took my hands in his and kissed me. 'Thank you, Mary. That is a comfort.'

I had been about to say that my sorrow was not for the failure of his mission, or his recall to the ignominy of a reduced place in government, but for my loss of this precious city and the life I had made for myself here. But his sorrow meant I could not explain what I truly felt, and so I said instead: 'We might make the most of our journey home . . . explore the ancient sites as we could not on our way here, since we were in such a hurry?'

'Yes,' he said, not really hearing me. 'Yes, I suppose we might.'

'We must return to England,' I said to Nell as we walked to an engagement with the wife of the Swedish ambassador.

'Oh?'

I turned to see her expression, but she moved a little

ahead of me in order to deny me that opportunity. 'Yes, Edward will tell the household of it tomorrow. He is quite shocked as a matter of fact. Out of sorts.'

'I see. Will you wish me to remain in your service, madam?'

'Good God, Nell. Of course! Why on earth would I not?'

'Well,' she said, slowing a little, and I could see that her face was flushed. 'Our agreement was that I would accompany you to Constantinople. I thought perhaps . . .'

'No, no, Nell. I should wish you to remain in my service for as long as you may.' After some moments of silence, a penny, or possibly a heavy gold sovereign, dropped. 'Unless . . . there is some reason, or some *person*, to keep you here?'

She stopped and faced me. 'Mr Thomas Lodge, one of the factors, he . . .'

'The pretty fellow, who plays the lute?'

'Yes, he . . .'

'What of him?'

'He has asked me to marry him.'

When had Nell the opportunity to court with a man? I could not think, unless on evenings when I had been engaged at dinners and parties and so on, and she had been doing rather more than reading her books and studying Italian, as she claimed. 'You would become the wife of a factor?' I asked, straining to consider whether such a marriage would improve her social standing.

'Were I to accept his proposal, then yes.'

'And is that your intention?' I struggled to conceal my indignation that she might be on the very cusp of abandoning me, and deeper still a wisp of jealousy.

'I should prefer to remain in your service, madam. If that is your wish?' she said quietly.

'Oh, Nell, yes it is!' I declared, and most indecorously embraced her right there in the middle of the bustling street.

Releasing her, I thought I ought to say more. 'Unless, of course, you would wish to become Mrs Lodge? I should not like to think I am getting in the way of your passions.'

'I do not love him. I like him, but love is another matter.'

'It is, Nell, it is. And a dangerous thing it is altogether,' I confessed, close to admitting to the growing feelings I held for her. After all, had she not just declared that she chose me over Mr Lodge? I almost skipped along to the Swedish embassy, so happy I was to have almost lost and then regained Nell.

Later, as we walked home, Nell asked me about the reasons for Edward's recall, and as we tended to talk freely when alone, I told her what I knew. 'He is not skilful in diplomacy. Edward is decent, straightforward and trustworthy and those are qualities that serve a man well in politics, provided they are combined with others, those being craftiness, guile and agility. To have the latter talents without the former is to make a man a fox, and disbelieved; but to have the former without the latter makes a man a sheep, and thus ignored, and that is Edward's fate, I'm sorry to say.'

'Yes. Mr Wortley is a man who believes an arrow flies straight.'

'He is.'

Nell then took an imaginary arrow from an equally imaginary quiver, leant back, drew back her arm and let her invisible missile fly through the air. 'It flies thus, in a parabola.'

'It does!' I said encouragingly, wondering where Nell's interesting mind was taking me.

'Diplomacy is the skill to weave the flights of many arrows into a single purpose, to make a truth, as it were, from many untruths, and one that is irresistible to all.'

I stood back from her, my hands on my hips in admiration,

and saw that her eyes were alight with all her sparking thoughts.

'I have been reading Machiavelli, you see,' she said. 'In Italian. It is not difficult.'

Oh, Nell, I did not say. How dare you make me fall in love with my maid.

I wrote to my sister to tell her of our imminent departure, and the prospect of our reunion in London. It would, of course, be many weeks before she received my letter, and I had no expectation of a reply, but the day before we sailed, I received one from her, written some two months before.

London
5 May 1718

Dearest Mary,

I am happy! Yes, happy! For I have at last heard from John that I am to come to him in France. And His Majesty has most graciously consented that I may join my husband in France without impairment to my jointure or any of those possessions that will, by right, pass to any son John and I may have, which as you know was not the arrangement when first I was permitted to go into exile. Isn't it a great blessing? And I feel so much less tired than before and filled at last with purpose, for the waiting has been a torment.

I am sorry that I write only one letter to your ten. Do not think I do not care for all you have told me of the sights and sounds of that faraway city you love, or for the intrigues between the Russian ambassador and the wife of the French consul. And your little sketch of young

Mary was very sweet. I had it put in a silver frame to sit alongside the portrait I keep always of you, but it has vanished, and I can only think that one of the servants stole it for the frame. They are not loyal to me, though I am nothing but kind to them. But I want you to know that you are not forgotten by me for one moment, and never shall be.

There is more to say, I'm sure, but I shall write another letter soon, and many more.

I am your ever-loving and affectionate sister,
F

What a comfort to know that Fanny was happy, though I feared her happiness would not survive that reunion she so longed for since, blinded by love, what she had failed to notice was that her husband was both unpleasant and absurd. Though I supposed it possible that years of exile had humbled him. But if I should ever discover he mistreated my sister I would go to war with him, of that I was certain.

Having settled into our Turkish life, I thought that we might try to continue it in some way in London, and so I resolved that we should bring close to twenty of our household on our journey. I had engaged a Circassian wet nurse for little Mary, but she was reluctant to leave Constantinople, arguing, not wholly unreasonably, that she had three children of her own, and a husband who worked at the docks. Mary was still not weaned and wet nurses were in short supply, so we decided to bring the whole family with us to England, a docker always being employable and the children unlikely to be the cause of great trouble.

Mrs Van der Kamp resigned her position to become

housekeeper for His All Holiness, the Greek patriarch of Constantinople, a decision on her part – and for that matter the patriarch's – that was no less baffling than it was welcome.

I was obliged to make a pretence of eagerness for London, for resuming court life and my literary acquaintances. Mr Pope had been an assiduous correspondent, though his eagerness for my approval of some of his poorer work was lamentable, and I sometimes found it difficult to be sufficiently diplomatic in response, as if the great poet were a nation with whom I had a treaty that had outlived our alliance, and a word out of place might spark war. My sister would, I felt sure, take many months to assemble all she needed for her emigration to France, and I hoped to have one more opportunity to make her see that her marriage to John Erskine was a prison, and that she should seek to have it dissolved by parliament and be free.

In my heart I held a great dread of England, for it seemed to me a land where I had known Death, and Turkey the place where I had known Love, not of any one person in particular but of life itself. London would be rain and mud, false talk and chimney smoke and puking in the alleys, and a people who exalted ignorance, thinking it a fine jest to hang a man for stealing a loaf. We English thought it barbarous to chop off the hand of a thief yet considered it a mercy to hang him from a rope so that his neck broke. In Constantinople the baker was hanged for short-changing his customers; in London the shopkeeper who swindled those who bought his bread was the toast of all his fellow aldermen for turning a better profit. It was hardly a surprise to me that the Turk regarded the Christian as the heathen.

13

THE FINDING AND LOSING OF THE TROJAN STONE

Summer 1718, The Mediterranean

(Mary)

A vessel, the *Preston,* sent under sail in all dignity to fetch the English ambassador from Turkey long before Edward knew he was to be fetched at all, anchored on the Golden Horn on the nineteenth of June. At least I did not need to worry about leaving behind what we had acquired, a ship being commodious enough for all of it: costumes, servants, furniture, carpets, four horses and a son and daughter.

We sailed late on the fifth of July, passing Gallipoli in the night, and next day anchored on the Hellespont. I bid the first mate, a pretty fellow of good physique, that he emulate Leander and swim across the strait. 'But where is my Hero?' he asked, showing his knowledge of the myth, and of the priestess who lit her light each evening.

'It is daytime, sir, and there is no storm on the horizon,' I averred, 'and so you may safely make Leander's time across the strait and even better it.'

The mate, whose name was Shovell, a nephew of the late admiral, bowed and awarded himself a little smile in anticipation of what he was about to say. 'Madam, you may whisper in my ear, you may flatter, entreat, promise, protest and swear, but I shall not swim, I will not dare!' Thus demonstrating the admirable education of at least one British naval officer, since Marlowe's unfinished poem was not greatly known in those days.

As I scrambled up the rocks where the broken remains of the fort of Abydos lay, I had a thought: in all probability Shovell could not swim; it was a superstition held by English sailors, after all, that to learn to swim was to invite the sea to come and take a man off his ship and into the cold water. Yet Leander *could* swim, and so could most of the other heroes of Greek myth. Perhaps it was only that the Greek seas were warmer, and their vessels more inclined to capsize, that made swimming a necessity for the Greeks as it was not for the English. Though I also then thought of Thoresby, and a hot summer's day, and of Nathaniel Shaw, and of how I watched him strip off his vest and hose, of his bare white buttocks and his perfect stroke in the lake, and of the surprising strength of feeling, of *need*, I had for him then. I had never felt that way about Edward, or perhaps a little in the first months we were married, but not since. I could not bear to think that I should never be able to love freely again, nor ever be loved free.

We sailed on that day until evening, before anchoring below a sandy, scrubby hill above which it was believed by some credulous souls lay the fabled site of ancient Troy. Edward, concealing his own enthusiasm for seeing the sites of classical history beneath a mask of weary acquiescence, undertook to rise with me early the following morning to explore whatever ruins we might find.

At dawn Edward, Nell and I were walking in fields, the landscape flat and uninspiring about us, here and there old stones, bits of Doric column, a broken slab of marble not of any great age bearing a Latin inscription hinting at Roman or Byzantine construction. A little after seven we stumbled upon a low, stone Greek Orthodox chapel, where we encountered the priest who was going about his labours. He was a shabby fellow, draped in dusty black robes, his beard dark and wiry, flecked with breadcrumbs and the remains of his last several suppers. He implored us to come within to inspect his fine icons, which were of the usual variety – gaudy, flat saints with wide, dead eyes and garments unduly burdened with gold leaf. We nodded with insincere approval, welcoming at least the damp and cool of his little church, which like all such places smelt of wood and wet, of old paint and a little of cats. We pretended to speak barely any Greek so that we might not find ourselves in dispute over questionable interpretations of the scriptures. As we made our leave, the priest bid us observe a stone outside that, he claimed, was a relic of Troy itself.

It was old, most certainly, for it bore several different scripts, Greek and Latin, but also triangular and arrow-shaped symbols such as we had never seen before, though I had heard reports of such letters found on a stone at Persepolis. In addition were the more familiar Egyptian symbols of birds and axes and so on that we know as hieroglyphs. Edward was already squatting in the dust, tracing with his fingers the words in Latin which were at the very bottom of the stone, almost as an afterthought, and then above them, at about head height, was the rather strange old Greek, and higher still the other two scripts, so that the very topmost rows would require a ladder for close inspection. When Edward looked up at me from where he was crouched, I saw him as I had never seen him before, as he must have looked as a boy of fourteen or fifteen, his eyes bright, his lips moist with excitement. 'Mary,' he exclaimed, 'it's extraordinary!'

I could not disagree. 'If we can have a canopy sent up from the *Preston* for shade,' I said, in business-like manner, 'and my notebooks and sketching paper and some pencils, I shall make a copy. Nell will go back for my things.'

She hesitated, assessing whether she should or should not go to fetch those objects from the ship.

'Hmmm,' said Edward, standing and staring up at the stone, which was about twice his height, perhaps a little more, his hands pressing into his sore back. 'We should take it with us.'

Before I could voice my opinion, the priest, seeming to sense the drift of our conversation, interposed himself between us and the stone, in a manner clearly meant to be understood as proprietorial. While I doubted the wisdom or prudence of removing the stone from where it had lain for some thousands of years, the notion that it should belong in some way to the priest decided me. I observed Edward take a step backwards, as if ready to retreat from his resolve, but I did not hesitate. 'We shall pay you in gold,' I declared in Greek.

The priest's eyes slid from me to Edward and, quickly comprehending that it was I with whom he should negotiate, slyly announced that a Frenchman had inspected the very same stone a week before and had made clear his intention to return with a work party and a hundred livres.

'A hundred livres?' I said, dismissively, despite knowing that would be as much as four gold Louis. 'We shall give you five English gold sovereigns for it.'

It is notable that a man of limited education but nevertheless great shrewdness will haggle for hours to win a good bargain but strike quickly if he sees that the advantage is momentarily considerable, and so the priest agreed to my terms in that instant.

'There probably was no Frenchman,' said Edward, quietly.

Nell, to Edward's great surprise, though not to mine, announced, 'The French are busy all over acquiring such stones, sir. I saw such at the Marquis de Bonnac's.'

Her prompting reminded me that I had, indeed, been shown an Aphrodite, presumably Hellenistic and bearing but one arm and only half a nose, at the French ambassador's residence the week before. 'Well, then,' said I, before assuring the priest that I would return with generous payment later that morning.

The captain was extremely reluctant to take on board his vessel an object of such weight and uncertain provenance. 'It may be cursed, Lady Mary,' he said in his strange manner, hovering somewhere between a bluff Norfolk drawl and a more gentlemanly tone.

'Good gracious, Captain Jessop,' said I, 'surely you are not a man to believe in such superstitions?'

He scratched at something beneath his heavy, full-bottomed wig and gave an apologetic shrug. 'Naturally, madam, *I* do not, but the sailor is a creature fashioned almost entirely out of superstition. Should they form any impression of bad spirits relating to this . . . this . . . stone, they will become truculent . . . difficult.'

'Do they need to know?'

'You shall need a party of twenty men to shift it down to the ship and get it aboard, if I have understood your description. There is a jetty a mile down the coast where we might load it without great difficulty,' he said with distaste. It was apparent that Captain Jessop was a man who persuaded himself into things and then out of those same things with alacrity. 'It would be better by far that you make your sketch, but quickly, since the winds will be less favourable by evening, and we sail on by noon,' he announced, as if in conclusion.

'I have a counterproposal, Captain. If I were to instruct only our household staff, of whom we have a good number—'

'A most goodly number, yes,' he interrupted, it being clear that he had been awaiting the moment to express his exasperation with the number of servants who were returning with us to England.

'. . . to bring the stone to the jetty,' I continued, 'and we wrap it in sailcloth so that the crew will not know its nature, and we inform one and all that it is an ancient Greek blessing from Poseidon for all who sail, might that be enough to allay your concerns?'

He pulled a face, his long features becoming longer still and putting me in mind of a camel. He was not a man whose fears were easily allayed, but he consented all the same, sensing that some form of compromise was the best he could hope for.

Our household staff were at first enthusiastic at being put to useful labour since they were in want of amusement, even though we had been at sail only a matter of days; but as soon as they were up on that sun-drenched field away from the cooling effect of the sea and labouring beneath the great weight of the stone, their enthusiasm melted away as surely as the sweat soaked into their vests. The foolish priest, as if my handsome payment had secured some additional service, insisted on walking in advance of our party swinging a censer of some perfumed wood or other. Two of our footmen, Circassians, were burly fellows, but as for the rest . . . Edward and I did not employ our staff for their biceps, and it was clear that a mile of walking with the ancient slab, which we had taken to calling the Trojan Stone, was beyond the strength of our party, if not its will.

The stone beginning to slip from the dozen hands endeavouring to keep it aloft, Edward handed me his jacket and went to assist. Next, to my amazement, stepped forward Nell, who seemed to get good purchase on the object with ease. 'I carried great weights for my Lady Wentworth,' she said quietly, turning her head to address me, 'for the baroness was much inclined towards the moving of heavy furniture about a room, and never could be quite satisfied with its position.' She said this without resentment, almost as if in affectionate memory of her time in service to the lady.

I took off my jacket, grateful that I was wearing Turkish attire as was my preference, handing it to one of the maids who had come along to witness the spectacle, and went to help. Between us the burden seemed lightened, perhaps as much through solidarity of gesture as what muscle we brought to the endeavour.

We sailed at four, too late for the captain's inclination but before the winds were so unfavourable that we would not get out into the Aegean Sea proper. I spent a little while with the children, took a stroll around the deck and only then wondered what had happened to Edward. He was down in the hold, holding a flickering candle to the stone and reading off its inscription. 'Here,' said Edward, handing me the candle and directing me towards a particular section of the Latin script. And there I read that it was an account of war – not, perhaps, the Trojan War, but one not so different, for it told of blood flowing so deep it turned the river red, and of the shore scattered with drowned men, of grieving women and slaughtered infants.

'It is . . . terrible,' I said excitedly. 'But also marvellous, to have such an account, and in tongues that no man living today may know. If we assume that the accounts in the other scripts give the same history, then it is the key to unlocking the writings of the past.'

'We must not let anyone on board know what it says,' rasped Edward. 'We must cover it and leave it here in the hold, or else we shall fuel the worst superstitions of the hands.'

'But . . .'

'Does the captain read Latin and Greek, do you suppose?'

'Jessop? Perhaps not. He seems a decent sort of block-head. But the first mate, Shovell, he will know them.'

'Then let not Shovell come and see it.'

'You would have me guard him night and day?'

Edward gave me that look of his. 'We cannot prevent the first mate from inspecting his own hold, but we may – or *you* may – distract him.'

'And how do you propose I do so?'

'Madam, you are well known for your powers of persuasion. Should Mr Shovell speak of inspecting the Trojan Stone, talk to him of other things instead.'

'What other things?' I said obdurately.

'Not of the weather, madam. But of the Greek tongue, perhaps, and the language that might be found in Persepolis that is plain there on the stone.'

'But that might only tempt him to inspect what is carved on the stone.'

'You will make your descriptions so fascinating that he will find your conversation infinitely more satisfying than dead words carved into cold stone, as indeed he should.'

Was that a compliment? Perhaps.

*

Over the next days and weeks, we sailed on past distant isles and mountains, I always with Homer in my hand, guiding me through the topography and history, though this guide of mine had been dead several thousand years, and perhaps had never lived at all, or not as one being but as many. Edward took trouble to spend time teaching his son grammar and numbers, he in English and Eddie, to his father's consternation, repeating them in both English and Flemish. I would interrupt them when given cause, bringing the boy up on deck, little Mary in my arms, pointing out the peaks of Mount Pelion where the centaurs lived and Chiron nurtured the young Achilles, or a day or two later the ancient acropolis above Athens, or the workings of the half-built canal at Corinth, left unfinished by Nero some sixteen hundred years past. How I longed to go ashore on the Peloponnese but was informed firmly by Captain Jessop that it was the domain of pirates and scoundrels.

'Then, sir, it sounds much like London.'

'London may be a nursery for rogues, madam, but these lands are where they perfect the art of knavery, and with pistols and sharp blades too!' he announced with a glint in his eye, as if he longed for it.

We made port at Candia, took on fresh fruits, bread and wine and sailed on most serenely to Malta, the flames of Mount Etna visible at night on the dark horizon and perfectly thrilling. Making port at Tunis I insisted we remain three days and nights to afford me the opportunity of acquainting myself with ancient Carthage. Having done so as best I could in darkness, it being too hot for daytime inspection, we left at the beginning of August, bound for Genoa, our sails seeking the strong southerly that is called the scirocco or khamseen, meaning the wind that blows for fifty days. Captain Jessop, for all his strangeness, knew his winds. The gentle breeze that carried us out of the port of Tunis he declared to be deceitfully beguiling. 'I trust that damned rock of yours is well secured,' he grunted.

'Certainly, Captain,' said I, in fact being uncertain of the nature of its fastening.

'I'd better go down and see to it, all the same.'

Edward appeared at my side. 'But you may leave all that to us, I assure you,' he said.

'It's my damned ship, sir, and matters of its cargo and its ballast are my domain. I shall send Mr Shovell down to inspect it.'

'No, sir!' said I, desperately trying to think of some reason why it would be better for anyone other than Shovell to see it. 'For I do believe that his esteemed uncle made some declaration against his heirs ever setting sight on Egyptian symbols, for fear of . . .' Though as I spoke, I realized that I was calling up the very notion of curses that it was my purpose to suppress.

Captain Jessop eyed me for a moment as he might a horse that had sat on its haunches and crossed its front legs in refusal to be of service. 'What fucking nonsense,' he muttered before calling out for Shovell. But before the first mate could go about any business down below the wind that his master had anticipated began to blow as if a spell had been cast by Poseidon himself. Soon a full storm was raging, tossing the *Preston* about like a twig in a weir. I went below to comfort the children, but Nell was with them and they, as if engrafted with her perfect serenity, were playing marbles upon a board, watching them move this way and that as our vessel mounted one wave after another as if climbing and descending a succession of Alpine peaks. Most of our household were puking wherever they might, their various hues all a good deal greener than the white or brown or black they had been hitherto. But Nell and the children were no more queasy than they might have been on a carriage ride across the park.

The next morning we found ourselves mercifully in calmer seas. I remarked upon our good fortune to the captain, whose face resembled in its exhaustion a candle that had burnt all night long and was now melted into something quite estranged from its original form. 'Good fortune? Good fortune be damned. We have, madam, been obliged to sail far to the east to outrun the storm and are now at the mercy of the fucking Spanish, whose fleet is at Sicily.'

Mr Shovell appeared at the captain's side, raised his hat, gave me a cursory bow and sought to explain his master's mood. 'I fear, Lady Mary, that we nearly did not make it through the storm at all, but for Captain Jessop's extraordinary skill. We were not helped by, let us say, a certain amount of shifting of our ballast.'

'Damned right, Shovell. We came that fucking close to sinking –' Jessop raised his thumb and forefinger and pinched them together '– and that were only half the storm's doing and half that of your fucking stone.'

'By which the captain means to say—' said Shovell.

'I am perfectly well acquainted with what the captain is saying, and in his manner of saying it,' I assured him.

Captain Jessop gave me one nod of his mournful, camelid head before marching off, instructing over his shoulder: 'The stone must be thrown overboard, for another storm is on its way.' The sky above us was a clear blue, but to the west and south great dark clouds could be seen amassing on the horizon.

Edward blanched. 'But the stone is of inestimable value,'

he protested to Shovell, thinking him a man more reasonable than Jessop. 'It cannot be sunk to the bottom of the ocean.'

The captain, hearing what Edward had said, spun about. 'It will be sunk to the bottom of the ocean with us or without us. Which is it you would prefer, Mr Wortley?'

The work of hauling a stone weighing a ton or more is a good deal more taxing in raising it up from a hold than in lowering it there, and it took the crew a half-hour or more to bring it on to the deck and position it ready to drop over the side. I begged permission to make a quick sketch of the letters before it was consigned for ever to the depths.

'You have twenty minutes, madam,' said Jessop grudgingly, his inclination for compromise not entirely diminished.

I had most of the Latin, and some of the Greek and what may have been Persepolian script transcribed, though had not begun on the hieroglyphs when I heard Jessop declare, 'I don't believe it!'

Glancing up from my sketchbook I saw on the distant eastern horizon what at first looked like very low white clouds, yet within a minute they had formed into a line of a dozen sails. Looking to the south I could see that darker clouds were gathering, too, and the ship began to buck upon the burgeoning waves. Jessop commanded his men to push the stone into the water forthwith. It was all I could do to jump out of its way. 'The mainsail,' commanded the captain, as we caught the stiff breeze, but the line of Spanish galleons was already sailing towards us, as if they were driven by a different wind, one brought to them by their own prayers.

'Fuck it, fuck it,' declared Jessop.

'We are not at war with Spain presently, Mr Jessop,' said Edward, reasonably.

'We are as near as, dammit, Wortley. 'Tis Sicily that is the cause of our dispute. They will see us as fair game.' He turned to Shovell. 'The cannon at the ready, sir!'

'Dear God,' declared Edward. 'Get below, madam,' he instructed.

I felt torn between a fervent desire to protect the children from the battle and an even more heartfelt wish to witness the drama that was about to unfold. What woman gets to witness a naval battle? A moment later we heard the first cannon shot from the distant fleet, and in the same moment felt the first squalls of rain. Puffs of white smoke were visible from the sides of the galleons an age before we heard the resound of the blast. Death was in the waves, in the wind that filled our sails, in the eyes of the sailors who were running to their stations. If ever I feared Death it should have been in that moment, for he had us in his talons, all of us. Yet I felt alive – more alive than I ever had before.

'Fire our cannon, Shovell!' ordered the captain.

'We are a league or more out of range, sir.'

'And so, sir, are the Spanish,' replied Jessop. 'This is a polite dance, a bow before the fucking gavotte, though let us hope it is the bow alone, and not the dance.'

I went then to go below to reassure the children and the more fearful of our household, but the *Preston* lurched and bucked as Captain Jessop brought it round to fire its cannon. 'Hold on to the rail, my lady,' bellowed Jessop, 'or you'll be in the water soon as you can say . . .' Though his last words were drowned out by a sudden, strong gust of wind and so I hung on as instructed, and trusted that Edward had gone below to be with the children, no doubt cursing me for my impetuosity.

The *Preston* shuddered as she let loose her cannon, the scent of sulphur oddly pleasing against the salt smell of the sea.

'Another round, and quick,' came the captain's command, and a moment later another blast. 'Now we outrun them!' shouted Jessop, and once more the ship lurched and bucked like an untrained stallion as the sails filled, and we chased northwards at above ten knots, the coast of Sardinia distant to our west under the surly sky.

My exhilaration subsided as it became clear we were not pursued by the Spanish fleet, until reason brought with it a great swell of relief. 'No battle, then, Mr Shovell?'

'Be glad of it, madam, for we should have been outgunned and sunk in an instant.'

I thought then of the stone that we had let sink to the bottom of the sea, of how it contained in all probability the key to ancient learning – for those men and women of history knew so much, their knowledge now lost in fire and flood and war. It was as if I had glimpsed the gods sitting upon their clouds. 'I am so terribly sad about the stone,' I said.

'I, too, am sad, Lady Mary, for I read some of what was written there before it went overboard, and it seemed Homeric, and in four tongues. It might have been a window on antiquity.'

'And how casual we were with it, for our lives are but a beat of this old planet's heart.'

'It was not worth the drowning of ninety souls, I think.'

Could we not have kept the stone and our lives, too? I held on to the rail a little longer, and breathed in the living air, and saw that a school of porpoises was escorting us, drawn perhaps by our great speed. It seemed they were beckoning us home, to safety. I went below, where Nell was describing the manner of firing a cannon to little Eddie, though where she had acquired knowledge of saltpetre and sulphur and fuses, I could not imagine.

*

Five days later we made port at Genoa. Edward was eager to return to London, which would be quicker overland, and so we went ashore and into a most delightful quarantine with Mr Davenant, the British envoy, and his wife, Catherine, an intelligent woman who ensured that while we were quarantined there we received many visitors, the rules of the quarantine merely requiring that no touching should take place – though such a rule might sensibly be required for all social discourse, for why should perfect strangers touch each other at all? And if this was a suitable precaution against the plague, then why not also against the smallpox and other maladies? I resolved to write to Mr Walpole on my return, proposing some form of domestic quarantine to impede the spread of distempers and malaises of all kinds. Indeed quarantine combined with inoculation, which I wished to prevail upon all society to adopt, might hold back all manner of disease. Why was it that I could see the sense in such a thing, when all the learned men of the Royal Society could not? Was it because they were so concerned to gain the approval of their fellow men that they wished to do nothing, say nothing, write nothing that might cause controversy? Since I was unlikely to ever gain the approbation of such men, I resolved to say precisely what I wished.

Meanwhile, the *Preston* sailed from Genoa for London bearing our children and most of our household. To see my children sail away caused me no little grief, though I knew they would be in the very best of care with dear Nell. Young Eddie gave me a low bow and expressed his hope that Allah should watch over me – it was his habit of late to think of himself as a little Turk. Mary clung to my neck and cried heartily. To be parted from Nell was barely the cause of less pain to me than bidding farewell to Eddie and Mary, for I had come to depend on her so completely that it was as though I was bidding farewell to my own spirit.

As the *Preston* loosed its ropes and its sails began to fill I allowed myself tears, though I dried them before turning and walking to the carriage where Edward waited. He had come to see our party safely away but had not condescended to stand with me at the quayside. As I clambered up into the carriage he said: 'All well, Mary?'

'Yes, all well.' Though I suddenly doubted it. What if some further misfortune should afflict the *Preston*? What if I had just seen the last of my little family? I very nearly ran from the carriage and hollered at Captain Jessop, Come back, come back!

Edward placed a hand upon my knee almost as if he read my thoughts.

'All well,' he said again, as if such a simple and familiar phrase was a charm.

But all was not well.

14

A MOST UNEXPECTED REUNION

Autumn 1718, Paris

(Mary)

Paris was absurd. The fashions made the women look like gin-soaked babies, with their tightly powdered hair, rouged cheeks and idiotic grins. Courtesies were observed not as sincere gestures of respect, but as tedious and much exaggerated ceremony, more suitable for an opera stage than a salon. Yet it had its graces, for all that. We came first to Fontainebleau and were able to make a tour of the palace, with its great abundance of rooms, so many in fact that one could imagine kings and queens and princes and ministers seeking yet never finding one another, which would make affairs of state slow indeed were there need of policy. But policy is rarely made in palaces. In England it is made in coffee houses and inns, and in France in brothels and bedchambers, and the outcome is much the same, which should not surprise us, for reason does not rule in either domain.

The architecture of Paris was pleasing, being built of stone, with parks well laid out and, moreover, furnished with fountains and flamingos. Like London the city has a river flowing through it, but the Seine is serene whereas the Thames is a churning mass of boats and rafts and fish heads and bobbing excrement. The great church of Paris, Notre-Dame, is nobler than Westminster Abbey. But Paris was not alive to me as Constantinople was, nor as London, even in that city's foul disorder.

I was ready to leave not long after we arrived. Though I had never wished to quit Turkey and was in no hurry to return to England, being happy to linger on my travels and record all, the proximity to journey's end began to exert a pull on me, as a spinning top seems to whirl in upon itself faster and faster before it topples. So it was, walking in the Jardin des Tuileries, lulled by the odour of lavender hedges giving the last of their scent, that I was thinking only of resuming London's duties and obligations, when I saw crossing the path before me a figure so familiar and beloved that I imagined for a moment that I had caught sight of a ghost, despite my disbelief in such things. Determined to scold the apparition for frightening me so (in truth trusting that if I laid chase I might dispel it), I ran towards it and, on hearing the tread of my slippers on gravel, the ghost turned and revealed herself to be none other than my dear sister, and a living, breathing sister at that! We embraced, at first in disbelief and, as doubts were confounded by embraces and tears and exclamations, with the greatest fervour.

Over the days that followed I learnt that Fanny had arrived in Paris at the end of the summer, on the understanding that her husband had finally made arrangements for them to be together. But at the last moment he was called back to Rome and his master's court, and so it was left to my poor distracted sister to find a house to rent and to make a life, once again, alone. Much as my inclination was to counsel her into renouncing her husband I forbore, for I could see how Fanny longed to see him again. I trusted that she would come to her senses in time, and instead of giving her advice, I resolved instead to go about visiting every part of Paris in her company.

We were as merry together as we ever were but I had been frightened by that premonition of her as a ghost. In an attempt to allay my sense of ill portent I bid her have her portrait painted so that I might take it back to London in her place. Consenting, she posed with her two-year-old daughter, Frannie, and in the mornings when she was sitting I went sometimes and watched, we all in a companionable silence, the smell of oil and linseed, of the artist's turpentine-soaked smock, even of the old floorboards putting us into a sort of stupor. Little Frannie wore a light blue satin dress that drew the eye away from my sister. The child was very pale and rather sickly-looking, and when she was not standing for the painter would retreat to her nurse's lap and curl up there, eyeing the scene like a wary old owl from a hole in a tree trunk. Yet I could see that her daughter gave Fanny great comfort, and since she was likely to be the only child of that unfortunate marriage, I prayed she would not succumb to any malady.

When it came to the time three days later for us to part, I could hardly bear to let my sister out of my embrace. It was she who broke our clasp, seemingly eager for what was to come, whereas I dreaded it. Feeling compelled to try one more attempt to make her see that her disastrous marriage could bring her nothing but catastrophe, I said, 'You know that Erskine will always let you down, Fanny, don't you? Just as he has ever since you married, so he will again and again until . . .'

'Until what, Sister?' Her eyes welled with tears, and I cursed myself for making her unhappy when I should have been attempting, in that moment, to bring her happiness. 'Until he drives me mad perhaps? Do you think I am not already driven to a kind of madness? I'm mad with shame, with loneliness, with worry. Do you not think I know my husband's failings better than any woman alive?'

I took her hands in mine, but she pulled them roughly away. 'Do not, Mary! Do not.'

'Forgive me, Fanny.'

Irresolution crossed her troubled features, and then she said something most unexpected. 'There is more, besides, which I cannot speak of.'

'Oh? But what is this that you cannot speak of? Give me some hint, at least, so that I might not leave you beside myself with worry.'

She looked about to see that we were not overheard and said, very quietly, 'Papa has given us hope that we might both return one day to Scotland.'

'Oh?'

'John is . . . is . . .' Again, she glanced about and put her lips against my ear. 'John is no longer loyal to the Jacobite cause,' she whispered and to my amazement let out a giggle. 'Isn't it wonderful?'

'Why have you not told me this before?'

'Never speak of this,' she hissed. 'It might cost him his life!'

I wanted to tell Fanny that a spy who changes his loyalties with the seasons is never likely to be trusted and runs the risk of succumbing to some man's sword, but seeing her unexpected delight that she was involved, even if only vicariously, in espionage, I said simply, 'Naturally, Fanny. This great secret is ours alone.'

I left her happy then, if only fleetingly, saddened that my dear sister could only find happiness in a delusion.

15

HOMECOMINGS

Winter–Spring 1719, London

(Mary)

The arrival of the *Preston* was much delayed, and I suffered ever-increasing anxieties that I might never see my children again. Why had I so thoughtlessly gone ashore with Edward at Genoa and let them proceed by sea? Was it that I wanted one final adventure before returning to London? Was it that I feared England would be a kind of death for me?

On our arrival in London we received word of the terrible storms that had sunk three vessels in the Alboran Sea. The crow that had once settled upon my heart returned to peck at it once more. All the way from Genoa to Gibraltar, Death stalked that ship carrying my children, my Nell, my memories of Turkey, tossing it in storms and breaking its mast, so that it was delayed weeks at Gibraltar, and then Death bore down on the ship again as it made its voyage across the Bay of Biscay in the storming seas of December. But Captain Jessop could cuss Death into a retreat and outrun the storms and in such manner at last Eddie and little Mary, dear Nell and our other servants, rugs, clothes and effects arrived at Rotherhithe on a bitter January morning. I stood at the quayside as the great ship docked, heedless of the sleet and wind, eager for sight of my children. At last they came down the gangway, Mary in the arms of her nurse and little Eddie clutching Nell's hand.

I took Mary into my arms, the nurse giving her over gladly before she tumbled over, so unsteady was she after all those weeks at sea. Nell was calm. 'Go to your mother, Eddie,' she said to him softly, giving him a discreet shove in my direction, but he shook his head firmly and declared that he would prefer to stay at sea than be in England.

I squatted down beside him and whispered in his ear that he would be able to go to sea just as soon as he was old enough and might even one day be captain of his own vessel. He looked at me distrustfully. 'Do you promise, Mama?'

What is a promise to a child of five? 'Yes, Eddie. I promise.'

Nell, the children, the nurse and I all squeezed into one carriage, the rest of the household coming along behind, and we set off for London. Pressed against Nell I found myself unable to resist allowing our bodies to feel each other's warmth. It was as if she was my talisman, and to touch her was to revive her magic. 'We have much to do, Nell,' I told her eagerly. 'London society is all a frenzy with, well . . . with the usual frenzy.' Certain of the letters I had written from Constantinople to friends had been published, naturally without my consent, and had created a stir which resulted in yet more invitations to parties and salons and to the courts of both the king and the Prince and Princess of Wales. I informed Nell of all this, though she seemed unmoved by these excitements, and I wondered whether the long and dangerous voyage had made her regret her decision to turn down the hand of Mr Lodge, the Levant Company's factor.

'How is Mr Wortley?' she enquired, as if of an elderly uncle.

'His career fares less well than my own, I am sorry to say,' I confessed. 'He is stubborn, as you know, and determined to displease all who might please him and ally himself with the most miserable men in parliament.'

Nell looked at me with a hint of mischief. 'I am sure you have assisted him in all manner of ways, and he has willingly sought your advice.'

The coach lurched violently to the side, hitting a deep puddle, before regaining its composure. 'You are laughing at me, or perhaps at my husband, or is it at us both, Nell?' I said, amused.

She stifled a smile. 'I would never dream of laughing at you, not only because you are my mistress, but I hope too that I am your friend. And as for Mr Wortley, he has never made me laugh, nor ever will.'

To the consternation of Hayriye – the nurse – and Eddie, and the confusion of little Mary, we laughed a good deal at that, Nell and I, and to have my Nell once more in my company made me feel whole and, in some way that I could not quite place, less susceptible to the many small criticisms that I had become aware were being made of me in London.

Edward and I rented a house on the piazza at Covent Garden to accommodate our large and various household. I had many engagements about town and often would have Nell come along with me, particularly for my daytime appointments, to carry my papers or go ahead if I was running late, as I so often was. And if I went to evening salons and returned home well after midnight, she would always be there to undress me and listen to my report of events. I sensed from time to time a certain unease in her, even a degree of dissatisfaction, and one night to my surprise she said: 'What is it that I am to you, madam?'

'What are *you*, Nell, to *me*?' I said, wondering if she suspected that my affections were greater than they ought to be, and only reined in with much effort.

I saw that she immediately regretted having spoken. 'I meant to say, well, I mean to say . . . I am not always certain how I can best serve you,' she said at last, but I felt sure that she had meant more than that.

I might have spoken more boldly, so convinced was I that we had become much closer than mere mistress and servant. I might have said something about desire, and then she might have spoken freely too, and next we would have been in each other's arms. But how could we have done so given our positions? And so my guard went up. 'I am not at all sure what you mean, Nell.'

Nell stood and went over to the window, and for a moment I thought that she might climb out of it. After looking down at the street below she said, without turning, 'It is just that I am not sure when I should be your friend and when your maid.'

'Why, Nell, I hope you shall be both, for what are friends but willing servants, and what is a good servant but a willing friend?'

'Yes,' she said quietly.

I had disappointed her, and no less myself with my too-clever reply. After she left I went over to the window, but beyond I could see in the shadows nothing but beggars and men pissing against walls.

*

As the months went by, I noticed from time to time how Nell was regarded by the rest of the household. As she was seen as not quite servant, being my steady companion, she was mistrusted, and therefore lonely. I could not think how to help her, though I wanted to. Edward had conceived the notion (how or why I did not know) that Nell had a brother, and each time he saw her would ask after him, and Nell, being too polite to disabuse him, would assure him of his health.

'What is this brother's name?' I asked her.

'I have no brother,' she confirmed.

'Yet you have one when my husband asks after him.'

'Since it pleases Mr Wortley that I have a brother, so I have a brother,' she said briskly.

'Well, we had better give him a name, at least, and perhaps a profession.'

'Hmmm. Shall we call him Thomas?'

'Yes, that is as good a name as any for one so doubtful.'

Nell concurred. 'And he shall be a . . .'

'A butcher?' I offered.

'Oh no. No brother of mine would be a butcher. Let him be a gardener. In a great house, perhaps.'

And in such manner Nell and I made her a brother, and in addition a private joke against Edward, which made Thomas-the-Brother better still.

16

A CAMPAIGN BEGINS

Summer 1721, London

(Mary)

Even neglectful mothers feel a deep affection for their children, or so I often heard, and though I was not neglectful, I confessed (if only to myself) that I felt no natural affection for little Mary. In truth I was not finding motherhood any more amenable with my daughter than I had with my son. I felt guilt at my lack of natural sentiment towards Mary. As a result, I made up for that lack of feeling with excessive attention, investing much time with my daughter in the months after our return to England, seeking to inoculate her, as it were, against the conceits that little girls are too readily given by their elders, such as thinking they must be pretty or be kept out of the sun or not learn Latin. I read to her at night for half an hour from Virgil, and though she was too young to follow the sense of it I trusted that the grammar might seep into her, for how else does a child learn any language, English included? We had Eddie sent to Westminster School, which was not two miles away and so he came to see me for supper once or twice a month.

It was the summer of seventeen twenty-one that smallpox ravaged the whole country, a most particular contagion that took children readily in its grip. If I could not show my daughter a mother's love in the conventional manner, I knew one thing I could do for her that would be better than any traditional form of affection. I resolved to resume the campaign I had begun in Constantinople and summoned Dr Maitland.

The man who came into the parlour one week later was not quite the one I remembered from Turkey. He was older by a decade in the three years that had passed, as happens sometimes to gentlemen who, fit and lively while with purpose, gain a belly and gout from too much time spent in a chair before the fire and too many glasses of malmsey wine. 'My lady,' he said, bowing low and removing his hat, which sat atop a wig of old-fashioned design. Nell was sat close by, and Maitland had the good manners to ask also after her health.

I: *Gesturing to a seat, for he was surely in need of one.* My dear Maitland. How are you? Not as well as you might be, I see. Why do you not take a wife? Some kind woman who would give you useful tasks to do about the house and garden?

MAITLAND: *Smiles tolerantly.* I suspect, madam, you have tasks enough for me in mind.

I: Ah yes, Maitland, but I am not kind, nor am I your wife.

MAITLAND: *Not inclined to parry but obliged to respond.* Madam, you are kind, but you are not gentle. People too often confuse the two qualities.

I: If by gentle you mean mild, then no, I am not mild, for I prefer strength. And the kindness I have in mind is a kindness to all humanity.

MAITLAND: *Bemused.* Indeed?

I: Dr Maitland, I wish to have my daughter engrafted against the smallpox.

MAITLAND: It is not a procedure that has ever been done in these isles, madam.

I: And yet there must be a first time, Doctor. Where do you suppose we should be had Mr Caxton resolved not to print because printing had never been done in England? Or had the first blacksmith declined to shoe a horse because if horses were meant to be shod, God would have given them shoes? The first is simply the first, and as far as smallpox is concerned, let it be us who bring inoculation to this land, resolute in the knowledge that we have seen it performed with such success in Turkey.

NELL: *Squeaks.*

I: Nell?

NELL: I wanted to cheer, madam, but then thought better of it.

I: I am roused, Doctor. Roused!

MAITLAND: *Coughs uneasily.* And Mr Wortley's opinion?

I: Is of little interest to anyone these days.

MAITLAND: *Glances at Nell, as if for confirmation.* The Royal Society showed some interest in the paper I sent them, though they published another.

I: I saw it, the paper they published. It was poorly writ, making engrafting seem like a curiosity, an amusement or, worse still, a sensation. It was light on its benefits and cast doubt on its certainty of prevention.

MAITLAND: Physicians must be cautious in their claims.

I: Cautious! They are not cautious when charging two guineas for bleeding a man to death. They are only cautious when it comes to a proposal that may reduce their income.

NELL: *Quietly.* Hurrah!

MAITLAND: *Calmly.* It is not uncommon for any profession to defend tradition from what is new and unfamiliar.

I: Let us begin, at least, with my daughter.

MAITLAND: *A look of horrified realization crossing his features.* You have other persons in mind?

I: I wish to see *every* child in the land engrafted, Doctor. Whyever would we not? And what is good for my daughter will surely be good enough for all. Why should a farmhand's daughter be pocked but a duke's son unmarked? No, no, we shall protect every child from that scourge.

MAITLAND: *Seeming to wish to make himself part of the upholstery.* I do not think I could perform such an undertaking.

I: If it is but you and I, Doctor, then we could only manage some dozen or so in a day, assuming the children do not live too far apart . . .

MAITLAND: You?

I: I shall assist you.

MAITLAND: *Not attempting to conceal his distaste at the prospect.* A dozen a day, in a year we might only protect some few thousand.

I: Once the benefits of engrafting are known, then even the most venal doctor shall wish to emulate our example, and no doubt will find some unnecessary potion to charge a tidy sum in addition.

MAITLAND: *If* we are to proceed, it would be best if we invite distinguished members of the Royal College of Physicians to observe the procedure.

I: Why? So that they may decry it? So they may in some way belittle my part in it?

MAITLAND: *Patiently.* I suggest it, madam, merely so they may attest to the procedure's efficacy. And they should be able to come and see how young Mary fares from time to time, just as we did with those children we observed when in Constantinople.

I: No! I will not have those overstuffed boobies pacing through my house and pronouncing on the health of my daughter.

MAITLAND: *Shakes his head regretfully, for all the world as if this had been much the reaction he had been expecting.* Then, my lady. *Stands, bows, also to Nell.* I must bid you good day, for those are my terms.

Surprised by his abruptness and prompted into stiffness, I said, 'Good day, Dr Maitland. Nell will show you out.'

Maitland had perhaps expected some argument, but I was not going to plead with him. I gestured to Nell that she should do as I bid. She was gone some minutes, and when I went to the window to see whether Maitland's carriage had departed, I saw that the two of them were in animated conversation.

Nell, on her return, asked whether I thought the doctor might soften his stance.

'He will, of that I am sure,' I said.

'You might consider writing to him to suggest that you are willing to give him another hearing.'

'Might I, Nell?' I asked, suspiciously. 'What did you and he speak of when I was out of earshot?'

'Of the great virtues of compromise, madam.'

'Did you, indeed? His or mine? The trouble with compromise is that it requires, well, compromise.'

'I suppose it does,' she said, pinching the head from a faded rose in a vase before looking at me with a strange expression I could not quite read.

My daughter's inoculation was observed by three gentlemen from the Royal College of Physicians, one a hawk-faced sceptic who could not bring himself to look me in the eye, another who feigned neutrality, a self-satisfied gentleman as wide as he was tall who went by the name of Grives, and the third, Dr Keith, an exhausted-looking man who had lost all but one of his children to smallpox, and who was fervent in his wish for its success. I made no effort to ingratiate the procedure but was content to let my daughter's recovery stand in proof of my case. They returned, these gentlemen, at various times over the succeeding fortnight to witness little Mary's health. While she showed some symptoms of that disease we all feared so greatly, she was in other respects cheerful and lively.

Nell, too, was subject to their investigation, being that rare creature – one inoculated against the distemper – and all my prejudices against physicians were confirmed when she came to me in a condition as close to distress as I ever witnessed in her.

'Madam?' she asked, standing at the doorway to my study.

'Nell, what is it?' I regret that I sounded impatient, but I was in the middle of writing to the Princess of Wales on the very matter under consideration, since I wished Her Highness to hear of the successful inoculation of one of the king's subjects from my own hand.

'I wish to ask, madam . . .' It was not at all like Nell to be so uncertain of herself.

'Yes, Nell. Spit it out.'

'Whether I am to comply with the wishes of the gentlemen from the College?'

'That depends on what it is that they wish.'

'It is, rather, only one of them, madam. Dr Grives.'

'Yes?'

'He came to me and . . . and he asked that I remove certain of my garments.'

She had my absolute attention. I stood, bid her come and sit in my own chair at the desk. 'And what did you say to Dr Grives?'

'I asked him why he wished so.'

'And?'

'He said that he wished to examine my form for any sign of blemishes or pocks.'

'Did he indeed,' I said. 'And what did you do next, Nell?'

'I came here, madam, to ask for your advice.'

'My advice is that you remain in this place until that

ungentlemanly gentleman is out of the house, which he will be in very short order, I assure you.'

'Oh, madam,' she said, grasping my hand like a woman saved from drowning.

I found Dr Grives chuckling at something or other with the hawk-faced physician, whose name I have since tried to forget. 'Dr Grives, I wonder if you would do me the honour of accompanying me to the withdrawing room?'

He gave a puzzled bow, and he and the hawk guffawed, presumably at the prospect of his conference with me. 'Certainly, Lady Mary.'

A footman stood at the door of the drawing room, and I bid him enter and remain, not that I imagined Grives would propose that I remove my own garments, but more that I wished the humiliation I was about to inflict upon him to be witnessed and thence, no doubt, reported on below stairs. 'Dr Grives, you are a family man?' I asked.

'Madam. I am glad to say I have a wife and three sons and two daughters, and lately a grandson. You are no doubt to ask me whether I intend to have them engrafted against the smallpo—'

'I have no intention of seeking your opinion on that matter or any other.'

He raised an indignant eyebrow.

'But I have a question.'

'Yes?'

'Your daughters are, what, around twenty years of age?'

'The youngest is but eight, the oldest sixteen. I married late.'

'And if your sixteen-year-old daughter were to be asked by a physician who had no business with her to remove some of her garments so that he might examine her, what would you say to that gentleman?'

He reddened. 'My enquiry to your maid was merely one of medical interest, I assure you.'

'Was it?' I said, not concealing the pure anger and contempt I felt for the man.

'It was and, Lady Mary, I may add that my daughter is not a lady's maid.'

I felt a strange gratification in his vile slur, as a soldier must feel when a man he is obliged to slay casts some foul accusation at the provenance of his mother. 'Dr Grives, if it is flesh you require then there is a whorehouse in Shoreditch where you may gratify yourself with any amount of female anatomy, some of it marked by smallpox, some by other diseases, and yet all of it sullied by the attention of men such as yourself. Now get out of my house and, if you are wise, get out of London, too, for your reputation now rests in my hands, and I am likely to drop it into the gutter where it belongs!'

A wheeze emitted from his rotund form, the sound of his pride escaping. He gathered up his hat with fumbling fingers from where he had placed it so nonchalantly upon the console table a few minutes before and scurried away. I glanced briefly at the footman, who gave me the barest hint of a smile.

Mary's successful inoculation was reported on by the Royal College of Physicians and then widely in popular journals, though to my consternation more as a matter of novelty and entertainment than as an important medical development.

I felt it was therefore important to oblige Edward to be my ally. Edward and I saw each other infrequently and then only when the House of Commons was sitting. We would have dinner together once a week to discuss family and business matters and, if invited to the court of either His Majesty or His Highness the Prince of Wales, would pretend to an amiability that we hardly felt. Other than that, our lives were led separately, which avoided argument or dispute.

'Edward, I wondered whether you might raise the matter of inoculation in the House. You might even propose a bill to encourage the practice.'

'Might I?'

'Yes, you might. Do not be so obtuse.'

'Public health is hardly an issue of concern to Members of Parliament, Mary.' He pulled a wing from the partridge that sat upon his plate, observed it with disapproval and set it carefully to one side.

'Quarantine is regulated.'

'That is a measure against the plague and aimed principally at the preservation of the nation's trade in wool rather than human life. If you had your way you would have physicians provided to the public by government and charge it to the exchequer.'

'And why not? It would guard against all manner of disease, and disease does not discriminate between the houses of the rich and poor or choose only the virtuous or the wicked. Death laughs at us for our meek compliance to his great appetites.'

'You are being fanciful and trying to provoke me. The notion of physicians providing a service for free . . .' He shook his head, chuckling at what he regarded as my outlandish notions. He then stood from the table, pulled from his pocket his watch and declared that there was a vote in less than an hour.

*

News of the success of engrafting against the smallpox spread, at first only amongst families of my acquaintance, for those who read of it in newspapers and journals would have understood it as a heathen custom, something akin to placing a dead man's tooth about one's neck as a cure for the toothache, which some ignorant folk in the countryside still fervently practised. Maitland's initial reluctance to have me accompany him when administering engraftings reduced when he saw that I could be of use in making the necessary introductions to the houses of the high-born, and I did not resent him charging a goodly fee to those who could afford it. My desire was to see inoculation universally practised for the benefit of all, but I reasoned that if dukes and earls adopted the protection for their own children, then in short order greengrocers and ostlers would, too. And so it was that a trickle became a rising tide, and soon a flood.

17

PARISIAN MISERY

Summer 1721, Paris

(Frances)

How strange to think now of happiness, yet I recall happiness when first I came to Paris, as one might recognize a distant landmark from far out to sea. But I am ever sailing away from it, further and further, and now it is no more than a speck and soon I know I shall not be able to see it at all. Was I happy, though? I think not. There was perhaps that deceiving and cruel sentiment we call *hope*, sweet and beguiling at first but, like an injured wild creature we take in to nurse back to health, the thing called hope one day turns and bites, revealing that it was never yours to possess. And what was it I hoped for? A happy reunion with my husband. I hoped Mar might find himself admired by his exiled king and court, since admiration is his only comfort. I hoped, too, that Paris society might welcome me, and that we should have enough income with my father's allowance and from Mar's positions with his King James to establish a modest but respectable household. There was, too, the thin hope that he might, through secret service to ministers in London, find a way for us all to return to Scotland. And there was that brief but joyful reunion with Mary, which seemed to me such a good portent, she brimming with stories of Turkey and the Levant and of all the people she had met so that it was like bathing in a warm and fragrant pool.

Oh, but how chill I am now.

First and last is Mar. When I came to Paris and soon after took this house on Rue Mouffetard, a most unfashionable and noxious street, but with good rooms and a cheap rent, he chided me. What choice did I have? I was obliged to find a home. 'You were in Aix, my dearest,' I pointed out, trying not to show my hurt. 'And did you not command me to find a house at this rent?'

'Are you rebuking me, madam?'

I forced a modest smile and looked at the clock that ran always ten minutes slow, wishing it might stop, might run backwards, and take me with it – from that day to the day before and then to the month and the year before, from Paris to London and to a time before my husband's disgrace. I said softly, 'I think it is I who am reproved for taking this house, and perhaps rightly so.'

'Perhaps!' And off he marched. He is a great one for marching off.

Later that day, or was it some days after, I asked him whether I should come to Aix.

'Why should you come there?' he asked, as if I had suggested going to the North Pole.

'To join you at court.'

'The court has moved to Avignon,' he announced.

'Oh? Avignon? Then we shall join you there.'

'You shall not! You shall stay where you damned well are.'

I had needlework in my hand and let the point plunge

deep into my finger to make my tongue still. 'Very well,' said I.

Realizing he had spoken too harshly he softened, as he so often did. 'It is not that I do not want you there, Frances. It is that the court flutters about like a bird from place to place. This house may stink of hides, and is noisy withal, but it is cheap, I grant you, and you and the children are comfortable, I think.'

'We are,' I said, though we were not, not in the least. I looked down at the bloom of blood upon my gown.

He pretended not to see. 'I am away to the Swedish ambassador.'

'Good,' I said a little abruptly, prompting him to turn in surprise. 'Good fortune!' I declared, attempting to better present myself.

He had told me of his triumph in securing an agreement with the Swedish king, a matter of the utmost secrecy. If it was so secret, then why tell me? If only he didn't feel the need to boast all the time and to anyone who might be impressed by him, he might not appear such a fool. Would the Swedes go to war with England? They took the Pretender's money willingly enough, for who would not take a bag of gold from one so desperate to be parted with it? Their invasion was delayed first for reasons of poor weather and then for some difficulties with the Russians and later still because their king became ill. Soon it was obvious to all that John Erskine, Duke of Mar (for our king-who-was-king-of-nowhere-at-all had bestowed upon my husband that title), had been duped. Or perhaps bankrupting the Jacobite treasury was a secret service he performed for King George? Though I doubted he would have been so efficient.

We went to Avignon, little Frannie and I, after all, and then on to Rome, but what we saw there was like a party that had ended long before, and the few who lingered were possessed by the creeping realization that they were no longer destined for a court with true power but had become the bearers of empty rituals that would only grow ever more cobwebbed and dusty. Since they could not turn their anger upon their king without being deemed traitors, they turned it upon my husband, already suspecting he was less loyal to their cause than he pretended to be. I do not say he did not deserve their distrust. My own presence at the Jacobite court was no less miserable for me than for John, and most probably brought greater suspicion on us both, since my antecedence was well known, and I hastened back to Paris with my daughter, enduring three weeks on muddy roads, feeling certain it was right to flee, but knowing that the house on Rue Mouffetard was not truly my home. It was a journey without hope, and hope is what any journey should contain if it is not to be wretched.

The smell in the house seemed to have grown worse in our months away. It was late April, and as lilies of the valley were in bloom I filled every room with them, hoping their fresh, pure scent would dispel the baser odours. The servants, to my consternation, took it upon themselves to steal most of the bunches I had set out. Had I committed some faux pas, I wondered? Were these flowers known to bring ill fortune? My maid, Cendrine, perceptive enough to grasp my ignorance, explained that there was a tradition of giving a bunch of the flowers to a loved one on the first of May, and so the servants, thinking I had brought them into the house for exactly that purpose, had taken them to give to those they loved.

'But if they thought me generous in bringing the flowers for them, why not say something to me of it?' I said, not concealing my hurt.

She bit her lip, Cendrine, embarrassed to tell me the truth but incapable of telling a lie. 'They pity you, madame,' she said, 'and do not know how to speak to you, because they are . . .' Her voice trailed away into silence.

'Are what?'

'Embarrassed.'

'Why should they be embarrassed? Do I embarrass them?' I could feel indignation rising in my voice, and all my loneliness, too, but it was not fair to blame Cendrine, for her honesty was what I had demanded.

Lacking the guile to dissemble, she held the brush she had been using on my hair a little above my head but seemed unable to move her hand. I could see her in the looking glass, and perhaps it was because she spoke to me through our mutual reflection that she felt emboldened to say, 'Your husband is not here, and you are not in your true home, and we see that you are sad. And we are afraid to speak to you of anything happy –' she brought the brush to my scalp and began to work it with uncharacteristic vigour '– to speak of anything like love.'

Whether she was brushing too hard, or whether it was a symptom of my loneliness I do not know, but since that day my hair began to fall out, and now there are only tufts and strands, and I am obliged to always wear a turban, day and night.

18

MERCY MISSIONS

Summer–Autumn 1722, London

(Mary)

It was in the early summer of the second year of my campaign that we found ourselves at the house of the Earl of Pitlochry at Beaconsfield. In many respects it was a typical ceremony of inoculation.

> DRAMATIS PERSONAE: *The earl, widowed, sixty years of age, florid of face, a retired navy man weighed down with his own sense of redundancy; two uneasy daughters-in-law, wives of his older sons, one of whom was absent on business in London, the other at sea guarding the recent peace with Spain; John Cargill, a kindly young uncle and third son of the earl; Dr Maitland; Dr Forbes as witness; myself, distantly acquainted with the late countess who had succumbed to smallpox the previous year; Nell, to run errands; five infants, four girls and a boy, solemnly prepared for their engrafting; various maids, footmen and others.*

The procedure conducted to the satisfaction of all, a low hubbub of relieved conversation ensues, and I am approached by John Cargill, the young uncle.

CARGILL: Lady Mary. *Offers a neat bow.* I have read your work and am in awe of it.

I: Really, Mr Cargill? That is flattery, but kindly meant, I'm sure.

CARGILL: *Surprisingly earnest.* No, madam, I assure you. 'Where gentle streams will weep at my distress/ Where no false friend will in my grief take part/And mourn my ruin with a joyful heart . . .'

I: *Surprised that he quotes my poem on smallpox, and noticing how pretty Mr Cargill happens to be.* Then, sir, I am complimented more than I am flattered.

CARGILL: Knowing you were to come here today I took the liberty of a gift I wish to give you.

I: *Seeing a book in his hand, and fearful that it will be a collection of this man's poems, I hold up a hand to make him desist, for a poet giving out his own poetry is a contagion to be avoided as surely as the plague.*

CARGILL: It is Ovid's *Metamorphoses*, and I am certain you have many editions, but this Italian translation I acquired on my tour of Italy last year, and I thought it unusually pleasing.

I: *Taking it and glancing through its first pages.* I have not this edition, Mr Cargill, and am indeed greatly pleased. Really you could not have chosen me a better gift, even if you had offered me a coach of beaten gold.

CARGILL: *Bows and smiles with boyish satisfaction. His legs are very fine.* Perhaps you would do me the honour of permitting me to pay you a visit? You have moved recently to Twickenham?

I: Regrettably I am very often at my husband's home, Wortley Hall in Yorkshire. *A lie, since I never go to Yorkshire, but it is my invariable response to any person who invites themselves to my home.*

CARGILL: Oh? Then I shall simply continue to admire your work from afar – and not only your poetry, Lady Mary, but also your work to reform medical ignorance.

I: *My resolve crumbling.* Though I am not due to leave for Yorkshire until June, and so you may find me at home in the coming weeks should you care to call, Mr Cargill.

On our journey back to Twickenham I asked Nell if she had noticed Mr John Cargill, the infants' uncle.

'No, madam. Was he the fellow with one eye?'

'One eye, Nell? One eye? I saw no one with one eye.'

'Then it was perhaps a footman.'

'Perhaps.'

I thought a good deal about Mr Cargill in the week that followed, a good deal more than was sensible or seemly. He called a week later, and we talked of literature, and of Rome and Naples and the flames of Vesuvius, of Catullus and Plato, and I was obliged to concede after three pots of tea and many macaroons that I had rarely spent an afternoon in such amenable company. I had Nell sit with us, and at some point asked her to play the fortepiano, a new piece by Mr

Bach, which she played far more fluently than was her general practice. Three pots of tea being one pot too many, I was required to withdraw to my chamber pot, and on my return I saw that Cargill and Nell were engaged in quiet conversation, which they had the courtesy to cease on my return.

'As you see, Nell,' I said after he had left, 'Mr Cargill is in possession of two eyes.'

'Indeed, madam,' she replied, blushing crimson.

'He has asked if he may pay us another visit tomorrow, and I have agreed, so if I am otherwise engaged, do instruct the footman to give him admittance and come find me.'

'Certainly.'

About once a month I would be granted a private audience with the Princess Caroline, and we would talk of many things – things that could not be spoken of at a banquet where all conversation had to be about nothing at all, for conversation about something leads to disagreement, and disagreement leads to indigestion. When the Princess of Wales and I met alone, or more or less, for some few of her ladies-in-waiting would be present, we spoke principally of literature and music, but also of the many divisions amongst the Whigs, of the prospects for a continued European peace, and of her father-in-law's court and its great dreariness. It was high summer, a day when the afternoon sun threw long lazy shafts of light across the polished floors of Leicester House, giving out the smell of beeswax and dust. Somewhere in a room on the floor above us or below a chamber orchestra was practising a piece by Purcell. Almost as soon as I entered her presence the princess asked me whether the time had come to have her own children engrafted against smallpox.

'Your Highness,' I said with a modest smile, 'only you can tell me whether that time has come.'

'Has there been a single case of death following inoculation, Mary?'

'Yes, there have been two out of some five thousand. But in one case we learnt the child already had the disease, and in the other that the little girl choked on a button.'

The princess placed a hand upon my gown at my knee (I still almost always wore Turkish pantaloons, but on visiting royalty dressed more conventionally). 'You see, Mary, that is why you have my regard. Any other would have said *hardly any* or *I believe not* or some such dissembling vagary, but you are specific, and you know your facts.'

'Facts are weapons that we may use deploying only our tongues and our pens, and yet they may win more territory than a thousand men and a hundred cannon.'

'Yet not all are amenable to facts. Indeed, far too few.'

'I agree, ma'am. The Church seems most particularly resistant to fact.'

One of the ladies-in-waiting gasped.

'I shall have to seek the permission of His Majesty, naturally,' said the princess of her father-in-law, 'and he, too, has a tendency to be resistant to facts and, regrettably, also a resistance to me!'

I realized that it was more than likely that if the Prince and Princess of Wales were for something, then the king would most likely be against. 'Then we must present him with facts so unarguably persuasive that he is bound to give his consent.'

'Yes,' said the princess, uncertainly.

'The king is interested in experiments, is he not?'

'So I believe. You see more of him than I do.'

'He professes enthusiasm for science and progress, insofar

as he professes enthusiasm for anything, and he also has some interest in prisons. I have a notion that we might conjure facts from royal enthusiasm, as it were, that will satisfy even King George.'

'That is another thing I like about you, Mary. You have *ideas*. Oh, to have more women about me with ideas!' The princess looked around the room at her ladies-in-waiting, who cast down their eyes in shame before, as soon as they were able, awarding me a look of the purest hatred.

The governor of Newgate Prison was perfectly in agreement with the proposed experiment, since he was a man ever keen to inflict misery upon those in his charge, he under the misapprehension that it was certain to lead to an agonizing death far more satisfactory than mere hanging. The experiment would, by royal order, be supervised by the president and members of the Royal Society, certain of which fervently hoped for the experiment's failure. Engrafting was to be performed upon six prisoners, three men and three women, all of whom were otherwise to be executed but who would, if they lived, be pardoned and freed. I was told that the experiment quickly became the subject of a gambling frenzy, with good odds being offered on all dying or all living, and the least odds on one or two failing to survive. Since I enjoyed a wager, I would have been tempted to place a thousand pounds on all living, since I knew the near-perfect efficacy of inoculation, but Nell talked me out of placing a wager on myself, as it were.

On the appointed day, Dr Maitland, Dr Forbes and I, together with a dozen members of the Royal Society and others from the Royal College of Physicians, and the Lord Chamberlain and others from the king's court, including the page boy Peter, a pretty mute boy discovered wild in the

Hanover forest and given to unaccountable fits of laughter, were gathered in a room to witness the engrafting. It was freshly painted and suitably appointed for distinguished visitors, bearing the portraits of the king and the late Queen Anne upon the wall. Yet the anointed room was not immune to the other smells of the place, of piss-soaked straw, of stale sweat, of lank hair, of sour milk and drains. We all inhaled these same odours, yet none confessed to their effects.

There was a strange lightness to the ceremony, presumably because the failure of the experiment would cause the prisoners no great suffering beyond the torment of the disease and would cause no public outcry since they were to die anyway. We knew not what crimes had been committed and assumed they might be sheep stealing and such like, given the prisoners were to be released if they survived the procedure. One of the women looked more child than adult, and I remembered what Nell had told me of a woman she knew who was hanged for concealing a stillborn. But it was another of the female prisoners who was noteworthy, for she had a look of blazing defiance about her and, seeing me – one of only two free women in the room, the other being one of the guards – she directed her words at me and no other.

'The elixir of life this is, and I have Lady Mary to thank for it!' she declared, pointing a long finger at me. She had a Spanish look about her, her hair black and long and, though surely not clean, bearing a lustre still.

Her statement was greeted with an appalled silence, broken a moment after by Peter the Wild Boy's high laughter, a sound like rain on corn ready for the harvest. I looked closely at the boy, whose eyes were upon me. Because he could not speak a word and had, it was said, been raised by wolves, he was thought to have no soul. Yet there was a deep intelligence in his gaze, and it seemed to me that he was in possession of some understanding that surpassed all the learned, pompous men who surrounded him.

I stood towards the back of the room and a few of the portly gentlemen of the Royal Society turned to look at me accusingly, as if my presence was bringing the whole matter into disrepute. The female guard being close by, I whispered: 'What has this woman done to be here?'

'She murdered her husband, she did,' she hissed. 'Like this,' she gestured with relish, drawing an imaginary blade across her throat.

I paused for a moment and wondered at the dark-haired woman being inoculated who was sure, in a week or two, to be freed, and pondered on why she might have slain her husband, for it was not unknown for certain husbands to deserve such slaying. I wondered if she might marry once more, this defiant young murderess, and whether that new husband might also find himself with a slit neck, but I kept my imaginings to myself.

The experiment was deemed a success, but further trials were demanded before the royal children could be inoculated, since it was the view of certain learned men that convicts were unlikely to die from mere disease, and only a rope around their necks would satisfy God and justice. And so it was that twenty-two orphans of St James's parish were commanded by royal decree to be inoculated, an experiment which delighted me, for I wished to see all children protected. And, all those orphans surviving, at last the royal princesses were engrafted.

By the autumn I felt that my work, which had occupied me so greatly for the best part of two years, might now be done, for surely all society would wish to follow the example set by the Prince and Princess of Wales. Yet, as is so often the way when a victory seems to be won, there was resistance from certain quarters of the medical profession and most particularly from the clergy, who considered inoculation an unconscionable interference in God's desire to bestow on mankind fatal diseases.

I was weary from the battle, and tired of being an object of curiosity and, too often, of contempt. I might have retreated altogether into pleasanter pursuits when I found myself the subject of a great provocation from one of those distinguished members of the Royal College of Physicians, a Dr William Wagstaffe. His paper had perhaps been in circulation for some weeks before I came to know of it. My friends were keeping it from me, I suspected, but my husband was always to be relied upon to bring me bad news.

'You have no doubt seen Wagstaffe's attack on you, Mary?' he said, pretending to disinterest over a supper I had arranged for my friend Lord Hervey and his companion (some said husband), Stephen Fox.

Much of the talk that evening was of politics and court intrigue, which I pretended interested me only a little, though I found it, in the main, fascinating. It was also a means of spending some time productively in the company of my husband, for left alone we fell to bickering over the children, in whom Edward showed little interest and unjustly accused me of showing even less.

'I have not seen Wagstaffe's attack. Have you, John?' I asked Hervey.

'Regrettably, Mary, I have. As indeed, have all. But none of your friends wished to trouble you with it.'

I reached out a hand, and Edward duly obliged. And I read:

> Posterity will scarcely be brought to believe that an Experiment, practised only by a few Ignorant Women, amongst an illiterate and unthinking People, shou'd on a sudden, and upon slender Experience, so far obtain in one of the Politest Nations in the world as to be received into the Royal Palace.

'How very amusing,' I said, controlling my fury admirably.

'It is naturally not worth dignifying with any form of response,' said Hervey.

'Naturally,' I said, as lightly as I could manage. 'Now, what think you of this pardon for Bolingbroke?' I asked, wishing to turn the conversation to other matters. 'Shall every Jacobite be permitted to slink back to England, and how long before they win a majority in parliament?'

'I wonder whether Mar might be permitted to return?' mused Hervey.

The notion of a pardon for Mar jolted me. I dearly wanted to have Fanny back so that I could protect her, for, based on her infrequent letters, her exile in Paris seemed to be sucking the very life from her. Yet if her return also meant the presence of her unfortunate husband, I wondered whether I would be able to help her as I wished. 'He should be able to return, but then be banished to some Hebridean island, and Fanny allowed to stay in London,' I said.

'Lady Mary,' said Mr Fox in his gentle accent, a northern tinge to it, 'the Earl of Mar is your brother-in-law. For you to wish to see him banished is a little Shakespearean, is it not?'

'Shakespeare would have him murdered in a dozen different ways, and then have his ghost haunt us all, for ever. That is the last thing I should want.'

Edward cast me a puzzled look across the table.

*

In truth I'd been rattled by the attack from Wagstaffe and knew I would not rest until I had dealt with it in suitable manner.

Next day I wrote a riposte, disguising my identity as *A Turkey-Merchant*. I sent my essay, with which I was well satisfied, to the *Flying Post*, a London newspaper which had a good-sized circulation, and entitled it *A Plain Account of the Inoculating of the Small Pox*. It began thus:

> Out of compassion to the numbers abused and deluded by the knavery and ignorance of physicians I am determined to give a true account of the manner of inoculating the small pox as it is practised in Constantinople with constant success, and without any ill consequence whatever. I shall sell no drugs, take no fees, could I persuade people of the safety and reasonableness of this easy operation. 'Tis no way of my interest to convince the world of their errors; that is, I shall get nothing by it but the private satisfaction of having done good to mankind, and I know no body that reckons that satisfaction any part of their interest.

My essay continued along the same themes, exposing the greed and ignorance of the generality of physicians, apothecaries, surgeons, charlatans, frauds and swindlers. I did not spare the clergy from my assault, though the editor of the *Flying Post* saw fit to temper and smooth and moderate certain of my allegations, to my regret.

19

A BRIEF FORGIVENESS

Winter 1723–4, Paris

(Frances)

He left the court in Rome and came to Paris in the fifth year of my exile, my husband, returning to the house on Rue Mouffetard, to his unhappy wife who found herself unable to confect smiles for him any longer, who found, indeed, that she spoke of herself as if she were not herself at all but someone she hardly knew. And my loneliness became greater still for there is nothing more solitary than being with a person who makes you feel alone.

John had attempted to be a Jacobite and a Hanoverian in one and the same person, yet that was a creature that nature could not allow, any more than a wolf and a sheep might exist within the same skin. Having betrayed first King George and next King James, and running out of causes to be disloyal to, my husband spent all his time in his study constructing a model of his estate at Alloa, which he believed one day he would return to with a fortune sufficient to restore the house and grounds. He is a great one for dreams, and since every man with a high opinion of himself is bound to be disappointed, life never being able to match the grandeur of such delusions, he began to slide into embittered discontent, which he directed at me, as if I had been responsible for his manifold misjudgements.

My sister wrote to me, letter after letter, telling me pieces of gossip, news from court, scandals and outrages, thinking them for my amusement. I would sit to answer but found I had nothing to say. I sat for hour after hour, the nib in my hand, the inkpot drying before me, but what could I tell Mary? That I was unhappy? That my servants hated me? That Paris was damp? Should I have written that Frannie was listless or that my stepson treated me with contempt? Would she have been amused to learn that Mar spent all day making oak trees from green-dyed wool and laying pipes for fountains made of goose quills? Mary rebuked me for my silence, and my silence in turn rebuked her by growing ever louder. It seemed to me that she must sit night and day writing letters to all, but mostly to me, word after word pouring out of her like lava from a volcano – molten, dazzling and insufferable. Yet if only we were together, Mary would look at me with those all-seeing eyes and I would speak as I could not write, of Mar's quiet cruelties, of the cold solitude of Paris, of how I should have known all this would come to pass, and how she had warned me and how obstinately I refused to listen.

We have grown poor, not that John was ever rich. The Earl of Mar's estates were ruined long before he rose to high office under the late queen. Since the Jacobite court will no longer employ him and the Hanoverian court has no use for him, we are in much the same circumstances as our maids and servants. Were they in a position to employ us rather than we they, all should be fitting.

One day, most unexpectedly, my husband began to speak

to me kindly, which he had not done for so long that I could not remember him ever doing so, though I suppose he must have at one time. His tone was that which an uncle might use to a somewhat simple child of six or seven years of age. He wished me to petition my father for release of my inheritance, so that we might have some income to live upon. I told him that he would be given it, even as an exile, were I to die, since my father is always scrupulous when it comes to contracts, but instead of growing angry Mar placed a hand upon my cheek and told me he would rather die himself than have money to live without me.

'If *you* were to die, sir,' said I, 'then the household expenses would be manageable and I should be able to afford a new green silk turban.' (My hair had not grown back.)

'You shall have a new turban, Frances. As many as you should like. Your father will not want you to live in penury, I am sure.'

'I shall write to him, then,' I said, though the thought of writing any letter to any person, least of all my implacable father, filled me with dread.

'Letters are intercepted. You should go to see him, though you will need the king's permission to return to England. Ask if I may come with you, since you are not well.'

'Am I not well?' I had not thought myself ill, only miserable, but illness is a great deal easier for the world to understand, and so from that moment I became ill.

I sought permission from His Majesty to return to England, which was granted, though it was made clear that John Erskine, formerly Earl of Mar, would not be permitted to return to British soil. I had no wish to go to London as ambassador for my disgraced husband. But to see my sister would be a fine thing, for all the words I could not commit to the page I believed I might find upon my tongue.

20

A VERY GREAT DISAPPOINTMENT

Winter–Spring 1724, London

(Mary)

Pursued by Death, and a little by Love for the first half of my life, another spectre raised its form as I entered my middle years, and its name was Betrayal.

The handsome Mr Cargill called several more times in the weeks after that first encounter at Beaconsfield, but I was then obliged to pay a visit to the Duchess of Marlborough, necessitating a week out of London, and after that his visits ceased. I thought little more of him until one afternoon months later when I came home to Cavendish Square, in a rush because I was due for cards with Lady Oxford in half an hour, Nell trailing along in my wake, a little distracted as she had been for months. Though I had implored her to tell me what troubled her, she always succeeded in turning my attention to some other matter, often reassuring me of her great loyalty and affection for me, which in turn prompted me to offer her a squeeze of the hand, or an embrace if I felt certain we would not be seen by one of the household.

'Nell, take my hat and have Mrs Higgs give it a tidy, will you,' I said as we entered the hall, 'and then come up to me and get me dressed, for if I miss the first hand I shall be at a great disadvantage the rest of the evening.'

'Yes, ma'am.'

As I placed my foot on the bottom stair, the footman said, 'There is a message here for you from Mr Cargill, ma'am.'

I turned, saying, 'Mr Cargill? I have not heard from him for six months or . . .' when I saw Nell glare at the footman with fierce animosity.

'He did not say Cargill,' she said quickly. 'He said Carter, the coalman, who is late with his account. I will deal with it, my lady.'

'Carter?' However distracted by other matters, I knew the household accounts better than any other, and Carter had been paid in full the week before. 'Let me see,' I demanded, extending a hand.

The footman stared at me dumbly, the colour draining from his face. I took the sealed paper, Nell looking on with tears in her eyes. 'It is addressed to you, Nell, though I recognize the hand as Cargill's.'

'Oh,' she said feebly, as if surprised. Then: 'You will be late for Lady Oxford's.'

'I think Lady Oxford shall not be worried by my absence, but I shall be worried if I do not know the truth of what is going on here right under my nose.'

'Oh, oh . . . I . . .'

'Come upstairs with me, Nell.'

I was sat upon a chair in my chamber with Nell upon the bed, where she sobbed.

'Nell. We have been together now for the best part of what, seven years? And in that time have I ever been cruel to you?'

She shook her head, her pretty face, prettier, I realized, than it had ever been before.

'I will not be cruel now. But you must tell me all.'

'It is that I have deceived you . . .'

'It is. You have deceived me,' I said, calmly. 'But the truth will untangle that.'

'Mr Cargill, even on that first –' she took a great gulp of air '– on that first occasion he came, and you had me play the fortepiano, even then, when you were out of the room, he declared to me his love.'

I almost urged her to admit that she must have been mistaken, and that it was I for whom he had declared his love, before realizing that, all along, it had been Nell in whom he had been interested. To that young man I must have seemed nothing more than a pockmarked dowager. How ridiculous of me to have been deluded by his flattery. And yet how much more cruel to think that my great affection for Nell had been no less a delusion. I looked at her solemn features, for so long wholly delightful to my eye, and saw instead a visage that was deceitful. 'I see.'

'I did not accept his declaration, madam. Not for a moment.'

'He is the son of an earl,' I pointed out, thinking the gulf in their respective stations was so obvious and insurmountable an obstacle to their affections that it hardly needed stating.

'As I constantly reminded him, but he talked to me so convincingly of love . . .'

'Oh, that,' I said, dismissively.

'. . . and said that his father had no ambitions or purpose for him, and was anyway bound to live for another forty years, and then that he had not one but two older brothers, and so our classes were not so very much divided, and he said . . . he said . . .'

'What did he say?'

'He said that I had the grace and charm and intelligence of a countess, and he could think of plenty of countesses who had not an ounce of what I had in abundance. But madam . . .'

'Yes?'

'I learnt all that from you.'

'Not all, Nell.'

'And . . .'

'And he writes to you here, and the footmen all know of it, and no doubt every member of this household but its mistress. I daresay you have all had great amusement at my expense.'

She looked down at her lap and began once more to weep.

Determining that I must exert my authority, I said, 'Nell, this is most unlike you. What is important is that you do not allow yourself to become this man's mistress, for while a woman of means may be some man's mistress and it do her little or no harm, for a person in your position it would lead to ruin. I could not, you understand, countenance your continued—'

'He has asked me to marry him!' she interrupted.

Plainly I had misheard. 'He has what?'

'He has asked, and I have . . . well, I have not said no. I do not have a father to ask for permission, nor a mother, nor any other to ask for advice, and I had wanted to ask you, but I did not know how or when I might do so, and feared you would hate me if I did, as I see now you do . . . and so the letter, which you may read if you wish, will be a continuation of our long correspondence on the matter of my reply to his proposal.'

I was hurt. Hurt that Cargill had made me think that I was the object of his interest when it had been Nell all along; hurt that Nell had conducted a love affair behind my back; hurt that she was on the very cusp of abandoning me, when I had loved her; but in that moment, most of all, I was outraged at such a breach of the rules of polite society, and that it should happen under my roof, thus no doubt confirming what all London thought most likely to happen here. What a thorough betrayal this was.

'I have no wish to read your letters, Nell,' I said coldly. 'You are dismissed. You may remain in this house tonight. Thereafter you must map your own course through this life. I will give you your wage for the year in advance, so that you will not be destitute.'

Her composure returned to her in an instant, as a cat falling from a high roof might tumble through the air yet land perfectly upon its paws and walk nonchalantly away. 'Very well, my lady.' She got up to leave, but hesitated at the door, and asked: 'What, then, of equality, of which you speak so often?'

'Equality is *within* the classes, Nell. Not across them. Fairness, honour, respect – these matter for all. But for a servant to marry the son of an earl is none of those.'

She looked at me then, dead in the eye, nodded stiffly, and left, taking with her not only herself but a greater piece of my heart than she deserved.

I heard some weeks after that she and Cargill had, indeed, married, and gone up to his father's estate at Pitlochry, but his eldest brother fell from his horse on the very day of Nell and Cargill's arrival and lay insensible for days before an untimely death. A week after that his father died of an apoplexy, brought on, no doubt, by the death of his heir. And Cargill's other brother, briefly the Earl of Pitlochry, was sailing back from Gibraltar when his vessel was caught in a storm, and he was killed when the mizzen mast snapped and fell upon him. Nell was therefore raised to be countess, but surrounded by such a wreckage of death and misery that it must have felt like a curse, and I felt impelled to write to her, softened by recollections of her loyalty and affection, her great intelligence and, no less, her uniquely pleasing company.

Twickenham
17 April 1724

My dear Nell,

I have heard of your many misfortunes since you wed and am heartily sorry for them. I wish to state plainly why I counselled you so strongly against marriage, for the little I knew of Mr Cargill made me think him sweet, but there is not a man in all the world who pleases as well as he does before he becomes that great weight upon any woman – a husband. *I wish you to understand that my disapproval of your match rested as much on the secrecy with which it was made as its unsuitability. I should have counselled you against marrying a man of such covert habit, for men are creatures of inconstant nature, and must be seen at all times to be kept honourable.*

Your very difficult beginning to married life will have made you know your husband well, no doubt, and I sincerely hope you like what you now see. It is best that you know each other truly, your tastes and hopes and faults, before you commit for life, for in that manner you might at least accommodate *each other. There never was a worse match than one made for* love.

Sharing troubles does not make a mismatch a match, any more than two trees blown down in a storm and leaning, the one upon the other, are likely to leaf again. But you are a woman who has the qualities to make a fine countess, qualities of intelligence and beauty and good judgement, and I say that in a spirit of honesty and – yes – of equality. Society will frown upon you, but it may in time forget you and I can testify that being forgotten is very much the most desirable state, for to be celebrated as I have been means that condemnation comes in equal measure (there, equality again) and I would much rather now be left unnoticed and forgotten in some rural glade to live my life as I would wish.

There may be some foolish souls in your household or amongst your new relations or living upon your estate, who believe that you have brought a curse upon the House of Pitlochry with three deaths following your arrival in short order. Let me assure you, dear Nell, that there never was a stupider person than one who cares to believe in curses.

I will close with a confession. All my life I feared Death and I feared Love no less, for I formed a notion that where I loved, so Death followed. I have tried sincerely these past years not to love for fear that in so doing I should tempt Death to follow upon its trail.

But I loved you well, and I believe that you loved me. We survived, did we not, you and I? We shall live yet for many years, of that I am perfectly certain. Let us be done with Death, though perhaps not quite yet with Love.

Yours in affectionate memory,
MWM

21

A RESPITE

Summer 1724, London

(Frances)

It took some months to make the arrangements to travel to London, and all through the winter my spirits were lifted by the prospect of seeing my sister once more, and telling her all and receiving her advice, and though I dreaded making suit on my husband's behalf, I desperately hoped my father would soften and use his influence to bring the whole sorry business of John's defection to an end.

I brought Frannie with me, and we were lent a house in Soho by my old friends Lord and Lady Bateman. As with those suffering an unspeakable illness, I was treated kindly yet distantly for fear that my contagion, which was of poverty and loneliness and my husband's treachery, would infect others. Mary, on the other hand, embraced me passionately and wished to know everything. She insisted that we spend days at her house in Twickenham, which being two hours' ride from London was inconvenient when I had so many lawyers to visit and petitions to lodge about town.

'You feel your life is empty?' she asked incredulously when I told her that whenever I had sat before paper ready to write to her, pen in hand, I could think of nothing whatsoever to say, indeed that my life seemed like a vast empty desert, stretching both behind and ahead of me.

'Empty some days, yes,' I said, almost afraid to confess it, 'and then on others full, though full as a great dark cloud is full of rain and thunder and hail.'

'Then let us fill your days here with gaiety, Fanny, so that you may go back to Paris with happy memories.'

How could I explain to my sister that I had no wish for gaiety? That I couldn't conceive of what a happy memory would be. When I was not in Twickenham, she came to stay with me in Soho and took me thence to Drury Lane, and to salons and evenings of cards where she gambled extravagantly. I tried to appreciate it but could not put on enough of a show.

'You are suffering from a fit of melancholy,' she declared.

I could not deny it.

'We will ride, for that is a certain cure for low spirits!'

The next day back we went to Twickenham, and then off cantering about Bushy Park, Mary instructing me to appreciate the air and the leaves on the trees and the lovers walking a little ahead of their chaperones. It had rained early, and the ground released that smell of soil and grass and heat that is normally so comforting. She drew her horse beside mine and, the fresh air making her even more outspoken than usual, said, 'Mar? He shows you his appreciation?'

'Appreciation?'

'He loves you?'

'He says so.'

'In bed?'

'Not that.'

'Not ever?'

'Never in Paris.'

'But it's been years, Fanny!'

'I think if he tried to do that to me I would break completely.'

'Oh, Fanny,' she declared, and jumped down from her saddle (I rode side saddle, as decorum demanded; Mary rode like a man, wearing, as she favoured, Turkish pantaloons). She rubbed my knee to comfort me.

'But you and Edward . . . ' I asked, feeling emboldened.

'No, but Edward is always miles away, and when he is not we argue satisfactorily about everything, and find ourselves perfectly gratified. You have Mar brooding at close quarters. I am not surprised you are melancholic. Anyway, I have friends, good friends.'

'Bed friends?'

She gave me a look such as she did when we were fourteen or fifteen and had secrets we wished to be guessed at but not spoken of. I did not press her. She led both our horses by their reins back through the park to their stables, talking all the while, though I only caught half of what she said.

When we returned to her house I asked her about Mr Pope, whom I knew to be almost a neighbour, and recalling that they had once been so close as to be thought intimate.

'We barely see each other.'

'You were close friends, I thought.'

'We were.' She seemed ill at ease.

'Then, you fell out over something. He was too affectionate, perhaps?'

'Ah, that. Well, yes, but Pope likes to tease his friends by hinting at his love for them to see how far they will go in reciprocating.'

'And you did not reciprocate?'

Unusually for my sister, she evaded. 'Not as fully as he'd like, but it was other things that upset him so.'

For once I was the interrogator, and Mary the one reluctant to speak. 'What other reasons, Mary?'

'He stole some of my work and claimed it as his own,' she said, quickly, as if confessing to some wrong she had committed herself.

'But that is outrageous!'

'Is it? Perhaps I should have been flattered,' she said, unconvincingly.

'You protested?'

'I did not.'

'Why not?'

'Because . . . because it is beneath me. I have hardly ever claimed my work in my own name, or not since we were children.'

'Yet everyone knows how clever you are, how brilliantly you write, Mary, and I think your poems are well known.'

'But not with my name on them.'

'With Pope's?'

'Yes. But worse than that, Pope let some work of his that was poorly received be thought mine.'

'Then he has used you!'

'He has,' she said, sorrowfully.

'Yet it is he who is upset with *you*?'

'But that is how men so often are, is it not? They gamble away their fortunes and blame it on their mothers for not loving them enough, or they take to drink and say it is because their wives do not understand them, or go with whores because they need *satisfaction*. They disgrace themselves and find a woman to lay their disgrace upon, like a pair of misused gloves handed to their servant to repair. Isn't that what Mar has done to you?'

It was too much to think about, this matter of men being *this* or *that*. 'Are you sorry not to have him as a friend?'

'I only fear becoming his enemy, Fanny, for he can be cruel. It is why I have said nothing.'

'I am sure he would not wish to be your enemy. Why would he when you have been so useful to him?'

'There is something else.'

I had a notion of what Mary was about to confess – that she had made some jest at Pope's expense. She so often hurt people without intention, sometimes those she loved the most.

'He wrote a dreadful poem, absurdly complicated and maudlin. It was about a young couple struck by lightning, found dead in a haystack. You know it?'

'Yes, I read of them, but not the poem.'

'He was very proud of it. Wanted me to read it first, before anyone else. I thought it ridiculous, and that Pope was trying too hard to impress, which is his great failing. I sent him a note to say I thought it very clever, which I hoped he would understand to mean that I did not much like it. But he had it published. Regrettably my riposte was also circulated.'

'Your riposte?'

'Oh, Fanny,' she said, coming to sit beside me on the pistachio-green sofa on which I had been perched for the past half-hour, a teacup in my hand. The tea was cold. She took the cup and saucer and placed it on the lacquer tray that sat on the little table before us. Taking my hand, she said, 'I wrote to you of it. I know you do not answer my letters, but do you even read them?' She said this not unkindly.

There were so many stories in her letters, so many references to arguments and literary scandals, hints of infidelities by those we knew, and her words so often seemed to dissolve before my eyes into loops and lines and symbols, so that I might have been reading another language, in another alphabet. But I could not admit to that. 'Yes, but you know, I am not well, Mary, and I forget so much lately.'

She looked at me for a long minute without speaking, as if about to confound what I had said about myself, but seemed to think better of it, not wanting to contemplate my illness, if illness it was. 'The difficulty,' she continued, 'was the day that Pope sent me his damned poem, I knew I could not be rude about it, not to him, and I wrote a little parody of it, less of his poem, more of the situation, you understand, about these two lovers struck by lightning, who were out in a haystack doing what a young man and a young woman are wont to do in a haystack . . .'

I laughed, and the sound of it, so unfamiliar, surprised us both.

'But that evening Lady Oxford and Molly Skerritt and someone else I cannot now recall came to play *triomphe* and I showed them Pope's poem – I shouldn't have done – and also my skit on it.'

'Skit?'

'It is the latest term, Fanny, for something light and quick. And I did write it light and quick. It took me no more than ten minutes. I had no intention of showing it to anyone, or not while I live. But I showed it to these ladies, foolishly.'

'But they would not tell Pope of it, your friends?'

'No, I did not think they would. But I was called to deal with a message received from Edward, who was in the Commons and sought my advice on some debate, and so I attended to it, and left the ladies with my poem, and a copy must have been made . . .'

'By whom?'

'I don't know, I do not want to know.'

Her upset was obvious.

'May I read it?'

'I'd like you to since I've told you about it. And didn't we use to sit in the library at Thoresby and write together?'

I smiled at the thought.

'A happy memory.'

I agreed, thinking that I did have happy memories after all, and perhaps the desert that lay behind me was not so bleak, and the one that lay ahead might not be so barren.

Mary stood and went over to her rosewood bureau, its exterior orderly and elegant until, lowering the lid, she revealed the chaos within. Yet in the disorder was some pattern my sister understood perfectly for a moment later Pope's poem was in my hand, printed neatly for wide distribution. It was elegant and complicated and full of allusion which I did not begin to understand, and so like much of Pope's other work.

'It is very clever,' I said.

'Do you understand it?'

For a moment I thought Mary was trying to make me feel small.

'It's all words,' she said, 'but it doesn't really mean anything. There's no true feeling in it. It made me angry, Fanny, I cannot say why. I felt he was wanting me to admire him and praise him for all his damnable cleverness and I couldn't bring myself to do it. So I dashed off a response that I never intended to show anyone. I should have burnt it as soon as I wrote it.'

'Show me. Please.'

She shuffled about amongst her pile of papers once more and emerged, like a terrier with a rat. 'It is printed?' I said in surprise.

'Printed and distributed, more's the pity. Someone gave the copy made that evening to a villainous pamphleteer, and he printed it and ascribed it to *a lady of quality*.'

> HERE lie John Hughes and Sarah Drew.
> Perhaps you'll say, 'What's that to you?'
> Believe me, friend, much may be said
> On that poor couple that are dead.
> On Sunday next they should have married;
> But see how oddly things have carried!
> On Thursday last it rained and lightened;
> These tender lovers, sadly frightened,
> Sheltered beneath the cocking hay,
> In hope to pass the time away.
> But the bold thunder found them out
> (Commissioned for that end, no doubt),
> And, seizing on their trembling breath,
> Consigned them to the shades of death.
> Who knows if 'twas not kindly done?
> For, had they seen the next year's sun,
> A beaten wife and cuckold swain
> Had jointly cursed the marriage chain.
> Now they are happy in their doom,
> For Pope has wrote upon their tomb.

I laughed, this time heartily and freely and oh so happily, and the sound of that laughter in my throat felt like standing beneath a waterfall, not that I have ever done such a thing. I felt *amused*, which is just how my sister wanted me to feel. 'Oh, Mary. It is so clever and funny, too. And it is much, much lighter and wittier and *truer* than the verse Pope wrote.'

'Yet I feel I have set a flame to the end of a very long fuse,

Fanny, and one day a big barrel of gunpowder will blow up in my face.'

I knelt before her and set my cheek upon her lap and felt glad to be there, in her house, surrounded by paper strewn about the floor. Here I was with my sister, and it was where I belonged.

22

A RANCOROUS FRIEND

Autumn 1724, Twickenham

(Mary)

It being some time since I was in regular correspondence with Mr Pope, and still longer since we had been in each other's company, despite his home being barely a quarter of a mile from my own, I was intrigued to receive a card inviting me to pay him a visit. We had been in a long and uneasy truce, and this sudden overture to peace was no less unexpected than it was mysterious.

I had heard much about Pope's grotto, none of it good. In a manner that was typical of him, he succeeded in his invitation to make my failure to have yet admired his creation a matter of poor manners on my part. But I bear no grudges and am generally of the view that a person may change for the better, even if most only ever seem to change for the worse.

I was received at Pope's door by Tricksell, his manservant, an individual I had met before and who had, indeed, changed for the worse, being even more inclined to inappropriate merriment at every word uttered to him. Given Pope's habitually gloomy nature, for him to have this cackling giant at his side should have been a torment, but like small men who possess large hounds, or pretty women who cherish the company of a plain cousin, so Pope seemed to relish having this oaf at his beck and call.

I was led by Tricksell through the house, briefly seeing that my portrait, painted on Pope's commission by Godfrey Kneller, still hung above his fireplace. I was encouraged onwards and out down the steps that faced the lawn and to the bend in the river, invited to turn and trail down some mossy stairs that sank down below the house, the servant assuring me all the while of the great surprise awaiting me. I felt some trepidation, for I began to wonder whether I was to be greeted by a minotaur down there in the damp and dark. If I was to be gored to death no doubt Pope would write me a fitting and touching epitaph, marred by his overly clever rhyme and undue sentimentality.

The place smelt of rot and mould, and though the day was not cold, in Pope's cave it was midwinter. The grotto was lined with shells, pieces of glass, gemstones, broken tiles and, at its far end, lit by an oil lamp, its light flickering upon its creator's bony features, making him look more than ever like an apparition. This was the world he had created, then: not a paradise of sky and seas and rivers and birds, but a dank, shiny, cold pit in which he might stand but I could only stoop.

'My dear Lady Mary,' said Pope, coming towards me to kiss my hand. He bid me come and sit beside him on a red velvet cushion. 'It is from this aspect that one has the full sensation of light against the stones and shells and so forth. The water of the river makes everything shimmer.'

It was clear that he was immensely proud of what he had

created. 'It is like putting one's eye to a telescope and seeing stars,' I ventured, knowing the necessity of pretence to admiration.

He said nothing.

Unable to bring myself to offer yet more effusive praise, I said, 'I know that many of your friends have admired your grotto enthusiastically.'

'Ah yes,' he said wistfully. 'My friends. But where are they now?' He gave me a meaningful look.

Perhaps it was true that Pope had never had true friends, only admirers. Pope loved others only as Narcissus was transfixed by his reflection. Love is a giving of the self, almost a parting with the self. But I could not explain this to Pope. 'I think you have many friends. Your work is admired greatly.' I was conscious of how uneasy we were with each other when we had once been so comfortable.

'My work, yes,' he said. 'But I am not my work. I am a man.'

He could be like this – maudlin and self-pitying even when he was most flattered and fawned upon. Conscious of our proximity I stood and feigned a particular interest in a cluster of dark red stones. 'What are these?'

'It is carnelian, from Scotland,' he said vaguely, as if he did not wish to discuss his grotto at all, despite bringing me here to admire it. 'You are writing?' he asked.

'Letters,' I said. 'Little else.'

'Poetry?'

'Not at present. I daresay I shall write more, but lately I find I am too busy with the unimportant to find time for the important – if poetry is important.'

'The smallpox inoculations have fallen out of fashion, I hear,' he said with a degree of satisfaction.

If he wished to belittle my efforts in the direction of vanquishing that awful disease, I wouldn't let him. 'It seems medical progress rests too greatly in the hands of bishops,' I said, 'which is French behaviour, and not a desirable situation for any nation to find itself in. I do my utmost to confound such prejudices, but I sometimes feel I must raise my voice above the howling of the ignorant, and that is a mighty chorus indeed.'

'You are weary of it?' he asked.

'Weary but unbowed,' I said, believing he was speaking of the smallpox inoculations.

'Poetry?'

His aim was to catch me out, to diminish me. I knew I had to be on my guard. 'I am not weary of poetry, no. And certainly not of yours.'

Pope held up his hands, examining them as if seeing them for the first time. 'What a strange thing a hand is, when one considers it at all.'

I was well used to his inclination towards the non sequitur. 'We should struggle to write if we had webbed feet like a duck, shouldn't we?'

He smiled.

'Quack, quack,' I said, thinking to urge him in the direction of laughter, but his mood was too gloomy for that.

'I will not quack for you, Mary, for fear I might find it reported in next week's newspapers.'

Did he wish to accuse me of indiscretion? 'I have never spoken ill of you, Alex.'

'Sometimes it is as if my very thoughts have found their way into journals.'

Had I not had my own work and letters stolen and published, too? 'We all suffer such fates, and none of us knows how it is done.'

'You should write poetry. Better than pamphlets,' he said.

'I will write again, but my work is not so important as

yours, as I said. Your poetry has carried you to the shores of recognition of, of . . . veneration, I should say.'

His expression changed in a manner that I knew all too well, one moment pleading lapdog, next spiteful wasp, a metamorphosis worthy of Ovid himself. 'Yet you think little of me, madam.'

I had been running my hand across the gems and shells on the wall. I stopped and said, not looking at him, 'I don't know what you can mean.'

'You have ridiculed me.'

'I have done no such thing.'

'*Here lie John Hughes and Sarah Drew/Perhaps you'll say, "What's that to you?"/Believe me, friend, much may be said/ On that poor couple that are dead.*'

I considered the possibility of denying my authorship, for I dreaded Pope's unconstrained animosity, but to lie would have been pointless, and if I am anything I am honest. 'My little jest from so long ago was not worth the memorizing, I think.'

He turned again, from wasp to injured pug, his eyes moist with tears of self-pity. 'It is not that you wrote what you did, but that I wrote what *I* did for *you*, thinking you would be moved by it. Not laugh at it.'

'It was nothing. Surely you can see that. Your own work was much admired. Mine I meant for no one's eyes but my own.'

'But you did it. You wrote those cruel words. That is why it hurt. And it is not the only thing you have done that is hurtful.'

I might have asked him what else, but Pope could so easily have been offended by any one thing I had done, however small, that the list of my imagined misdemeanours would easily have filled the entirety of that afternoon and the night, too. 'I have given you, sir, my friendship, and I never once did intend to hurt you, I assure you.'

He stood, and though I had need to crouch where the roof came low, poor Pope who was always stooped did not, and I was reminded of his suffering, and felt a pang of pity for him. I was about to speak thus when he said, 'Not that anything you might wish to do to hurt me could possibly matter, madam.'

'Oh?'

'Your poems you write for your friends. You say so yourself. You have no wish to have your name known.'

It was one thing for Pope to attack me for the inconstancy of my friendship, for there was some truth in that. But I would not accept him deriding my poetry and my life's work. I felt that I had to stand up for it. Far too many had retreated before him already, and I knew it to be in the nature of bullies to attack those they think too weak to defend themselves, and only to cease their attacks in the face of strength. 'I have had no choice in that,' I said. 'But that does not mean I am ashamed of my work. And, moreover, I would rather that my work was not thought yours, nor yours thought mine.'

There was heat now in that cold place. 'What of mine has been said to be yours?'

'You know full well. When something of yours is not well received, you let it be thought mine. Or Gay's perhaps.'

He laughed bitterly. 'You think so? And what would someone make of yours that was mine?'

'You dismiss my work, then?'

'I do not dismiss it, madam, for it does not bear the attention that dismissal would demand.'

I pulled a stone from the wall, not intending to. I turned it in my hand. It was green and dull and might have been envy itself. 'I do not say you are not talented, sir. You are. But I have my gifts, too.'

'Your gifts are great. For a female.'

'*For a female*? And what might a female be? Does she not have a brain, a heart, a hand to write? Does she not have an eye to see, and an ear to hear? Might a female's gifts not be every bit as great as those of a man? What is it that separates the sexes but flesh?'

He raised his head, as a horse does when smelling something unfamiliar. He was unpractised in the art of argument, I could tell. His guests of late had been only of the flattering sort. Surely he knew I would not have come to do that? 'It is more than that,' he said, having considered how he might best dismiss my argument. 'A woman is less than a man as a lake is not a sea. A lake may be pleasing, and may be deep, but it can never be the sea.'

'A woman is less, then?'

'Certainly.'

'Am I less than you?'

He laughed, though a little awkwardly, I grant him. 'Would you like me to say you are more?'

'How much less is my work than yours?'

'Let us say it is half.'

Half? In the very moment I told myself not to be provoked by him, my tongue was moved into saying something I should ever regret: 'At least I am a whole woman!'

'And I?' he said, seeming almost to will what must come next, as a dog, having stolen a joint of meat from the table, lingers for its beating.

'You are but half a man,' I uttered, as inevitably as Cleopatra put the asp to her breast.

He smiled, the smile of an assassin sighting his victim, and held out his hand. I placed in it the dull green stone I had plucked from the wall. 'It is a bloodstone,' he said quietly.

I foolishly stood proud as I made my exit, hitting my head

on the roof of his absurd grotto, and heard his sigh of satisfaction at that small injury, no doubt the first of many he would inflict on me. I had insulted him and that had been precisely what he had wanted me to do.

Oh, Pope, you sad, bitter, clever creature.

23

THE MELANCHOLY MADNESS

Winter 1724–5, Paris

(Frances)

After two months in London my husband demanded my return, requiring the notes and deeds and bills I had acquired during my visit. Our daughter had enjoyed getting to know her cousins, and my own health was greatly restored. Paris reared before me like the sheer face of a mountain, granite grey, too steep even for snow to cling to, and I knew I was not prepared to scale it. But I had no choice. The money I had succeeded in wringing from those few hands willing to even contemplate helping Mar would not be enough to dent our debts, let alone give us a good living in Paris. And John lived too well, since the notion of not entertaining grandly, of wearing simple clothes and eating plain food would have been as good as death to him. I did not much care how I lived, so long as our numberless creditors stopped hammering at our door day and night.

My husband knew the extent of my success and the

measure of my failures long before I arrived back on Rue Mouffetard.

Something had shifted in my absence. I was unhappy before I left, but it had been a familiar unhappiness, as familiar as the distasteful smells of the street and the furtive looks of the servants. I had grown inured to it. But now, my health restored by my London visit, my predicament was clear.

'I cannot stay here,' I declared to Mar, walking into his study, though I did not get very far since the entire floor was occupied by the model of his Alloa estate, which had grown considerably while I was away, having been comprehensively redesigned to meet the demands of his burgeoning imagination. I was obliged to step carefully across a miniature parterre before I succeeded in finding a square inch in the deer park in which I could stand before him.

'Indeed, madam,' he said, not looking up from where he was affixing chimney pots, perfect in every detail but their size.

'I have been here almost a week and you have barely acknowledged me. The servants are even more insolent than before. I think I am not wanted.'

'You are not wanted, no; you are of no use to me or to any man. But you are necessary, and that is that.'

'Necessary? To what end?'

'To my ends, to my purposes.' He stepped across his paths and fountains, his maze and lake, his ha-ha and his pergolas and seized my arm, squeezing until I could not help but cry out in pain. 'You are my wife. Here you shall remain.'

I sat that night at my bureau, ready to write to Mary and ask for her help, but it was as if the house had begun once more to exert its spell over me, and each time I set the nib to paper, no word would appear. Only tears fell upon the sheet, and they dried too quickly to leave any trace.

Over the following weeks I tried to rally my spirits. I endeavoured to spend time with my daughter, but Mar had engaged a French governess for young Frannie, a woman whose constant lessons seemed to be comprised solely of reciting the order of the kings and queens of France. I knew that Frannie was bored, yet when I sought to interrupt, they conspired together to exclude me, picking up needlework or a novel they had been discussing, and seeming all of a sudden to be the greatest of friends. Even my child did not wish to be with me.

The servants whispered about me incessantly and, as I grew ever more melancholy, they whispered about that, too.

I thought of what Mary would tell me to do: she would say, 'Take air!' and so off I went walking along the banks of the Seine, but that only earnt me accusations of being a whore from the stallholders, and so from then on I stayed home, the windows shut against the smell of the tannery, my loneliness enveloping me.

A mouse, dead, is in my bed. When I confront the chambermaid she merely shrugs. 'It's a mouse. It's dead,' she says. 'Why shouldn't it die in your bed as well as anywhere else?'

I sleep ever more badly, imagining cockroaches and snakes and all manner of beasts at my feet. I can no longer speak, not even to little Frannie. I find I can survive the days if I say not a word. But I worry greatly about the bestiary in my bed. Sometimes in the darkness of night I feel the slither of lizards, the claws of cats, the brush of a feather, the prick of a hedgehog's spine and I fumble for the tinderbox, which I have taken to keeping at my side. But by the time I have a flame and light a candle and pull aside my covers the animals have scrambled away. I search under my bed, and more often than not I find a feather, or some dropping that shows me I am not mistaken. They *have* been there. Where they go I cannot be certain. I check in every closet, fling open the windows loudly. The servants are summoned to get me back into bed, to give me opium tablets to calm me, but I spit them out. I know it is they who put the creatures in my bed.

They listen outside the door awaiting sounds of my distress, all of them. The servants, my husband, my daughter. The tutor. The fishmongers from along the riverbank. I will not explain myself. They want me to accuse them, but I will not. Cendrine, who I thought my friend, is worse than the rest, for she sits with me, waiting for me to fall asleep, so that she can slip some new animal at my feet, a biting monkey or a stinging insect, and I know I must do all I can to stay awake.

Mar brings physicians to examine me. They pull at my eyelids, prod my spleen, look in my ears, listen to my heart and try to bleed me, but I will not consent to it, for I know they wish to feed the creatures with my blood, so that they may grow stronger and I weaker. I make clear my objections through squirming and grunting and shaking my head with great violence.

They try to tie me, and I am obliged to bite the hand of Monsieur Lafitte, the surgeon. I draw blood, and there is a fitting irony in that.

24

FATHERS AND SONS

Spring 1727, London

(Mary)

It was not the first time our son had run away.

The first time Eddie had got as far as Oxford and sought admission to Balliol.

'You are unhappy at Westminster?' I asked him, he sitting opposite me on the new yellow sofa, dropping crumbs all over it since he was eating a bun the maid had brought for him together with a glass of milk. The servants took pity on him, pity being something the boy had a talent for creating in that class of person.

'Not really,' he said, his mouth full.

'You have few friends?'

'I have friends, Mama.' He looked up at me, chewing slow as a ruminant. He had the broad, flat features of his father, beginning to resolve into handsomeness as they had in Edward, though at present the boy looked ponderous, his eyes a watery grey and not lively, his chin large and face long. His clothes were dusty from the road, and there was a fishy smell about him, as is often the case in boys of that age.

'Did you go with one of your friends to Oxford?'

'No, I went alone.'

The many friends he claimed for himself might anyway have been a fiction. He had an imagination, which was something. 'Your masters are unkind at Westminster?'

'Not to me.'

'Then why leave? You have at least two more years before you may go to Oxford. And I must tell you that the reports I receive of your work are not encouraging, Eddie.'

He smiled at this, his boyish face twisting into that of a man who has happily sold a horse for well above its value. *Oh, at least be better at your deceits*, I longed to say to him.

'It is too simple for me, the work there,' he said, 'I need something more interesting than Latin declension and sets of numbers to multiply.'

'I see,' I said doubtfully. 'Then what would you study?'

'Everything! I should like to learn the language of the Arabs. I learnt a little when in Turkey if you recall. And Flemish too. I have not lost it. And Chinese! How fine a thing to speak the language of such a faraway place, Mama. And I should like to sail around the world!'

'Hmmm. Well, your Latin might be better first.'

I let him sleep at Cavendish Square that night and instructed him to bathe. We had no clothes of his fit, so I had the housekeeper send out for new hose and breeches and vest, and gave her five guineas, not imagining she would spend more than two but she was another who indulged the boy, and so she returned with no more than three shillings in change and a fine pigeon-grey silk coat, white silk breeches and a nicely embroidered waistcoat. The next morning I sat with him while he ate a good plate of eggs, kidneys and tongue and drank a jug of beer, I imploring him not to spill it down his new suit. 'Eddie, dear,' I said, 'you are eager to be out in the world as a man, I know, and you have great spirit, and that is a fine thing . . .'

He looked up from his plate, wary.

'But you must *learn*, you must *study*. And you most particularly must learn some patience. Your father and I—'

'Why is Papa not here?' he asked, failing to conceal his resentment.

'Papa is busy with his mines, Eddie. You know that. He is all contracts and wages and profit. I am sure you would benefit from some time as his assistant.'

'I am not interested in contracts and wages and profit any more than you are, Mother,' he said, obstinate over a kidney which determinedly escaped his fork.

'Are you not?' I said, unable to pretend to an interest I did not possess. 'Nevertheless, you must show some application. Our love for you is great, Eddie, but in return we need some, some . . .'

'Faith?'

'Faith. Yes,' I agreed, a little surprised at his quick reply. It was as good a word as any. 'Faith that we have your best interests at heart.'

He did not acknowledge my comment, but took a swig of his beer, his eye upon me, as if measuring me.

I kissed him on the cheek before he was driven away on the chaise. He looked back at me, his expression in that brief moment one of pure terror, as if he was being sent to the gibbet. I felt something for him then, knowing that all his boyish bravado about his cleverness and his friends and his certainty was bluff, and that he was just a small and fearful child, unsure of what he was or what he might become. It was the love for something that one knows to be sad, the pity one feels for an empty purse in a house that is poor, or for a parson who tries to cover the patches in his breeches with his coat. It was not the healthy, unbridled love I should have felt for my own son. I stood out in the street and waved my hand, which I would not have done for any other.

We received reports of some improvement in his behaviour from Mr Freind over the succeeding months, though also an incident where Eddie climbed up inside a chimney wanting to know what it must be like to be a chimney sweep. Nevertheless, I imagined that my counsel as to how he should comport himself had been understood.

But at Easter he vanished.

We placed an advertisement in both the *Daily Courant* and the *Public Advertiser*.

> Reward, Twenty pounds for boy, Edward Wortley Montagu, fourteen years of age, of low height, fresh coloured, lightish brown Hair, grey Eyes, two Marks on his arms. If the Boy will return himself, he shall be kindly received and put to sea if he desires it. Apply to Edward Wortley Montagu Esq, MP, 5 Cavendish Square, London

We heard no word, and I began to despair. I tried at first to make light of it, since he was a boy given to adventures, and to creating some commotion where he would be the centre of attention, and he might not have come to any harm. But then again, he might have been robbed of what little he had or been put to work in some place where he was beaten and mistreated. Or he might have fallen into a river and drowned. These and a clamour of other terrors took possession of me. I had grown too casual with Death, and I began to fear that he had seized his moment to take my son.

Each morning I awakened with the old crow sitting upon my heart, its claws flexing and making it hard to take so much as a breath. I rose, dressed and made every attempt to walk, eat, make polite conversation, and yet the crow did not fly away but stayed clawing, and with each passing day it seemed to grow and I diminished.

My father came to see me just once while Eddie was missing. I received a card one noon announcing that he would call that evening. Appearing past eight o'clock, his chair parked in my entrance hall, he emerged from it looking like the god of weariness, in the same moment both grand and absent. He offered me no greeting but walked stiffly into the library, seated himself upon the sofa and looked about for a servant from whom to order sustenance.

'Papa,' I declared, bowing low before him. 'It is so kind of you to come.'

'Kind?' he growled. 'You do not think me kind, nor am I. But your son is missing, and I come to tell you in person that I am sorry for it; though I did not have so much hand in it as you no doubt suppose.'

I had not imagined my father had done any such thing, yet the strangeness of his comment provoked my curiosity. 'I have not supposed you having any hand in it, sir. How so?'

'I know you have your ear at every door in London, madam, and so you must know that he came to see me at my chambers some two months past.'

I controlled my fury, as I so often had to with my father. How could he not have thought to mention this to me before? Edward and I had been searching for Eddie for a month and had even got so far as placing the advertisement in the newspapers.

'Yes,' said my father, a fond glint in his eye, 'young Edward found some way into my presence, and spoke with great fervour of the stupidity of his tutors and his desire to go away to sea.'

'And what did you say to him?'

'I told him to obey his schoolmasters and his father, naturally.'

'You might have told him to pay heed to his mother, too.'

He cast me that look of his, not scorn exactly, but disdain. 'I gave him a gold sovereign and told him that all boys want to go to sea.'

'Why did you not tell me of this when first you heard he was missing?' I asked, crossly.

'It did not seem at all important. He is my grandson, and it is natural he should wish to seek advice from me.'

I laughed at that, which my father thought insulting, and he left soon after.

Eddie was returned to us from Gibraltar some two months after his disappearance, that rock being as far as my errant son voyaged upon a West African trading vessel before he tired of his lowly position and the hard labour. After three weeks of scrubbing decks he had boasted that he was the grandson of a duke, presenting his engrafting scars as testimony. He was fortunate that the captain of the vessel was a Quaker gentleman and thus disinclined to throw him overboard.

Edward and I agonized over what to do with the boy, before resolving to send him with a tutor to the West Indies, where he might learn something to his advantage, have his insatiable appetite for adventure rewarded and, most importantly, be kept well away from further trouble.

With the commotion of Eddie's disappearance over, I turned my attention to another drama, no less close to my heart, for I had been receiving reports from friends in Paris that Fanny was in great distress, out of her wits, and that her husband no longer knew how to care for her. I had long since ceased receiving letters from Fanny, and hardly expected to hear news directly from her husband. I thought it right that Papa should know all this and wrote to him seeking his advice on the matter, once more receiving his card informing me that he would call that evening. Again, his chair arrived in the hall, and on this occasion he emerged even more weary, needing a stick to help him make his way into the library.

'Father, are you ill?' I asked with concern.

'Not at all, Mary. No, just a pain here and there.' He had shrunk and the terrible authority I had known all my life was so diminished that I felt it possible to talk to him freely of my concern for Fanny.

'You always thought she married the Earl of Mar at my insistence.'

I did not disagree.

'You are wrong about that, Mary,' he said, with surprising gentleness. 'Frances really did love John Erskine, and so I concealed whatever misgivings I may have had and supported her in it, thinking I should for once give love its chance.' I thought back to the fiery arguments he and I had shared, and of how he had forbidden me from even attending my sister's wedding. He had been defending her all along, not himself, and I saw how I had misjudged him, and felt an affection for him that I had hardly known before. 'I am sorry I did not find her a better man than the Earl of Mar,' he said, a hint of despair in his voice.

He was *sorry*? I had never once heard my father express regret for any single thing he had done. In this spirit of mutual benevolence I ventured to ask after the health of my stepmother, the Duchess of Kingston.

'Isabella is well enough, thank you, Mary. She wishes I were less engaged at court, but affairs of state leave little time for family, as you know all too well. We shall have you and Edward for dinner soon. I am resolved to repair whatever breaches have occurred between us. And I shall do all that I can to see Frances is brought safely home.'

I went to my father and embraced him, and he permitted the gesture. I could not think of the last time I had done so – not since I was a child, I thought.

As he stood to leave, having taken a little malmsey wine and some sweetmeats, he gasped and fell back on to the sofa, and I told him I would call for Dr Garth. Recovering himself, he told me to do no such thing, he was a little tired was all, and with some difficulty he was back in his chair and on his way home.

Next day I received word that my father was gravely ill and to attend his bedside. I went straightway, though because our relations had long been so cool I was not familiar with his household. At the door I was met by a servant who seemed uncertain how to treat me, admitting me with only the greatest reluctance. Lady Isabella, my stepmother, could barely condescend to greet me, other than to say, 'He will not live out the day.'

'I must go to him.'

'You shall not.'

'But—'

'You will wait here,' she said, pointing to a chair in the morning room. I tried to reason with her, yet she would not accept my pleading. 'You have been a constant source of distress, unease and upset to your father, Mary. If he is to have even the faintest hope of rallying then I must protect him from you.'

What a sentence for her to pass, making herself judge and jury upon my loving if turbulent relationship with my father. He was *my* father. I tried once more to remonstrate, but Isabella marched out of the room without a backward glance.

Some hours passed until I was admitted to my father's chamber, where I was not able to speak with him for there he lay, his cold, grey body upon his deathbed. He was gone, and it felt to me as if the world had tumbled from its axis and I was falling from it, plunging headlong into the void that keeps us from the stars. That he and I had been at war for the better part of my life did not make his death any easier to bear, for I'd thought he would always be there, and I would ever need be ready for some new battle with him. There is a great comfort in being opposed, for in that opposition we find our true selves. I had never sought nor expected his approval, and I had not had it – or not since I was eight or nine years old. Yet it was his disapproval that had defined me, and his death left me wondering who I truly was. That our last conversation was a softer one than any we had had before was not consoling, for it held the prospect that we might have been truly reconciled given time. Perhaps he might have become the father I'd always longed for. But Death had come to snatch that hope from me, as always.

I wrote to Fanny, wondering how to soften the blow, and doubting whether she would truly understand my words.

We are orphaned, I told her, *and like orphans we must hold on to each other, more firmly now than ever before.*

25

SALT TEARS

Spring 1728, Paris

(Frances)

A man who claims to be my husband tells me if I do not get well I will have to be sent back to England. This man weeps. I reach out, touch his tears, taste them. They are salty. They are real. 'England?' I say, and my voice surprises me. I have not heard it for months or years, or perhaps it is only hours. It is husky and sounds like a nutmeg grater. 'What is England?'

26

IN PURSUIT OF A PINEAPPLE

Summer 1728, London

(Mary)

In May I received news that would once have gladdened me – Frances was to return to England from her exile in France and be free of her reprehensible husband. But the circumstances of her repatriation were far from happy, for her melancholy condition had worsened to such a degree that she had been declared a lunatic. This matter of Frances's insanity brought with it certain complications for those of us who were deemed to be sane.

First was the lunacy itself. It was a label commonly affixed to any woman who failed to comply with her husband's every wish. A man might be a lunatic and yet preside over a joint-stock company, or be a physician or lawyer, or sit in the House of Lords, and yet never have that name affixed to his person nor his rights to behave as his madness demanded in any way curtailed. A woman might weep from time to time or express a view a little too forcefully and be declared out of her wits and hauled before a court of law. My first task would therefore be to make every effort to bring my sister back to health, as I had succeeded in doing those eight weeks she was in London in the summer of twenty-four.

If Fanny was truly ill, then it would be my solemn duty to do all I could to protect her from the insatiable appetites of her husband's family. Those not disgraced and exiled were living in Scotland beyond their means and would be eager to gain control of my sister so they might possess her income – a much easier matter once she was on British soil and under their guardianship. James Erskine, the Lord Grange – Mar's brother – had been permitted by the king to purchase his exiled brother's estate in return for payment of one thousand pounds annually to my sister, and I had little doubt she would not see a penny of that were she to fall under Erskine's influence. He would spirit her away to Scotland and place her in a damp garret until she rotted away. But to resist them would require a fight, and I was only half ready for one.

Fanny was brought to London by her daughter, Frannie, whom I saw straight away to be a spirited girl, eager to find some place of safety for her mother, for being a girl of thirteen and having to care for such a troubled mama is a burden very great to bear.

When my sister entered my home at Cavendish Square she seemed for a moment to know me. Her face, so drawn and thin and grey, flared as a candle flame does in the moment before it dies, but her features seemed then to fall into vacancy. *Do not leave me!* I wanted to scream at her, but instead I took her in my arms and held her close, and though she did not respond, I told her again and again that I loved her and promised to make her well.

Turning to Frannie, my eyes wet with tears, I asked whether the journey had been very arduous for them both.

'The journey has been tolerable, thank you, Aunt. And Mama has not had one of her fits.'

'Fits?'

'Mostly she is quiet, like this, and sometimes calm and able to speak of the weather or dinner or such like. But other times, if something upsets her, she can begin to moan and sometimes even scream very loudly.'

'Oh, you poor dear,' I said to Frannie, embracing her in turn, but she was almost as impassive as her mother.

'We are all used to her, Aunt,' she said matter-of-factly, and I understood then that to her own daughter my sister had become little more than a difficulty to be managed.

'What things upset her?' I asked, thinking this would be useful intelligence.

'Oh, almost anything. And then again nothing at all. A bird flying into a window is certain to set her screaming. And if my father were to raise his voice, that does it, though also sometimes if he is kind to her. And lily of the valley. That makes her cry out most terribly, though none of us knows why.'

My sister observed her daughter as she spoke without any display of emotion, nor even comprehension. How cruel this was. Fanny had been much improved when she'd last left London – not quite herself, but well enough. I had made her swear to me that she would stand up to Mar and fight for herself. Yet she had not possessed the strength, and perhaps never had. And I knew now why our father had seemed to favour such an ill-starred match, for he had seen when I had not how Fanny truly loved Mar. How dare Mar do this to her! And how dare a man – any man – rob me of my own sister!

Knowing that I must not show my upset, I thought I should try to speak to Fanny as if she were not so obviously stricken by her terrible malady. 'Would you care for some tea, dear Frances?'

'Tea?' she repeated.

'Yes, tea is always good for the spirits.'

'Spirits?' she repeated.

'Warming and sweet.'

'Sweet?'

Wondering if she would simply repeat whatever I uttered next, I said, 'Or perhaps you would care for a pineapple?'

To my great surprise Fanny declared, brightly, 'I should like a pineapple very much, Mary.'

I was therefore obliged to send the housekeeper out in pursuit of a pineapple, at whatever cost. By the time Mrs Simmons returned, red in the face and peeved at being obliged to procure the fruit at a price equivalent to two years of her wage, Frances had forgotten her desire for the extravagant fruit, and asked only for a glass of warm milk.

'We shall have to hire out the pineapple, madam,' said Mrs Simmons firmly, not in a mood for contradiction.

'Very well, Mrs Simmons.'

My ready agreement seemed to cheer her. 'Cook will know of plenty of houses near by that will be glad to hire it at ten shillings a time,' she said. 'In that way it will make back some of what it cost before it rots.'

'But that we might all,' I said unthinkingly before noticing Mrs Simmons' expression of stern disapproval, making me realize what I had implied.

I turned to Frances, expecting her to burst into laughter as she would once have done, and we would have spent the afternoon giggling about the absurdities of the pineapple, and my implication that we might hire ourselves out, too, while fresh enough, but she was as blank as a slab of stone.

In those first weeks, having sent Frannie away with young

Mary to stay with their cousins at Acton, I found that a settled routine of needlework, warm milk, light foods and only the most softly spoken visitors allowed Frances to be a little more herself as she listened with care to conversations, and even sometimes spoke a word or two, though often what she said bore little relation to the matter at hand. Lady Oxford was a regular visitor, a kind and placid friend, who made no demands on Frances beyond asking after her health or commenting on her sewing, which would prompt a nervous smile and often the word *cheese*, which Frances seemed to have always on her lips, not in want of any to eat, but merely for the comfort of the sound. From time to time she became unaccountably distressed without obvious cause, which made me uneasy about leaving her in the care of the servants, and so my own social life became engirdled by my sister's affliction.

Having withstood the attacks of Alexander Pope, remorseless as the volleys of arrows released by the English archers at Agincourt, I was used to being portrayed in journals and pamphlets as dangerous, scheming and despicable, and so was well aware that James Erskine, Frances's brother-in-law, had begun to place stories about my seeking to use my sister's money for my own ends. The tale of the pineapple gained wide circulation – that I had indulged in such great extravagances with the assurance of Frances's thousand a year. It is a simple truth that people such as the Erskines could not comprehend that a woman might wish for her sister to have control of her own money for her own good, instead of being eager to put it at the disposal of her male relatives so they might fund their schemes such as new fountains on their estates or tables at the best gaming houses in the city.

Each hour I spent with dear Fanny convinced me more than ever that she was beyond recovery. My love for my sister did not diminish, but grew beyond all measure, for now she needed my protection as never before, and though hatred is a terrible thing to carry in one's heart, I found my hatred for the Erskines grew until I could barely contain it.

I soon received word that James Erskine was in London, seeing lawyers and consulting with judges. He was preparing a legal suit to win custody of Frances, and this obliged me to begin the wearying process of preparing a case in my sister's defence.

Erskine visited me one afternoon in July. It was a typical summer's day, a light drizzle making the roses droop and washing all the colour from the street beyond the windows. It was the kind of day that tempts one into the park and then scorns one for being so impudent as to imagine it might be a pleasant experience.

The man presented himself with a bow. 'Lady Mary, I shall ever be grateful that you have been so kind as to accommodate me this afternoon, and on behalf of my brother, and my niece and nephew, it is my honour to offer you our profound gratitude that you have given dear Frances a home these past weeks,' he declared, once more bowing, this time so low that his full-bottomed wig slipped forward and he was obliged to rise quickly and return it to its customary position.

I stood facing him, anticipating what he was to say next. He remained silent, waiting for some polite utterance that I was unwilling to give.

'May I see my sister-in-law?' he asked eventually.

'You may not, Lord Grange, for she is easily distressed,

and I am perfectly certain that the sight of you will cause her great anguish.'

'She barely knows me.'

'Precisely.'

'I must point out, madam, that I have every right to see my own kin.'

'I must point out, sir, that you have no such right, and she is not your kin, merely a relation by marriage. An unfortunate marriage, and an unfortunate relation.'

His rising fury was plain to see in the reddening of his face, but he showed admirable self-possession in maintaining a calm manner. 'I cannot agree with your description of matters, madam, but then again disagreement is where we stand in all things, I suspect. I act on my brother's – your sister's husband's – wishes to—'

'I am well aware of who your brother is,' I interrupted, 'and his relation to you, and to my sister and, for that matter, to the very devil himself.'

'Really, madam!' he snapped, before once more regaining his composure. 'I come merely to make clear that I am obliged to act upon my brother's wishes and ensure that Frances is brought under charge of law, and shall be given into the care of her family in Scotland, where I assure you she will be cared for without regard to any consideration but her own welfare.'

I laughed, though I should not have done. 'She would be cared for there as Sunday's leftover dinner is attended to by a hungry household on a Monday. She would be consumed by you Erskines little by little, or more probably in great gulps, and there would be not a thing left of her but a strand of her hair and a slipper.'

'Really, this is too much, madam!' he protested, his voice rising. 'We are not cannibals!'

'Oh, but cannibals,' I said steadily, 'is precisely what you are. There is only a little of her left, and that little I shall tend until my dying day so that she does not suffer more.'

'You will live to regret your manner today, Lady Mary.'

I rang for the footman and had James Erskine, the Lord Grange, seen out into the blustery street, though he needed little encouragement to bring our conference to its conclusion.

I knew that I would have to act quickly if I was to avoid Erskine outmanoeuvring me in the courts. I went to speak to Lord Carstairs, a friend of Edward and a presiding judge at Chancery, who had particular expertise in determining cases of lunacy, which were more common than seemed reasonable and almost always brought in cases of wives who had become troublesome to their husbands. Lord Carstairs advised me to have Frances live in her home at Knightsbridge, which she had inherited from our late father. He further urged me to have her attended by a household of her own servants and, being aware of my disapproval of the quackery of the medical profession, recommended the services of Dr Richard Hale, a physician of enlightened sensibility, a great expert in treating insanity, and who was known never to restrain or starve his patients, but instead was inclined in the direction of sedatives to calm them. In this manner Erskine's suit that I was keeping my sister unduly under my control could be resisted successfully, he assured me, and Dr Hale would be able to testify as to her condition, and to the care I had shown for her.

I followed Lord Carstairs' advice and was pleased to find my sister soon settled in her own quarters, if little changed in her general lunacy, which I was bound to concede, with a sadness that sat upon my heart with the weight of all the world, was her true condition. She would sit in silence for two or three hours, followed by an hour or more of screaming. But the servants understood that they needed only to ensure my sister came to no harm, that she ate and drank a little, and took whatever medicine Dr Hale prescribed for her.

Yet after only two weeks of this new arrangement I had cause to regret it. I had just returned from an evening concert, and my maid was undressing me when Mrs Simmons presented herself, her manner like a startled hen, which was essentially her manner always.

'Your sister has been seen at Barnet, my lady.'

'My sister?'

'The very same.'

'At Barnet?'

'Barnet,' she confirmed, as if it was a place so disreputable that this would be the last time she would utter its name.

'But I saw her only this morning at Knightsbridge, Mrs Simmons. Why would she have cause to go to Barnet?'

'She was heard screaming.'

'At Barnet?'

'Screaming at . . . at that place, yes.'

Since poor Frances regularly took to screaming without cause or warning, that in itself was not alarming, but I could not think why she would have gone to Barnet. I searched my mind for any significance to the place, before recalling that Frances's good friend Mrs Murray, who had also once been my friend until Pope persuaded her that I had betrayed her trust in some way, had family there. On further consideration I realized Mrs Murray was also known to Erskine. I threw off my maid, who was fiddling at my hair, stood, pulled on a sack dress and shouted for the chaise. 'It is past midnight, my lady!' declared Mrs Simmons.

'A chaise is capable of running even at night,' I assured her.

Soon I was out on the road and had taken the precaution, given the hour, of having Lamrock, once engaged as my husband's manservant, but lately become mine, to ride beside the coachman. Barnet was far off and we were all too likely to attract the attention of brigands, not that I was wearing any jewels or, indeed, stays or stockings. It was most liberating to be out on a summer's night being driven at speed, unconstrained by a bodice. Indeed, I was in possession of nothing but the force of my indignation, for I felt a growing certainty that Fanny was in the process of being kidnapped. But a problem occurred to me, and we were not far into Hyde Park when I realized that if indeed Erskine was behind this, I would need to prove that I had the law on my side. 'Stop!' I shouted at the coachman, who brought the two horses quickly to a juddering halt. He turned, the expression on his face one of unmistakeable insolence. 'M'lady?' he said, as if I were a troublesome infant.

'We must first go to Lincoln's Inn Fields.'

'Very well,' he said wearily. He turned the horses, and we headed for the home of Judge Carstairs, who I felt sure would not be pleased to be stirred from his bed.

Lamrock tapped at the heavy wooden door with the discretion only a manservant knows, murmured some words to the night footman and within five minutes I was sat in the judge's parlour before the last embers of a fire. Thankfully the good judge saw the urgency of the need for a warrant and, no less, the grounds for my state of undress, and after insisting that I take a brandy with him while he drew up the paperwork ordering Lady Mar to be returned to London *in statu quo*, I was able to resume the journey to Barnet a little before dawn. We arrived there to find that my sister had left only an hour before us, accompanied by her daughter and her stepson, who was an Erskine through and through and no doubt part of the scheme. Although Mrs Murray had regrettably become my implacable enemy, her parents, a kindly old couple, were unaware and guilelessly told me all: that Frances was being taken to Erskine's estate at Alloa for the Scottish air, which was said to be so marvellous in relieving lunacy. They kindly told me that I would be able to meet the party at Stevenage, where they were to stay the night with Lord and Lady Whempstead.

We rode on at noon and were at Lord Whempstead's before six, our arrival noticed immediately since the party knew full well they were fugitives on the run, and like all fugitives were eager to keep an eye out the window and listen for the sound of wheels upon gravel. We were therefore greeted by three footmen, a butler, the housekeeper, Lord Whempstead and the renegade little party comprising: my dear sister, who had colour in her cheeks and seemed cheerful if uncomprehending; her unpleasant stepson; Frannie, who had presumably thought herself on an adventure; Mrs Murray, who regarded me with distaste yet also unease; and James Erskine, the Lord Grange, who to his credit looked sheepish.

'Lady Mary. You come alone?' he said.

Did he think to overpower me? 'I hazard you would kidnap me along with my sister, but for the fact that your party must already struggle to squeeze into your coach, sir!'

'Oh, madam,' he said with a sad chuckle, 'it is not a kidnap.'

'That it may not be, sir, but I have here a warrant signed by Lord Carstairs for the return of my sister to London.'

Being a legal man, Grange stepped forward to take the warrant from my hand, though I would not permit him to place a finger upon it and presented it for him to read while

I held it at a sufficient distance from his grasp. I did not know Lord Whempstead, but he stood on the portico, witnessing the remarkable drama being played out on his doorstep with bafflement. I was by then renowned, and if my face was not known by all, my name most certainly was, which presumably explained Whempstead's plain fascination with me. Lord Grange may have wanted to play me, but he knew he would have to observe the rules of the game. 'The warrant is in order, madam,' he declared, as if it was his place to sum up its authority. 'Lady Mar shall be returned to London. Would you be agreeable to her spending the night here?'

'I would not,' I said, 'but I shall speak with Lord Whempstead, if I may.'

Whempstead bowed and gestured to me to approach him. What I required was fresh horses, and a carriage and coachman, since I could hardly ask more of my exhausted groom. Lamrock would return with my sister and me on a coach provided by Lord Whempstead who, as I expected, granted my request with good grace. I gave my niece leave to return with us, but she declined, having high hopes of continuing her adventure even in the absence of her mother, who was due a spell of screaming which, sure enough, began at Knebworth and continued as far as Hatfield.

Frances seemed immune to the disturbances of the past few days as I put her into her own bed in Knightsbridge and, as happened every day or two, she knew me for a few minutes: 'Mary?' she said, just before I blew out the candle.

'My dearest?'

'Why were they taking me so far?'

'Your brother-in-law wanted you in Scotland, Fanny, for the air.'

'Air is good though, isn't it?'

'Oh yes. Aristotle told us so. Even if we cannot get you the air of Mount Olympus, I shall get you out into the country air at Twickenham once we have all these legal questions resolved, and then you shall be well.'

'Am I not well?'

'Not wholly well, my dear, no. But we shall get you well, with good air. And we shall go riding together.'

'You always say riding cures all ills.'

'I do! I do!' I declared, so pleased that she had remembered my prescription for good health and the combat of melancholy.

'You really are full of horseshit, Mary. I always thought so.'

I withdrew my hand, not meaning to, but it seemed a reaction over which I had no more control than blinking. Did she really think so little of me? I reminded myself of her lunacy. 'Well, perhaps,' I said, gently, 'all mere mortals are full of horseshit, my dear, though some of us conceal the fact better than others.'

'Yes,' she said, satisfied with my explanation, and to my great joy she fell into a deep sleep with a smile upon her face, which I gazed upon for a good long while before blowing out the candle.

The next step was to arrange for a lunacy inquisition, since it was only by having my sister declared insane in law that she could be protected from the Erskines. The weather changed from cool and blustery into a hot, still August, the streets lying in a putrid torpor, the smell of excrement like a solid wall at every open window. I longed to go to Twickenham and take Frances with me, but legal matters consumed my every hour.

First came the petition for a commission of lunacy. This was held at the home of the Lord Chancellor, with Lord Grange having the services of the Solicitor General, Mr Talbot, and myself having the Attorney General, Mr Fisher, to put my side of the case. My role was to keep quiet, which caused me no little distress, but so long as Lord Grange did not speak I resolved that neither would I. The argument put to the Lord Chancellor by Talbot was that Mar had sent his wife from France intending her to be put into the hands of his brother, Grange, for her welfare. This was revealing of the widespread view that women, once ensnared in a marriage contract, were possessions to be placed wherever they might generate the most income.

'It is also the case, my lord,' continued Talbot, 'that it is more proper for Lady Mar to be in Scotland. She is married to a Scot and is therefore a Scotch person.'

I felt I would explode if I had to remain quiet much longer but contained myself.

'Lady Mar has lucid intervals and has expressed such a wish herself,' he continued.

She had not, I felt sure, or if she had it was with no more purpose than her constant repetition of her desire for cheese.

'No commission of lunacy may be granted,' Talbot asserted, 'for the king's custody of the body of an idiot cannot apply; instead she should be found a guardian under Scots law.'

My man Fisher then made his argument, seeming not to challenge the various gross lies uttered by Talbot, who was of course his friend. Indeed, we were all friends in that chamber, or had to pretend to be, for such are the obligations of class, and the fiction of being *Lord This* and *Lady That*. Titles are thought – by those who do not possess them – to be wonderful gowns that one may dress oneself in and remove at will. Instead they are brands, seared on to us by the hot iron of birth and visible to all; they mark us as surely as burnt flesh, and stop us from being free while permitting us only that which is not worth having. I sat in that chamber, Grange's pale eyes upon me, and wished only to flee, to comfort my dear sister and beg her to be what she had once been.

'The simple fact,' said Fisher, 'is that His Majesty the King appointed the house in which Lady Frances presently resides for her use on her return to England, and given there is no dispute that Lady Mar is not in her right senses, the case for a commission of lunacy to proceed, and to proceed in the place – or as close to it as may be – as the king has decreed, is irresistible.'

Of course! That was why Judge Carstairs had insisted that I place Fanny in her own home. And thus it was that the Lord Chancellor concluded in my favour, though only after some weeks and a further hearing, since the law must be seen to proceed with unhurried dignity.

I was appointed guardian to my sister and, after further negotiation with the Erskine family, who made the bargaining skills of the most wily trader in Constantinople's Grand Bazaar seem feeble and yielding by comparison, I obtained from them five hundred a year for her care, half of the sum granted to her by the king for the sale of Mar's estate, and her own fortune remained hers for use at such time as she regained her senses.

I had won, but how bittersweet was that victory. The sister I had loved since the day she was born, and whose company I had always longed for, was lost to me, her presence like a book with leather binding, a gold-embossed title of infinite promise, which, when opened, revealed only blank page after blank page.

I went to see her every day, and sometimes her face would brighten at my arrival, and we would talk a while. She liked a day when clouds scudded across the sky, and on those we would stand at the window and imagine what the shape of each cloud was – a dragon, a mule, a face, or a ship. But on other days she would only weep, and when I had spent an hour with her, I would go home to Cavendish Square and I would weep too. I sometimes feared that lunacy was a contagion and that I was surely succumbing to it.

27

MONSIEUR VOLTAIRE

Autumn 1728, London

(Mary)

My despair at my sister's distress was only compounded by Pope's attacks upon me, which grew ever more vicious. He belittled me, sullied my reputation, implied that I was loose in my affections, was not only pocked but poxed, and portrayed me as Sappho. Though I admired Sappho, I knew what it was he intended by bestowing that title upon me. No doubt he wished me to retaliate, and yet with each provocation I became more determined to forbear. I knew that if I was to reclaim my standing as a poet and *penseuse* I would have to do so through other sources. Who better, then, than a French intellectual whose talents were so great that he had sought refuge from his homeland?

It was at a dinner at my friend John Hervey's that the promising young French poet and playwright Monsieur Voltaire and I were introduced, and after the usual formalities we fell into lively and rewarding conversation. He told me that he was writing a series of essays on the English and wished me to read what he described as his 'clumsy first drafts'.

'I am surely ill qualified, monsieur,' I protested, as one is obliged to say when invited to do something one wishes to do very much. I knew he would ask others – Pope, no doubt, and Swift – but I trusted that my opinion would be of more use to him than theirs.

'I have it on the very best authority, madam,' he said, 'that you are the most intelligent woman in England. And since a woman's intelligence is always likely to be greater than a man's—'

'Really? Why?' I interrupted, fearing he was likely to say something about rarity or preciousness, which would have been enough to make me hate him.

His lips gradually curved into a smile. 'The female intellectual is no rarer than the male, but since men like to think it is only they who possess intellect, the woman who is acknowledged by the society of men for her brains has been obliged to earn the accolade a thousand times over.' He spoke English perfectly, though with a sibilant hiss, which he claimed was the result not of the bad habits of French pronunciation, but of missing front teeth.

How often was a man thought a genius for saying one wise or witty phrase, and yet a woman in the same conversation could say something infinitely wiser and wittier and be asked where she had heard such a thing, as if she must have stolen it from a brother or husband. 'A good reply, monsieur,' I acknowledged. 'You have escaped my disapproval with a duck and a weave and are perfectly unscathed.'

The next day I received from him a package containing three essays, written in English, that seemed both too good to be his, because fluent and witty and idiomatically correct, and yet also not good enough since they lacked the lyrical manner of his French. It was almost as if, in swapping his musical tongue for our deeply practical one, he had sacrificed his own tune. In content the essays were deceptive: some men stoop to flatter or charm, but Voltaire praised England by affectionately ridiculing it. He was fascinated by our tolerance of religious dissent, and there were moments in the essays when he seemed close to describing England as something of a paradise of reason and freedom, yet humour redeemed his words again and again, for he surely knew there were beggars starving on the streets, and mothers too soaked in gin to feed their infants. And no doubt he knew too that while parliament debated matters freely, each member guarded his own interests with no less vigour than the French nobles did theirs. I resolved to speak to him about these matters when we met for a supper, tête-à-tête, that evening.

'You think my English both too good, and yet not good enough?' he said, amused and yet a little insulted when I told him my opinion of what he had sent me.

'It is better than almost any Englishman would write, yet it seems somehow not yours,' I explained.

He smiled without concealing his sense of injury. 'Perhaps every man and woman who speaks in a language not their own sacrifices a part of themselves to acquire that new tongue, as a bull which is made into a bullock is made both fat and docile. And perhaps,' he continued, carried along by his own argument, 'words and thoughts are so much the same thing that our very ideas are changed when we must find new words to express them?'

'It is why I prefer to write in French,' I said, 'since I always feel more erudite speaking and writing in your language than in my own.'

'And why I prefer to write in English,' he replied, 'because it is both inexact and yet certain, and so more capable of surprise.'

'You make it sound untrustworthy.'

He chewed thoughtfully on a piece of pompion pie, before declaring, 'The English *are* untrustworthy, I think, or their words are, at least. To the French most certainly. Barely a Frenchman alive has been stirred to do what I have done and learn to speak the English language. The French believe that you English are pagans, since you have invented your own church, one that allows you to worship your king, though instead of worshipping him you ridicule him. And the French torture disbelievers for apostasy, whereas you instal them as your bankers. You make treaties with the firm intention of breaking them as soon as an opportune moment arises. I do not disapprove, you understand, I merely observe.' He smiled his twinkly smile and patted his thin lips with a corner of his napkin.

'If England is so perfidious, then what is France?'

He considered the question, searching for the exact term. 'Disdainful, and in its disdain for the world France imperils itself, for it has become lazy and slow and, like a man who has had too many pleasures in life, barely notices that it has slid into impotence.' He gave a startled laugh at the comparison he had drawn. 'Forgive me!'

'I assure you, monsieur, that no woman is shocked by the notion of an impotent man. Indeed, for many of us it is a relief.'

He did not laugh but looked at me quizzically, as if wondering whether this might in fact be true.

'And is it really the case that so few Frenchmen and -women learn English?' I asked. It seemed improbable, but then again I could not think of any French person I knew who had gone to the trouble of learning our language apart from the man sitting before me. Any educated Englishman – or -woman – most certainly learnt to speak French to a tolerably good degree.

'The works of Milton, Pope, Swift are hardly known,' he declared. And then, more enthusiastically, he added: 'I shall translate them all!'

'Pope might not be worth the trouble,' I grumbled, unable to help myself.

Voltaire frowned. 'I know of your dispute with Mr Alexander Pope.'

'His with me, I should say.'

He gestured airily, as if to wave away my objection. 'Disputes between two such distinguished people are impossible to assign, any more than the chicken is the egg's and the egg the chicken's.'

I made no attempt to press my point. I had hopes that Voltaire, being friendly with Pope and Swift as well as with my own ever-shrinking circle of allies, might work to bring peace between us.

'But how do I explain Shakespeare?' he asked. 'He is so violent, so unformed, so . . . rude!'

'Shakespeare is about character above all else,' I answered, feeling on firmer ground. 'About human frailty in all: kings and peasants. It is why we English think him great. He tells our history and our love stories, but is bawdy, too, and so his work is for everybody. You can see his play one day at Drury Lane and the next out in the street in some town a hundred miles from London. There will be a crowd of farmhands and washerwomen, old men and children, and they will stand in the rain for two hours and laugh and cry and go back to their poor dwellings and think they have seen kings and fools and storms at sea and magic too. Can Molière claim that? Can you?'

Voltaire thought carefully before he spoke. 'Molière perhaps,' he said softly, 'but few others. Myself, no. But should my ambition be to become like Shakespeare? I do not think the French will ever take to such a chaotic style.'

'You must only be yourself,' I said, reaching across the table and taking his hand, since he seemed in want of reassurance.

'I cannot translate Shakespeare. People will think me mad!'

'They may think you mad anyway, my dear Monsieur Voltaire. To be thought mad is the price we pay for thinking things anew. There is no risk in speaking and doing and writing as everyone else does and has done always. But there is hazard in speaking the truth, and the only reward lies in that other life, which is not lived in heaven but in the minds and hearts of others long after we are food for worms.'

We talked more that evening about the need for originality and courage in what we wrote, before Voltaire came at last to what he had wanted to ask me about all along, which was the practice of inoculation against the smallpox. He demanded an account of every detail, of what I had first witnessed in Turkey, of the engrafting of Eddie, and of little Mary, and my persuading the queen, who was then Princess of Wales, to have her daughters engrafted. We talked so long that the candles burnt down and I sent the servants to their beds, and at dawn I went down myself to the kitchen and made Voltaire a breakfast of eggs. Before he left, the air fresh as it is so early in the day, even in summer, I asked him at the door, 'Do you only admire the English so you may attack the French, monsieur?'

'Not only, Lady Mary, but also,' he said, skipping down the steps. 'Also!'

Not long after, another parcel of Voltaire's words arrived for my comment. This time he had written about the most intelligent woman in England and her work in encouraging the practice of inoculation, that woman being none other than myself. I wrote back quickly with a few small corrections, though I doubted he would find anyone to publish these *Lettres Philosophiques*, as he chose to call them. It was my strong suspicion that Monsieur Voltaire's career as a writer would be all too brief since he was determined to espouse views sure to infuriate all. He was a man for another time – somewhere in the future, when war would be thought absurd, religion a matter of private belief instead of public ceremony, and a woman might be a minister or ambassador. Despite my misgivings, I felt that I owed him my good judgement and perhaps the courtesy of at least one more breakfast of eggs.

28

EVERY TIDE MUST TURN

Summer 1736, London

(Mary)

Years passed, Eddie troublesome and kept out of England through bribes and much pleading, Pope's vitriol against me a bottomless well, Edward's political career stalled but his mines doing well enough, and my own health inconstant to the point of treachery.

I had been a week in bed with a fever, Lamrock these days both manservant and chambermaid and lately physician, too, so attentive was he in his care, so quiet, so discreet he was hardly there at all. And for the first time Death spoke to me.

DEATH: *A fat crow, feathers unclean, beak with scraps of flesh hanging from it.* You are old, and you are alone, and you shall never love again, nor be loved.

I: I am not yet fifty. I have friends. I have children and a husband. I have a sister whom I love. I am not alone.

DEATH: Your enemies outnumber your friends. Those few friends you have Pope peels from you one by one, like pelts from rabbits. Your daughter dislikes you, and you her. Your son is a rake and a scoundrel, and shames you. Your husband stays away from you, and you from him. Your sister is in Scotland, and you shall never see her again. You are too old to love or be loved. You are ready for me. *Pecks.*

I: You think I am afraid to be alone, but I have always been alone. I do not fear you, and because I do not fear you any longer, I am free. I shall leave this country and go where you shall not find me!

LAMROCK: Madam?

I: *Seeing the room, myself, my bed, my servant.* Lamrock?

LAMROCK: *Mopping my brow with a cool flannel.* You have been in a delirium, madam. But I believe your fever has broken.

I: What things was I saying, Lamrock?

LAMROCK: *Coy.* No words, madam, but that you were free.

As I grew well, I recalled what Death had said to me, and felt more and more that what I had heard in my delirium was the truth. Frances's daughter, Frannie, had remained in Alloa, and on reaching twenty-one became my sister's guardian and took her from me. But there was a mercy in it, for Fanny never was truly well again, and I believe her daughter really did care for her. My guardianship had, at least, seen my sister outlive her odious husband and witnessed her brother-in-law James Erskine's disgrace, firstly for incarcerating his own wife, and then for his vehement opposition to the Witchcraft Act, a most sensible piece of legislation that made witchcraft a fraud, not a sin. But Erskine believed fervently in the satanic power of witches, and he was now regarded as even more of a lunatic than his poor sister-in-law, though being a man had not been dragged before a court to declare him so. I persuaded myself that Fanny might live happily enough on that rain-swept estate.

Edward and I lived in perfect estrangement. We corresponded regularly, and always politely and often even cooperatively, most especially when it came to managing the contrasting affairs of our two children. Eddie was now living in Leiden, studying Arabic though in fact spending his time gambling, whoring and amassing debts so considerable that it would take several fortunes to clear them. He threatened every so often to come to England, and my task was to dissuade him from doing so, and to keep him in his place with bills good for fifty pounds or a hundred, just enough to keep him out of gaol. He had married, so we heard, a woman ten years his senior, an innkeeper's daughter. I doubted much adventure lay in her direction.

Mary was, by contrast, good and honourable but quite astonishingly dull, and had found a man who suited her, John Stuart, the Earl of Bute. Edward and I opposed the match on the sensible grounds that he was a Scot and a Tory, two considerations that did not bode well for our family. And yet, in the only daring thing Mary ever did, she eloped with him. She will not speak to me, and so I am obliged not to speak to her, and in such manner Death is not wrong: my children are a thing apart from me.

As for Pope, he does more than turn my friends against me, he writes poisonous verses about any person I love, and makes that person think them written by me. Voltaire is long ago returned to France, his attentions absorbed by the

Marquise du Châtelet, and he cannot concern himself with peace-making here in London. It is only those who are immune to Pope's lies, whether by means of intelligence or grace or a loyalty I barely deserve, who remain my friends. These include, mercifully, Her Majesty the Queen, and also Lord Hervey, who is out of favour with all, but not with me, nor I with him. We are like shipwrecked souls, adrift on a raft.

I had given up all hope of love. I did not seek it, nor even believe I wanted it. And as so often in life, what one has desired above all things arrives only when one has ceased desiring it. I had been expecting to dine with John Hervey alone and offer him solace, for he had been obliged to withstand the marriage of his great love, Stephen Fox, to Elizabeth Horner, a girl of thirteen. Since I was by then expert in love's many losses, I considered myself well qualified in the art of consolation. But on being shown into the dining room, who should be seated at the table but a creature so glorious that the sight of him made me gasp. The young man jumped to his feet, approached me as lightly as a cat upon a narrow branch, bowed low and placed lips upon the back of my hand – lips that were charged with a current of some force that confounded me. He looked up and declared, '*La Bellissima Signora Maria!*'

So shaken was I by this unexpected encounter, and by the melting away of years of disappointment, betrayal and grief, that I simply stared at the creature. He looked at me with eyes which, though a deep brown, made me think of Anne in their warmth and intelligence, and said in a sing-song Italian accent: 'Lady Mary, I have read all your work, and Lord Hervey has told me of your great loyalty to him. You must know that you are admired all across Europe and . . .'

I did something I never imagined I would do. I placed a finger upon his lips – female lips, not male, with beautiful cupid's bow. 'Ssssh. Ssssh,' I said. 'Who are you?'

'My name is Francesco Algarotti, and I am here to declare my love for you.'

Hervey, who had been watching our meeting with all the satisfaction of a matron introducing a spinster daughter to an eligible widower, clapped his hands and bid us take our places. As ever the fare was of vegetables and mushrooms and such like served with light sauces, for Hervey could not abide the sight of meat or fish. We talked with such animation about all manner of things: Algarotti's work, for he was well advanced in translating Newton's *Principia* into Italian; Voltaire's *Lettres Philosophiques*, and the French propensity to burn any book that was worth reading. We talked of opera and music; of Michelangelo's *David* and Botticelli's *Venus*; of platonic love and Greek love; of Padua and Venice; and of good wine and bad gin. In short, we talked of everything, and I felt that night as if I was not with friends but with spirits I had known long before I was ever born and whom I would know long after I was dead. When it was time to leave, well past three o'clock, Algarotti held my hand tight, and pulled me to him in a close embrace such as I had enjoyed with no man since Nathaniel Shaw, for my husband never embraced me with such fervour. The young Italian and I vowed to see each other the very next day.

Over the weeks that followed Algarotti and I went about together to the opera, to cards, to friends and acquaintances, and he charmed all in equal measure, bestowing his sweet looks and great intelligence upon all. Since he was young enough to be my son, I told all that I was Algarotti's patron, and had taken it upon myself to show him the sights of London. I thought it unlikely I would be able to dispel all danger of gossip and speculation but did my best when we were in public to treat him much as I would a nephew, which pained me for my whole being flushed with desire for him. I longed to caress him, but had to make do with small gestures, a hand on his elbow, a light adjustment to his collar, and each time I did I felt a charge of some force, surely the stuff the very stars are made of, and trusted that Algarotti did, too. He played along with our display most honourably, never revealing that bond that I felt perfectly certain was forming between us.

When days came that he and I could not be together the hours dragged most terribly. If I went riding or to a concert, I would imagine I saw Francesco at a distance, and my heart raced until I drew near only to see that it was some other young man. I slept fitfully, and if my dreams were of him, I awoke with a smile, and yearned that I might turn to see his angelic face lying there beside me.

I knew that I was possessed by a fever, and the delirium it gave me was no less perilous than those others I had suffered and barely survived. When one day John Hervey came to my door at a time when I had told him to call, I saw before me not Hervey but Algarotti standing there in my hallway, and my heart raced for I knew this was the moment I would declare my love for him. Just before I spoke the words, the young Italian's form resolved into the less pleasing one of Hervey. 'Oh, it's you,' I said, my dismay unconcealed.

'It is I, calling as you bid me to, madam.'

'Yes, yes . . . of course,' I said, pretending to some disturbance in the household that had made me forget about our appointment.

Hervey was as clever a man as any in Europe, and sensitive to my moods and desires. Once we had settled in the drawing room, he pressed me. 'I do believe you are enamoured with our young friend.'

'You mean Signor Algarotti?'

'I do not mean the Duc d'Orléans.'

'He is very charming, yes,' I said, fluttering like a dowager aunt.

Hervey was not to be deflected. He gave me the insolent smile of an interrogator who knows that he has cornered his suspect. 'You have fallen for his handsome looks and clever tongue.'

'I like him a good deal, and I confess that in all probability I like him better than is good for me. Are you going to warn me that I am making a fool of myself, or to tell me that he has told you that he thinks me a terrible, pockmarked old lady?'

Hervey's manner changed then from that of interrogator to the true friend he was. 'My dear Mary. He has said no such thing. We have talked of you, and he feels for you that deep admiration and affection that I feel too.'

There are times when deep admiration and affection are as much as one can reasonably expect from any man or woman. And there are other times when they are as good as insults. I smiled uneasily.

'But admiration and affection are not enough with Francesco, are they?' continued Hervey. 'You need him – you want him, body and soul.'

I would have not permitted any other to speak to me as Hervey did, but we spoke often of love, and of its many forms, and I confessed to him that my desires were as he suspected. 'I have spent all my life seeking true love, John, and not yet found it. Am I hopeless in thinking it still possible for me to stumble into heaven in the arms of some other?'

'You are not, Mary. We must all think love is possible, for if there is no love then what else is there?'

'Only death, and for me those two angels arrive always together. I fear that if I love Algarotti he will be the cause of my death – or I his.'

'I assure you our friend's affections are ardent, and generous.'

I heard John Hervey say what I wanted him to say, without quite grasping what he meant me to understand.

I wrote to Edward to tell him that I had taken young Algarotti as my protégé, showing him London, making introductions and assisting him in his writing. I told my husband that I felt protective of the young man, and although I was aware I was not being wholly honest, nor was I being wholly dishonest, as I knew how easily young men could take the wrong path. I thought of my son. Young Eddie was mired in scandal, sunk in debt, living now in Holland with a woman who was not his wife, or so we were told, he having swiftly abandoned the woman he had married.

I imagined I had taken sufficient care in the manner in which I spoke publicly of Algarotti, and in my comportment when we were out together, that I had kept scandal at bay. Even Pope had not issued one of his barbs for a while. Imagine my surprise when I received a letter from my daughter, newly married in far-off Scotland.

Mount Stuart
Isle of Bute
5 September 1736

Dearest Mama,

It is not the place of a daughter to urge discretion upon a mother, and I feel certain you would uphold this principle with no less determination than would I, if the circumstances were other than they are. I do not hear all the rumours and lies that are commonplace in London here on this Scottish isle. Indeed, I hear barely anything at all. But there has been a great clamour of late, and of such volume that it has reached as far as this place, and no doubt far beyond. It is that a woman of intelligence and high standing, much admired for her literary accomplishments and no less for her reforming zeal, a woman approaching fifty years of age, has acted imprudently for she has taken as her lover an Italian half her age. I am sure you would warn this woman that she exposes herself to ridicule, and in addition offers her husband, a man of impeccable loyalty and distinction, humiliation.

I shall not name this woman, for I have no need. You know her well and have always her best interests at heart. I beg of you, dear Mama, to make her see reason.

I am ever your faithful and loving daughter,
M

Good God! How had Mary heard of my dalliance with Algarotti? I had been most discreet, and gone about with him only as a friend, a patron, as I was to many a young writer. And yet how typical of Mary to admonish me for being . . . for simply being myself. I read and reread her letter, astonished by the force of her rebuke. She chose to say nothing of married life, or of Bute or of her journey there or of her household. Nor did she speak of her father except to imply he was a party to her rebuke. He had relented in his opposition to her marriage, not without some encouragement from me, and consented to settle an allowance upon them. Indeed, how dare she imagine I had not told Edward all, or something, at least, for that was our pact, to always be honest, and I had told him of Algarotti in my letters, if not everything I felt for him. My husband cared not for my love and understood that it was there to give to others.

And yet.

My daughter's stern, brief letter did give me pause, not for the love I felt for Francesco Algarotti, but for fear that I was indeed possessed by a sort of madness. I thought of dear Fanny, and how she could not see how her love for Mar blinded her to his gross imperfections. Yet what were Algarotti's imperfections? None. He was sweet and clever and obliging. He was affectionate and almost feminine in his charms. He was all that I had ever looked for in a companion, being the best of both man and woman. But did I truly know him? Was there some dark and troubled side to Francesco that I was blind to? I resolved to take my daughter's letter that instant to Hervey, to hand it to him without a word and observe his reaction, much as a moonstone may reveal the wearer's inner thoughts.

I summoned my chair and flew to his quarters at St James's where I entered through the open door and went straight to his chambers to see, to my great delight, not only Hervey but, a little way behind him and peering about his shoulder, dear Algarotti. Both men were stripped to the waist, and had pulled about their loins a bedsheet, so that they looked for all the world like Roman senators.

'Why, my dear friends. I am treated to a very fine display, worthy of being chiselled by Michelangelo himself!' I declared, cheerfully.

Neither seemed to welcome my arrival, which was not greatly surprising as it had been so thoroughly unannounced.

'What brings you here, Mary, and so early?' asked Hervey, somewhat gruffly.

'Is it early?' I asked, only then looking at the clock upon the wall to see it was not yet eight o'clock. 'Where is your footman?'

'Visiting his sick mother.'

'And the under-footman?'

'At church.'

'Is it Sunday?'

'He is Catholic.'

'Have you not so much as a maid at your service today, John?'

'Not so much as that,' he said, smiling, and only then did I notice that he was blushing. 'What brings you here, dear Mary?' he repeated.

'I . . .' I looked at the letter in my hand, but all of a sudden thought how unwelcome it would be for Francesco to read it, and so did not present it to Hervey as I had intended. 'It is nothing. Please forgive me.' I turned to leave, understanding that I would not be invited to stay for a pot of chocolate. I left as I had arrived, unannounced, and only a little chastened. That Hervey and Algarotti were intimate had not escaped me, and that I had disturbed them in their intimacy had given me pause, and yet still I thought that there must be room for me, too, in this triangle of affection.

My daughter's admonishment was not the only one I received, for a few days later I heard, as I did from time to time, from Eleanora, Countess of Pitlochry, who was Nell to me and ever would be.

Grant House
Pitlochry
Perthshire
14 September 1736

Dear Mary,

You are, as ever, much in my thoughts. The leaves are already turning here in Perthshire, and the early mornings carry that chill that portends the winter frosts to come. Yet we are cheerful, and busy about the estate. We have a new schoolmaster, a clever fellow who, like me, was orphaned when but small and brought up by kindly folk and given an education. Intelligence may be found just as easily in those who are born low as high, as I am sure you often told me.

The child you asked after who plays the trumpet so well, we are to send to the Royal Academy where Mr Handel was recently master, for I believe his talent to be prodigious and worthy of encouragement.

Intelligence is one thing, of course, and good judgement another, and reputation another again. One may be well read, learned and yet imprudent. Another may be quite ignorant of the world and yet always give good counsel – a wise fool, as it were. And a reputation is hard to gain and easy to lose. I know all this only because of what you taught me in those years I spent with you. And were I still in your company, and in your service, I would give you counsel, perhaps only as a wise fool could, and tell you that you should take great care of your reputation when it comes to the young Italian gentleman that you mentioned in your last letter, for a pretty fellow is as like as not to be inconstant, and your heart is too good a thing to be placed in such youthful hands.

Forgive me if I have spoken indelicately. I mean only ever to be your loving friend.

Yours affectionately,
Nell

Again, a letter of warning, and delicately put. I went walking in the park, seeking to settle my churning feelings. I saw that I was, indeed, in the grip of madness, driven to it by a creeping loneliness that had impaired my judgement and distorted my feelings. I determined to speak directly to Francesco that night, and to tell him plain how great my feelings were for him, but that because of those feelings I must forbear from seeing him again. It was not the fear of scandal that made me decide thus, but a sense that I was bringing myself, and Algarotti, into danger.

It was time I set my life in London on a different course now that Fanny was no longer my charge. I would put myself once more at the heart of society, set relations with my daughter and – if at all possible – with my son on better terms, and do all that I could to support the ministry of my friend Robert Walpole, who was attacked so bitterly by all out of envy and small-mindedness.

As it happened Francesco did not attend me that evening as he had promised. I wrote to him at his quarters to admonish him for letting me sit before a dinner, a glass of wine warming before me and a hot supper cooling. He arrived, flustered, at five the next afternoon.

'You had another engagement?'

'I did, I am sorry, Maria, that I forgot our own, which was more important to me a thousand times over.'

So he spoke, always. Why did not logic tell me that if his appointment with me had truly been a thousand times more important, he would not have gone instead to another? 'And who was this wholly unimportant person with whom you spent the evening? A princess, perhaps, or an actress?' I touched him lightly upon his chest, and he giggled uneasily.

'I am embarrassed to tell you, for I know how you will disapprove.'

'If you were at a whorehouse I would only counsel you to take care that the girls are clean. Or if at a Molly house the boys cleaner still.'

'Really, Maria. What do you think of me? No, I was invited for supper with Mr Pope.'

'With Pope!'

'You see why I could not tell you of it.' He reached out, took a lock of my hair in his finger and curled it, as only a lover would do.

'But Pope. I hope you did not speak of me. He decries me, demeans me, and turns all my friends against me—'

'Shhh, Maria. He said nothing of you but that you were once a great friend of his, and he was sorry that your friendship came to an end.'

'By his hand! And the accusations in his poems against me are so terrible that—'

'He is jealous. That is all. And why should he not be?' His voice like warm honey easing my firm resolve into liquid silver then, as the evening progressed, to something so vaporous that it might easily have escaped the room altogether.

Yet I gathered myself some time before midnight and said, 'I have something I must tell you, Francesco. It is important, and I need you to listen.'

He raised an eyebrow, cocked his head to one side, a smile, half intrigue, half mischief, on his lips.

'I have all my life longed for a true companion, someone

to love completely, and with whom I could be happy. Regrettably my husband is not that man. We are friends most certainly, parents to our children, though that has not been a wholly happy venture, and always respectful of each other, but we are not in love . . .'

Algarotti leant forward to speak, but I hushed him.

'I have gained a reputation in this country and have lost it somewhat these past years as friends have deserted me. I was until recently much involved in caring for my sister, who is said to be a lunatic though it would be fairer to say she has been grievously mistreated. And so when you and I first met I was something like a fledgling – a very old fledgling, I concede –' I summoned up a laugh, and he joined in sympathetically '– that finds itself in a nest that has fallen from a branch and is exposed. At the very moment when I wished to fly away, I walked into a room where you sat, and instead of flying I have been fluttering about you, imagining you were there for me to love . . .'

Algarotti leant forward, took my hand, but I withdrew it quickly, for it was not the response I desired.

'But I have misused you, and perhaps you have misused me a little, too. It cannot be right that I should think of you as a lover. No, that cannot be. And so I have to tell you that I must not see you again, Francesco, though it is a sort of death to me to say so.'

He was silent for a moment, observing me as a man might watch a leaf fall from a tree. And then he began to make a speech in his turn which changed the very course of my life: 'Maria . . . Mary. You tell me that you are unhappy here, and I see it, I feel it. You are a great woman. You are friendly with the queen, the king, with the most important ministers, with poets and natural philosophers, and all of them hold you in the highest esteem.'

I made to wave away his compliments, but he stopped me.

'And yet these great friends mean nothing to you. I feel that you are suffocating here in London, as surely as if a feather pillow were across your face. Why are you not kicking and screaming? Why are you so quiet, Mary Wortley Montagu? There is a whole wide world that awaits you and yearns to show its love for you.' He stopped then, drew back, almost as if he expected me to applaud him, before delivering his *coup de grâce*. 'I shall leave in a week or two for Venice. Come with me, come to Venice! Venice will love you, I promise, and you in turn will love Venice. There, let a whole republic be your lover!'

I could not speak. The decision I had so sensibly reached earlier in the day fell away from me like garments discarded late at night. I stood before him naked, as it were. 'Yes,' I said feebly. And then more forcefully, 'Yes, I shall!' and I leant towards him and kissed him, fully and deeply, his taste that of almonds and port, and beneath it something metallic and – lower still – the baser taste of maleness, of leaves and soil and bracken.

'I will see you tomorrow?' I asked as he stood to leave.

'Tomorrow and tomorrow and tomorrow, dear Maria.'

29

POLITICAL AFFAIRS

Winter 1737–8, London

(Mary)

Preoccupied as I was with preparations to quit England for good, it was most certainly not my intention to publish a political journal. Indeed, my heart had rarely felt so softened and poetical. I had been writing almost exclusively in French, sending my poems to Francesco, who was in Venice, or possibly Paris, or perhaps Turin. I received only one letter in reply to my six, and then asking for assistance on some London matter, but he would conclude always with reassurances of his love, and however much I told myself not to submit, my heart took possession of my pen, and I would write him another ten reassurances of my great and undying affection and beg for replies that never came.

It was as a pail of cold water thrown over a drowsy milkmaid that I found myself reading a new newspaper bearing the misleading title *Common Sense*. This weekly putrescence, this vomit, this pus-filled boil of a Tory tatter sought to besmirch our government, calling Mr Walpole *Sir Blue*

String and *Swindler* and such like. But worse, and what pricked me into action, was its casual and repeated deprecation of womankind.

> The Fair Sex in general (Queens excepted) are infinitely above plain downright Common Sense; sprightly Fancy, and shining Irregularities are their Favourites, in which despairing to satisfy, tho' desirous to please them, I have in order to be of Use to them, stipulated with my Stationer that my Paper shall be of the properest sort for pinning up of their Hair; as the new French fashion is very favourable to me in this Particular, I flatter myself, they will not disdain to have some Common Sense about their Heads at so easy a rate.

I was so infuriated that I groaned loudly enough to prompt Sara, my new chambermaid, to rush in. I thrust the newspaper at her and bid her place it straightway upon the fire.

'But the fires are not lit, m'lady.'

'Then light them!' I declared. 'For only flames are fit to consume such words!'

'Very well,' she said with a curtsey, taking the offending matter in her hand as if it were already aflame.

This accusation by men, and most particularly men of a Tory disposition, that women were good only for foolishness and that common sense might be found pinned to their hair but not found in their heads – *our heads* – was, in short, a provocation too far. Something in me snapped like a sparrow's bone. It was almost as if my fervent admiration for Francesco had been keeping me from what I most needed to do, yet now it was before me, as close and startling as a coach concealed in fog and seen only in the moment it is suddenly bearing down on one. I had no wish to behave in a manner that would confirm those vile authors' prejudices, so I determined that day to no longer pretend to any person, and least of all to myself, that I was ignorant of politics or uninterested in its battlegrounds, be they the chambers of parliament or the pages of the newspapers.

Over the next weeks I set about finding a publisher, negotiating clear terms for my journal so that it would not be edited except in such manner as to improve it, mindful of the fact that far too often my writings, which had left my nib sharp as a rapier, had ended up upon the published page blunt as a spoon. Finding no willing publisher I made arrangements with a printer and with shops that would distribute, and searched, though in vain, for willing advertisers. All that remained was for me to commence my campaign and decide upon my identity and my newspaper's title. For my name I chose *Author*, and for the title I could think of none better than *The Nonsense of Common-Sense.*

I thought it best to set out in clear terms why I had chosen to bring another newspaper into the clamorous world.

> The Title of this Paper would appear very absurd, if these Words, Common-Sense, were to be now understood in the same Manner they were when they were supposed to mean that low Degree of Understanding, which directed a reasonable Man in the Course of his ordinary Affairs. But these poor Words have since been applied very differently; they now mean a certain Paper with many Flights and small Reason, that is handed about at Coffee-Houses and Tea-Tables, for the Amusement of the Idle, the Entertainment of the Malicious, and the Astonishment of the Ignorant.
>
> Out of a real Compassion for these poor People, and being as sensible as the Author himself, of the Necessity

> of good Economy under the present Pressure of National Debts, I would exhort all his Readers seriously to consider the Value of Two-Pence, before they bestow it on a Paper not worth One Farthing.

I wrote the first edition primarily about the foul oppression of labourers in the wool trade, itself a sort of slavery. And if my readers grasped the barbarity of slavery in our own land, then I trusted they would think it no less barbarous when carried out in others.

I held off until the sixth edition of my journal before launching my volleys for womankind against the injustices of the male sex, and concluded that essay with these words:

> A Woman has Virtue of a purer Kind than any Philosopher has ever shewn; since she knows that Mankind is too much prejudiced against her Sex, to give her any Degree of that Fame which is so sharp a Spur to their greatest Actions.
>
> —I have some Thoughts of exhibiting a Set of Pictures of such meritorious Ladies, where I shall say nothing of the Fire of their Eyes, or the Pureness of their Complexions; but give them such Praises as befits a rational sensible Being: Virtues of Choice, and not Beauties of Accident. I would not have them place so much Value on a Quality that can be only useful to One, as to neglect that which may be of Benefit to Thousands by Example. There will be no Occasion of amusing them with Trifles, when they consider themselves capable of not only making the most amiable but the most estimable Figures in Life. Begin then Ladies, by paying those Authors with Scorn and Contempt, who would throw you below the Dignity of the human Species.

Did I hope to stir male opinion into abandoning its constant oppression of womankind? Had I expectations that parliament would legislate so that women would be freed from unhappy marriages, permitted to keep their wealth as their own rather than handing it meekly to their husbands, who might be wise with it, but were more likely to be foolish? Did I think it probable that women would be allowed to enter professions where men persistently demonstrated their incompetence and yet no less persistently scorned the notion that any woman could perform such simple functions as pleading a case at law or tending to a distemper? I did not, for I was a woman close to fifty (as I was lately so often reminded) and had seen enough of the world to know that the act of reform took more than a just cause. Indeed more often than not it took an army and blood and shot, and though I had no wish to put women to war against men any more than I was eager to put men to war against each other, I was determined not only to write but to act.

It was the pursuit of peace that motivated me next, and since I had begun to lose confidence and, to be frank, interest, in my newspaper, I resolved to take action in parliament itself, for it was high time a woman's voice was heard there.

There had been an incident some eight years earlier when the *Rebecca*, a smuggling brig under the command of a Welshman by the name of Robert Jenkins, was returning to England with its plunder when it was boarded by the Spanish navy and accused of smuggling. Naturally Jenkins protested his innocence, much as a fox denies eating every creature in the coop despite the blood and feathers on display about its mouth. The Spanish would have been wise to have slain Jenkins and set fire to his ship, which is what they threatened to do. Instead, given their inclination in the direction of torture, they lashed him to the mast and severed an ear. Why-oh-why they returned Jenkins' ear to him I cannot imagine, for without his damnable ear to show one and all, England might have been saved a great deal of trouble. But they gave Captain Jenkins his ear, and he placed it in a jar of pickles he had aboard. What happened to the pickles, history does not tell us.

On his return to England Jenkins, no doubt thinking he might create a sensation that would in some way be profitable to him, presented his ear to my friend Mr Walpole, who expressed little interest either in compensating him from the public purse or in demanding reparation from the Spanish, for what price might a Welshman's ear command? And there the matter might have rested, and indeed there it did rest for eight years.

His Majesty's Opposition had begun agitating for war, seeing several advantages in their case, none of which were honourable: first, they saw that war with Spain might bring them advantage in terms of the Caribbean trade, over which the Spanish still had undue control; second, they hoped to secure some benefit for the South Sea Company, and in particular that corporation's squalid trade in slaves, which was under licence by permission of the Spanish; and third, they viewed it as a means of weakening His Majesty's Government and Mr Walpole in particular, whom they knew to be opposed to war. In 1733 Mr Walpole had told the House of Commons: 'There are fifty thousand men slain in Europe this year, and not one of them an Englishman.' He was courageous in his defence of peace, and cheered to the rafters, but five years on and such a statement brought cries of 'Shame!', since it was thought a matter of honour to send sons and brothers and lovers to their death for a cause no sensible person could possibly discern.

The Tories, encouraged by stockholders in the South Sea Company, hunted for a *casus belli*. And then some one of them remembered Jenkins' damnable ear in its pickle jar, and trusting to the power of good vinegar, requested Captain Jenkins return to the House of Commons and present his ear once more, this time encouraging reporting of it in all the newspapers. Why public sentiment is not moved by the injustice of slavery or starvation wages but is enraged by the notion of a Welshman's ear being cut off by a Spanish cutlass I cannot conceive. The Tories had judged the timing of their move well, and it was clear that, if men were not to speak out against their lamentable warmongering, then women must.

I asked Edward to come to Cavendish Square. I let him sit while I paced about the room, deciding how best to make my concerns known, though he knew the nature of them as we had been corresponding about the growing clamour for an unnecessary conflict for several weeks already, my letters direct and persuasive, his replies evasive. I decided on the plain and simple manner to permit him no equivocation. 'How will you vote on this matter of war?'

'In favour, if it comes to it.'

'*If it comes to it?*'

'Yes.'

'I demand that you do not!'

He smiled that bemused, tolerant smile of his that he had been presenting to me for nigh on thirty years. '*Demand*, madam?'

'Well, if not demand then implore. Yes,' I said, going to him and kneeling before him, my hand upon his knee, which was still a fine thing to place a hand upon. 'I implore you, Edward, to support Robert for this once. War is long and bloody and this is not a war for territory or trade or honour, but for injured dignity, and that is not a thing young men should suffer for, since one man's dignity is another's ignominy. You might as well see your reflection in a looking glass and fire your pistol at it for want of its beauty.'

'Is that so?' he said, still seemingly amused.

'The matter is serious.'

'Your friend the prime minister . . .'

'He hates being called prime minister.'

'But such he is. Mr Walpole has already accepted the argument is lost. That is why I said *if it comes to it.* I do not think there will even be a vote in the Commons. There might be a vote of some sort in the Lords, but sentiment has shifted, Mary. The Spanish navy thinks it has a right to regulate the trade of all the Americas, and it is time we showed them they do not.'

'*We? We.* Are you one of those who would agitate for war?'

'Oh, Mary,' he said wearily. 'There is a time for peace and a time for war, and however much we would wish for better times, as winter must follow autumn—'

'Oh shut up!' I marched away, having no wish to hear sanctimonious platitudes from him or any other.

I went immediately to my friend Lady Huntingdon's, since I knew her to be as fervently opposed to war as I. She received me with good grace and reported that she had heard from Lady Saunderson, whose husband, Sir William, served in the House of Lords in a ceremonial role, that a decision had been taken to close the galleries for a debate taking place next day, saving that only serving members of the Commons would be permitted. We both surmised that the debate would be the very one my husband had mentioned, and that this might be our last opportunity to prevent war. Lady Huntingdon and I spent the rest of that evening writing to our friends, and by midnight we had already received replies from Lady Saunderson, the Duchess of Queensberry, the Duchess of Ancaster, Lady Westmoreland, Lady Cobham, Lady Charlotte Edwin, Lady Archibald Hamilton and her daughter, Mrs Scott and Mrs Pendarve.

We would be a considerable party and no doubt joined by others. A female rebellion was to rise in all its glory!

We gathered at the door of the Lords at nine next morning, to be met by that very same Sir William Saunderson, who had no doubt caught wind of our invasion though I felt certain not from his wife. He met us politely, with as many bows and courtesies as our multitude of titles deserved. 'It is with regret, my ladies, that I am informed by the Lord Chancellor that I may not give you admittance.'

'Sir William,' said I, 'we ask only to be allowed to observe the proceedings.'

'I am afraid, Lady Mary, that shall not be permitted. Even if there were not so many of you to fit, given your number and the width of your gowns . . .'

'Sir William,' said Lady Hamilton, 'we may remove our gowns and sit in our stays if that would assist matters.'

Sir William Saunderson reddened. 'That, madam, will not be necessary, I assure you.'

'Sir,' said Lady Saunderson to her husband, 'we must speak to the Chancellor on this matter.'

'You may speak to me about it, Frances.'

'I may speak to you at any time and get no more sense from you then than I do today!' replied Lady Saunderson, as furious as I had ever seen her, but provoking laughter in the gathered party.

Sir William remained unyielding.

A half-hour or more had passed during our argument, and

a crowd had gathered to watch this spectacle of twenty or more women gathered at the entrance to the House of Lords. Deciding that she did not wish to become street theatre, the Duchess of Queensberry declared, 'Enough, Sir William, our authority is greater than yours, and we shall enter,' and she began to push past the poor man, urging us to follow in her wake.

'By God!' declared Sir William, his resolve finally sheering away. 'You shall not pass.' And he retreated rapidly within, we following in close pursuit. He was just far enough ahead to order the doors to the chamber to be bolted before we reached them.

From our new position outside the chamber we could hear the noble lords within deliberating upon the possibility of our admittance and resolving against. At least our action was delaying them from approving a motion in favour of war. There we stood for the next several hours, hollering and thumping and kicking upon the great doors so as to disrupt their proceedings. In time we were joined by members of the Commons. They did not join in our protests, naturally enough, but regarded us with detached bemusement, as if we were a string ensemble they had engaged for a house party that was playing loudly and badly and out of tune but was to be tolerated none the less.

Hour after hour passed and still we stood protesting, without sustenance or relief. At five in the afternoon I had a thought and beckoned to the Duchess of Queensberry, and whispered in her ear. 'If we all fall silent, the lords will think us gone for our dinner, imagining that ladies could not possibly keep up a protest beyond eight hours.'

'Agreed,' said the duchess, who immediately hushed the entire party. The MPs were uncertain how to act. They could hardly take up the hollering and thumping on our behalf, and so they found themselves involuntarily colluding in our stratagem. Sure enough after twenty minutes we heard the Chancellor, thinking us departed, give the order for the doors to open, and we all rushed in, ladies and MPs alike, we women making sure that we took the front row of the gallery before the MPs from the Commons were able to have them for themselves. And there we remained, somewhat hungry but emboldened, jeering and cheering and clapping and making clear our views regarding the absurdity of war with the Spanish over a man's ear.

It was approaching eleven at night, the debate drawing to a close and my friend Lord Hervey, presumably disconcerted by our presence, having spoken uncharacteristically miserably, when I felt impelled to address the lords from my eyrie. 'My lords, you have endeavoured to exclude us women, thinking us not fit to be in this place and sit silently. And so we will not be silent, but have a voice for once. We are not going to plead or flatter or say that we are—'

'Madam!' declared the Chancellor. 'You have no right, Lady Mary, to utter so much as a word in this place.'

'I agree, my lord. I have no right. But has reason not the right? Has good sense not the right? Has the voice of all those young men whose last breath will be spent on a battlefield or aboard a ship blasted from the seas by cannon not the right to say, *Be still, my lords. Think, my lords, of the price you ask us all to pay*? And for what? For a penny more profit in the pound? For another thousand slaves to be sent to Jamaican plantations to be whipped? For an ear in a pickle jar?'

A rumble of approval at my words went across the government benches, but I knew if there was to be a chance of my case carrying the day I should resume my seat and silence, and pretend I had not spoken at all. I saw Hervey glance up at me, but if I had hoped for his approval, I was to be disappointed. His expression was that of a boy disgraced by being in the company of an embarrassing aunt.

We did not carry the day because, as Edward explained to me later, the matter had been settled long ago, and even had I been in breeches and wig and with a barony to my name, even if my speech had been the most eloquent ever heard in that place, the vote would still have been for war, because in our new age of profit and dividend and the clamour for sugar and cotton, it was money that ruled the world, not reason. And I knew he was right, though it gave me no comfort to be reminded once more of my powerlessness.

It was time to leave England. It was time for me to find love at last.

30

MASQUERADES

Summer 1739, Venice

(Mary)

Venice brimmed with indulgence, sensuality, carnality. It was a city designed for the pleasure of its every inhabitant, rich or poor, man or woman, young or old; and for its every visitor, too, whether wise or foolish, whether seeking inspiration or degradation. All fell under the spell of its carnival of excess. Venice was a city of the night. The canals, which at noon on a warm spring day bobbed with excrement and cabbage leaves and smelt of rank decay, at night seemed almost perfumed, growing so still and catching the light of the stars so perfectly that one felt one could almost walk across the liquid gold of them. Every window glowed with warm candlelight, and the sound of distant violins made it seem that the whole republic had been given a musical accompaniment by God Himself.

There was a darker side to Venice, though, its nuns locked away in secret convents, its licentiousness causing pain as well as pleasure. In my first weeks I saw, when masks were pulled aside, the sure sign of syphilis eating away a nose, a cheek, an eye. Indeed, it was a place where masks were worn even when they were not, where all pretended to a blissful happiness they can hardly have felt. For all that, the city brought me back to life and made me see how my London life had not been living at all, but a kind of steady slope into death. I felt certain this was my one chance at resurrection, and I was determined to make the best of it.

I took a palazzo on the Grand Canal, reacquainted myself with old friends and made many new ones, while I awaited the arrival of my love, Francesco Algarotti.

I waited and waited.

Algarotti did not come.

He was first in Paris, next in London, then Potsdam, also Padua (so close!), but then he was away again to Rotterdam.

Yet in Venice I met a person who was of even greater interest to me in my newfound state than Francesco Algarotti. She was a woman who wrote as she pleased and thought as she pleased and spoke as she pleased, and she was not condemned for it. She was known for certain of her letters and poems which had been published, unbeknownst to her, in Italy, also for her work in medical reform and most particularly for spreading word on the virtues of inoculation. She was invited to every great house and given a place at dinner tables as guest of honour. That woman's name was Mary Wortley Montagu. Never before had I felt so at ease, so truly myself. My days and nights were filled with entertainment, and with a succession of visitors whose company was pleasurable. I went to concerts when on any night I was not otherwise engaged, with or without company since all could go about Venice *in domino*, wearing a loose cloak and a mask on the upper part of one's face, affording that freedom to women I encountered so long before in Turkey.

The Spanish ambassador, Prince Campoflorido, and his wife treated me with all the honours I should expect if I were myself an ambassadress, sending me regular invitations which I was happy to accept. That our two countries were at war seemed to be no obstacle to our cordial relations, though it lingered in the background, like a stranger standing in the shadows. I found myself given access to intelligence remarkably indiscreetly, particularly by men who, wishing to charm and impress a woman as men so often do, told me what they hoped would dazzle and amaze. Had I been a man I am certain they would not have done so. Men with other men tend to show their prowess by giving away very little, as if taciturnity were itself a show of strength.

This gave me a thought. I had been unable to prevent war, unable to take a place in the Lords which would rightfully have been mine had I been born a mewling boy, nor could I win a seat in the Commons where I might have set about making a party for peace and equality and proper schooling for girls and boys alike. But there were other ways to influence the course of wars. Indeed, it is intelligence that makes empires and it is the lack of it which extinguishes them. I sensed intelligence was here in the streets of Venice as abundant as the fogs that rose from the canals on cold winter nights. To catch the fog, to hold it and send it where it might be useful was the trick I needed to master – and master it I would.

I wrote to Edward to ask whether he might find it useful if I were to send word of what I heard from the various foreign ambassadors resident in Venice. He replied with a degree of enthusiasm untypical of my husband, but with very clear instructions that my hand and his interest must be concealed with care. He recommended that I write to him by the hand of my maid, and have the letter sent to him under the name *Jonathan Stoat* at an inn at Holborn. Though I certainly thought discretion wise, the level of intrigue he suggested was suitable for one of Mr Shakespeare's comedies. I nevertheless acted as he bid me.

'Sara?'

'Madam?'

'You write?'

She reddened, not from embarrassment but ill-concealed annoyance. 'Certainly I write, my lady!'

'Your hand is good?'

'You've seen it. It is very good!'

It was a messy, barely legible hand, which was precisely what I desired. 'I have seen it, and it is serviceable.'

She puffed with pride. Sara was plump, short and strong, rose-cheeked and the very model of a good-hearted English country girl. John, the footman I had brought from England, fortunately took a keen interest in her honour. Were it not for his constant guard I think she would have been seduced by many a young Venetian boy. 'What is it you want me to be writing, then, ma'am?' she asked.

She sat at the table I had set out with pen, ink, paper and candle.

Appreciating that I was asking her to do something greatly beyond her normal duties, and conscious there was some danger in it, I thought I should offer her some comfort. 'Would you like a glass of wine? A peach or apricot, perhaps?'

She looked at me with deep suspicion. 'Who would get

that for me but me myself?' she said, not unreasonably. 'Excusing me, ma'am.'

'Well, let us take a glass together when you are done, Sara, as a reward for what I am to ask you to do, for I must tell you there is some jeopardy in it.'

She held the pen above the paper. 'Tell me,' she prompted, awaiting my instruction and I saw that her hand had an almost imperceptible tremble to it.

'Set out first the address.'

She began to write the name of our palazzo.

'No!' I ordered. 'Put instead *Palazzo Bognoni*.'

'But I know of no such place.'

'Precisely.'

She wrote out the name I gave her, spelling it *Bonononi*, which was no less correct than the spelling I had intended.

'Next, address the letter to *Mr Stoat, sir*.'

She did so.

'Next: *I have overheard the Prince of Saxony, Fred, say to the Prince of Wolfenbuttel that there shall be agreement between them as soon as they may take their crowns to move once more against Poland*.'

She looked at me dumbfounded but proceeded to write. 'How do you spell Wolfenbuttel?' she asked.

'As you please, Sara, as you please.' She had spelt Saxony as *Sackshoney*, and I anticipated seeing her interpretation of Wolfenbuttel with relish, before thinking better of it. I'd had the benefit of an education, albeit much of it on my own initiative; Sara had been granted only the most rudimentary schooling until the age of ten, after which she had been put to work as a scullery maid. I said softly, 'You write very well, and in your own manner, which is more than acceptable to me.'

Sara gave me a doubtful glance, but I could tell she was pleased to have been praised.

After giving her two further pieces of intelligence to write, including something the Duke of Milan had told me most indiscreetly about the incontinence of the Duke of Savoy, I invited her to sign off the letter, '*A friend.*'

She wrote as I had asked and stood. 'This has been a peculiar business, ma'am.'

'It has, I grant you. But then perhaps *I* am peculiar.'

'Perhaps you are, if you don't mind my saying so, ma'am.'

'I don't mind in the least.'

'Will that be all, m'lady?'

'It is. Now off to bed. I shall undress myself tonight.'

She looked at me sceptically, knowing that I would not lay out my clothes in the correct manner, and that by undressing myself I would only make more work for her in the morning, but unable to make further protest she departed with some relief that there was to be no more letter-writing.

It was only as I was falling asleep that I recalled my offer of a glass of wine, but it was too late for that.

Every stranger who arrived in Venice called on me. It was as if there was a map of the city, and upon it, marked by a drawing of a dragon blowing fire, was written *MWM*. The sons of nobles from Austria, Saxony, France, Piedmont all came and, being well raised and grasping the rudiments of *conversazione*, repaid my hospitality with tales of their travels, whether impressions of Rome and Naples or gossip about ill-run palaces where predatory duchesses called upon them late at night to ensure they were settled in their bedchambers. But the Englishmen on the Grand Tour were different – an inundation, being mostly shallow young men, boastful and foolish, travelling in groups of half a dozen; they were rowdy, talking to each other only in English, learning nothing of the culture they had been sent to appreciate, and spending their days attempting to outdo each other in eating, drinking and acquiring diseases beneath their breeches that they would one day bestow upon some unfortunate young woman destined to be their wife.

Not all English visitors were so lacklustre. The young Lord Strafford came for the *carnivale* and was modest and genteel, and Lord Lincoln came for the summer and spent many an afternoon in my company. If a few years younger I should have felt flattered by these youths' seductive charms, but there was only one man I desired, and he was proving to be maddeningly elusive. Intelligence of his whereabouts reached me unreliably, for he could not be in Berlin one day and Paris the next unless in possession of a flying machine, though such was I told and other things besides, including that he was the favourite of the new Prussian king, who was setting up a court to rival any in Europe. I knew that Algarotti had a talent for gaining introductions where they could be of most advantage to him, and no less a gift for prodigious flattery. He was like a mouse that lived in a hole beside the emperor's banqueting table, scuttling out whenever there were crumbs to be had, and scampering back into the dark when there were not. I tried to persuade myself that I must see him for what he was, and that was a creature of little use or interest to me.

Settled in Venice, with new friends and a new life of great fulfilment, free of English politics and English hatreds, free of court battles and publishers stealing my work, free of slights and accusations, free of troublesome sons and haughty daughters, and so far distant from my husband that we became, through our correspondence, close once more, I felt confident that I was making a life for myself in precisely the manner I had always wanted – as an independent woman. It was therefore not in the least welcome when one morning almost two years after I had moved to Venice the name of Francesco Algarotti rudely interposed itself between me and my strong black morning coffee.

31

ALGAROTTI AGAIN

Summer 1741, Venice and Turin

(Mary)

Lamrock was a small, unobtrusive man, who managed the affairs of my household with admirable efficiency and discretion. He was about my age, his close-shaved grey hair neat when he was not wearing his wig, and he was grey of face, too. He was always willing to do as I asked, and yet never offered me an opinion on any matter. That he'd been left behind by Edward at Cavendish Square like a spare valise was very much my gain and my husband's loss. He had helped me find first Sara and then John, had come willingly abroad, arranged passages, coaches, baggage and, indeed, the rental of this palazzo. I had, in short, taken the man wholly for granted for years.

It was Lamrock, therefore, who informed me about the persistence of a messenger who had called each day that week, and whom he had declined to admit. 'He claims he has been sent by Count Algarotti,' he said with distaste.

'*Count* Algarotti?'

'The gentleman once of your acquaintance has been made a count by the King of Prussia, I believe.'

I was beginning to understand that Lamrock had access to intelligence that, for one reason or another, was withheld from me. 'Indeed? Well, show him in.'

He hesitated. 'I will do so, my lady, but . . . if you may permit me?' He gave me his odd smile, crooked and self-conscious, as he did when he feared he was overstepping his authority.

'Say what you must, Lamrock. I wish for your advice, given freely.'

'Whatever it is that Count Algarotti wishes from you, I advise you to place your own happiness above his.'

There would have been a time, and not so long before, that I would have been infuriated by his presumption, but I had asked him to give me his frank advice, much as a court jester is freed to speak truth to a despotic king. Besides, he was only telling me what my own reason did in stronger terms: I would not allow myself to be ill used by Algarotti again. 'Thank you, Lamrock.'

The messenger was a youth of little more than sixteen, dusty from the road, with dark curls that fell to his shoulders. He bowed deep. 'My master bids you, Lady Mary, to attend him in Turin.'

'Turin. Why on earth should I join him in Turin?'

'He has written you a letter.' He handed me said letter, sealed with a splendid crest, that of his new Prussian rank, presumably.

'Why did he send *you* and not come himself?' I asked the boy before taking pity on him and ringing for Sara to bring him a glass of lemonade.

'I am to tell you . . .' He coughed, and it was apparent that he had learnt the lines he next recited. 'That my master understands full well that you might be inclined to read his letter and disregard it, for he has been sinfully neglectful of a true friend whom he loves as dearly as his own life. I am to return with your reply, even if it is to say that you never wish to set eyes upon my master again.' The boy bowed once more. I almost offered him a round of applause.

I broke the seal and read Algarotti's letter quickly. Amongst flamboyant apologies, a brief account of the wonders of the Prussian court and of the new King Frederick, he revealed that he was in Turin as Prussian envoy and had delicate negotiations to conduct in which he wished for my assistance, having heard reports of my subtle diplomacy in Venice. I could not think from whom he had heard this, unless it was from John Hervey, to whom I wrote regularly, and who I knew would have kept in close contact with him.

I sat to write my reply. I was intrigued by his request for my assistance in his 'negotiations', having little doubt that he planned some subterfuge, a practice for which I'd developed a certain appetite. I began with a witty retort, implying that the damp air of Venice had softened my brains much as tanners use dung to soften their leather, yet as my nib flew across the page, I found myself writing words of affection, even of passion, just as I had before. Was it that my limbs felt that affection for him that my heart had lost? And next it seemed my fingers afflicted my heart, for its beat increased to a gallop, and I was once more in the grip of that deluded passion for Francesco Algarotti that I had thought thoroughly vanquished.

I sent the messenger away with my reply and bid Lamrock come see me.

'Lamrock, we are to go to Turin.'

'Oh dear,' he said in his mournful monotone. He saw all, of course. 'When would you wish to depart?'

'Tomorrow.'

'How long will we be in Turin?'

'Some months, I suspect. We had best pack up the house and end the lease.'

'You are leaving a place where you have been happy and safe, my lady.'

'What are you? My conscience?'

'I shall try to be. It is naturally not my place to ever do other than you please, but you bid me to give you advice, and my advice is that you are leaving certain happiness in Venice for uncertainty and potential misery in Turin.'

'Lamrock, you tell me true, and I appreciate it. But I must find out whether there is to be anything more between Algarotti and myself, as I once thought there would be.'

'And what if there is more, but it is not good?'

'Then so be it. I shall have had an adventure.'

My first sight of Francesco was in the street. Lamrock had arranged rooms for our party for just a week at a palazzo on the Piazza Reale, his intention being that our stay in Turin would be brief. We had arrived late the previous evening, and I had not announced my presence in the city to Algarotti, for I had not yet decided what it was I would say to him.

I was taking the morning air in the piazza, wholly different from that of Venice – not sea air, but mountain air, flavoured with the smells of a great city: of horses and wood and vegetables from a market near by, of coffee and spices and naturally of drains. The journey had been long and dusty and taken a week, and I was glad to be settled if only for a handful of days. Having just resolved to return to my rooms and send a short note to Algarotti's residence as soon as I did so, I caught from the corner of my eye a figure moving at great haste through the archways to the side of the piazza, pursued by a rough-looking youth who was gesticulating and demanding money.

How odd it is that a person deeply loved or much feared is recognizable in an instant, even if at great distance, even if one's vision is generally not what it once was. It is something like the facility a sparrow has for knowing when a sparrow-hawk is in the air, even when a mile away. And thus I knew Algarotti from his shape, his gait, his gesticulations to his tormentor, who was now raising his voice and attracting unwanted attention. I drew nearer, as did others, for Algarotti had stopped and appeared to be trying to reason with the youth who, it seemed, had rendered some service to my friend, and not been paid for it.

Was Algarotti in debt? Had he asked me to Turin only to plead with me for money? I felt indignant at the thought of it. Naturally I expected to be misused in some way, but if it was money he wanted he might have simply written to ask me for a loan as was customary – a loan always being easier to request and harder to decline than a gift.

He had not seen me, I felt sure, and when I returned to my rooms I wondered whether to declare my presence at all, but curiosity rather than longing impelled me to do so. Besides we had come a long way, and if I was to be made a fool of, better this time that it was done swiftly than slowly.

He had aged, but that only served to make him more handsome. He was broader, more muscular, dressed in the Prussian style rather than the Italian, more soberly and tastefully than before. As I entered he dropped to one knee, like a suitor, and looked up at me with his enchanting eyes and swore that he had only been half alive until that moment.

'But which half, Francesco?'

He laughed, stood, and kissed my hand, seeming to understand that his blandishments were unlikely to succeed. In truth my blood ran faster and hotter in my veins, I felt my cheeks flushing red, and all that old desire came rushing back, like a guilty secret unwillingly confessed. This he noticed too and did not fail to understand, and I cursed my body for speaking what my tongue would not, for I knew too well he would use the power he had over me. 'Let us spend the next days in the pleasure of each other's company, Maria, before we set about the business I have in mind for us here. I wish to know all that happened after I left London and am eager to tell you of Potsdam and the wonders of Frederick's court.'

'You will no doubt tell me all of that, and I may tell you something of my life in Venice, which I went to at the invitation of a certain gentleman. But can you believe he was so discourteous as not to be at home when I called, nor was he ever at home, nor even in that city at all, for he had invited me to be with him without the slightest intention of honouring his invitation?'

He narrowed his eyes, an uncertain smile upon those cupid lips, before deciding that he would parry my fury with laughter. 'That man sounds despicable, dear Mary. Let us hope you never encounter him again.'

'Let us hope not.' I placed a hand upon his chest and his eye fixed upon my own as sure as a hawk upon its prey. Without wishing to do so in the least, I kissed him full on the mouth, tasting him once again as I had imagined so many times – too many times – in those first months after we had parted. Pulling away, I declared: 'No, he is not the same man at all, and I am not the same woman. Well, there's a mercy.'

*

We continued in such manner in those first days we were together. Each time he talked of Frederick I made a swooning gesture and declared, 'My prince!' since it was so apparent that Francesco was in love with Prussia's new king, and whenever I spoke of my son he declared, 'The monster!' and if I mentioned a letter from my daughter he would say, 'The mouse!' and in this way we treated each other with that toleration that comes from pretending that those things that matter to us most matter least, which is the kind of game played when the stakes are so high they can never be paid.

I asked him one evening about the scene I had witnessed on the Piazza Reale, the youth demanding money, he fleeing from him. 'You saw that?' he asked, horrified.

'Yes. Do you not have money, Francesco, because if that is—'

'No, no. It was not money. Well it was, but . . .'

'But what?'

'He . . . He had made me a waistcoat, or his master had. He is a tailor's assistant, and I thought I had paid for it, but it seemed . . .' He flushed red with embarrassment.

'You are lying!' I declared.

He shrugged. 'What can I tell you, Maria. The boy wanted money, and I had already given him enough.'

'And is he still pursuing you?'

'No. I am glad to say he is not.'

I had no need to press him further on what service the boy had provided him. It was all too obvious. But by then I knew enough of the plot we were to hatch together that any unpaid debts, of whatever nature, were likely to bring unwelcome attention. 'Try to keep out of further trouble while we are about this business, Francesco.'

*

The business began in my second week in Turin. Our task was to poison relations between the Duchy of Savoy and the Republic of Genoa, which had been hitherto perfectly harmonious. This was to be of some benefit to the Prussian king in his war against the Austrians, since conflict between domains subject to Austrian protection would distract Frederick's great enemy. The purpose of the plot was less important than its subtle execution. I cared nothing for Frederick, but to be engaged in subterfuge was intellectually demanding, and held the deceptive enticement that my low cunning might change the course of history. That I also wished to impress Francesco may have been a small part of it. Very small.

Algarotti was already known as Frederick's man, and since Prussia was trusted by no one, it was my duty to use those many invitations I had received and connections I had made at the dinner tables of Venice to attend salons where I obliged my hosts by allowing myself to be entertained by court gossip. Men who should have been more prudent before reporting on a duke's impotence, a page's presence in a duchess's bed or the provision of rifles to Corsicans because *to cause trouble there greatly inconveniences our brothers in Genoa*, thought little of it when rewarded with my laughter and assurances that I had drunk far too much wine to remember a thing. All of which helped to make more plausible the lies Algarotti and I were to spread about what the Duke of Turin had said about the Doge of Genoa and what the doge had said about the duke. We worked on our plan together, found confidants and spies in each court and spent happy hours forging letters that we sent out into the world to foment confusion. Should I have felt more loyalty to the truth, and to honour? Perhaps. Yet to have an opportunity to influence the course of war and peace satisfied my desire to live as fully and adventurously as I might, and it was not inconvenient that in pursuing these activities I was also able to show Algarotti that I was indispensable to him. And hadn't Aphra Behn been a spy, and a good one?

After two months of stirring the pot of enmity between the neighbouring states to the point that the Savoyard ambassador to the court of Genoa was recalled to Turin and the Genoese ambassador returned to his city, Algarotti abruptly announced that our work was done. It seemed that the Prussian king had decided that conflict in Italy did not, after all, further him in his war with the Austrians, and he asked Francesco to return to Berlin, which he consented to with an eagerness that was as wounding as it was unsurprising, for I'd known perfectly well from the moment Algarotti's messenger had appeared in my palazzo in Venice, nervous and dishevelled, that his master would wish only to use me and dispense with me, as he had done so many times before. It would be absurd to feel hurt, to fear abandonment, yet the human heart *is* absurd, pattering on with its feelings despite whatever reason the brain strives to impose upon it.

'Will you return to Venice, Maria?' asked Algarotti as his belongings were being placed in crates ready for the long journey to Prussia.

'I? What concern is it of yours where I choose to go next?' I had in fact not considered any other possibility.

'You know Venice well now, I suppose,' he said, in a manner I found intolerably condescending.

'I shall probably *not* return to Venice, as it happens,' I said, surprising myself.

Algarotti turned and looked at me. 'Ah. I see. You are returning to London. That makes good sense, Maria.'

I felt furious – so furious that I said: 'I have no need to go scuttling back to anyone. Unlike you, who cannot wait to be admiring your preening prince.'

He reacted to this as if a two-year-old had kicked him below the knee, with a fond chuckle.

'I shall go to Avignon!' I announced, for no better reason than that it was the first place I could think of, perhaps because it began with the letter A.

'Avignon? Whyever there?'

Whyever there? Naturally I did not know the answer to the question. In our weeks of intelligence-gathering I had heard it said that Avignon, a papal city, was a place of great intrigue where the affairs of Europe were decided in whispers and looks, in messages in code and secret signals. I had gained a taste for espionage and fancied to continue it. Though these reasons, which I now repeated to Algarotti, had only come to me in the moments before I uttered them.

'Be cautious, Maria. You make a good spy – better than any man – but there is great danger in it. And the passage there will be difficult now it is autumn, with brigades of Spanish troops here and there in the mountains,' he said.

'You need not worry yourself about such things. I shall proceed there within the week.'

Algarotti began to give me more advice, but I held up a hand. 'Our paths part in this moment. You go north, I go south.'

'South-west.'

'Oh do shut up!'

'Write to me to tell you have arrived safely at Avignon,' he insisted.

'I will do no such thing. And please do not write to me. I have no wish to be thought a *Prussian* spy.'

'I shall think of you always, Maria.'

'You only ever think of yourself, Francesco. There is no one else in the world who matters to you, no friendship that exists except to be used for your ends, no passion that cannot be manipulated to your advantage. Your heart is shrivelled. If surgeons were to cut you open they would have to search long and hard for it and if they were to find it in that empty void they would mistake it for a dried pea.'

To my surprise, he appeared genuinely hurt by my denunciation. He came to me, took my hand. 'You are wrong, Maria. I am filled with love. But it is not and cannot be a love for just one person. I am not yours, any more than you are mine. We are free spirits, we two, and so we must live and so we must die.'

It was a pretty speech, and I was obliged to fight an inclination to soften towards him. But I had heard more from those lips than was good for me. I removed my hand from his. 'Goodbye, Francesco.'

Lamrock, who had witnessed our sullen farewells, scuttled ahead of me out of the room.

Once out into the street, he asked, 'Avignon, my lady?'

'Avignon, yes,' I said, unconvincingly.

'If you're sure.'

I might so easily have changed my mind in that moment, returned to Venice where I had friends and a life easily resumed. But pride took possession of me. I would show Algarotti that I could live anywhere, that I was not done with adventure just because I was done with him. I did not need him or any man. 'Perfectly sure, Lamrock.'

It took some days for the necessary arrangements to be made, I in truth feeling weary at the prospect of yet another journey. My bones ached, my teeth ached, my feet ached. Part of my delusion in coming to Turin had been a belief that I was, or could pretend to be, youthful, but now that

Algarotti had dispensed with me, the illusion shattered, and I was left a woman staring into the abyss of old age and poor health.

Apart from physical considerations there were those of sentiment, too. When I had left England for Turkey it had been with Edward and in expectation of a great adventure, and I had not been disappointed. When I left England for Venice, it had been in the prospect of making a life with Algarotti. Now I was setting out once more, with no true notion of whence I was bound, and no promise of companionship.

Turin had been the end of something that had never truly begun.

Where was love now? I had known love only ever as one knows the colours of a rainbow – a pleasing but fleeting illusion. I'd once thought I loved Edward, but that love had turned quickly into the dreary acceptance of familiarity. My children I'd loved, but my love for them had been cruelly repaid. And as for Algarotti, his had been the sorriest delusion of all.

Was it too late for love? My heart was cracked open, and I did not know where to take it except on yet another journey in the thin hope that it would mend.

32

BETTER LONELY THAN PITIED

1742–6, Avignon

(Mary)

All of Europe was at war but for Avignon, yet Avignon was hardly at peace. It was like the still, dead eye of a storm, and though I spent my days peacefully reading, writing and in discussion with the distinguished persons of the city, it was with the uneasy feeling that the great encircling calamity might sweep us away at any moment. As a papal city, visitors came and went, and though the entertainment was not so great as in Venice, there were concerts and operas to attend, and an excellent newspaper, *Le Courrier d'Avignon*, free of French censorship, its editor regularly inviting me to dine with him and to write occasional articles on whatever subject I chose. Sometimes these were on nothing more than the abundance of the mulberry crop, at others on the tragedy of the European war. The vice-legate of the city became a friend, and so I secured the ear of the most powerful man in the city, and more usefully my ear was placed near to all he had to say.

Most importantly, as the court of the Pretender was in Avignon when not in Rome, the place simmered with Jacobites talking treason. If I was to make myself useful I knew that I could not appear to be what I always had been – a firm and unwavering Whig, loyal to the House of Hanover. I somehow had to find a way of making myself acceptable to the rebels, and I did so by decrying the new government in London – not hard to do, for the so-called Patriot Whigs had stabbed my dear friend Robert Walpole in the back. I let it be thought that my sympathies had shifted, and in such manner was invited to dinners where I overheard schemes being hatched for landings of rebels in Ireland or on Scottish islands, for the forging of banknotes and plots to persuade King Louis of France to restore his plans for an invasion of Britain.

I hinted at this intelligence in my letters to Edward, though I could not state them too plain, since correspondence was intercepted, but Edward's replies carried only his usual complaints about ill health and business interests and questions about certain of my bills, with no mention of my hints at all, except for a thinly veiled reminder that all my letters were opened in Paris.

It was my dear old friend Lady Oxford who wrote to me with news that troubled me to a surprising degree: Alexander Pope was dead.

Pope had never been in anything but imperfect health, and that he should have lived to the age of fifty-five was itself a triumph of his determination and stubbornness. It was reported that Pope had said, when told on his deathbed by his physicians that his condition was much improved, *Here am I, dying of a hundred good symptoms*. Typical Pope, witty and self-regarding to his last breath. Yet his death unsteadied me. The remembrance of him as a friend, confidant and collaborator was fond, and in some strange manner the loss of his unwavering hatred these past twenty years was unsettling. It had fixed me like a butterfly pinned to cork. Without Algarotti, without my sister, who though she breathed was little more than a ghost, without the slightest wish to see my son and no likelihood of seeing my daughter, Pope's death reminded me of how alone I was. I thought of returning to London, but I feared that if I went back to England, I would only find myself pitied. Better lonely than pitied.

The Duc de Richelieu held parties from time to time in Nîmes, less than a day's ride away, and I was persuaded by some ladies whose acquaintance I had made in Avignon to attend, despite finding increasingly that carriage journeys jarred my bones and rattled my teeth. Arriving in Nîmes I found myself of interest to the duc, whose inclination towards seduction was infamous. I hardly imagined that I might truly fascinate him, but so it appeared, for he and I were soon in deep discussion on all manner of matters. I raised the persecution of the Huguenots, which he claimed to deplore as much as I did, and next my admiration for Voltaire, whom he deplored no less. He then began to speak to me most indiscreetly about the position of the Jacobites, what encouragement there was for their cause in both England and Scotland, and of French plans to support a landing. I wondered whether my claims to sympathy for the Jacobite cause had been so successful that I was now taken into confidence by one of the most important French generals, though I was not oblivious to the possibility that this was an attempt by the duc to use me as a channel for false intelligence. I pretended to know more than I truly did and professed a sympathy for the Pretender that I hardly felt, and by the end of the evening felt sure that I was in possession of military intelligence of the utmost value.

But how on earth was I to impart this secret to ministers in London?

At first it seemed a stroke of mixed fortune would solve my difficulty. My servants Sara and John had married when in Venice, greatly against my wishes though not, it seemed, nature's, as they now had three young children. John came to see me one day, ushered into the room by Lamrock, and was clearly reluctant to say what he must. He coughed, took a step towards me, and then a step back. It was a surprisingly chill day for October, and he had brought in on his clothes the cool air, a pleasant smell against the coal of the fire. Eventually he declared: 'My lady, we are resolved, that is, Sara and I have decided. Or I should say we are agreed . . .'

'You are in accord, then?'

'We are.'

'And yet you have not told me about what.'

'We are to return to England,' he announced, looking sorrier about it than I imagined he truly was.

'You are?' I responded, surprised, before I was seized by the realization that I could not wish for more dependable or honest bearers of my secret message than Sara and John.

A smile must have formed on my face because John said next: 'You are pleased? Well, I must say, m'lady, I have been building myself up to tell you this news and had been imagining some upset. I asked Mr Lamrock to tell you, but he said that we must do so ourselves, for it is only right that way.'

'And so it is, John. Lamrock is right in all things.'

'You are not sorry we are leaving you?'

'I am truly sorry for it, John, that is, I am sorry for your departure. You are certain?'

'We are.'

'Well, that is a shame, but I appreciate that you may wish to raise your family in England.'

He seemed so disconcerted by my reasonableness that he choked on the words he had prepared to deliver. 'I . . . I . . . it is . . .'

'I can plead with you to stay if you wish. I might point out that you will find no better employer, and that the climate here will serve your palsy a good deal better than the damp and noxious air of London.'

'I should rather be a chimney sweep in England than a lord here in France.'

'Then I wish you well in being a chimney sweep, and I shall help you to establish yourself in that or in whatever other trade you choose. Though I suggest grocery. You are good at striking a bargain, John, and if in time you are able to purchase a shop you may have the vote, and I know you well enough to know that you would never vote for a Tory.'

'I wouldn't – not even to annoy you, my lady.'

'Well said!' I laughed. 'Now, when are you proposing to travel?'

'I hope we may depart within the week.'

'I shall ensure you are given some assistance on your arrival from my husband.'

He had not expected this. 'Oh? That is very kind.' He bowed.

'In return I wish you to take a letter of the very greatest secrecy to him. I know that I can trust you.'

Suspicion crossed his face.

'It may save many lives, John, this letter, and will not imperil yours unless you are careless with it.'

'I have no wish to become a spy at my age.'

'You are but thirty, John. And anyway, I am only asking you to carry a message. The spying you may leave to me.'

'I shall have to discuss it with Sara.'

'Most certainly you shall. Indeed, it will be best carried by Sara, in her stays.'

'Then perhaps it will be best if you discuss the matter with her directly, m'lady, since you have the greater expertise in the question of what may be hidden in a bodice than I.'

'John, you are impertinent!' I said, succumbing to laughter, as much from the relief that I had found such a convenient way to convey my secret to London.

John and Sara had been gone a week when, in the middle of the night, there came a loud rapping at my door. I took the tinderbox, fumbled with it, lit a taper, and next a candle. By the time I reached the door Lamrock was there. He bid me be silent and snuffed out the candle.

'We know you are within, Lady Mary,' said a rough Scots voice. 'And would bid you parlay with us.'

I could just make out Lamrock's head in the gloom. He was shaking it, a finger to his lips.

'We promise fair treatment, but you have betrayed us, and it cannot go unremarked.'

I whispered to Lamrock: 'We cannot skulk within like rabbits in a burrow.'

'Would you run out of the burrow into the jaws of the fox, my lady?' The door shook again, with great force. 'They are most likely in their cups, and in the morning will see reason,' he hissed.

I had not told Lamrock of the secret letter and feared now that Sara and John had been apprehended at Paris or Calais. They would have suffered if that was the case and I was almost beside myself with distress at the thought of it. The shouting subsided, as Lamrock had predicted, and we sat together in the kitchen where I told him of the message, and my fears for Sara and John.

'It may be that the letter has not been discovered,' he said. 'Indeed, we must hope not, for yes, it would have brought great danger to that good family. But if you had intelligence to take to England, most likely the Jacobites will have discovered from some other source that you are in possession of it. Go in the morning straight to the papal vice-legate and seek his protection.'

In the morning, dazed from a sleepless night, my joints stiff as they so often were of late, I gathered together a few items in a valise, since I was in want of a maid to prepare them for me. I stepped out in the direction of the papal vice-legate's palace, which was but three hundred yards from my residence along two narrow alleyways. It was a fine spring morning and I was somewhat lost in my thoughts when I heard footsteps behind. Before I could turn, a hand was over my mouth, and I was grabbed and pulled into a dark, low doorway.

Moments later I was sat in a filthy room, shuttered and with the leavings of a meagre dinner from the night before still upon the table. Two rough men stood before me. 'You are Mary Wortley Montagu?' they asked.

'You know full well who I am.'

'Give us no lip, woman,' said the rougher of the two.

'What do you want?'

'To have you confess that you have been sending intelligence to the curs in England.'

'I have not!'

A knife appeared, a small, sharp blade, its point catching a shaft of sunlight that glinted in that moment through a crack in the shutter. 'This, madam, will have your blood upon it if you do not tell us the truth.'

I used every fibre of my being not to let the terror I felt be heard in my voice. 'What makes you think I have anything to tell?'

'We know the Duc de Richelieu spoke to you very freely of French plans, thinking you one of our leaders –' he turned and spat on the filthy floor '– and if you have not yet sent intelligence, then you are not doubt intending to. A knife across your throat would silence you.' For a moment, the relief that my letter had not been discovered outweighed my fear. I inadvertently allowed myself a small smile at the thought of Sara and John being safe.

'You are amused at this, perhaps?' the man exclaimed with a leer, bringing the tip of the knife to my chin, and then pressing it down upon my hand so that it drew a bead of blood, in the exact place that the crow had pecked me as a child. That memory returned to me with the force of an apparition, almost as if it had prophesied this very moment, for once more I faced Death, and knew that to disdain it was the only way to live.

In moments of great crisis it is said that one can recall one's life entire, and so I did, though I saw it before me written out as in the pages of a book. I thought what a fine entry in my diaries this strange incident would make. If Death was to come to me on this morning, my great regret would be that I had not put my papers in order. 'I cannot think my murder will do much for your cause,' I said.

He glowered, and to my surprise sat heavily at the table opposite me, the blast of his stale breath making me reel. 'You know nothing of our cause.'

'Perhaps I do not.'

'It is to bring justice and the old ways to the poor – to crofters and farmhands. The Whigs are all about this and only this,' he said, rubbing two blackened fingers together in the universal gesture for money.

'Your cause is not mine, but I do not decry it, nor do I scheme against it,' I lied.

'You were leaving the city?'

'I was not.'

'Then why the valise?'

'I would hardly be quitting the city with just a sack dress and some stockings! I was on my way to see the vice-legate.'

My interrogator blanched. 'He's expecting you?'

'Certainly,' I lied once more.

He glanced up at his companion, who shifted uneasily. 'Tie her up and gag her,' he instructed.

There is no pleasant way of being tied and gagged. I was bound roughly to the chair on which I sat, and my mouth had a filthy cloth stuffed in it, presumably to prevent me from shouting for help. I had a great urge to pass water, and to my shame did so where I sat. The two men left me alone in that dank, gloomy space, uncomfortable in my puddle, and all that was left to me was to listen to the scratching of rats.

I do not know if I was there for an hour or six, for I slept. I had slept not at all the night before and was desperately tired. And what a mercy sleep is to all who suffer. Sleep brings dreams even to the man awaiting the gibbet, to the starving child and the ailing grandmother, and in our dreams we grow wings and horns and are giants or fairies and we feel no pain and are glorious.

I was woken by the sound of splintering wood, and the sight of Lamrock with six of the vice-legate's guards. I was freed an instant later. 'Oh, madam, what a thing to befall you. Such indignity!'

'Water,' I croaked, for I found I could barely utter a word. A cup of water was brought to me, I swallowed and spoke. 'I have my head upon my shoulders, Lamrock, and had not expected it to be here.'

'These men who took you, they are now gaoled.'

'How the mighty fall.'

'They bring the Jacobites no credit, for all in this city must behave peaceably. They were a renegade gang.'

'How did you know to find me here?' I asked.

'I have good intelligence, madam, always. Besides, you were barely a hundred yards from your own front door.'

In a city like Avignon a murmur whispered into one ear is, within the day, a roaring symphony deafening all, and over the next week I had an inundation of visitors, some saddened for they had heard about my assault, others because I was in need of servants and wished me to employ those they had no further use for, and others again applying for the positions of maid and manservant. I filled those positions the moment I met Marianne and Fribourg, a Huguenot couple found for me by Lamrock, for they were modest and sensible.

Life in Avignon was not – could not – be the same for me after the incident as it had been before. Tranquillity had vanished as surely as if a cat had appeared amongst birds on a branch. I needed to fly, yet that was not so easy. Despite the senior Jacobite gentlemen of the city assuring me of my safety and no less of their esteem, I felt a growing anxiety, which increased greatly with news of the landing of Charles Edward in Scotland in the summer of 'forty-five. News reached me, as usual, with agonizing slowness, but what I heard from my Jacobite neighbours made me doubt my reason, for it seemed that the Young Pretender triumphed and was sure to take London by the year's end. What future would await me, my family and every friend I had ever known, were that to happen? No doubt there would be a cruel vengeance wrought upon those who had governed England so sensibly for thirty years and more. My own predicament hardly improved when the news turned in the spring of the following year, the rebellion coming to its bloody end at Culloden. In the months that followed, I learned of Hanoverian cruelty wrought upon those who had fought for the Jacobites. Had I been in London, I should have made the case for mercy, for blood begets blood, suffering begets suffering, and pain begets pain, and no lesson was ever so often given nor so poorly understood as that.

It was the beginning of 'forty-six before I was packed and ready to leave the city, and even then I was uncertain where to go. And then came a certain young man, of good bearing and a kindly enough face, by the name of Ugolino Palazzi. His card was presented to me by Lamrock, who handed it to me with raised eyebrows, which was his certain sign of censure.

LAMROCK: The young gentleman claims to have made your acquaintance before, my lady.

I: *Reading the card, which bears the title 'Count U. Palazzi, Representative of the Prince of Saxony'.* Show him in, Lamrock.

LAMROCK: Very well.

In walks a man of around thirty, a short, alert-looking fellow of pleasant countenance.

PALAZZI: *Noting the disarray of the house with evident satisfaction.* Lady Mary. *Bows.* You did me the great honour of having me at your table in Venice.

I: *Having no recollection whatsoever of the gentleman before me.* Of course. Count Palazzi. Indeed. *Spying Lamrock lurking in a corner, I gesture to him to leave.* And what brings you to Avignon?

PALAZZI: Certain business on behalf of the Prince of Saxony. I am not at liberty . . .

I: . . . Naturally.

PALAZZI: But, dear lady, I am informed that you are soon to leave Avignon. *He glances about at the packing cases.*

I: We are.

PALAZZI: And you are bound for?

I: I am not at liberty . . .

PALAZZI: . . . Naturally. *There is an awkward silence. He smiles. His teeth are very white, though one at the front is chipped, most delightfully.*

I: *Wondering whether he has surmised that I have no notion of where we are to go, the road back to Venice being far too hazardous given the war raging between Spain and Austria, and the road to England being fraught with danger and devoid of any appeal.* But soon, as you see.

PALAZZI: It is simply that I am bound for my mother's home at Brescia, and I know how honoured the contessa would be to have you and your household stay in her palace. It would be a great privilege for me to escort you there.

I: That is a most charming offer indeed, Count Palazzi, and I shall give it careful consideration. Will you stay for tea?

PALAZZI: Perhaps I may return tomorrow?

I: *Encouraged that he gives the correct reply.* Certainly. Come at three. *I ring the bell, and Lamrock appears. I hear him quietly interrogating my visitor as he escorts him out.*

Palazzi left a smell of something heady in the air, jasmine or such like, and something more, a certain atmosphere. Lamrock appeared before me, lips pursed.

'You do not trust the young count?' I asked.

'You remember him from Venice?'

'I . . . I . . . might.'

'I do not,' he said, with resolution.

'He offers us some path out of this place.'

'I will make enquiries,' said Lamrock, unhappily.

Over the week that followed Lamrock found that Palazzi was a mystery, a cipher, a unicorn, a nought. No one seemed to know him, no one seemed to have heard of him and no one would vouch for him. Nevertheless, since neither of us could think of any better place to go than Brescia, nor any other person to go with than Palazzi, it seemed that Palazzi had arrived as good fortune sometimes does – at precisely the right moment. He was educated, seemed to know many people who were friends of mine, and wanted nothing in return but my company on a journey he assured me he was bound to commence no later than the end of the week. He called each day for tea and was the model of courtesy and charm and discretion.

It was on the very morning of our departure that he presented himself in great anguish.

PALAZZI: *In theatrical distress, performed for those in the very furthest seats.* Oh, Contessa!

I: My dear Palazzi. Whatever can it be? Are you ill? Has something befallen your dear mother?

PALAZZI: Oh, the shame, the shame! *He falls to his knees.*

I: *Urging him to his feet.* Tell me, dear count, what is it that mortifies you so?

PALAZZI: Oh, it is terrible.

I: *Becoming impatient.* What is it that is so terrible?

PALAZZI: I have to confess, to confess . . .

I: To confess what?

PALAZZI: That all of my property is in my mother's hands, and I receive only the smallest allowance, and I am sorry to say I have debts which may prevent me from being permitted to leave Avignon.

I: *Recognizing that I am in precisely the same situation that I was some months before, when gagged and bound, a hostage, though at least on that occasion I did not need to pay for my liberty.* You need money?

PALAZZI: *His whole compact, muscular frame twitches. A part of the drama.* I assure you if you are able to extend me a loan of a certain amount, I will give you a note in return, which my mother will be pleased to honour on our arrival at Brescia.

I: *A note! How many notes I have issued in good faith but with little or no expectation of their redemption. And here, no doubt, would be another.* For what sum?

PALAZZI: *Squirms again.*

I: *Now I wish to kick him, yet if I were to do so I know that I would only be kicking away my own ladder, and I am absolutely resolved to leave Avignon today, for to stay would mean not only misery but also humiliation.*

PALAZZI: Three hundred sequins.

I: Three hundred! *It is a considerable sum. More than a hundred and fifty pounds.* Very well.

PALAZZI: Oh, Contessa! *He falls again to his knees and kisses my hem.*

I: *Unable to resist the temptation to kick him away.* I am not a contessa, but the daughter of a duke. You may call me Lady Mary or madam, as you please.

PALAZZI: *Weeps.*

Had I consented to pay him half of what he asked, the years that followed might have been less costly for me. Yet to have bargained with him would have demeaned me. My power rested in my ability to pay for his freedom from the city – I did not wish to buy him half his freedom, any more than I wished him to be only half an escort on the perilous journey now facing us. And so I paid what he asked. But I had given Palazzi some understanding of my wealth, and that I should not have done.

33

IN THE SPIDER'S WEB

Autumn 1749, Gottolengo, Venetian Republic

(Mary)

I had set out for Brescia on that bright morning, some four years after I first settled in Avignon, in the company of Palazzi, believing I knew the measure of him, while Lamrock watched him with the patience of a wolf watching a lamb. Yet Palazzi was no lamb, nor was he an envoy for the Prince of Saxony, nor any of the things he claimed to be. He was a spider, and he was leading us ever deeper into his web.

First came the matter of the journey, and in this the spider showed great skill. For all his unsatisfactory nature, he was good enough company: intelligent, eager and, when pressed, resourceful. Though I had been shaken by his sudden and unexpected demand for money before our departure, it seemed to me that on that journey he was determined to do his utmost to show that he deserved my trust and, since I had no choice in the matter anyway, I found myself giving him what he craved. Palazzi used his considerable gifts at confabulation to convince the Spanish forces that we were travelling at the command of Don Philip himself and, when we had crossed the lines and arrived in territory occupied by the advancing Austrians, he drew on my acquaintance with the Austrian Empress to win us every privilege. The miseries we witnessed in those lands ravaged by war were and remain terrible to remember, and entering Venetian lands, at peace, was as travelling from the depths of winter to the heights of a bountiful summer, though what lay between those territories was not time but merely the matter of a mile and a frontier. War is mankind's doing, and it is humanity's greatest pestilence.

How he had engineered it I did not know, but as we came to the gates of Brescia there was his mother, Countess Giulia Palazzi, awaiting us in her coach and six. She insisted then and there that I lodge with her, treating her son with that manner that sits tentatively between love and disdain that I recognized only too well from my own relationship with Eddie, and that made me feel a sense of uneasy camaraderie with her. She was charming, solicitous and, once there were no men present, surprisingly frank. The countess assisted me over the next days in finding lodgings of my own in the town, but before I was able to occupy them, I fell into a malignant fever that left me weak as a butterfly in a storm, battened down on to my bed and unable to raise myself from the sweat-soaked sheets. Throughout the weeks that followed the countess treated me like a sister, sitting with me, mopping my brow and bringing me an improbable variety of salves and potions. She arranged for a succession of physicians to visit me, each one pronouncing my prospects more hopeless than the last. For two months or more I existed on that bleak frontier between life and death, unaware of what was going on about me, and unable to give even the simplest instruction.

After what sufficed for my recovery I was left weak and unsteady, and felt an exhaustion so considerable that I wondered if I would ever again possess that energy that had brought me so far. Lamrock told me how, while I'd been ill, he'd been sent away from the house to find lodgings elsewhere in town and had learnt certain things about the Palazzis that put me even further on my guard, for though the countess herself was blameless, her three sons each had a reputation for lawlessness, extortion and tyranny.

Feeling exhausted and ever more reliant on Lamrock, I considered what we could do, and resolved to move to the countryside where the air would assist my recovery. Inevitably Palazzi had a proposal and offered to take us to the village of Gottolengo where, he assured us, a castle stood empty that would be perfect for my purposes. I consented to inspect the place and Lamrock and I were accompanied by the count and his mother. The journey across the flat fields that lay between Brescia and the village took us all day and we arrived at Gottolengo after dark, to find the 'castle' a half-completed building in need of a roof and floor. But there were two chambers amenable to occupation. Oddly I slept that night as well as I had in many months.

The next morning, I could see that my new residence was set delightfully, though it would need considerable sums spending on it to make it into a habitable home. The countess announced that, with great regret, she was obliged to return to Brescia on urgent business but assured me that her son would remain for a few days to ensure I had all I needed. While I hardly wished for the spider's company, I was truly grateful for his mother's kindness. What followed was all too predictable.

I: Palazzi, I wish for your advice.

PALAZZI: I am at your unconditional service, Contessa. You must feel free to command me to do anything whatsoever in your aid.

I: *I had by then given up attempting to dissuade him from calling me* Contessa. I must make some gift to your mother, some mark of gratitude for her great kindness to me.

PALAZZI: *Contorts his face, wrings his hands, paces the room.* My mother, you must understand, Contessa . . . she is a proud woman. Proud in her poverty, do you understand?

I: *Wondering where this will lead.* I understand that she has self-respect, yes.

PALAZZI: And she is determined, always, absolutely determined to observe the . . . the rules of propriety, and to a woman such as she the rules include welcoming a visitor into her home, and most particularly a visitor in need. You understand?

I: Yes. Well, we will leave the matter there, then.

PALAZZI: And were you to give her a gift of, let us say, some cloth or jewels, she would feel bound to reciprocate.

I: As I say . . .

PALAZZI: . . . It would be to thank her, yes, I understand. To thank her for the care she has shown you. But she would . . . *Tears springing from his eyes as easily as words from his tongue.* She would, despite having so little, buy a jewel or some cloth or a parrot, perhaps, or a fine table, to give to you in turn, so that you and she would endlessly be giving each other gifts, and yet she . . .

I: She could not afford such extravagances. I understand. I wish I had not mentioned it. I thought only of some small gesture. Perhaps some little thing she likes particularly to eat.

PALAZZI: *Feigning sudden outrage.* You would insult my mother with a sack of nuts?

I: Does she like nuts?

PALAZZI: *Moodily silent. At length he sits on a chair and stretches out his surprisingly long legs. He is like a frog, all leg. Short body, bulging eyes, and short arms with alarmingly expressive fingers at the end of them. Odd that I thought his features pleasing when first I saw him.* I have a thought.

I: Yes?

PALAZZI: A gift may be given to her secretly, as it were. Something she would greatly appreciate and yet would not embarrass her.

I: *Knowing what is to come.* Oh?

PALAZZI: Money! You may give my mother money through myself. I would leave it for her in some place she would be certain to find it most readily, and, ah . . . *He fans out his long fingers and widens his eyes, as if seeing her delight before him.* And she would be made most happy by it. I should leave her only the faintest hint of from whom it came, and some slight insinuation of it being her reward for all the kindness she had shown to you, and yet she would be under not the slightest obligation to acknowledge it or reciprocate.

I: *Knowing perfectly well what he is about, and yet unable to resist, for if he was swindling me, so was I teasing him*. That is very subtle.

PALAZZI: We are subtle, here in this region. We are a subtle people. It is our culture.

I: To weave webs of fine silk.

PALAZZI: Yes, yes! We are weavers of fine silk!

I: And how much would be a suitable sum, do you think?

PALAZZI: Ah no, Contessa. I could not suggest . . .

I: Well, then, perhaps . . .

PALAZZI: But let us say two hundred sequins.

I: Two hundred? *I had been about to suggest fifty.*

I determined that this would be the last occasion I would submit to one of his stratagems. For more than a year I refused to give him so much as a sequin, except in return for some genuine service he provided, and his appearances in Gottolengo became mercifully less frequent. I busied myself with gardens which I took possession of by the river, a positive arcadia of vines and blooms that, together with three gardeners engaged from the village, we brought into such order that they became an object of pride for all the residents of Gottolengo, who gazed down on them from the village's single bridge that gave a fine view of my orchard and rockeries and roses. I did not mind being watched as I went about my pruning and planting, always giving a cheery wave to whichever of my neighbours stood viewing me at work, and I found my various agues eased as the months passed. In such manner I felt at last to have found a place where I could be happy without fearing death or yearning for love.

As my presence in the village became known in the province, I was subject to legions of visits not only from the ladies of Palazzi's family but from all the quality thereabouts. All were most solicitous, and determined to make me a part of their social circle whether I wanted to or no.

I was invited to attend a daytime party to celebrate the feast of Martinmas at the palace of a contessa who lived some five miles distant, and declined, since the days of early winter were short, and I had no wish to be on the road in the dark.

Palazzi appeared to urge me to change my mind. I could not think why.

PALAZZI: Everyone will wish to see you there, Contessa. It is a fine day.

I: I am not feeling very well, Palazzi. I think it best if I rest.

PALAZZI: You will disappoint so terribly if you do not go. And it is at the Contessa Cigole's mansion, which is not two miles from here.

I: It is five miles. And too far.

PALAZZI: It is a beautiful day.

I: *Looking out of the window. It is, undeniably, a beautiful day for late autumn, and I conclude that perhaps a short ride, a charming meal and a return before dark will not be so unpleasant.* It is. Very well, I shall go! *I instruct Lamrock to guard the rooms, since despite all the work done to the castle over the preceding year, it has not yet any locks or keys.*

PALAZZI: It is most important that you take your manservant with you, Contessa, and your maid and footman. Custom demands it. To arrive alone, without the dignity of servants, would be regarded as a grave insult.

I: Then I shall remain here after all. I cannot leave the house unguarded.

PALAZZI: *His moist, bulging eyes light up, impish.* But I have a solution! Two very trustworthy men shall guard your castle, Contessa. I shall present them for your approval. They are of long standing in the village. Indeed, Bertolo was mayor not ten years ago. Let me bring them to you.

These men were, naturally, waiting but yards away, for Palazzi's spontaneously helpful proposals were always well incubated. I was thus presented within moments with two men I had seen only once or twice before in the village. They looked like a pair of scoundrels, though many of the menfolk thereabouts did, and it was a far from reliable indicator of their characters, which were often perfectly gentle. Yet I had an ill feeling about the arrangement. Why did I consent to these men guarding my home, despite knowing full well that I would most likely have cause to regret it? Part of it was pride, no doubt; and another a desire to trust Palazzi, or at least test his trustworthiness; and lastly I did not wish, in turning down these two men, to gain a reputation in the village for high-handedness.

The Martinmas party at the Countess Cigole's was no less delightful than promised, the company lively and welcoming. It was apparent that I was regarded as a local celebrity, and if the stage was more modest than Venice and the entertainments simpler, I felt that it was none the worse for that. My opinions of the different lands I had travelled through were sought by all present, and I was asked to confirm the truth of stories they had heard that I knew the King of England and was a good friend of the Doge of Venice, and that I had met Voltaire and the Austrian Empress. I did all but sing an aria (which I would naturally never do, for my reputation would be forever shattered). But for all the entertainment, it was November, and the feast was taken in the courtyard of the mansion. After two hours of conversation in Italian, a little goose and less bread, together with some large amount of red wine, I was not only exhausted but very, very cold. I called for my carriage.

'No, no!' protested the contessa. 'You have only just arrived. There is a bright moon tonight, and look,' she said, pointing up at a sky the distracted blue of early winter, 'no cloud! No need to worry about the dark. Your coachman will find his way home easily.'

'I confess, dear lady, that I feel very tired, and must to my bed.'

Countess Cigole clapped her hands and a footman in a uniform covered in so much gold brocade that he resembled a gilded maypole appeared, to whom she fired out instructions so rapidly I could not follow them. Ten minutes later I found myself in a well-warmed bed before a roaring fire in a chamber in her mansion. As I fell into a deep and comfortable sleep I lapsed into delicious dreams of Francesco Algarotti just as he was the first day I set eyes upon him, but for the fact that he had a crow upon his head, and one on each shoulder, and it was the crows that spoke to me of love and a life together, while he was mute.

Next morning, I awoke feeling quite purged of both tiredness and what I'd feared was to be a recurrence of the fever I had suffered in Brescia. I thanked the countess for her hospitality and found that Palazzi, too, had remained at the Cigole mansion, apparently concerned for my welfare. We returned to Gottolengo together with Lamrock, Marianne and Fribourg, whereupon, entering my chamber at the castle I immediately saw that all was out of its place. The men assigned to guard my home had long since left to go on a hunt, and when I checked the place where I had left my jewel boxes I found them gone. My heart pounded, I felt weak, and yet I knew I had done this to myself as surely as any other had done it to me. When I told Palazzi of the theft, he threw himself to the ground in his habitual manner, wailing all the while at the dishonour brought upon his family's name.

'The dishonour might easily be repaired,' I ventured.

'How, how, dear Contessa?' he pleaded from his prostrate position, looking up at me as a pug exhorts its mistress after it has done its toilet upon her silks.

'By the jewels' recovery.' I pulled my slipper away from his chin and retired to bed.

Next day Palazzi reported to me in great distress where I lay prone that he had searched the whole village without success. 'My honour . . . my honour,' he protested.

Was it now my role to restore his honour?

'But I have a notion of who the thieves may be,' he said.

'I'm sure you have, knowing your subtlety.'

'Indeed, Contessa, indeed. And I believe they will have gone as far as Milan.'

'Really?' I wondered what his next ruse would be, though by now I was truly weary of him.

'I am happy to go in pursuit of them, for even if there is a chance in a hundred of recovering your jewels, and no less—'

'Your honour, yes.'

'Then I feel obliged to make the journey.'

'Go, then.'

'But such a journey will be costly, dear lady.'

I was so sick of Palazzi I would have paid almost any sum to win some peace. As it happened, he needed only forty sequins for this latest adventure, which I felt certain would not produce my lost jewels. But I reasoned that with the money from my jewels together with the other sums he had stolen from me he had probably accumulated sufficient to return to his former diplomatic position at the court of Saxony and Poland, if he had ever held such a thing, and I fervently hoped I would soon be entirely rid of him.

34

THE MOST BEAUTIFUL PLACE ON EARTH

Summer 1751, Lovere, Venetian Republic

(Mary)

The return of the fever I suffered in Brescia arrived as I feared it would, and for months I was too weak to visit my gardens, entrusting them to the villagers I had employed, who repaid my loyalty many times over. The contrast with Palazzi was not lost on me.

Gottolengo, surrounded by streams and marshes, was not conducive to good health. Italian physicians were no better than English ones for their propensity to bleed, having an even greater inclination in the direction of leeches. Though in one respect their medical services were immensely superior to those of England, for the town levied a tax on every household to pay physicians, in return for which they were to receive no fee, and to never refuse to visit the household of any person, whether rich or poor. So impressed was I with this that I wrote to Edward again urging him to introduce a bill for a similar system in Britain, notwithstanding his previous aversion to such an idea.

Lamrock eventually secured for me the services of Dr Baglioni, who was bright-eyed, quick-witted and spoke without pomposity. His instructions were clear: if I was to survive the next bout of fever it was imperative that I travel to Lovere and take the waters there.

The journey to Lovere was along rocky tracks and over precipitous passes, and I wondered if I would live to see the fabled place. But when I first set eyes upon it from high above the town, and admired the placid lake on which it stood, I truly believe I saw our world as the gods once did – pristine, unspoilt and at peace.

I took a house almost on the shores of the lake, and each morning threw open my shutters to a heavenly vista of water and mountains, of forest and pretty little houses dotted on the hillsides. The people of Lovere were generous, intelligent and industrious and I soon acquired pleasant company. In all I felt better than I had in years.

To further lift my spirits, I began to receive letters more reliably, making me suspect that the postal system at Gottolengo had not been one to trust. Edward's letters were, as ever, concerned with the price of coal, with the number of trees on his land and, more legitimately, with fears for our son, who was reported married for a third time, despite having not dispensed with his other two wives, and worse still of having been arrested in France for setting fire to the home of a man who had lent him money. He was imprisoned for three months in the Bastille, and subsequently banished to Holland. Eddie wrote to me regularly bemoaning his father's meanness towards him, but Edward and I were united in our conviction that whatever was given to our son would be lost in short order.

My correspondence with my daughter became more frequent, infused with a warmth that was perhaps kindled by our long time apart and our many miles of separation. Mary told me a good deal about my various grandchildren and their quite distinct personalities. She was expecting an eighth child and seemed to think there was nothing unusual in continuing to produce heirs for as long as she was able. Her husband had recently become tutor to George, the young Prince of Wales, and so had risen most unexpectedly to a position of great prominence. I trusted that she would be able to bear the talk that would now trail in her wake sure as a muddy gown, for that is the price one always pays for status. She took my advice with polite grace, and so I took hers.

To Nell I wrote letters filled with the colour of my Italian life, and she responded with the watery hues of the Scottish Highlands, and with small details about her family and estate, but they were none the less appreciated for that.

I wrote to dear Fanny regularly, receiving replies written on her behalf by her daughter, which were as carefully composed as the steps of a sarabande, slow and stately and hinting at a meaning that eluded the reader as fully as the author intended. Yet I hoped that my own words were read out to Fanny. I wished I could have told her all about Palazzi and sought her advice on what to do, for so often she saw the simple course, when I only ever imagined the crooked path. But Fanny was lately content to embroider and walk and care for a small puppy, and had ceased her fits, or so Frannie informed me. I could but hope that Fanny was happy to be with her daughter and her painful memories had been lost, even at the cost of the better part of her reason.

*

My husband regrettably heard some rumours about the behaviour of Palazzi and delicately sought assurances that I was not falling under the influence of a man of unreliable character. I had not informed him of the theft of my jewels. It was dear Lady Oxford, ever guileless and frank, who informed me in a letter of what might have been more truly on Edward's mind – that the London papers were carrying stories that I had taken Palazzi as my lover. What bitter irony! I had unsuccessfully pursued love all my life and approaching my dotage was rumoured to have fallen in love with a tarantula.

This latest foul rumour reminded me of the importance of bringing all my papers into proper order, for everything would be distorted if my own voice was not heard: I would be thought dirty, unfaithful and immoderate, as Pope had so unfairly alleged; my work would be claimed by others, and that which others had done poorly would be attributed to me. It would be as if I had never been born at all. The word can live for ever, even though the heart cannot. I resolved to publish my Turkish letters first, bringing them all into a single volume so that anyone who cared to read them would know what Constantinople was truly like and understand how I came upon the science of inoculation, the humbling faith of Islam and the various freedoms enjoyed by Turkish women, contrary to the prejudices and ignorance of English writers who had all had the misfortune to be men. I went to the trunks containing my diaries and copies of the letters I had written, to find them in hopeless disarray.

I needed a secretary.

'Lamrock, I need a secretary. A person of unimpeachable honesty, someone capable and literate. I intend to spend what time I have left preparing my writing for publication.'

As was his habit he thought a moment before he spoke.

'We are likely to find in Italy only an Italian. Would an Italian be acceptable, madam?'

'Why not?'

'His English might not be as good as it need be?'

'True. He will need French, also. Many of my letters are in French. And my diary entries are sometimes in Latin or Greek. And sometimes in a special code.'

Lamrock gave me a look. 'Then we shall require a person of very particular aptitude.'

'There must be educated young men, or for that matter women, in Brescia or Padua?'

'Or old ones, even better educated. Perhaps a priest?'

'Oh no, I shouldn't want a priest.' I thought of all that was in my diaries, and how a priest would most likely shudder at their contents. 'No. No priests, Lamrock.'

To Lamrock's credit he found a succession of candidates over the next month, and we interviewed them together, I asking questions of their reading and experience, Lamrock of their character and family. The first was a foppish youth of not more than twenty, eager to show off his Latin and Greek, his French and his fine hand. Had he stopped a moment to ask about the task I wished to give him I might have granted him the position, since he would have been pretty as a parrot to have had each day in my study, but like a parrot he would have squawked a good deal and comprehended nothing.

Next was a solid gentleman of about forty, corpulent and breathless and needing a stick to relieve the weight from his gouty foot. He was erudite and spoke English fluently, having served for several years as secretary to the East India Company in London. He was solicitous and attentive to the great work that was needed, and indeed knew something of my poetry and work on smallpox. The difficulty arose when it came to set terms, for he wanted to be paid a sum greater than my yearly living expenses and when I questioned why he told me that he had it on good authority that I could afford his services, that authority being none other than his friend Count Ugolino Palazzi.

Two women also applied, and I naturally was well disposed to think that a woman might make an amenable companion as well as secretary, yet each came with some flaw, the first being so deaf that I was unable to make myself understood, and the second arriving with her two small children, assuring me that her mother would normally take care of them but that she had unfortunately broken her arm that morning when stepped upon by the milk cow.

After a month of interviews, I was beginning to despair when at last came a very fine candidate, a doctor of letters who had recently retired from the University of Padua. Indeed he seemed perfectly well qualified, but for the fact that he addressed all his questions to Lamrock. Lamrock naturally urged him in the direction of seeking his answers from me, but he simply refused to acknowledge me.

'Dr Morisini,' I said at last. 'It is not Lamrock's diaries that are to be put in order but my own!'

'Madam,' he declared, 'no woman's intimate thoughts should be put before a world of men.'

'Dr Morisini, the world is half full of women, or have you not noticed?'

At which the distinguished gentleman stood so abruptly that the powder from his wig erupted in a cloud about his head. 'I bid you good day,' he said, bowing to me in a cursory manner and much more thoroughly towards Lamrock.

I asked Lamrock how such a misunderstanding might have arisen, and he confessed that in his advertisement for the position he had described me simply as Dr Wortley Montagu in order to encourage applications from all quarters.

'But I hold no doctorate,' I assured him.

'In a just world, madam, you would hold a doctorate and many other titles beyond *Lady*.'

'I do not think I can endure interviewing another man,' I said.

'And I fear I have exhausted the supply of suitable persons in the whole province.'

'I am determined to have my papers put in order, for gaps to be filled, for certain small elisions to be made. I . . . I . . .' I felt all of a sudden a great emotion, for the impossibility of making my words live long after I had taken my last breath was obvious. And if that should be the case then they would die with me, and Death would have won his long battle.

'You must not despair, my lady,' said Lamrock, calm as ever. 'The task is not so difficult, and I feel certain that, with patience, we will find someone. I have taken the liberty of preparing two early chapters of your diaries to show the relative simplicity of the task.'

'*Simplicity?*' I was conscious of how my papers were arrayed across half a dozen trunks, all out of order, my entries from childhood interspersed with pages from the twenties and thirties, and my script often illegible, even to me. 'I cannot even think how to begin the task. Bring me what you have done,' I asked, somewhat peevishly.

Lamrock brought me a volume containing my childhood entries, neatly written out, well ordered, so perfect a display of my memories that I wept over the pages and had to dab my handkerchief upon the ink to stop it from spoiling. 'Oh, Lamrock! How have you done this, and when did you do so?'

'Over the evenings when you have been out dining with friends. I should have asked your permission, but being conscious of our difficulty in finding a candidate I thought I might get some measure of the task required. Can you forgive me, madam?'

'Lamrock. *You* are my secretary! You are my guide; you are my very salvation!'

He granted himself the most diffident smile and bowed his head. 'Very well.'

'I must increase your wage to reflect your new duties,' I said hastily.

'That will not be necessary, but I have one condition.'

'Anything – anything at all! What is it?' I asked.

'That you permit me to deal with Count Palazzi on your behalf from this day on.'

'Oh, granted, granted!' It was all I could do to restrain myself from embracing him, though I knew that such an act would not only breach politeness but be unwelcome, for Lamrock was possessed of the sensibilities of a clock, and whoever heard of giving a clock a tender embrace?

But if I hoped to spend the next months and years in peace working with Lamrock on my letters and diaries I was to be disappointed, for there was to come a murder, a dispute over a statue in which God was required to intervene, and one final outrage from Palazzi.

35

PALAZZI'S WEB BREAKS

Autumn 1756, Gottolengo, Venetian Republic

(Mary)

I found that in the village of Gottolengo, where I spent all but the summers, my counsel was sought on matters ranging from the insignificant, such as a dispute over the rightful owner of a gaggle of geese that lived upon the pond, to the very great, including whether a man should be hanged for having allowed his horse to trample his neighbour's child. That I was from England added significantly to my value, much as a Chinese vase is worth more in Paris than Macao, and a piece of French brocade will be talked about in Nanking but thought commonplace in Nîmes. I would say I was regarded more or less as presiding magistrate for the region and, being an Englishwoman, was more trusted since I had no association with the existing families who had, naturally enough, been in bitter dispute with each other for several centuries. I was able to resolve marital disagreements with a few well-chosen words and to settle arguments over land that had long proved intractable by taking my pen and drawing a line across a map. The fact that my eyes were too poor to see the various competing boundaries drawn upon it made my judgement wholly arbitrary, and it was all the more appreciated for that.

I thought little of the service I provided to the townsfolk, but my assistance was taken a good deal more seriously by them. To my dismay I discovered that they thought enough of me to wish to make a statue and put it in the town square. The mayor presented me with a very fine design; the monument would be life-size, of me seated and reading a book. Through the offices of Lamrock I made clear that I did not have time to sit for such a project, but this appeared to be no obstacle, for the sculptor would proceed on the basis of certain sketches he had made of me without my permission. How could I make clear that the statue must not be made? It was not modesty on my part, but plain fear. For if news of the statue became known in England it would be taken as yet more proof of my apparent vanity, of my earnest desire for notoriety and praise, and I would be ridiculed.

'Lamrock. How can I stop them making this damnable effigy of me and having it sit there in the village square for pigeons to use as their chamber pot?'

'There is one strategy I can think of that is bound to be effective: you must claim that your God forbids you. All here are Catholics and will believe anything you may care to tell them of what it means to be a Protestant.'

'Yet they might have heard of the statues we make of our kings and great men, all of whom are no more devout than myself, which is to say not at all.'

'Then we shall tell them that a statue of a woman may not be made in our faith. They will struggle to think of any statue of a female made in England.'

This was true enough, though it had nothing to do with faith and everything to do with the disregard held by men for womankind's accomplishments. Had it not been for my fear of being laughed at in the pages of the *Public Advertiser* I should, with this thought in mind, have marched down to the square and summoned the sculptor myself.

Lamrock went to explain to the mayor that our God forbade such an image, and that put an end to the matter, for a man may argue for ever with his fellow man or woman, but dare not take up his case with God, however wrong he may think God to be.

There were more serious conflicts in the town that required my involvement, most notably when Marianne came to me before light one morning, shaking with fear.

'What on earth is it, Marianne?' I asked, stirring.

'The maid of Signora Bellini is here. She says her master is dead.'

'Oh dear.' I could not think what this had to do with me. Signora Bellini was a woman of somewhat exhausted beauty in her thirties whose farm provided us with our eggs and meat and cheese and who had been kind enough to give me advice about planting in the garden. We took tea together on occasion and she sometimes talked to me of her great desire to travel, most particularly to China. She had been startled when I explained to her that China lay even further from Gottolengo than Rome.

'Signora Bellini bids you come, because . . . because she has killed Signor Bellini.'

'Goodness!' I rose, pulled on a sack dress and slippers, and went straightway to the house. On my way I reflected on recent conversations when Signora Bellini and I had been sat amiably together in the herb garden, she talking of salvia and thyme, and I had gently enquired about certain bruises upon her face and arms, and she had told me with conviction of doors she had walked into, and falls she had had about the farm, but there is not a woman in the world who ever walked into a door who was not also beaten by her husband.

The scene that greeted me was startling and gory. My nose was first assaulted with the smell of fresh blood, as surely as if I were entering a slaughterhouse. And the scene within was as if from hell itself, Signor Bellini's torso, blue-white, splayed face down upon the kitchen table, prongs of steel poking through his back like the jagged peaks of the Alps, their tines dripping with red. Gathered about the table stood the household servants, as if in some religious scene painted by Signor Caravaggio. Signora Bellini was sat quaking in a corner, alternating between giggling and wailing and clearly in the grips of an hysteria.

'He fell upon the roasting pan?' I suggested.

'I pushed the bastard!' she declared in one of her briefly ecstatic interludes, before weeping once more. 'He was coming at me, a pan in his hand, and I ran about the table, first one way and then another, and he had been drinking, you know, and so was not quick, and I do not know why cook had left the big roasting forks upon the table, I think she had been cleaning them, and I got myself behind him and gave him a mighty push and he fell right upon them.' She laughed, madly, and then gasped, 'I shall be hanged!'

'No, no,' I said, sitting beside her, wiping blood from my hands, for the very air in that room seemed to bleed. I placed an arm about her shoulder. 'I shall go and see the mayor and tell him what I have witnessed, a terrible accident, and an innocent wife who could do nothing to prevent it.'

'It is a sin, murder!'

'It is. And you averted the sin, for he did not murder you, but fell upon his own violence, and thus met his end.'

She looked at me in astonishment. 'He fell?'

'Indeed.'

'But how would he fall?'

I thought a moment, stood, and acted out how that dreadful man might have fallen, my eyes all the while on the frightful scene that was before me, the smell of the congealing blood becoming cloying and all-consuming.

'Yes,' she said, doubtfully. 'Yes, I suppose he might have fallen.'

'Your servants will all agree that they came upon the horrible scene and only then called you to see what had befallen your poor husband.'

'Will they?'

I knew where the servants' sentiments would lie – in favour of the course that would cause them least trouble. No man willingly goes to court, for a witness can so easily be turned into a culprit.

By the time I left, Signora Bellini was calm, and had sent her manservant off to fetch the mayor, so that he could bear witness to the unfortunate accident.

Every person in the village knew the truth of what had happened, but all chose to believe the story I had embroidered quickly out of early-morning light and blood, for there are times when the truth is inconvenient and lies may be precisely what justice demands.

After some eight years living in Gottolengo and Lovere, I determined to move back to Venice. Lamrock and I had by then put all my papers in English in order, and we had begun to work on an Italian and a French manuscript of my diaries, too. I had set about making discreet enquiries of persons who might be relied upon to publish them and found that Venice was the place to have the Italian editions produced. After so many years of quiet living I felt ready for more entertainment than the countryside could provide.

There was one other consideration, which was that I dare not send the manuscripts to England. It had become apparent that, despite our improved relations, my daughter was bitterly opposed to the notion of my achieving any greater notoriety (as she termed it) than I already possessed. I had imagined that I'd been quite forgotten in England, but it seemed certain piratical printers had produced occasional editions of my letters and poems, and these had been well received. Mary implored me not to have my letters and diaries published, and while I made clear that I would not do so in my own lifetime, she told me candidly in one of her more startling declarations that I was not to rely on her to assist in any way in their posthumous publication which, she said, would bring great hurt to all who truly loved me. I came to realize that when it came to protecting my reputation and securing my legacy, my own daughter would be my tireless enemy.

There was another enemy to overcome, for though he had not troubled me greatly for some little while I knew that Palazzi and Lamrock were locked in a battle as long and bloody as the Peloponnesian War, and from time to time I heard the distant rumbles of it.

As we began to make ready to leave Gottolengo, Palazzi came to see me more and more often. I directed him to speak to Lamrock on any matter concerning the sale of the castle or the arrangements for moving my possessions to Venice, yet he persisted, arranging for purchasers who never came and sending packing cases which did not arrive. As the date drew near for our departure, he grew frantic, telling us that plague had come to Venice (untrue), that the roads from Brescia east were impassable (also untrue), and even that five ladies had been murdered already that year on the road to Padua and I was most likely to be the sixth. This was said in the manner of a clear threat, and I threw him out.

But I had made one fateful error before Lamrock had assumed full control of my affairs, which had been to place all my ready cash, more than two thousand pounds, with Palazzi's banker in Brescia. I had not trusted Palazzi, naturally, and had made my own enquiries, satisfying myself that the man was of good reputation, despite his poor choice in friends. However, when I made the trip to Brescia to withdraw my money, I was informed that the banker had departed for America two years earlier, and my cash was lost. Even then I did not despair, for though the sum represented half my wealth, I remained in possession of notes good for another two thousand and was determined not to admit to the world how Palazzi had swindled me.

I went to the padlocked case in which I had kept the notes safe for all this time. But when I went to ready them for exchange, I saw that every bill was blank.

'Lamrock!'

He appeared, and immediately saw my distress. 'Madam. What troubles you?'

'These bills. They are blank. The villain must have found the case, picked the lock, and replaced every bill with blank paper so that I would be fooled into believing them untouched!'

'Enough. I will deal with Palazzi,' said Lamrock with a low growl such as I had never heard from him.

'Do not do anything foolish, Lamrock,' I said to him as he went to leave, his ageing bones suddenly made young by pure fury. My comment prompted a look from him, as much as to say: 'Why do you underestimate me now?'

A day passed, then two, then three, and I heard no word from Lamrock and none from anyone else, and I became ever more worried and was soon almost out of my wits at what Lamrock might have done and, worse still, what Palazzi might have done to him. Terrible scenes cast themselves into my imagination, of fights or worse, and on the fourth day I could bear it no longer and decided I must set out for Brescia myself.

Despite my infirm body, which ached all over most days, I struggled on to a horse and rode the four hours to the city, marching into the mayor's office, where I was greeted with the usual honours. The mayor of the city was a short, fat fellow, upon his wall a portrait of a man who might have been him, had he been thinner and a great deal more handsome than he had turned out to be. His office smelt of unopened files, of dust and of the geraniums which sat in a box at the open window. Noticing my agitation, the mayor said, 'Calm yourself, Lady Mary, please.'

I was in such distress that I felt I would pass out. I had lost everyone important to me and I simply could not endure the loss of Lamrock too.

'Oh, Signor Capaldi, please tell me what has happened here in the city.'

'Ah, madam. It is a great business indeed,' he said, with apparent glee.

'What on earth has been going on?'

'Dear lady,' said the mayor, puffing up with pride in anticipation of the tale he was about to tell. He stood, placing his short arms behind his back, and began to strut up and down behind his desk, almost as if he were a cardboard duck at a fairground, running on rails. 'Count Palazzi has been acting the brigand for some years, as you are well aware. He has stolen money from one and all, and terrorized respectable citizens. We had been gathering evidence that he had murdered his banker, and when your manservant—'

'My secretary,' I corrected.

'Your secretary, indeed. When he came to me reporting this latest outrage, I became aware that your notes had been exchanged for cash without your authority and sent my constables to Palazzi's residence to arrest him. He had his men ready for us, and fired upon the constables who were equipped with rifles and fired back. A fierce battle ensued, in which your secretary was held hostage.'

'Goodness, Lamrock! Is he well?'

'Quite well. Signor Lamrock was able to restrain one of Palazzi's men at a crucial moment, which may well have made all the difference to the struggle,' said the mayor. 'And now Palazzi is imprisoned, and two of his henchmen dead!'

Happy though I was with this excellent outcome for the people of the province, I could not help but say: 'And I am poor.'

'Regrettably, Lady Mary, yes.'

Lamrock entered at that moment, as if scripted by Shakespeare in one of his happier comedies.

'Lamrock!' I declared with profound relief.

He smiled modestly, unable to wholly conceal his pride in the affair, and he and I went from the pompous mayor in haste and directly to the finest inn in the city and ate and drank to excess in celebration of his great victory until I remembered that I had no means of paying for our feast. Lamrock, conveniently, did.

In my newly impoverished state I was obliged to sell the castle for what little I could get for it, which was barely enough to pay off Marianne and Fribourg. Lamrock and I then made for Venice, where, unable to rent a palazzo, we stayed some weeks with old friends, but Venice had changed and the ease with which we had found comfortable lodgings seventeen years earlier was not to be repeated. With Europe at war once more, Venice was teeming with all those who could afford to flee the approaching armies, and even modest rooms were not to be had. I could, of course, have confessed the reasons for my sudden penury to my husband and would have been furnished with whatever sum I required, but I had no wish to give him the pleasure of knowing that I had been robbed not once, not twice but perhaps a hundred times by Palazzi.

It was in Venice that a letter arrived from a most surprising person, a person that, in other circumstances, I should not have wished to hear from at all. I had not forgotten Francesco Algarotti – that would be akin to forgetting that I was in possession of a nose. But one does not think of one's nose except when sneezing or suffering from a chill, and so it was with my memories of him. *Forgotten* – what a word. How often do we say *forgotten* when speaking of something that occupies our every thought. As a child we claim to have *forgotten* our whereabouts when, for instance, a precious vase is broken; and when a little older we claim to have *forgotten* that we gave a certain encouraging look to an unsuitable young man. And now, as an old woman, I say to anyone who may ask that I have forgotten all about Francesco. But it is no more true than saying I have forgotten my nose.

Algarotti, having heard of my straitened circumstances, in an act of great and uncharacteristic generosity, offered me the use of his house Mirabella in Padua, and so there we went for the summer. Had I hoped to see him once more? Perhaps, but more out of curiosity than from the last smouldering embers of an old passion. He was anyway engaged in business in Bologna and told me in his letters that he was aged and ugly and as likely to deserve being an object of my affection as a pile of bricks that had once been a mansion. I wrote to him of the various adventures and mishaps that had befallen me since our parting all those years before, and from that day on we kept up a lively correspondence, much of which comprised discussing our various ailments. Whatever pain Algarotti had caused me, his letters and his most unexpected generosity eased the memory of it. I only hoped he did not pity me, any more than I pitied him.

Both Lamrock and I were but a year or two short of seventy, and my sight was failing. Poor Lamrock was obliged to read to me my correspondence, and take instruction for my replies, and though he did not once complain, I became conscious that we were wearing each other down like two old millstones that had produced many a ton of flour. I discovered a canker in my breast which grew a little more with each passing week and that I had no doubt would be the end of me. I did not tell Lamrock, nor seek the advice of any physician. My old friend Mary Astell had, very many years before, a cankerous breast removed by a surgeon, but she suffered in great agonies after, and it did not extend her life significantly. I would not take that course. My only fear was that I would not have time to put in place satisfactory arrangements for the publication of my works, and that is what Lamrock and I spent our days in planning, and it was just as well that we did, for the obstacles put in the way of my writings were to become very considerable indeed.

36

DEATH COMES CLOSE

Autumn 1761, Padua

(Mary)

I fancy the moon gazes upon the earth with awe and not a little fury: with awe for upon our planet live the endless glories of verdant forests, cool waters, snow-topped mountains and scorched deserts, while the serene moon is home only to that silvered silence which fills the starlit universe. But surely the moon resents the relentless gravity which traps it in our orbit, as Newton has decreed. If the moon were free from the earth, would she wander off into a new corner of the heavens and live a wholly other existence?

When I received the terrible news of my husband's death, I understood that we had been moon and earth to one another. He the cool sphere in our long marriage, I the one with storms, volcanoes and flights of brightly feathered birds. But he had always been there, stern yet generous, unyielding yet considerate, untender yet not without sympathy, and I had lived in his silvery light. Gone, and my world was unanchored. For days and weeks I could not think what to do, for there had always been Edward; all my life I had made a show of not needing him, and it was only now I knew that I did.

The will he left caused a storm, inevitably. He succeeded in appearing mean by settling amounts on his daughter's children and very little on his wife or son, and if there is one thing the public detests more than a wealthy man, it is a wealthy man who is miserly in death. Eddie, having presumably thought hard about how he might hurt me most grievously, chose to contest his father's will not on his own behalf, but on *mine*. It was impossible for me to make known the deep estrangement between Eddie and myself without appearing to be a heartless mother, and so I was obliged to extricate myself from his suit in the most tortuous manner. I received a letter of condolence from my niece Frannie, and at the bottom of it a few words written in my sister's own hand, a scribbled phrase about my long limbo, and I took that as an encouraging sign that her condition must be improved to some degree.

The need to sort out the mess of the will, to see my daughter and grandchildren and, I hoped, to hold my dear sister once more in my arms, all said but one thing: the time had come for Mary Wortley Montagu to return to England. Lamrock and I began to make arrangements for the long and necessarily modest journey home, having very little in ready cash or notes. There were delays of one sort or another all through that spring and summer, with various farewells to be made to friends in Venice and Padua. Algarotti promised to make the journey to Mirabella, where we had stayed through many seasons, and we awaited his arrival one month and then the next, but true to form he did not appear. I was told by a friend that he was ill with consumption, and by another still that he was already dead, which seemed unlikely since he continued to write, though with Algarotti anything was possible.

A further letter arrived from Scotland and the news it carried was the worst I had ever received, for my dear, beloved sister was dead. Fanny was gone. And though I had lost her not once but half a dozen times, she had always been there in my heart and no less in my thoughts. I'd imagined that if my racked body allowed me another year or two of life I would see her again, embrace her, and be reassured that she was happy. But no, Death had stolen that last love from me, and I was more alone than ever. I had Mary, and all her children, and no doubt we would observe the courtesies a mother and daughter must show towards each other, but it would be uneasy, I knew.

Grief battered me like a storm, such as we used to see from time to time in Avignon, when the skies would darken, the winds would howl and it seemed that the end times had come. My sister's death was my private storm, and I did not know whether I could endure it. Death was close to me now, relentless, taking every last person I loved.

Lamrock saw me through my grief, tenderly bringing me a little warm milk where I lay in my bed, and speaking only of easy things, like the leaves turning and the abundance of lemons on the trees.

'Lamrock!' I declared one day, grabbing his hand so hard that an uneasy look flashed across his tired features.

'My lady?'

'Do not die! At least, please do not die before me.'

'I will do my best, my lady.'

I knew little about Lamrock, despite all the years we had been together. He had lost his parents when only a small child and he and his brother had been raised by an aunt and uncle, stern, devout folk, and though childless they had never treated the two boys as their own. Lamrock was put into service at twelve. His brother, Joseph, went to America. 'Why did you never marry, Lamrock?'

He raised an eyebrow. 'I married, my lady. In seventeen thirteen, it was.'

'Oh, Lamrock. I didn't know.'

'She died of the smallpox the year after, and so . . .' But he did not say more, and I saw tears in his grey eyes, and though it is terrible to confess it, I had never thought until that moment that Lamrock could weep at all.

'My brother died in that same outbreak,' I said. 'It is a terrible disease and, were it not for the greed and ignorance of physicians, easily preventable.'

'The Royal College of Physicians now recommend inoculation for all, I am glad to say.'

This was news I had not heard. 'How so?'

'Edward Archer is now in charge of the smallpox hospital and is a great advocate of inoculation.'

I could not help but be surprised that no one had thought to inform me. 'The smallpox hospital? I did not know of that either. This Archer, why has he not sought my advice on the matter?'

Lamrock became uneasy. 'You would like to write to him, madam?'

What could I say? What would be the purpose in a letter? My campaign, for which I'd been ridiculed and hounded, had finally been taken up by men, and no doubt my own efforts roundly forgotten. 'I am too weary,' I said. 'Perhaps tomorrow.'

As our last summer at Mirabella turned to autumn, we began to fear that the roads would prove impassable if we tarried any longer. We sent the trunks containing my diaries and some of my letters to a convent in Venice where the Mother Superior was both learned and reliable. Lamrock would retrieve them once we had the funds and means to ship them safely to England and had found printers who could be relied upon to await my death. And with that, armed with the Turkish letters which we had gathered into a neat and publishable volume, the adventure of my life was drawing to its close. This, I knew, must be my final voyage.

37

RAGGED REMNANTS

Winter 1761, Rotterdam

(Mary)

It was late October when we arrived in Rotterdam, but with war once more raging we were bound to wait our turn for places on one of the few vessels that was able to cross the German Sea safely. We lodged with the Anglican minister, a generous and kindly man by the name of the Reverend Benjamin Sowden, who seemed in no great hurry to see us gone. Night after night he had me at his table, while I entertained his dinner guests with accounts of my long life, so that I began to wonder he did not weary of these tales. Lamrock he had work on his register of births, marriages and deaths, which one might have thought few, given his congregation was not great, but Lamrock reported it to be in utter confusion.

Sowden considered himself a man of letters (notwithstanding his incompetence in keeping church records) and indeed reviewed books published in Holland for the *Monthly Review.*

'Madam,' he declared after I had been with him almost a

month, the weather preventing any passage to England, even had the French navy allowed for it. 'Madam, I am conscious that you have with you a work that will illuminate all the world.' Sowden spoke thus, with wheezy pomposity and always with a degree of exaggeration. 'If your collected letters are written with an ounce of the elegance with which you speak of them, I am certain they will be read by every literate man and woman in Europe.'

'That is kind, Reverend, and I hope that may one day be so. But I am resolved to see them published only after I am dead, so that I shall not be subjected to derision, for I am truly weary of all that.'

'Then allow me, my dear lady, to make a proposal. As you know, the Dutch authorities are very liberal when it comes to publication, and if you were to leave the matter in my hands, I can promise you that the letters would be well produced and printed in affordable editions.'

I would have dismissed Sowden's offer out of hand, but for consideration of the fierce opposition I knew I would face from my daughter and her husband, who were now raised into positions of great influence, for my son-in-law was the new king's favourite.

I asked Lamrock's opinion of Sowden.

'He is a decent enough man, no doubt, but if, as you suspect, your family were to try to prevent publication, is he of sufficient guile to resist them?'

'But if we take the collection of letters to England, I am placing all the responsibility upon you, my dear Lamrock, to resist whatever pressures are placed upon *you*.'

'Rest assured, dear lady, that I may not be strong, but I am crafty.' And he winked at me, something so surprising that I stared at him in plain astonishment.

What meant he by that wink? I thought back to the

making of the manuscripts and realized that it was almost certain that the copy I possessed was far from being the only one in existence. 'Might it be sensible to have an edition published in Holland, and that we leave that to Sowden?' I suggested.

'It might.'

And in that manner, I bequeathed to the Reverend Benjamin Sowden the only copy of my Turkish letters that I knew for certain to exist.

38

THE FLARING OF THE FLAME

Spring 1762, London

(Mary)

It was January when at last I came into the Pool of London, to be greeted by my daughter, grown matronly and stern. We embraced with not a little trepidation. The grandchildren I had longed to see were there, too, or the older of them, for there were so very many. They each regarded me as they might a shire horse brought to them to ride, with a dash of wonderment, a little reverence, and a good dose of fright. But I was familiar with small children, for Marianne and Fribourg had their two, and before them John and Sara had three, and so I was able to say the soft things that put children at their ease.

After a fortnight in which tender words of affection were soon chased by bitter acrimony over what I had written or said, I moved from my daughter's home on South Audley Street to the house she and her husband, Lord Bute, had rented for my use at St George Street, not three hundred yards from their own. It was the shape of a harpsichord, and not much bigger. Lamrock I sent off to Norfolk to visit the place where his aunt and uncle had lived, a house he had inherited at some point in our long exile and where he had a tenant and no doubt repairs to be made and so forth.

To my surprise and consternation, I found once in my own quarters that I had upwards of forty visitors a day and was obliged to cram them into corners. It seemed that I was a sensation, a curiosity, an exotic. Had I been a great deal younger I might have felt flattered but, having experienced such great criticism from English society, though not from the more enlightened minds of Italy and France, I felt uneasy with this unexpected admiration, which landed on my lap like a large, amenable cat. I thought in those first days my attraction rested solely in the novelty of someone long forgotten and presumed dead, who had mysteriously returned to life, as if I were Anne Boleyn arrived back in London, her head elegantly tucked beneath her arm. But it was not, or not only, the spectacle of curiosity that my visitors sought. To my relief they talked to me of my poetry (and inevitably of their own), also of my work on smallpox and of the latest medical discoveries. The conversation, particularly from the younger of my visitors, was altogether a pleasure. I was pressed for my views on the new king, yet another George. Though I am ill equipped to criticize any family for a shortage of names, I do wonder that we might not have had a Henry or an Edward, or even a Richard. They asked too, these young people (for at my age everyone is young), what I thought of the political situation with the French and Indian war, and whether I approved of my son-in-law, who had been made prime minister by the new king. Bute was making unpopular concessions to bring the war to an end. Naturally I spoke freely, for when have I not?

'He is a Tory, you see,' I explained, 'and I am a Whig, and have never known much good come from Tories. But that said, my son-in-law is against war, which may not get him very far with his own party but meets with my approval. Although Tories, it has to be said, are in the main only interested in peace if it is more profitable to them than war.'

This and my other pronouncements were listened to with an eagerness I found gratifying.

Having not seen my daughter for a week, and despite my exhaustion and the pain in my every limb, I felt I owed her my kind attention, and so walked the short distance to her house, making my way through a small gathering that was for some reason assembled in the street before it. I rapped upon the door and was greeted by her footman with as much surprise as if I had indeed been carrying my head beneath my arm. I was shown through to the drawing room and instructed to wait.

'Mother!' declared Mary with alarm as she entered.

'Yes, my dear. Now we are at last at close quarters it seems only right that we should spend some time in each other's company.'

She made no attempt to conceal her unease. 'It is just that . . .' She went over to the window, looked out at the men in the street. 'It is a difficult time.'

'Is it? I am sorry to hear that.'

'And you have made things so much worse,' she declared.

I regarded her with astonishment. 'Oh? How?'

'Why must you speak so, of everything and to everyone?'

'What on earth do you mean?'

'You are visited by all manner of person, and say whatever is in your mind, and next day it is reported in the newspapers.'

'You would have me silent? I shall long be silent in my grave.'

My daughter laughed in disbelief, as if she could not believe I would ever die, however much she wished for it. 'I doubt that.'

I stood, not without difficulty.

'You do understand, don't you,' she said, emotion making her voice, usually so dispassionate, high and unsteady, 'that most of those who come to see you wish only to provoke you into saying something that will undermine John, so that they might write of what his mother-in-law has said and have it printed next day?'

Did she think so little of me that she could not imagine I might have opinions that mattered in the world? I had lived a long life, met so many men and women of importance. I had travelled and written and formed my own view of all, which I was happy to impart to others. 'Even Horace Walpole came to see me yesterday and sat with me for two hours listening to my impressions of Italy. And he has always hated me, having formed the view that I was a bad influence upon his father. If he can soften towards me, why cannot you?'

'Oh, Mother!'

I made to leave. 'It was wrong of me to come unannounced. I see that. I shall return at a time more . . .'

'My husband is in great political difficulty, and your presence . . . it . . . it . . .'

'Is unwelcome?'

'Yes! Yes, it is, for you are . . .'

'I am not and never can be an admirer of a Tory, Mary. But John is your husband, and I offer him all the respect I am able. I have said nothing against him.'

'You remind people of . . .'

'Of what?'

'Of yourself!'

'Well, that I cannot help. I even remind myself of myself from time to time. What is it that is so unbearable about Mary Wortley Montagu?'

She sighed, as if I ought to know.

'I am sorry, my dear, if I have made life more difficult for your husband. Being prime minister is no easy place to be, as my good old friend Walpole would attest if he had not been harried into an early grave by his detractors.'

'Mr Walpole was near seventy, Mother, and enjoyed a comfortable retirement in the House of Lords.'

'I am older.'

She came to me, condescending to show some affection, and took my hands in her own.

'How cold your fingers are,' I said, before realizing she would think it a rebuke.

She pulled her hands from mine in an instant, the gesture accompanied by the sound of shattering glass. A brick landed not a foot from where we stood. I went to the broken window to see that the crowd beyond had swelled to more than a hundred, and they were baying for the blood of Lord Bute, my son-in-law.

'I shall go and speak to them,' I said.

'Mother! Are you out of your senses? It is a mob. They will molest you.'

I took her in my arms and said quietly and with as much force as I could, 'I vowed when I was young never to be afraid, and though in truth I have always feared death greatly, and feared no less that I should never find love, now I am so near death and so very far from love, I find myself perfectly unafraid.'

I walked down the steps, leaning heavily on my stick, and out on to the street, the crowd drawing back, as I knew it would. 'Who was the brick intended for?' I asked, politely.

'Not for you!' said a boy.

'For the fucker Bute!' declared another.

'I doubt a brick will make him change his policy, if that is what you intend. Besides, he is not at home. Whether you like the king's first minister or no,' I declared, 'throwing a brick through the window to frighten his wife and children is no way to behave.'

A murmur rippled through the crowd, a sound like wind rustling long grass, and someone said, 'It's Lady Mary Wortley!'

Another repeated it, until a moment later they were all shouting 'Mary Wortley, Mary Wortley!' as if I were the leader of their motley crew.

I had not expected the common people to know me. They appeared to regard me much as my grandchildren had, as a startling curiosity. The crowd began slowly to disperse, and I hobbled along behind them back to St George Street and my harpsichord house. Glancing back, I saw my daughter watching me through the shattered window.

39

THE CROW

Summer 1762, London

(Mary)

Everything is difficult. Writing a letter takes an age, and reading is impossible. Every part of my body gives me pain, and there is nothing I wish to eat apart from fresh figs, and they are not to be had. My son has written to me five times this past week begging to be permitted to sail from Holland to come and see me. He thinks in my decline I will weaken, and naturally hopes that this bed is my deathbed. It may be. Once here he would show all what a fine son he is, no doubt, and make great claims upon my estate that would be gambled and drunk away within a year. I tell Lamrock to say to Eddie that I am beyond writing a letter, and also that my will was settled more than a year ago, should that be his purpose in expressing filial concern, and if Eddie has a notion to challenge the will, he will find he is like Laelaps the hound, chasing a fox that can never be caught.

What was the name of that fox?

There, I forget. Was it the Cadmean vixen? Yes, I am the Cadmean vixen, that can never be caught. Except by Death. We are all caught by Death, in the end.

And Zeus grows bored. 'Zeus grows bored,' I say to Lamrock.

'What's that, madam?'

He grows deaf. 'Why are you here? I thought you were going to Norfolk?'

'I have been, thank you, my lady. And now I am returned.'

'That was quick.'

'I went to Norfolk in April, my lady. Now it is August.'

'Is it so? August. Where were we last August?'

'In Padua, my lady. Preparing to leave.'

'I don't want to see my son.'

'No. Your instructions are clear.'

'Mary tells me that he has married another woman. Perhaps she will make him sensible. I wonder where he puts all his wives?'

Lamrock does not answer. He may not be here. I reach out for him and knock some object to the floor.

Algarotti was here this afternoon, not aged a day. He vowed his love for me and told me that he would meet me in paradise. 'A nice thought,' I said to him, 'but you will have found somebody more important to lie with, and there I'll be, waiting in paradise and everyone pitying me for being alone.'

'Didn't Algarotti look well?' I say to Lamrock. 'And weren't we told he was ailing?'

'Algarotti, my lady?'

'Yes, you remember him.'

'Not an easy gentleman to forget. But he is in Bologna. I

read you a letter from him this morning if you recall. And a very pretty one it was. But he said he was very ill and so could not come to you.'

'Oh. Not here, then?'

'No.'

It is dark, though I believe it to be not long after midday. I ring the bell, and it is Jane, the maid, who is always flustered and out of breath, though she is a slender little thing. I know that she spies on me, and reports all to Mary. 'Why hasn't Edward been to see me?'

'Edward, ma'am?' she asks.

'Yes. My husband. He is busy in the Commons, I suppose.'

'Oh, ma'am!' she declares and flees. Foolish thing.

'You were asking for Mr Wortley Montagu?' asks Lamrock.

'I have no wish to see Eddie. Did I not make my instructions clear?'

'You did. Perfectly clear. The maid had a notion you were asking after your husband.'

'Don't be ridiculous, Lamrock.'

'Yes, madam.'

Terrible pain today. Mary came and sat for an hour, telling me all about the children. She is expecting another. 'You are not a rabbit!' I told her. She takes offence with the greatest ease, though it seems only from me. All I hear from every quarter is what a graceful, kind and intelligent woman she is. Other visitors came today, too, though I can see only shapes, and voices come to me as if from a great distance, and then all of a sudden loud and close.

*

My sister comes and holds my hand and tells me she has recovered her reason and is truly happy. 'Are you living in Scotland still?' I ask. 'No, Mary,' she replies. 'I am dead.' I cannot be consoled. There is no consolation that can be given me now. That is the worst thing about dying. We dead and dying are inconsolable.

Anne Wortley's lips are upon mine, her eyes clear and sparkling, and I kiss her with such fervour that I surprise myself. 'You are recovered, dear Anne. Well, there's a mercy!' Yet her lips turn to nothing but air, and mine are so very dry.

'Lamrock!'

'I am here,' he says, tenderly. He presses a damp cloth to my lips, and I take a sip or two.

'Lamrock. My papers. Do not let them fall into Mary's hands. I beg you to see them published.'

'Yes, ma'am. The Turkish letters are already being printed in Holland. I received a letter from the printers today.'

'Be careful of my daughter, that is all. And the diaries?'

'All safe in locked trunks in the convent in Venice.'

'Truly? Oh, that makes me happy. That makes me very happy.'

Each breath a torment. Something so easy as breathing. I have done it every minute of every day for seventy-three years. You would think I would know how it goes, but I am forgetting even that. Here is the crow, back upon my chest. 'Hello, crow,' I say.

He pecks and pecks, right into my heart.

'Do not break his wings!' I shout. 'Not this time. Do not break his wings!'

*

A hand is upon my brow. I do not know whose. Is it Lamrock? His touch makes me think of Nathaniel Shaw all those years ago, his pale form at swim. My body, smooth and lithe, and shedding all my garments, and the feel of that cool, clear water, and swimming to him and taking him into me, there in the water, his lips on mine, that ecstasy that life can bring, that love can bring, be it lifelong or just a moment's brief possession.

'I have known love,' I say.

'So have I, my lady. So have I.'

EPILOGUE

INTO THE FLAMES

November 1794, London

(Mary Stuart, Countess of Bute)

Louisa, my youngest, has been here all afternoon, going only at eight o'clock to Gloucester Place, and it is as well she has gone, for now I may proceed with what I have known all my life I must do. She came to comfort me in my illness, sitting with me and making entertaining conversation. She has always been my good companion; people used to say that we were more like sisters than mother and daughter, though she was my last child. It is not age but temperament that divides character, and we share to some extent a temperament, though, perhaps surprisingly, she of all my children is most like my mother, what with her desire of reading all and writing all, and that has been where these past few years we have had our disputes.

The fire in my chamber is banked high. I think it the case for us all as we face death that we think of those who have died long ago, our parents most particularly, and our brothers and sisters; our children if we have suffered that great misfortune of enduring the death of an infant.

I raise myself from my bed, quietly since I do not know to what degree the servants will have been persuaded by my daughter to oppose what I must compel my failing limbs to do. It must be this night. How many more remain to me? Her diaries are in a trunk, neatly bound in leather and ready to be sent to the publisher, for that had always been her wish. I have not the strength to pull the heavy trunk towards the fire, and so I know that I will have to spend the night feeding the flames piece by piece with her words, shuffling to and fro from trunk to grate, and in the morning I shall be spent, and shall be found lying amongst ash and charred remnants of paper, and how fitting that will be. I have lived a life unimpeachable, seeking to absolve all those sins my mother committed, and yet here sit her diaries, recovered from – of all places – a nunnery in Venice. We'd paid good money to buy her Turkish letters, John and I, from the minister in Rotterdam, who gave them to us knowing our intention to have them destroyed, but some other copy must have been in existence, and they were published, and caused a very great sensation.

There will be no more sensations.

I have read these diaries, every word, as has Louisa. I have done my utmost to honour the wishes of my mother that came to me in a letter after she was dead and have hesitated in their destruction. Her secretary, Lamrock, came to me again and again demanding the diaries, pleading for them, yet I would not yield. I gave a promise only that I would guard them safely until my dying day, the same promise I gave to the Mother Superior of the nunnery where they were found. And now my dying day is upon me, and my promise is spent.

It is such effort though. I have a stick to steady me, but oh my knees are weak. I must make the light bright, to read her words one last time, to make my resolve firm. I have read these pages a thousand times or more, each time wondering whether I can honour my mother's wish to see them published, but I cannot. *The king I allowed run his fingers over my breast, since it amuses him so, and since he is king why should he be denied?* Such things she wrote, that might have been thought amusing half a century ago, but today are most certainly unacceptable. *Algarotti tonight spoke to me of how a man may make love to another man, and how pleasurable it is for both parties.* The outrage! And then she goes into detail, as if her readers might wish for a manual of instruction. She writes of proceedings in parliament: *We would do better by far to take the first five men and the first five women to be found in the street and seek their opinion on matters of war and peace and find more sense between them than the entire House of Lords*. My mother would think differently today, now that in France they have tried her prescription for government and found it leads them to wade knee-deep in the blood of their betters. And then there is this: *Mary is such a dull bird, a sparrow, or perhaps a wren. Eddie is a parrot, all squawk and flap and worse. How is it that Edward and I gave the world two such awkward creatures as these?* What would she say if she knew that my brother had died of a bird bone that pierced his throat? She would have laughed at the irony of it, I suppose.

The fire makes a choking smoke as I feed it, page after page. Midnight turns to one, and that child's hand grows into a woman's and is soon the script that is so familiar to me from her endless letters, words tumbling from her, incessant, rapid, clever, apt, and I cannot and never could still her tongue or her pen. Her voice is loud in my head, and I am five, six years of age once more, and lectured on manners or wickedness or the orbits of the planets. I push the pages into the flames more and more rapidly, fearful that I will not finish my fateful task, yet it is as if as fast as I feed the flames, she is here in the room with me, writing more and more and more. And the clock face shows two, then three, then four . . .

'Mama?' It is Louisa, knocking on the door. A thin light comes through the window, the sound of horses' hooves beyond on the rain-slicked cobbles. 'Mama?'

She enters, and yet she does not see me, only the charred paper, the ash, the cold grate.

'Mama!' she declares, but I have spoken all, heard all, done all.

There shall be no more words. Not one.

AFTERWORD

MARY WORTLEY MONTAGU: FACT AND FICTION

Although Mary's diaries were burnt by her daughter, many of her letters survive, as does some of her poetry and other writing – together forming the inspiration for this novel. But the rest is invention. One of the difficulties and joys of writing both history and historical fiction is what source material is left to us, and what gaps. For the serious historian the gaps must be filled with imagination based on evidence; for the novelist, the evidence can sometimes get in the way of the story we wish to tell. In the case of the remarkable Mary Wortley Montagu, the gaps are very great and yet far from obvious, for though we have those letters and many contemporary accounts of her, Mary was careful to conceal her emotional life from all but her private diary. Mary lived so fully and did so much, her life could easily fill three or four novels. But Mary was in a sense absent from her letters, hidden beneath her witty words and all the famous people she knew, who variously adored or detested her.

After her mother's death when Mary was three years old, she and her brother and two sisters were brought up by their paternal grandmother, Elizabeth Pierrepont, at West Dean in Wiltshire, but Elizabeth died when Mary was ten years old and the children were divided, Mary's youngest sister, Evelyn, being sent away to Chelsea to be raised by her Aunt Cheyne, her father's sister. This physical parting may have fuelled Mary's deeper estrangement from 'Sister Gower' in later life. She, Frances and William returned to Thoresby, though William was soon sent away to school. Nathaniel Shaw and Joseph Snape are inventions, though there are hints in Mary's letters of youthful love affairs, and it seems likely that as a very young woman she did have a 'heaven', probably a man her father would never have consented to her marrying. Her friendship with Anne was close, though perhaps not quite as close as I suggest in the novel.

Mary's father, the Earl of Kingston (later Marquis of Dorchester and later still Duke of Kingston), arranged for Mary to marry the improbably named Irish heir to a viscountcy, Clotworthy Skeffington, prompting Mary's elopement with Anne's brother, Edward, with whom Mary had been conducting an on – off clandestine relationship for some time. Whether Mary would have married Edward had it not been that elopement was her only way to avoid a miserable life with Skeffington we cannot know. Mary certainly loved Edward, at least in the first years of her marriage, but she was disheartened by his aloofness and the great majority of their marriage was spent apart. They remained friends, regular correspondents and were always respectful, routinely defending each other from the many attacks that came their way.

I have changed the sequence of certain events in the novel, since my focus has been, as far as I am able, Mary's emotional life rather than chronological accuracy. Mary was appalled by the marriage her father arranged in 1714 for her beloved sister Frances to John Erskine, Earl of Mar, Mary correctly foreseeing that he was unreliable both politically and personally and would bring her sister misery. (Note: in the novel I have made the marriage a year later.) Mary published a satirical essay on marriage in the *Spectator* that year under the name 'Mrs President', a riposte to an article critical of women who marry several times. In her lampoon, Mary amusingly pointed out that women who remarry have often had to endure a good deal of unpleasantness from the husbands they were obliged to bury.

Mary survived smallpox in late 1715, two years after her brother died from the disease (William died in 1713, though I have made his death a year later in the novel for narrative convenience, and for the same reason have brought Mary's illness forward six months). Mary was scarred and lost her eyelashes, which had the effect of further accentuating her large eyes, which were often the subject of comment. She quickly resumed her activities at court, frustrated that Edward was not more adept at gaining high office, his principled stance on a number of political issues probably holding him back. Mary was a natural courtier; she sought stimulating company and was equally sought after for her wit and intelligence. She made friends easily, had an innate understanding of political power (though she often claimed otherwise), and her influence probably helped gain the offer to Edward of the ambassadorship to Turkey that was to have such a huge influence on the rest of Mary's life.

In the period before leaving for Turkey, Mary, Alexander Pope and John Gay collaborated on several satirical poems which gained praise and notoriety. Authorship was not clearly attributed – the pattern for much of her literary work throughout her life.

Mary's journey through Europe and her time in Turkey as described in the novel are broadly consistent with the account given in her *Turkish Embassy Letters*, published only after her death, and rightly regarded as one of the outstanding pieces of travel-writing in English of that or, indeed, any age.

Mary's correspondence from this period reflects her open mind and determination to judge everything as she saw it without regard to convention. She sought to debunk Western notions that Islam was ignorant and less worthy of respect than Christianity and saw much to admire in Turkish society, particularly – and surprisingly – in the rights held by women. She also very quickly grasped that undue power lay in the hands of the janissaries – the military elite – and that this led to political instability in the Ottoman Empire. It is possible that her enthusiasm for Turkey influenced Edward's diplomacy – he was regarded by both Austria and his political masters in London as compromised by his partiality to the Turkish cause and was recalled, much to Mary's dismay. Before they left Turkey she had her son, Edward, 'engrafted', or inoculated, against smallpox, having observed how few people bore smallpox scars in Turkey, and how few fatalities there were from the disease, and she made it her business to learn about the process.

The long voyage back to England from Constantinople afforded Mary an opportunity to see at first hand the places recorded in her beloved Homer. Though she and Edward wished to bring antiquities back from ancient Troy, Crete and so on, the captain of the ship declined them permission to bring them on board. The incident of the 'Trojan Stone' is therefore a fiction, as is its throwing overboard during an attack by Spanish vessels. Their ship, the *Preston*, was fired on by the Spanish navy, though we do not have Mary's detailed account of the incident.

On her return to London, Mary resumed her literary friendships, and her work was published, again mostly anonymously. She had her daughter, Mary, inoculated – the very first smallpox inoculation ever to be recorded in Britain – and began to campaign to spread the practice, going from (aristocratic) house to house to personally bear witness to its safety and effectiveness. One of Mary's concerns was the tendency of physicians to overcomplicate the process, largely so they could charge exorbitant fees. Her opposition to their practices, including bleeding, brought her into conflict with the medical establishment. Ultimately, Caroline, Princess of Wales (and a friend), decided to have two of her daughters inoculated, though only after an experiment performed upon prisoners awaiting execution and held at Newgate and the inoculation of all the orphans in the parish of St James. The royal inoculations paved the way for general acceptance, although there was still opposition, notably from sections of the medical profession and the Church. Provoked by criticism of inoculation as 'the practice of ignorant women', Mary went on the attack in print, under the pseudonym of 'A Turkey-Merchant':

> Out of compassion to the numbers abused and deluded by the knavery and ignorance of physicians I am determined to give a true account of the manner of inoculating the small pox as it is practised in Constantinople with constant success, and without any ill consequence whatever. I shall sell no drugs, take no fees . . .

The practice of inoculation was not approved by the Royal College of Physicians until 1755, and the eight-year-old Edward Jenner was inoculated two years later, protecting him from the disease. Arguably we have Mary to thank for Jenner, and for the process of vaccination that he discovered in 1797.

Mary tended to enjoy great loyalty from her servants, particularly later in life. But Nell is an invention, intended to represent the close and often complicated relationships Mary had with a number of her servants. That a servant rose to become a countess is based on truth – that of the servant of an Italian neighbour of Mary during the time she lived in Gottolengo and Lovere. The poor but beautiful servant's name was Octavia, who became the Countess Sosi. There has never been an Earl or Countess of Pitlochry; the invented John Cargill is not so fanciful, as Mary encouraged the attentions of young, educated men throughout her life.

Mary became aware only gradually of her sister Frances's distress in Paris and wrote her a succession of letters intended to be cheering but that must have only made Frances feel even more despairing. Around this time (the early to mid-1720s) Mary befriended Lord Hervey and Molly Skerritt and became close to Robert Walpole. Walpole began an affair with Molly Skerritt, and when his wife died, he married Molly. Walpole's son from his first marriage, Horace, held Mary responsible for introducing his father to Molly and also in some way for his mother's death. This led to his frequent criticisms of Mary throughout her life and beyond.

Mary famously fell out with Alexander Pope, soon coming under sustained and vicious attack by him. The reasons are unknown. Lady Louisa Stuart, Mary's granddaughter, wrote an account of Mary's life based largely on the recollections of her mother, Lady Bute, Mary's daughter, which suggested that Pope had declared his love for Mary who, having laughed at him, caused him to turn against her with much bitterness. This seems far too simple an explanation. Another story that gained wide acceptance was that Pope was greatly offended when Mary borrowed from him some bedlinen and returned it unlaundered. This, again, seems far too trivial a basis for one of the great schisms of literary history. In the novel I suggest that the dispute arose largely from intellectual jealousy, and in particular Mary's brilliant lampooning of Pope's overly sentimental poem about the death of two lovers struck by lightning, though Pope knew of the lampoon earlier than I suggest in the novel, since he sent the original poem to her in Constantinople and she, somewhat insensitively, wrote him the lampoon as her reply. She had fatefully overestimated Pope's sense of humour. He was more than capable of bearing a grudge that could last centuries – and indeed, has!

Mary's son, Edward, to whom I give the diminutive Eddie in the novel to help distinguish him from his father, ran away to sea at the age of fourteen, causing his parents to place advertisements in the newspapers offering a reward for his return. Eddie was ultimately identified by the captain of the ship on which he was employed as a cabin boy by his inoculation scars – unique at the time, particularly as Eddie's were on both arms after the abortive first inoculation by an elderly Greek woman in Constantinople. Mary's father, the Duke of Kingston, died in 1726, a year before Eddie ran away to sea, and the scene in which he confesses to encouraging the boy is therefore my invention. Eddie's early behaviour proved to be the pattern for the rest of his life: he grew to be a 'rake', drinking, gambling, marrying bigamously, running up huge debts and borrowing in the expectation of an inheritance he was never to receive. Mary left him one guinea in her will, though she knew that he would receive the allowance from her late husband's estate that had been hers, and so the single guinea was intended as a warning to him to not be profligate rather than as a punishment.

Mary met Voltaire several times during his period in London from 1726 to 1728. We know that he showed her his writing, and that she gave him her frank assessment of it being both 'too good and not good enough' to be his. Voltaire's time in London influenced the rest of his writing and philosophy in many ways. He praised Mary and her work on inoculation in his famous *Letters on England/Lettres Philosophiques*, published in French in 1733; and after Mary's death thirty years later, Voltaire reviewed her letters (which were published in various editions) for the *Gazette littéraire*, describing her as a 'woman for all the world'.

Mary's sister Frances became severely mentally ill in her penurious exile in Paris and was allowed to return to England permanently in March 1728 where she was declared by a panel of judges a 'lunatic'. There followed a bitter custody battle, ultimately won by Mary. Mary's position was represented by her enemies as motivated by a desire to control Frances's income – which was not great, and certainly had not been enough to fund her exiled husband in France. It is much more likely that Mary sincerely wanted to care for her sister as best she could.

Mary probably suffered from periods of depression herself in her forties. Her son was a constant source of worry, she was the subject of sustained attacks from Pope and others, and while she took consolation in a number of close friendships, particularly with Lord Hervey who was a senior minister in Walpole's administration and himself the subject of constant rumour because of his bisexuality, Mary seemed at this stage of her life to lose energy. And then along came the twenty-four-year-old Francesco Algarotti. At the age of forty-seven Mary fell passionately and hopelessly in love, perhaps for the first time since the mysterious affairs of her youth. Her love for Algarotti was largely unrequited, at least physically. Algarotti was gay. But Mary became quite obsessed with the young Italian, who had an exceptional intellect, devastating charm and no doubt relished Mary's company and the connections she and Hervey made for him. The affair, whatever its terms, lasted sporadically for much of the rest of her life.

Approaching fifty, Mary felt increasingly alienated from the cultural life of her homeland and began to think of living abroad. She devised a plan to live in Venice with Algarotti, which he did nothing to encourage, but also seemed not to actively discourage. Mary's daughter eloped with John Stuart, Earl of Bute, who had sought Edward's approval for the match, but it had not been forthcoming, possibly for financial reasons, but more probably because Bute was a Tory and a Scot, a combination that filled neither Lady Mary nor Edward with confidence given the misery John Erskine, Earl of Mar, had brought to Frances.

In 1737, provoked by a Tory publication called *Common Sense* which expressed views about the place of women and the poor that she found abhorrent, Mary began to publish a periodical, *The Nonsense of Common-Sense*, which allows us to learn her views on a range of matters not mentioned so fully in her letters, but which may well have been more evident in her (destroyed) diaries. Nine editions of her periodical appeared, including memorable essays on workers' rights and on feminism. The two extracts in Chapter 29 from her publication are genuine. In March 1739 there was an anti-war 'sit-in' (as we would term it today) in the House of Lords, led by several aristocratic women. Mary wrote of the event in detail and approvingly to her friend the Countess of Pomfret, but it is not clear whether she led the protest or was even present. Since Mary often elided herself out of her own history, it's hard to be sure either way.

In July 1739 Mary left for Venice, accompanied by two servants, Mary and William (to avoid confusion I have changed Mary and William's names to Sara and John). Lamrock is an invention, who takes the place of several reliable friends and servants who became particularly important to Mary as her health began to fail in her fifties and sixties.

Mary was surprised and delighted to find herself celebrated and honoured in Venice. She was received by the most noble houses and was able to form friendships that served her well. After about two years in Venice and travelling in Italy she was finally reunited with Algarotti in Turin. There it seems she assisted him in an ultimately unsuccessful diplomatic mission on behalf of Frederick of Prussia, by now almost certainly Algarotti's lover. We know very little of what happened during their two months together and my account is speculative.

Over the next two decades Mary lived variously in Venice, Avignon (then a papal state), Brescia, Padua and the villages of Gottolengo and Lovere. She had a difficult relationship for much of this time with another minor nobleman, Count Palazzi, a sort of mafioso figure who swindled Mary out of much of her money, manipulated her and, towards the end of their tumultuous relationship, kept her captive for a short time. It seems Mary knew the nature of Palazzi's character, and there were probably times when he defended and protected her as well as exploited her – which is in the nature of protection rackets, after all. During this period Mary, on the recommendation of Palazzi, engaged a Dr Bartolomeo Moro as her secretary. He remained with Mary for the final seven years of her life and was one of very few named beneficiaries in her will. He had access to all her papers, though the role he played in her posthumous fame is unclear. The invented Lamrock takes his place in the novel.

Mary and her husband kept up a constant and warm correspondence throughout her long exile. There was no real acrimony between them, it was simply that neither cared to live with the other, and even though Edward visited Europe on a few occasions, he never made any effort to spend time with his wife. I have somewhat compressed the years from 1755 to 1761 in the novel to move the story along as Mary nears the end of her life. Edward Wortley Montagu's death in 1761 shook Mary, and subsequent rumour and dispute over his will, most predictably from their wayward son, assisted by the relatives of the long-dead Earl of Mar, compelled Mary back to England. She also had a genuine wish to spend time with her grandchildren, even the eldest of whom she barely knew. Mary was by this time unwell with breast cancer. Before sailing from Rotterdam she made the strange decision to entrust her *Turkish Embassy Letters* to the English Minister in Rotterdam, the Reverend Benjamin Sowden, with clear instructions that he should publish them (for his own profit) after her death.

Several accounts seem to bear out the view that Sowden lent the letters for a day and a night to some travellers, who returned them to him. He was then induced not long after Mary's death to part with the letters by her son-in-law, the Earl of Bute, in return for the then huge sum of five hundred pounds. Mary's daughter and her husband were determined to suppress the letters. Yet a matter of months after Mary's death they were published and were sensationally popular and have remained in print for the past two hundred and sixty years. It seems that a copy of the *Turkish Embassy Letters* was made by the mysterious travellers who were lent the letters for a night by the Reverend Sowden. The great upsurge of interest in all things 'oriental' in the latter part of the eighteenth century was probably fuelled, at least in part, by the publication of Mary's Turkish letters.

Mary made and kept copies of hundreds of the letters she

wrote, and no doubt kept many of those she received. Those who received her letters also tended to keep them, and at least some have made their way to us largely through the efforts of her great-grandson Lord Wharncliffe, who published the first reasonably reliable collection of her work in 1837. His editing, however, left much to be desired. In common with so many Victorian men who wrote about women, he emphasized the domestic and 'feminine' aspects of Mary's character over her political and intellectual interests.

Mary's last words are said to have been *It has all been very interesting,* which would be an accurate if unduly plain summary of her long life. She died on 21 August 1762.

But what of Mary's diaries? Mary Stuart, Countess of Bute, her daughter, kept them under lock and key throughout her life. She allowed no one to see them except for her scholarly daughter, Louisa, who took a keen interest in them. In the novel I suggest that the Countess of Bute burnt the letters shortly before her death (as indeed she did) against Louisa's wishes, but we know from Lady Louisa's own account that she consented to their destruction, albeit reluctantly, given the distress she could see their existence caused her dying mother.

Mary Wortley Montagu is remembered today, if at all, for her *Turkish Embassy Letters*, for a few of her poems and for her work on smallpox inoculation. There are a number of scholarly biographies, and a couple of twentieth-century novels inspired by her life, but there are no statues to her, and the only street named for her is in Lovere, Italy – fittingly a promenade on the shores of Lake Iseo, a view she truly loved. There is a plaque in a church in Lichfield, and an obelisk in the grounds of Wentworth Castle, Barnsley.

In an age when we are reappraising the many public statues that celebrate the lives of men we now regard with suspicion or disdain, how ironic it is that when Mary was offered the honour of a statue it was in a village in Italy, and that she felt obliged to decline the honour for fear that she would be ridiculed for it. Mary kept no slaves and led no armies. She thought the world unjust and said so using great wit and humour. In bringing the practice of inoculation from Turkey she saved countless lives. If there are empty plinths to be filled perhaps we might consider placing Mary Wortley Montagu upon one.

TIMELINE OF EVENTS IN THE LIFE OF MARY WORTLEY MONTAGU

15 MAY 1689: Birth of Mary at Arlington Street, London (though the principal family home was at Thoresby, Nottinghamshire).

8 JUNE 1690: Birth of sister Frances.

6 SEPTEMBER 1691: Birth of sister Evelyn.

21 OCTOBER 1692: Birth of brother, William.

1693: Death of their mother, Mary Pierrepont, née Fielding. Mary, Frances and William are sent to live with their paternal grandmother, Elizabeth Pierrepont, at West Dean, Wiltshire. Sister Evelyn lives with her paternal aunt, Lady Cheyne.

1698: Death of paternal grandmother, Elizabeth Pierrepont. Mary, Frances and William return to Thoresby and into the care of an inadequate (in Mary's opinion) governess. Mary and Frances begin to educate themselves by stealing into their father's well-stocked library.

23 AUGUST 1712: Marries Edward Wortley Montagu (an elopement, having escaped her father's confinement at West Dean).

16 MAY 1713: Birth of her son, Edward ('Eddie' in the novel, to distinguish him from his father).

1 JULY 1713: Death of Mary's brother, William, aged twenty.

AUGUST 1713: Mary rents Middlethorpe House, near York.

20 JULY 1714: Mary's sister Frances marries John Erskine, Earl of Mar.

1 AUGUST 1714: Death of Queen Anne, accession of George, Elector of Hanover, as King George I.

APRIL 1715: Mary's friendship with Alexander Pope begins.

9 AUGUST 1715: Lord Mar (Mary's brother-in-law) declares for James Stuart ('the Pretender') and rides north to lead the first Jacobite rebellion.

DECEMBER 1715: Mary seriously ill with smallpox.

FEBRUARY 1716: Pirated copies of Mary's eclogues in wide circulation.

1 AUGUST 1716: Mary, Edward and Eddie set off for Constantinople (Istanbul).

8 JUNE 1717: Mary arrives in Constantinople, after travels in Germany and Austria and a stay in Adrianople (modern-day Edirne).

19 JANUARY 1718: Birth of Mary's daughter, the future Countess of Bute.

18 MARCH 1718: Eddie is inoculated against smallpox.

5 JULY 1718: Mary leaves Constantinople aboard the *Preston*, following Edward's recall as ambassador.

30 SEPTEMBER 1718: Arrives at Dover, England.

APRIL 1721: Mary's daughter is inoculated against smallpox – probably the first ever inoculation performed in Britain.

JANUARY 1726: Death of Mary's father, the Duke of Kingston.

JUNE 1727: Becomes friendly with Voltaire during his exile in England.

11 JUNE 1727: Death of King George I, who is succeeded by King George II. Caroline of Ansbach, Mary's friend, becomes queen.

JULY 1727: Eddie runs away to sea, aged fourteen.

8 MARCH 1728: End of friendship with Alexander Pope confirmed with publication of his 'The Capon's Tale'.

APRIL 1728: Arrival of Frances, Lady Mar, from Paris, severely mentally ill.

MARCH OR APRIL 1736: Mary meets Francesco Algarotti.

24 AUGUST 1736: Daughter, Mary, elopes with John Stuart, third Earl of Bute.

20 NOVEMBER 1737: Death of Queen Caroline.

DECEMBER 1737: First edition of Mary's political journal *The Nonsense of Common-Sense*.

JULY 1739: Mary leaves England for Venice, in pursuit of Francesco Algarotti.

16 MARCH 1741: Mary arrives in Turin and spends two months with Algarotti on a 'diplomatic mission'.

MAY 1742: Settles in Avignon, a papal state and refuge for prominent Jacobites.

5 AUGUST 1743: Death of Mary's friend and confidant Lord John Hervey.

30 MAY 1744: Death of Alexander Pope.

19 AUGUST 1745: The 1745 Jacobite rebellion begins, ending in defeat at Culloden in April 1746.

AUGUST 1746: Mary meets Count Ugolino Palazzi, and leaves Avignon, settling in Gottolengo, Brescia Province, Venetian Republic.

JULY 1749: Mary is ordered by her doctor to spend the summer in Lovere. She subsequently spends her summers in Lovere.

SEPTEMBER 1756: Breaks with Palazzi, moves to Padua and Venice.

25 OCTOBER 1760: Death of King George II, who is succeeded by King George III (patron to Mary's son-in-law, the Earl of Bute).

22 JANUARY 1761: Death of Mary's husband, Edward Wortley Montagu.

JANUARY 1762: Mary returns to London, ill with breast cancer.

MAY 1762: The Earl of Bute becomes prime minister.

21 AUGUST 1762: Death of Mary, aged seventy-three.

7 MAY 1763: Publication in Holland of Mary's *Turkish Embassy Letters* – causing a sensation.

6 NOVEMBER 1794: Mary, Countess of Bute, dies, having burnt her mother's diaries shortly before her death.

FURTHER READING

The Life of Lady Mary Wortley Montagu, Robert Halsband (Oxford: Oxford University Press, 1956)

Lady Mary Wortley Montagu: Comet of the Enlightenment, Isobel Grundy (Oxford: Oxford University Press, 1999)

The Letters and Works of Lady Mary Wortley Montagu, ed. Lord Wharncliffe (London: Richard Bentley, 1837)

Mary Wortley Montagu: Letters (London: Everyman's Library, 1906)

Lord Hervey, Eighteenth-Century Courtier, Robert Halsband, (Oxford: Oxford University Press, 1973)

The Pioneering Life of Mary Wortley Montagu, Scientist and Feminist, Jo Willett (Barnsley: Pen and Sword Books, 2021)

Indamora to Lindamira, Lady Mary Pierrepont, ed. Isobel Grundy (Edmonton: University of Alberta, 1994)

Portrait of Lady Mary Wortley Montagu, Iris Barry (London: Ernest Benn, 1928)

A Toast to Lady Mary, Doris Leslie (London: Hutchinson, 1954)

Reflections upon Marriage, Mary Astell, third edition (London: R. Wilkin, 1706)

A New System of the Spleen, Vapours and Hypochondriack Melancholy, Nicholas Robinson (London: A. Bettesworth, 1729)

The Country Housewife and Lady's Director in the Management of a House, and the Delights and Profits of a Farm, Richard Bradley (London: D. Browne, 1736)

ACKNOWLEDGEMENTS

This novel began when my editor at the time, Eloisa Clegg – who had been pondering a different novel I'd sent her – called me to say: 'I wonder if you have anything that feels more *connected* to your last book?' After a day or two of panic because I hadn't, the penny (or gold sovereign) dropped, and I realized that the character of Aunt Frances in my novel *The Second Sight of Zachary Cloudesley* was inspired by a certain Lady Mary Wortley Montagu. I went back to Mary's *Turkish Embassy Letters,* which I'd read as research for that novel, then read Mary's published letters and poetry, and next every biography I could lay my hands on. Soon I was utterly and hopelessly in love with Mary and have remained so ever since. Charlotte Trumble was the editor who took my wobbly first draft and transformed it with patience and sensitivity into a book very close to the one you have in your hands, and Kirsty Dunseath added further editorial magic. Kirsty has been a mentor as much as an editor, and I am hugely grateful to her. People sometimes ask me whether it's hard having one's work edited, but I feel immensely lucky to have had the care of not one but three editors.

Thank you, too, to my remarkable and endlessly supportive agent, David Headley, to his colleagues Emily Glenister, Helen Edwards, Kirsten Lang and everyone in the DHH Literary Agency team.

Thanks go to the talented design team at Transworld, and particularly to Marianne Issa El-Khoury, and to my kind and thoughtful publicist Izzie Ghaffari Parker, to the brilliant Alison Barrow, and to Sara Roberts, who performs all sorts of wonders in marketing. And to the astonishingly thorough proofreading and copy-editing skills of Kate Samano, Holly McElroy and Bella Bosworth, who kept me on my historical toes!

A very special thank-you goes to Professor Isobel Grundy, the author of the definitive life of Mary Wortley Montagu and Professor Emeritus at the University of Alberta, Canada. I was fortunate to be able to ask Isobel questions, test out theories and share with her some of my wilder speculations. Isobel gave me all manner of research tips which I pursued with enthusiasm. Thank you to Linda Uda at the Lovere information service in Italy, to the staff of Lovere library and those of Accademia Tadini. Lovere is the only town anywhere with a street named for Mary, a promenade right on Lake Iseo. It is a place Mary loved above all others, and deservedly so. Thank you to Jo Willett, whose 2021 biography of Mary raised her profile at a time when almost all of us were benefiting from inoculation against COVID-19, and too few of us recognized the part Mary played. Enormous thanks to Elizabeth Ingram, Lynsey Nairn and the team at the Bute Collection at Mount Stuart, Isle of Bute, who gave me access to their archives. To have Mary's lively, vivid letters right in my hands was simply unforgettable. Thank you to Geoff Pope and his fellow trustees at Pope's Grotto Preservation Trust for a tour of Alexander Pope's grotto and a thorough test of just where Mary might have bumped her head.

Thank you to all those who continue to sustain me in my writing life, and who have given me notes on this novel or generally encouraged with coffee, cake and the occasional glass or three of wine. The Barmoor writers: Jo Bell, Nell Farrell, Rosie Garland, Tania Hershman, Sarah Jasmon, Robbie Burton, Chris Eagles, Matt Black and Lesley Richardson; and fellow writers here in Scotland: Meg Pokrass, Helen Sedgwick, Shona Maclean, Ange Cran, Rachel Humphries and the team at Moniack Mhor. And to Bill Macmillan, Jo Cunningham, Catherine Jarvie and the rest of the CBC gang.

Finally, thank you to my family, who have been endlessly supportive during the many ups and downs of this writing life: to Jess and Rory, Ben and Poppy, to Molly, whose memory lives on, and most of all to Sally, who knows that my best ideas come before breakfast. And to the three little people to whom this book is dedicated. I hope you live your lives as courageously and adventurously as Mary did hers.

Sean Lusk's debut, *The Second Sight of Zachary Cloudesley*, was a BBC2 *Between the Covers* pick, a *Sunday Times* Historical Fiction Book of the Month, and longlisted for the Walter Scott Prize and the Goldsboro Books Glass Bell Award. He is also an award-winning short-story writer, winner of the Manchester Fiction Prize and the Fish Short Story Prize. He has lived in Greece, Pakistan and Egypt and now lives in the Scottish Highlands.

You can find him at www.seanlusk.com or on Twitter/X @seanlusk1 and Instagram @seanluskauthor.